STOOP TO CONQUER

A Tenth Ave. Trip

John Michael Bolger

ISBN: 978-1-68222-274-4

Dedicated to the loving memory of my friends, Howie Nesto and Clayton Brooks,...and to all of the troubled kids in all of the Hell's Kitchens of the world.

PERSONAL ACKNOWLEDGEMENTS

To Agnes and John... for giving me yesterday;

To Philomena, Bernadette and Charlotte... for giving me today;

To Gina, Jude, Olivia and Rory... for giving me tomorrow;

and

To the Dominican Sisters of Blauvelt... for teaching me penmanship;

To M.J. Karmi... for reaching down to pull me up when I was
all the way at the bottom;

and especially

To David Milch, "Teacher"... for giving me permission;

Thank you.
From the depths of my heart.
I am forever grateful.

I am Francis Doonan.

Staring out the window of a southbound Greyhound, I have just left Dannemora Prison, the only home I've known during these last fifteen years. The bus knifes through the countryside to carry me back to my pre-incarceration home in New York City, past the farms, fields and rivers of the Upstate. *can't help but wonder if monet and manet lied about the locations of their subjects; such simple beauty and air... free air.* A large, salty tear wells in my eye as my thoughts shift to the memory of a funeral I wasn't allowed to attend for a dear father who won't be waiting back in the neighborhood for me... not today; not ever. The drops ski down my cheeks as I recall those great, twinkly-eyed, Irish-smile "Hellos" and "Welcomes" the man was famous for. *my god, i miss him; i'll never stop feeling terrible about the pain i caused him... but that was the "then" francis. up 'til now, everything was "then." now is new; start again. my god, that's frightening.* As a hint of desperate panic starts to come over me, my body manages a smile through the tears. *ah, but my lovely irish mother, agnes would be there; she always is.* My mother is, hands-down, the toughest person I've ever known. No three-bill thug fighting bouncers for fun was ever tougher. But I also knew that we weren't tough at all. *just as afraid as you, francis... a thought that has actually kept me alive these fifteen years.*

Agnes would have a steaming hot meal ready with every kind of food I'd ever mentioned or even looked at in her presence... new clothes, some spending money and advice. *something i've never listened to before, but life somehow has removed the cemented-in wax from my ears.* There, waiting for me will also be my apartment on Tenth Avenue... immaculately clean... with fresh sheets and my stuff. My mother has paid the rent for fifteen years and never let anyone stay there, a shrine of sorts to "Saint Francis." *it's amazing how you can get caught up in a window's reflection, catching the mirror of your own eyes, and you end up watching "this is your life." god, i gotta puke, but back to the show....*

Waiting there in that apartment will also be the letters that I sent myself at least once a day – over 7,000 in all – some containing only blue Bic ink smudged to illegibility *mostly by tears and snot*, some poetry, some confession, some drooling, some prayers, some hope. *too many suicidal, but i'm still here.* Better than the newspaper, and certainly more effective for keeping my head in the right place, I plan to open one a day for more than the next twenty years.

I really can't wait to get back to my music collection, though: massive and extensive and complete. It provides the soundtrack to my life. Like most people, I associate specific songs with certain significant events in my life and, not surprisingly, although the world has changed, pretty much anything after 1981 is mediocre noise. *nah, i gotta change my thinking; that's not fair. shit, i wish i had a letter to open, to lose the arrogance and just be me.*

The truth is that Francis Doonan is not, and never was, a tough guy... not even the 32-year-old, ex-convict version. My childhood dream was to be a florist. *yes, a fucking florist.* From the sixth grade until graduating from Holy Cross Catholic School, I worked in the Flower District, on Sixth Avenue, down in the 20s. It was my little piece of floral paradise in the middle of concrete and glass, and I did it all there: swept floors, delivered arrangements, cleaned out the refrigerators, trimmed roses and generally learned the business while soaking up the beauty. I learned the most from this old Spanish guy named Chonley Diaz, who had no one better in the business than God Almighty. It was due to a combination of talent and practice. He just had this perfect eye for design... what looked good going together... things average people would never even dream of. But he got plenty of chances to perfect his skills because Chonley worked for everybody... <u>had</u> to work for everybody thanks to his destructive thing for women, intoxicants and ponies. But some words of advice Chonley gave me once stuck in my head and became my own pearl of wisdom to give out: "In a world of weeds, there's always gotta be a flower." As a result, I became known in the neighborhood as "Frankie Flowers." All of the neighborhood micks had a ball with that while the goombahs envied the name and wondered if I was "connected." But anybody who knew anything knew there was no way that was possible since I couldn't be Italian. I've got red hair, blue eyes and drank like all the other bastards from the Green Isle. *but not all the irish have the red hair. i distinctly remember one who was the most golden of blondes.*

Sandra O'Casey... the prettiest girl ever to bless the streets of Hell's Kitchen... and the love of my life, no doubt. She told me early on that she would wait... that we would see where things stood once I got to this point, when I got out... but we see how long she remembered that promise. *stop, francis. all she's ever done is be supportive. even after all of your attempts to push her away. just how long did you imagine she was going to wait? still... claudio pozzo? fucking claudio pozzo... is a lucky man. but i'll just never understand how she could marry a guinea who has probably never read a book before in his life. ...because that was sandra's passion: books.*

I'd noticed her from afar since we were very little, but I was always afraid to talk to her, usually because there were too many people vying for her attention. Anything that was living wanted to do it in this girl's world; she was <u>the</u> flower in a world of weeds, and everyone was stroking her petals. We actually talked face-to-face for the first time in the New York Public Library on Tenth Ave., when we were both about fifteen or sixteen. I asked for directions to the horticulture section from the fat librarian with the sweat crease on her nose from those Ben Franklin eyeglasses just as Sandra emerged from behind a large cart of returned books and said, "Hey, Frankie Flowers. Follow me." *i would've done it even if she hadn't offered.* She was tall, about 5'9" with flowing blonde hair that fell around her shoulders like a curtain of molten gold. Long, athletic legs carried her along while blue eyes guided us... a blue like God must've chosen off the pigment chart when he was coloring the oceans of His universe. Everything in or on my body reacted, sped up, heated up, stiffened up until the sound of her voice snapped my daydream. "You know, Frankie, I think it's great that a kid from Tenth Ave. loves flowers like you do. Better than all the other nitwits who just screw around and get into trouble all the time. Do you have any specific title or author?"

"I just like to look at the pictures." I confessed, "I'm not too good at reading."

Sandra started, "I'll make a deal with you, Frankie. You teach–" but I interrupted her to point out that my name was Francis... if she didn't mind. Rather than being put off, she just smiled and said, "Okay. I like that better anyway. So, if you'll spend some time teaching me about flowers, I'll help you with your reading. That okay with you?" If it weren't for the close proximity of a shelf of musty, well-read books as we rounded the corner, I would've hit the floor. "Here's the section. I've got a lot of books to re-shelve, so I could be just about anywhere in the building, but I hope you find me before you leave. We could set up a time to meet if you want."

I managed to stammer, "That'd be swell." *swell! swell! what a fuck-ing moron!*

If she thought I was a dork, she didn't let on. She just smiled, saying, "Have a good time, Frank... Francis," she corrected herself. "There are a lot of books on flowers."

My version of "This is Your Life" goes off the air when the bus driver shouts out, "We're gonna stop at this hot-shoppe for twenty minutes. No more, so be sure to be back by then or I'll leave without you." He laughs, but something tells me he's serious. I bound down off the bus, using some of the energy I've stored up for this first day of freedom... and for the rest of my life... the beginning. I enter the hot shoppe like a stranger in a strange world, which is really what I am since I chose not to watch television for a decade and a half. Instead of keeping up-to-date on fashion, trends, looks and things, I'd decided that, if I were not physically a part of the free world, I didn't want to know anything about it. *that's the donkey-mentality irish in me.*

I marvel at how much things seem to have changed as I follow along to join the line in front of the coffee counter. *like a cow being led to the slaughterhouse.* After waiting for several minutes, it is finally my turn to order a large coffee and a sweet bun. One of the workers hands me the roll while he turns around to make my coffee. I immediately take an enor-mously satisfying bite of the sugary pastry... and almost choke on it imme-diately when the cashier demands payment. "Four dollars?!? I just ordered a coffee and roll. Are you sure?" I ask with simple amazement. The groans of the crowd behind me are more than barely audible.

"Hmm. Well, let me check. Yep, it's still four dollars," she snaps back sarcastically, adding, "What do you live in? A tree?" *yeah, kinda.* I hand her a five and tell her to keep the change. This time she retorts, "We're not allowed to accept tips, but here's one for you: Snap out of it." I take my cup and baggie over to one of the tables nearby and begin tearing the bun apart, dipping each piece into my coffee. When it is gone and my coffee is half-way behind it, the call of nature sends me scanning the area for the restroom. During the search, I spot a clock and can't remember if we've been here fifteen minutes or twenty. Jumping up awkwardly, the coffee goes flying and everyone in the vicinity is looking at me, including the bitch behind the register, who is slowly shaking her head in disgust.

As I dash into the restroom, I pass some hippie changing his baby girl on a board that he's swung down from the wall. *shit. how can i piss with that baby staring at me? that ain't right to have her in here with all these swinging pricks.* Although I struggle initially with a little stage fright, I soon let out the deep sigh of satisfaction that comes with knowing what a five-dollar-piss feels like. But then I notice there's no handle to flush. Stepping back to get a broader view, it flushes by itself and I bolt for the bus. The bus driver is literally in gear, rocking the bus a little.

Slipping back into my seat next to the sweet little old lady, it doesn't seem as though she's budged, smile still the same. I smile back and ask if she'd like the window for the rest of the ride. "No," she replies, "You need that." *what did she mean by that? must be an angel sent to guide me home.* I return a soft "Thank you," catching the date on her newspaper: June 27, 1995. *wonder how the yankees are doing. hell, they're always great even when they're bad.* I allow myself to float on the memories of Daddy getting off the Jerome Ave. subway stop, going to see Roger and the Mick... holding his hand, baseball glove in the other... hoping, praying for a foul ball. The tears form behind my lids. *may you rest in peace, daddy. you will always be my hero. "this is your life,"* back from commercial....

The face of Danny Albanese comes into frame, the little Guinea-thug bully of my childhood. "Hey, Flowers, I hear you take it in the ass. That true?"

It's like I'm back there again....

Just as I passed the noise of a clearing throat, Danny's spit flew through the air to land on a parcel of flowers I was carrying to deliver to St. Clare's. I could hear all of his cronies laughing and clearing their throats, one by one. I picked up the pace so that spittle from every direction fell short like spears in an Errol Flynn flick. But I made it to "the fort" and the gate lifted to grant me sanctuary. But I couldn't deliver the flowers like that; ducking into a bathroom, I wiped off the spit that managed to find its way onto my pants and hoped there was none on the back of my shirt. The entire time I was making the delivery, I kept wondering to myself why Danny was like that. I'd known him since kindergarten and we'd never had a problem. I knew he came from a "connected" family... so maybe he'd watched "The Godfather" too many times. *but doesn't he realize i could be tom hagen, for christ's sake?*

My mind was filled with equal parts dread and excitement. I hoped like hell that Danny's boys weren't still out there, but I also knew I was on my way to meet Sandra up at 72nd and Broadway so we could hang out on the Great Lawn in Central Park. We'd had little platonic dates for the couple of years we'd known each other, and we had planned to get some food and stroll through the woods that afternoon. *i wonder if she realizes that i'm actually madly in love with her. shit, i should have grabbed some flowers from the discard bin; there were a few good ones there... but i've given her a million flowers.* Before I realized it, there she was. That must've been the way Columbus felt when he spotted America, but I wondered if she felt the way the Indians felt when they spotted Columbus.

It wasn't that Sandra didn't look happy to see me, but she still looked... well, less than happy. Before I could say a word, she started, "Francis, I gotta tell you something. I can't stay. Danny Albanese's father got great tickets to the circus at the Garden and he invited me to go with him. Then, afterward, we're gonna have dinner with the ring master at some great restaurant down in the Village." She might as well have ripped out my heart and stomped on it. "I'm sorry," she continued, "but I gotta go. He's sending a car. My mother's so excited about it. I wonder if it's black or white. See you soon." She gave me a sheepish glance over her shoulder, hoping I'd be just a tiny bit as excited for her as she was for herself.

I'd never uttered a word, and I remained just as silent as she ran off. I stood frozen in place for what felt like hours as thousands of people brushed past. Then, without thinking totally about it, I broke into a westward sprint across Broadway – zigzagging like Gayle Sayers through a field of lions – then across the West End, down to the river. Where the pavement ended, I let out a dead-raising yell that was the most primal moment of my young life. There were no tears. Just... in the distance... New Jersey. *jesus fucking christ, what a pathetic sight. nothing but retards over there.* Fury rumbled up from the pit of my stomach, gurgling through my lungs and voice box. "I fucking hate you!" I screamed across the Hudson. The echo screamed it back. *the feeling's mutual.*

It was dusk, and that would soon become darkness. *great, nothing to do. god, my chest hurts. i hope i'm not having a heart attack. it's your heart, alright, but it ain't no coronary.* I felt like the Tin Man, only Dorothy skipped on down the Yellow Brick Road with some midget monkey from the Wicked Witch's crew. *i'd like to crush his fucking sicilian skull. but that's not who you are. you're just going to rise above it and have a florist shop that'll blow them all away. they'll see. ...but the pain is still enormous.*

Off in the not-too-distant distance, I could see the flames from a burning 55-gallon drum French-kissing the night. Around it, a United Nations of humanity was all in the same pain. As I approached them, a gravelly voice seemed to come from nowhere. "What's up there, young brother? Five dollars gets you in. We's offerin' whatever floats yo' boat: booze, songs, laughs, tears, dust–"

"What do you mean dust?" I cut him off.

"Angel dust, mo'fucker," the old man came back, slightly annoyed. "Dust" sounded different, and that's all I wanted right then: different. I peeled off a five, took a stiff swig and made the acquaintance of one weird fucking angel. Before long, things went pain-free; my body went numb, and those flames kissed deeper. Credence Clearwater Revival's "Lodi" blared inside my head: "Oh, Lord, stuck in Lodi again." Over and over. Seriously off-key. *this is nice, like one of the caves in "catcher in the rye." only problem is i'm staring at fucking jersey.* I had no idea how much time had passed, but I abruptly found myself in a haze... nothing like I'd ever felt before. I was tingling-numb from head to toe. I could still think about Sandra, but I couldn't <u>feel</u> about Sandra. *yes... salvation. hey man, this is cool.*

Through the burning barrel's sparking tongues, I could see the old black man laughing hysterically. Obviously at me. "You are without a doubt one of the most fucked-up white guys I have ever met in my life, Irish," he coughed out between guffaws. "For the last half hour, you been yellin', whoopin', cryin', laughin' and lookin' generally fuckin' psychotical all in one place... without moving. It's gotta be pussy, parents, or both; you's too young to be this crazy." I just kept staring at him. I think I had forgotten how to speak English, but he continued on, "Name's Sonny Blue. They call me Blue cuz I stays that way... blue. And this is my can... sort of my spot, ya dig? But don't worry. You's in the right place, Irish. You don't wanna say and I don't wanna know; too personal. I don't do personal.

"Ya see, I gots the <u>real</u> United Nations here, not that sham on First Avenue. 'Round this can comes everyone. Oh, yeah. I've had Congressmen, TV producers, models, doctors, priests.... Even had some young yogi dude who had a thing for Nicky Barnes' Uptown "H." See? I'm eclectic. Tonight my offerin's dust; tomorrow it could be smack. Next week, some drummed-up, hippie-shit LSD. (But I tries to save that for full moons. Heh heh. What a fucking show, Irish.) We don't do much speed here, 'cept for the beans from Jackson Heights. Been beginning to show up with some nice coke, though. They claim it's pure candy. Shit. I know my shit. Pure would kill you; they cut it with speed, but it's a nice number.

"I don't know how you found me, but it's cool. I like your face anyhow. You welcome here." He started to turn away and then remembered, "Oh! Also, if you see any wood layin' around next time you come back... and you will come back... bring it with. You know, keep the home fires burning." I didn't know if I was supposed to stick around or leave there and then, but I thought I thanked him, or at least I did the best I could manage and walked slowly away along Tenth Avenue on legs of Twinkies.

I floated into the deli on 56th to the sound of Mrs. Allesandro's customary "Hello, Francis. How is a-my favorite flower delivery boy in all of a-New York?" But this time the owner's wife added a quick "You look sick." Mumbling something about having the flu, I tried to change the subject by asking after her son, Michael. Singing out in her thick Italian accent, Mrs. A. barely took a breath. "Oh, he's alright. He's at a-fencing class. A-fencing class. Worthless! How he's going to use this in a-life, I don't know. Maybe slice-a the eggplant with the sword." She laughed from her toes. "I'll-a make-a you some hot minestrone soup; make-a you better, eh? Sit down over there." Moments later, a steaming cardboard container with speckles of red hot pepper on top got deposited in front of me. "That's-a the secret; burn it right out." I was so starved, I wolfed it down without savoring a bite... not that I could've tasted it anyway. I couldn't taste. Nothing. Nor feel. Mrs. Allesandro had stood over me the whole time, watching me inhale the soup. The concern was clear in her voice, "That's on me, Francis. You say-a hello to your parents now, okay? Such a-nice people." I tried to make a stoned notation: *remember to remember to bring this lady some flowers.* I knew I'd forget, though.

back to the street. four steps exactly to the alleyway: lurch... launch... minestrone is bottle rocket city. move. sweat. fuck. really? everything in my body tells me i'll never get home. now twelve blocks to go. keep seated, folks; the captain has put on the no smoking sign. landing in just a few minutes. umbrella weather in the kitchen, dank. and thank you for flying air angel dust; know you will again, so please don't forget to take your personal items with you... while you've got them. fuck, i'd just left half of them on the wall. Halting my run, I finally saw the stoop. Easy steps to home: 602 Tenth Avenue. Safety: the whole while, I'd been telling myself that, if I could just get there, I'd be safe. Essentially like being on base in *Ringolevio.* Lazy passers-by headed north. Roving in all directions was the standard human traffic: hookers, pimps, westies, easties, toughies, trannies, fucking wannabes. All was well in the Kitchen. *hey, 'night, stoop.* Clumsily, I stumbled up five flights to crash.

Yawning, I turned off my alarm and rose the next morning feeling surprisingly good until I noticed a smell like a barn yard animal. *but what are all these carrots doing in my clyde fraziers? nevermind.* Eventually, the memories of the previous night answered the question, but there was no time to dwell on that since I had to go to work; that was actually unusual for a Saturday. The boss, Benjamin Levine, was Jewish, and Jews don't work on Saturdays; it's their Sabbath. That particular Saturday, though, I had been told to report to work at 10:30 sharp.

I showered and dressed, scarfing down a bowl of corn flakes with some O.J. and a sip of cold coffee, before bounding down the stairs. Rocketing out the door and to the left, I headed east on 43rd until I passed Le Madeleine, that new little café that had opened up the year before, and then took a right to run all the way down Ninth Ave. to 27th Street. Week in and week out, I'd trod this same path over to Sixth Avenue a million times... the corner of Sixth and 27th, to be exact. Surprisingly, the door was locked at the Levine Floral Company. Alarmed, I looked down at my Timex. *well, it's 10:30 a.m. killed it, but shit, maybe i'm wrong; maybe that dust fucked up my mind and gave me amnesia. ohmygod, what's that hissing sound? oh.... but am i hearing things? shit, the dust made me retarded. i'll end up one of jerry's kids.*

"Hey, Francis, over here." The unmistakable voice of Benny Levine pulled me back to reality. And if that hadn't done it, I would've recognized Benny by his hand. I turned around to see a black limo with smoked windows, out of which stuck a solitary hand. There was only one other person in the world with a better manicure: Barbra Streisand... but none with a pinky ring sporting a "B" made of diamonds as well. "Get in."

The car slid away from the curb, "Good morning, Benny. How's everything?"

"Never better, kid. Just give me a minute. This is my new driver and we're sort of getting acquainted. Eddie, turn right onto Broadway." The driver gave a quick nod. "So, how are you doing, kid?"

"I'm great, thanks," came my reply, "but not doing as well as you are. That's some suit you've got on. I've seen you decked to the nines before, but you look like you just stepped down off of the screen. You going to a funeral or something?"

"No, no, my boy. Nothing like that. Just some personal business to take care of. But you like the suit?" I nodded emphatically. "Well, you should. It's 100% Mongolian cashmere... Hart Schaffner Marx. The shirt? Custom-made by some Chink over on Madison. I've got hundreds of them in every hue of the rainbow. The shoes are Italian leather, also custom-made by some peasant whose every meal his whole life will be eaten with a spoon and a bowl.

"So why am I telling you all this?" he continued. "Because life is about circumstances... and what you make of them. 'Custom' is the word, my boy. Everything 'custom.' A nice station to reach in life, 'custom.' That's what you want to be working towards. That's your goal. Remember that, kid."

I was just barely following his train-of-thought with this lecture, but I worked at paying attention all the same. "I'd do anything to be as successful as you are, Benny."

"I appreciate that, but that's not my point. Do you think I got all of this from flowers? Hell no. I do alright at the flower shop, but not enough to live the way I like. How you get to be where you like... how to get to custom... that's what I'm going to teach you. And your education starts today.

"Eddie," he said, giving new directions to his driver, "keep going all the way down to the ferry. Just drive on; we're going to go over and back." Benny picked up one of the bags that had been sitting in the seat next to him and took a deep sniff. "Mmm. Deli food. Jewish Heaven. You like, kid? I got Hebrew National hot dogs, knishes, cream soda, some strudel. Oh, and stuffed derma. But you wouldn't want that. And you really wouldn't if you knew what it was," he added with a chuckle.

My stomach lurched a bit as I revisited the alleyway scene post-rocket launch. "Thanks. I'll take a dog, Benny."

"Eddie, put on WABC-AM so I can hear Cosell. There's just something about his voice on a Saturday, you know?" Benny seemed to enjoy his Saturdays like a kid would. "Besides, I've got money on nine college games today, kid. You hear me loud and clear, though: that Cosell, he's on the pad; I know it. Francis, any Jew working on a Saturday is on the angle." I laughed out loud at the irony of what he'd just said.

The distinctive drawl of Howard Cosell broke through the laughter and rustling of bags in the back of the limo: "Today we'll be discussing Joe 'Willie' Namath, Muhammad Ali and St. John's at The Garden...."

"Louie, what color is your sweater today?" Benny shouted over Cosell's voice "Eddie, Francis, I'll bet you both a yard Carnesecca wears a Scottish cardigan with diamonds. If he does, I'm betting the ranch; it's a lock." Eddie and I caught one another's look of confusion in the rear view mirror, but neither of us wanted to interrupt Benny's gambling rambling. We continued eating from the white sacks, listening to Cosell's broadcast with periodic interruptions from Benny. It wasn't long before Eddie hit the ramp and glided to a stop on the ferry. Benny instructed him to cut the engine and crack the windows a little. Pushing a U.S. Grant into his hand, he added, "Go up top for a while and get some air while I talk to the kid. You'll discover that one of the perks of this little part of our trips is that, between the snack counter and the wild pussy you can always find onboard, you'll never have any trouble keeping busy. Once these broads get over to Staten Island, it's over, but believe me: the snatch drips across the Hudson. Get lucky and throw a hump into one in the bathroom... usually black or P.R. Just buy them some soda and chips and they'll polish your helmet while Lady Liberty blushes."

Eddie looked totally dazed as he walked away; I was speechless. But Benny just roared with laughter. I'd never seen this Jekyll and Hyde side of Mr. Levine before, but maybe it was because I'd always liked him, no matter what. Benny Levine had been an oasis of kindness.

I could hear the sound of the shit-colored water slapping against the piss-colored hull as it lurched from the pier and Benny began my education. "Francis, you met my boys, Eli and Ari, when their mother brought them into town to shop, right?" I nodded. "They're good kids and I love them with all my heart. I'd step in front of a bus for them without thinking, and have no doubts that Eli will go to school, be a lawyer, while Ari becomes a dentist. Hell, he's already talking about giving his little rabbit a root canal for Christ's sake!" Benny let out a chuckle that lifted the mood a bit as he put his arm around me lightly. "I would like nothing better than to teach them my business... and not just the floral business, if you understand my meaning, but they're not like you: tough, rough and tumble, black eyes, skinned knees. They don't know how to jump a roof or play stick ball... leap off the point. Understand?

"And, you know, they've got no idea that some of the greatest boxers of all time were Jewish – Whitey Bimstein, Charley Goldman, Ray Arcel. These guys taught me how to throw dice in the back room of Stillman's Gym, the fucking Mecca of boxing for all time! They lived in Cedarhurst, LI, and I'm from fucking Rivington Street!" Benny became more animated as he went on. "My heroes were the John Garfields, the Meyer Lanskys, the Benjamin Siegels (you probably heard him called 'Bugsy'), Barney Ross.... But, Esther's father and the boys' grandfather is who the whole community calls Rebbe. It's a religious position of great esteem and importance. We tolerate one another, but it would just never do for Eli and Ari to inherit my business. Do you understand?"

"Sorry," I stammered. "I'm not sure that I do."

"I love my boys; don't get me wrong. In order to give them the things that we've always wanted... to make sure that they <u>could</u> grow up to be lawyers and dentists, I've had to do some things that I shouldn't have... things I couldn't necessarily talk about. But it doesn't mean I'm ashamed of what I've done. In fact, I'm proud of the business that I've built, on the books and off. And when a man gets to be my age, he starts thinking about who will carry on his work after he's gone. That can't be the boys, but I see the potential in you to be good at this line of work. And believe me: I mean that as nothing but a compliment. I've always seen that something special in you... and so I'd like to teach you the ins and outs, the subtleties of my business. But you have to learn it from the ground up. Are you following me now?" Intrigued, I nodded and stuffed more fries in my mouth. "Good. So here's the skinny. I want you to work for me."

A bit confused, my tongue pushed half-chewed French fries to either side of my mouth to make room for a muffled, "But I already do, don't I?"

"Yes, but I mean <u>really</u> work for me. What I need... what I want you to start doing is serving as my Shabbos Goy." He could see that the look of befuddlement on my face wasn't lifting. "It's a Jewish thing. Ultra religious Jews can't even flip a light switch on Shabbat (that's our Sabbath), and that puts me in a squeeze. All my action heats up on Saturday, and being that my wife is the offspring of a man everyone thinks is holier than Swiss cheese, I'm screwed. I have to abide by the rules. Fortunately, when he kicks there's a massive inheritance in it at least. Anyway, what I need is for you to lay some bets, pick up money, bring messages to whatever broad I happen to be seeing, that kind of shit. I'll give you a hundred bucks cash a day, and then match that in a bank account I'll set up for you. You know we Jews excel at money management, right?" he asked, punctuating the question with a slight smirk and an observant, raised eyebrow. "You won't be able to touch it because I ain't gonna tell you where it is."

"That all sounds great, but would I only work for you on Saturdays, then?" I asked, still trying to take it all in.

"Oh, no. Part of learning the business includes the legitimate side too. And there's still a great deal I will teach you about the floral business. You've got a true talent with flowers, and you can learn even more from Chonley than you can from me, so you'll still work side-by-side with him.

But, it would be best that you not tell him about the extra work and the extra money I give you since being my Shabbos Goy <u>used</u> to be his job. I mean, don't get me wrong; I like him a lot. He's the best flower man there is, but I need someone a little more dependable for my non-floral-related business. I think that someone is you. So what do you think, kid?"

The stream-of-consciousness slowed to a halt, and although I didn't quite understand everything that he'd said, I knew a good deal when I saw one. "Sure, Benny. Of course I'll do it for you. I could use the extra money anyway."

"Excellent," he replied. "Then here's your first assignment: take this letter to Yolanda Gomez at 524 West 55th, Apt C. Tell her, 'Same place as usual, tomorrow.' Francis, I'm telling you – this woman has honey nectar dripping from between her legs. I have to double-shvitz when I leave her or else stray animals would follow me around." I laughed. "I also need you to deliver these receipts to the Eighth Ave. Blarney Stone on 56th. You'll give them to the owner, a big Irish fella who's always sitting at the end of the bar. Goes by the name of–"

"Patsy," I finished his sentence.

"Ah, shit. That's right. Patsy Doonan. He'd be your uncle. Hmm. Well, we can't have you making that delivery then, can we? He's one tough bastard, your Uncle Patsy, infamous all up and down the West Side. They used to tell a story about him during the St. Patrick's Day Parade, when he backed off five Guinea scumbags who came in to shake him down by yelling as loud as he could, 'Bring on the punting unit!' Those wops bolted as if the Celtic militia was on its way up from the basement."

"Yeah," I responded, "I've heard that story at family gatherings ten million times... nine million of them from Uncle Patsy."

"Well, part of working for me is figuring out a way to solve problems. If you don't want Pats knowing what kind of work you're up to, you'll have to figure out a solution." Benny had clearly intended that as a test. *had he known he was going to do that all along?*

I knew that Uncle Patsy wouldn't have taken too well to my new duties since his greatest wish for me was the priesthood, but there was no way I was turning down the opportunity to make that kind of money by working with Benny to avoid keeping a family member in the dark. *wouldn't be the first time; won't be the last.* I'd already figured out how to deal with the problem anyway. I'd subcontract some of the stickier work to my best friend, Howie. *i'll throw him $20 and he'll be happy.* "Not a problem, Benny. Is that everything for now?" He gave a brief nod as Eddie climbed back into the driver's seat while trying to shove his shirttails into his waistband.

"Thanks, Mr. Levine. You're nothing short of a prophet. I met this young Puerto Rican beauty topside," Eddie began.

"Who'll blow up to 200 pounds within a few years... and grow a mustache," Benny added to me under his breath while I did my best to stifle a laugh.

"There wasn't a whole helluva lot of room in the toilet and she was calling me every curse word in the Spanish language," Eddie continued. "I kept wondering if there was anybody waiting to use the bathroom and if the cursing scared them away. One thing's for sure. The rocking of the ferry was helping my stroke!"

We all three laughed heartily as the ferry ground to a stop at the river's edge. "My pleasure, Eddie. You can disembark the ferry and drive Uptown." Benny continued reading through a short stack of newspapers as we headed back up to the west side of Midtown. As we were approaching the store, he turned to me and said, "Go inside and grab your mother some roses from the store. It'll be a nice surprise to take home."

Ever since Battery Park, I had been trying to put together the right words to say to Benny to express my gratitude appropriately. "Mr. Levine...

Benny... I just don't know what to say. I don't know how to thank you enough for this chance. I promise I won't let you down. You have my word on that. I just don't know how I'll ever repay you for all the unbelievably nice things you've done for me... and continue to do for me all the time."

"Just keep our arrangement between us and do a good job; that'll be payment enough. And maybe sit Shiva for me when all is said and done." He could tell from the look on my face that I had no idea what that meant, so he explained, "It's when you mourn someone's passing in the Jewish way. Not as exciting as an Irish wake, I'll give you, but it's about respect."

"You can count on it. I feel like I should kiss your ring or something," I joked.

Unexpectedly, as a father would, Benny leaned over and kissed, pinched and then patted my cheek. "Don't forget the flowers, kid. I'll see you during the week."

I got out and the car pulled away. I strode into the shop to get two dozen of the nicest roses we had in every color, and heading home, my mind replayed the events in Benny's limo up until I walked through the front door of our apartment. Daddy was watching baseball and Mommy was cooking some sort of roast for Saturday dinner. My sisters, Philomena, Bernadette and Charlotte were at CYO girls' basketball. Nobody spoke. It made me wonder if they'd been fighting again. Whatever the reason, it was as if I were invisible. I suddenly felt overwhelmingly sad and eventually just laid down the flowers and went right back the way I'd come.

Once I reached the stoop, I saw my best friend, Howie Nesto, an Italian Jew... who swore he was Irish... approaching from across the avenue. He was more than just my best friend. As the saying went, he was my "brother from another mother." We were inseparable and went everywhere... did everything together. Nothing could come between us. With the Donegal cap he always wore leaning to one side, talking out of the side of his mouth like Leo Gorcey, he called out, "Frankie Flowers, my boy, how the hell are you?"

"Good, brother!" I replied. "Listen, before you pop a squat, run this up to my Uncle Patsy at the Blarney Stone, would you? But don't tell him it's from me."

His look of quizzical defiance was unmistakable. "And what do I look like to you, fucking Hop-Sing or what?" I took a twenty from my pocket and pinched it between both thumbs and forefingers. Closing his eyes to slits and sticking his lower lip behind his front teeth, Howie's tone changed. "Uh, would you rike a sta'ch on those shirts, sir?" Giving him the bill for the errand, but not the Chinese impression, I had to laugh at Howie scampering down the avenue.

boy i sure wish i knew where sandra was. i got some extra money; we could go to the village for good pizza... or even the movies. i wonder if that "blues brothers" flick is out yet. ah, it wouldn't matter anyway. i still have to deliver the letter for benny. Yolanda Gomez buzzed me up and was waiting at her door for the letter, looking like Sophia Loren. She looked right into my blue eyes as they were roused from the sight of two big, black nipples busting through a tee shirt. Smiling slightly, she said, "Thank you, papi," and slowly closed the door.

Despite the quick "hello and goodbye," I had a hardon you could dangle five wet serge suits from... on wooden hangers... and I had to do something about it, so I ran straight to the Show World Sex Emporium over on Eighth, at 42nd. Ah, the Street of Sin. You could get some tokens, pick a girl, head into a booth and jerk off till you were dizzy... or out of tokens. I'd usually slip away quickly after the deed was done, though, before the old black guy with the mop had to come in and clean up the nut. That always made me feel guilty, but I was usually more worried that Sandra would see me. *but, whatever. a stiff dick has no conscience.* That time I got some kind of Eastern European contortionist. *easy cum, easy go. the pleasures of youth.*

As dusk was falling, I found myself wading through the sea of Cleopatra Jones-look-alike hookers on my way past a fruit store. Piles of wood were stacked up out front from broken orange crates. *that would burn real good.* I gathered some up and headed Uptown to the "United Nations," wondering what kind of offering Sonny would have that day. I ran into Howie returning from the Blarney Stone.

"That uncle of yours is whacked, Francis. He made me drink three shots of Irish whisky with him, toasting some guy named Adam Day Crayola. Who the fuck's that?"

"Eamon De Valera," I corrected him. I didn't have the slightest clue who he was either, but my Uncle Patsy had done the same thing to me, so I'd heard the name. "I don't know, but maybe it's one of his old, dead bartenders. He gets real close to 'em and takes things about them all personal. A lot of them probably die trying to drink with him and keep up."

"No fuckin' way," came Howie's reply, to which I just smirked. Noticing what I was carrying, he added, "Where you going with all the wood, a boy scout meeting?"

It dawned on me that Howie would get into visiting the U.N. too, so I invited him along. "Yeah, you could say that. You wanna come?" I could tell by the look on his face that Howie was in, but his words were drowned out by Sinatra music that had to have been louder than if you were sitting front row at The Garden. Cruising by on our left was a cherry red Oldsmobile Delta 88, carrying none other than J.R. Albanese (the father of my neighborhood nemesis, Danny), and a few members of his crew. Most of us knew that J.R. was short for Johnny Rugs, the nickname he'd been given because his hair piece looked like a bad carpet remnant from a Sears fire sale. But nobody had the balls to tell him that to his face.

Howie chimed in what we were both thinking, "I wonder if he knows how ridiculous he looks."

"Oblivious," I added. All the members of the Albanese crew scrunched up their noses in disgust at us. I couldn't understand what their problem was, but I did understand Danny a little. The kid never had a chance; his old man was only third from the left on the Darwin Chart. *better to break out than stay here and deal with their shit.* "C'mon, Howie. Let's go." 72nd and the Hudson had become a kind of West Side Shangri-La for me, and Howie strode by my side without question. In fact, there was a lot of silence on the way, that great, unforced, comfortable kind that can only exist between true friends.

Sonny saw me coming and shot me a big, rotten-toothed grin, gazing at me over his shades, "Table for two? Right this way," he motioned, looking down at my bundle. "Nice looking wood." *that comment could get your ass beat in the wrong neighborhood.* I chuckled to myself. "Thanks for the contribution to the barrel, my man. Would you like to have the 'Special of the Night?'"

I was intrigued and amused, so I decided to play along, bowing. "Why yes, I would, my kind sir, but first say hello to my best friend, Howie."

"Whaddaya say, whaddaya know, Howie. Sonny Blue's the name. They call me Sonny cuz I stays that way... sunny." A great, smoker's-wheeze laugh accompanied the handshake. "Pleased to meet you, Howie. Tonight we're offering the opium plate; fresh catch of the day. It will blow your mind, gentlemen. And to cleanse your palates, we have some MD 20/20, compliments of the wine cellar of Mr. Clarence... Bigblackmothafucka." It was clear that Sonny didn't know the last name of the enormous, jet black man towards whom he'd just gestured. *does he know any of our last names?* Clarence caught the acknowledgement and nodded, a case of red "Mad Dog" 20/20 at his feet. "Francis, you stoke the fire while I stoke this pipe." Another wheezy laugh. Passing the pipe, he added, "Howie, you're up. Hang onto your hat, my little brother." Sparks flew and so did the time.

Eight hours later, we were all still smoking, some laying on the ground, some leaning wherever they could find a spot. Howie and I were sitting together in a far-off land where we could be or do anything we wanted. *but were our pain and rage too much to allow us? that shit was the thief of potential. we were lost in the night with dozens of black men who would've traded places with either of us in a heartbeat.*

stoke the pipe, stoke the fire, stoke the night.

A couple of days later, I'd walked down the block and a half to grab some breakfast at the Kraft Diner, when the counter person greeted me with, "Well, good morning, Francis. I'm glad you also came to visit us before you left. We're all going to miss the Doonans around here." Now, Rohit was one of the nicest Indian guys in NYC, so I knew he was being sincere, but that didn't make what he said any less confusing... and he could tell that by the look on my face. "Oh, I'm sorry. Am I wrong? Your mother and father were in here yesterday, and I thought I overheard them telling the owner that they are moving to Long Island soon. Were they talking of someone else, perhaps? I was sure they had said something about better schools and opportunities for their...." his speech slowed and then stopped, doubtlessly because of the look of questioning disbelief on my face. "... Three daughters," he finished quietly, swallowing uncomfortably. I didn't know whether to feel hurt or angry. To break the awkward silence, Rohit threw in, "But I'm probably wrong. I'm sure I didn't hear it right. Don't listen to me. Coffee?" I started to nod yes, but then realized I wasn't hungry anymore. As I stood to leave, Rohit clearly felt bad and tried to change the subject in hopes of getting my mind off what he'd revealed. "Oh, did you change your mind? Well, okay. No problem. I wonder if you could do a favor for me. Will you tell your friend, Howie, that I need to see him soon?"

"Sure," I said, almost absentmindedly, wondering what he wanted with Howie nonetheless. Back out on the street, the spring air helped to lift my spirits a tiny bit as I started for "flower world." I didn't know if it was because I was hurt by the shock from Rohit, but I was craving getting high so bad. The temptation to head Uptown was heavy, and although I did my best to focus and do what I was supposed to do, the self-intervention failed.

As I approached Ninth, it was like a firefight: seven different kinds of black guys scurried up to me, creating a din of voices overlapping one another, "Smoke? I got some hash too. All the way from Turkey," one rang out.

"How much?" I focused on him.

"Ten dollar pieces. This shit is lovely, homeboy, and the bodega on the corner has some nice little pipes." Without giving it another thought, I hustled to the corner and bought a little purple pipe – my favorite color – and a disposable lighter. Ducking into a doorway on 39th Street, I broke up the hash... jet black with little white marks inside. *suck, inhale, suck, inhale, hold it... a little longer.* Gasping for air, I finally exhaled, but as the pipe burned my fingers, their pain couldn't match my pain inside... and so it was neutralized. A light rain started to fall.

Back on my journey, with things feeling a little bit better once the medicine had been administered, I reached work and actually got into it... I mean <u>really</u> into it: sorting, cleaning, packing thousands of flowers from every reach of the world. *this must be what heaven smells like.* I was a real cool worker: meticulous, conscientious and immaculate. Eight hours passed by in a clip. On my way out, the secretary, Susie, stopped me. "Don't forget this envelope that Mr. Levine left for you. 'Night, Francis."

"Thanks, Susie," I mumbled back, more interested in the manila envelope... but not as much as I was in the hash that had been calling to me from my coat pocket all day. I stopped two doors down to smoke the rest of it and then opened the envelope. Inside that were three more white envelopes, each marked: "Patsy @ Blarney Stone" *more work for howie*, the fat one read "Lucky's on 48th @ Ninth Ave." with a little note scribbled next to the address that said, "Make sure you tip the kid, you cheap cocksucker." And, of course the third envelope was the one I'd been expecting: one for Yolanda Gomez. One final item slid out of the manila envelope, a sheet of paper, folded in half, with a Ben Franklin inside. *ben franklin nothing. they oughta have ben <u>levine's</u> smiling mug on there!* The sheet of paper held a note from Benny:

Yolanda thought you were sexy. Don't even think about it or I'll cut your putz off! Are you even circumcised? Ha ha.

Ben

All I could do was laugh. *damn i'm stoned... and hungry. those go together like a horse and carriage. shit! dinner time! should be on the table right about now.*

At home, the family was gathered around the table. No one would look at me. Something was definitely up. I was unsurprisingly late, so I kissed everybody and went to wash my hands. The usual silence was room tone. I decided to break that silence. "Listen, when you guys move, I've decided I'm gonna keep the apartment as... you know, sort of a homestead. Besides, I'm not too interested in Long Island and I gotta start saving money for my floral shop. Benny's gonna teach me the business-end of flowers." I sat back for a second to take in their reactions. I couldn't determine if there was more relief in their faces that they didn't have to tell me or surprise that I had turned the tables with the newscaster role. My mother smiled at me with a glisten in her eyes that could've been tears. *or was it concern that i wanted to stay? weird.* I forged ahead. "Daddy, if you could talk to the super and tell him I'm staying, that would be cool. So you girls must be excited, right?"

"Yeah," they said in unison. "We can't wait," added Charlotte.

Daddy finally spoke, "Francis, your mother and I have been meaning to tell you for awhile now. It's just so hard to get your attention lately."

I couldn't really argue. I didn't know that I really wanted to. "Pass the potatoes, please. They're great as usual, Mommy." Dinner went on pretty much as usual after that, and once I'd helped clear the table, I went to my room. I was actually tired from the day. I dropped the needle onto the Beatle's "White Album" and clamped on a gigantic set of headphones attached to my Harmon Kardon stereo *(top of the line; clipped by none other than howie, himself, the master booster who could steal the beanie offa the pope's head during mass in st. peter's. ah. now i know why rohit wants to see howie.)* Sometime during "Rocky Raccoon," I drifted off to sleep.

The next morning found me back on the stoop, bright and early, on the lookout for our super. Castillo was a real fucking hustler, one arm longer than the other... and that arm was always in somebody's pocket. I met his gaze so he lumbered over to tell me he'd spoken with my father and everything was cool. *i wonder how much he hustled out of the old man.* I just nodded and dismissed him with a stare. That stare quickly shifted, though, when I caught sight of Sandra O'Casey and two of her friends coming up Tenth Avenue in their St. Agnes Catholic School uniforms. We locked eyes and she instinctively smiled, which wilted into a frown when she saw the look of intentional indifference on my face. I tried to disguise that I was hurt about her going to the circus. I wished I could tell her, but I just couldn't. The two shanty Irish, big mouth, fat, fucking cows who were with her started singing "Tiptoe Through the Tulips" in Tiny Tim voices as a way to get under my skin about the florist thing. I refused to give them the pleasure of a reaction, so one of them called me a scum bag. *talk about the pot and the kettle, bitch.*

She was the sister of none other than Kelly McCluskey, a.k.a. Kelly the Mick, the self-appointed local head honcho with the Irish gang world. I knew she was just parroting him; there was no love lost whatsoever there. Kelly the Mick had offered me a lot of opportunities with his "gang," but I'd declined them all. I wasn't interested in crime, but even less into working for Kelly the Mick. I had the looks, the stature, the voice and the balls, sure... but I'd chosen to live life on the level and that pissed Kelly off because no one said no to him.

Sandra stepped up onto the stoop in an effort to talk to me, but I brushed past her and took off. Her other friend sneered at my back, "You're a real prick, Flowers. Somebody should put you in line. Sandra was quietly sad; she hadn't meant to hurt me. But I couldn't see her remorse. I'd hoofed it to Ninth Ave. with nowhere to go, tears streaming down my face. *how can it be like this with a whole new world in front of me? fuck it. i'm gonna join the army. i could just walk right over to that recruiting station in times square. hell, i'm almost there.* But the feeling evaporated. I knew I'd be the one sticking flowers in the ends of the soldiers' guns, not pointing them.

I hopped on a Downtown Broadway bus, taking it all the way to Spring Street and then hanging a left on my way to Little Italy for some pesto pasta and a little idle wandering. Exploring The City always made me feel like a lone wolf on the frozen tundra. I kind of liked that feeling. Heading over to Washington Square Park, I just wanted to sit at the fountain among the Bohemians for awhile. For some reason, their world always appealed to me: the smells of patchouli, smiles, music and the sounds of guitars. *shit, i wish i had a joint.* All of a sudden, a Frisbee came out of nowhere and hit me square in the head and I went down as if I'd been shot.

From my back, I could see the silhouette of a girl standing over me, with little wisps of golden hair glowing in the sun like a halo. This hippie girl with long, flowing hair, cut-offs, and a peasant shirt that <u>almost</u> hid two big tits and a pair of equally large bushes of hair under each arm leaned down to ask my forgiveness in a manner of speech that was only heard in the Woodstock Nation. "Oh, my God. I cut your head." She must've been right because I realized that salty taste in my mouth was from my own blood. A thin stream ran right down my face like the sort you get in a fight from a head butt. *how the fuck did a frisbee do that?*

I didn't realize that another girl had been with her until she bent down and said, "Let's take him to our dorm and fix him up." I wasn't rejecting the offer, and thought I'd even pretend to be dizzy so they'd practically have to carry me the couple of blocks over to 4th. I'd put it together that they were NYU students, and found out on the walk that Monica and Sally were both from San Francisco. *god, but they smelled good.*

Their room looked like a Moroccan opium den. There had to have been eight bongs on a coffee table. Closing the door after us, Sally said, "Francis, we should smoke some weed to get you anesthetized, okay?" *no arguments from me!* Monica was like Florence Nightingale. She put me down on her water bed and started to clean me up with a washrag. The wound was really small, but it spurted blood like a geyser. Before long, Sally had a bong gurgling and smoking. "Here. Take a hit," she offered, holding her breath. "Hawaiian bud, primo shit." *did i die and go to heaven?* While I drew in a hit, Sally turned on The Dead's "Friend of the Devil" and swung back around like a dancer to grab the bong back. "You know these guys?" she asked

"Course," I coughed back, blowing out two lungs full of weed smoke. "Garcia's a genius. Where are you two from in Frisco, anyway?"

"Well, we both live in the Bay Area, but we're <u>from</u> the Haight. What about you?" Monica replied before taking an impressively large hit on the pipe.

"Haight Ashbury?" I asked. "Wow. I'm just from here. Well, not here, here; not the Village. I'm from The Kitchen. Hell's Kitchen.

"Look at that, man," Sally mused. "Worlds collide through a Frisbee." *we are so fucked up. that is some primo shit.* The bong made its rounds again. And again. I couldn't be entirely sure at that moment, but I think Monica started to play with my hair, twisting a lock around her fingers. I was way too stoned to move even my head, sunk deep in the water bed.

"I want to kiss your wound and make it better," cooed Monica. And she did.

"Me too," chimed in Sally, and followed suit. The next thing I knew, we all had our tongues in each other's mouths and six hands were fumbling with buttons, snaps and zippers.

I stared up at the ceiling and exclaimed silently "YES! Who's better than me, huh? A fuckin' ménage à trois!" *my first. fuck, these girls are sexy.* They ate one another's pussies until they writhed and groaned with orgasms, both of them jerking my swollen, purple-headed cock. *purple. hey. my favorite color again. heh heh. yeah, i am fuckin' stoned.*

Flipped over from my back onto all fours, Monica stared up at me and growled, "Now fuck me while Sally tongues your ass." I noticed a single drop of blood fall from my wound, pass before my eyes and land right on her chest. I guess the pressure must've restarted the bleeding, but I didn't give a shit and neither did she. Monica moaned again and rubbed the blood into her tits like a porn star does a load. I obliged. Several times.

When our miniature riot had run out of steam, we all fell asleep entwined in one another's arms. The room smelled like the elephant house at the Bronx Zoo, but we all-had shit-eating grins on our faces in our sleep.

The naps only lasted about an hour since we all awoke, half-frozen, to see that we'd left the window wide open and night had fallen. Even though it was spring, the nights were still nippy. My frisky Friscoan freaks bid me a fond farewell with their tongues down my throat and told me to come hang out again. *i think i can probably arrange that. heh heh.* Monica walked me to the door, flashed me a peace sign and said, "Adios, amigo." As I was walking to the W. 4th Street subway station in what seemed like super slow motion, it felt like I'd been hit by a train, not a Frisbee. *the shame of the whole thing is that i can't tell the story to any of my friends or even brag to benny; who would believe me?*

I didn't stop replaying the events of that afternoon in my head until I was back in the Kitchen and made it onto the stoop. There was something about that stoop. It was like the captain's bridge on the greatest ocean vessel in the world. Everybody knew me: cops, old ladies, kids, good guys, bad guys, everybody. I had to laugh to myself at the thought that all of those people would be my customers someday. I was laying the ground work now, sort of planting seeds with water and time and sun. I felt truly happy. A rarity. Then Monica and Sally crept back into my head and I wondered if anyone could smell me... or if they had on the train. I had read somewhere that after pungent sex, other people react with attraction. My Uncle Patsy always claimed that the French fuck all day and then wring their sweaty clothes and bed sheets into bottles and then mix it with uric acid (which he was always sure to point out is pig piss). Then they sell it to us as "Eau de Parfum" for an arm and a leg. He claimed some guy told him that while he was buying a case of Chanel No. 5 off of him. But Patsy always got the better of them; he'd get them whacked on shots of whisky and then acquire a case by throwing them a twenty-spot... or else throwing them out. *musta been true. every female in the doonan brood has a bottle of that chanel.*

From my "captain's chair," I noticed one of my boys from the neighborhood crossing 43rd on his way up Tenth. Malik "Milk" Williams was a poor soul. His old man had been a "fallen" member of the Nation of Islam who was forced to leave the Black Muslim flock when he met, fell in love with, and impregnated, a beautiful Scottish immigrant. On Milk's tenth birthday, his father leapt in front of an Uptown "C" Train out of the blue, and his mother died with a needle in her arm only three years later... or so the word in the Kitchen went. Malik had been on his own since becoming a teenager. The Welfare Department paid his rent, and various families in the neighborhood tried to help out with money, clothes and food when he'd head home with a different friend each night for dinner. *it's real sad; that kid's got talent and looks – caramel-colored skin and bone structure like a* jet magazine *cover model. he's also talented beyond belief, both on wheels... roller skates, skateboards, whatever... and as an artist. there's not a building, doorway or train car on the west side that doesn't have his signature pint carton of milk tagged on it.*

I worried for Malik even though I'd seen his rage come out one night: a couple of guys from Jersey pulled up in front of the stoop, looking for a place to score some dope. Milk and I were deep in conversation, so we basically ignored the frequent requests of jerkoffs in cars with Jersey plates. But that night, one of those scumbags yelled, "Hey, nigger, I'm talking to you! Come here, slave boy. I want to see if you want to wash and wax my car, you motherfucker. I bet you could do a pretty good job with those big nigger lips." At this, there was no more ignoring those two Jersey greasers in their brand new Buick Riviera... sales receipt still on the back window. "Hey, shine," he continued, "Come on. We don't have all night." *big mistake.* Before they could put the car in gear, Malik came off the stoop and picked up an NYC Sanitation garbage can and laid it in sideways through the windshield. Glass was everywhere. Crossing to the other side of the car, dragging the driver half-way out of the open window, Milk beat the guy senseless while the other loud-mouthed cunt in the passenger seat was yelling and trying to decide if he should run for it. Milk had just grabbed a handful of broken glass and started literally turning the guy's face into a bloody pulp when I grabbed Malik from behind and pulled him off the guy.

I'd never seen anything like it. That rage had turned him white in complexion, and he had gone so berserk that he actually wanted to fight me as the next person in his field of vision. The Riviera squealed away as a couple of neighborhood guys had seen the commotion and rushed over to help me. Milk was still fuming so I told them to get him out of here before the cops showed up. *what a shame. milk had just been asking me about how he could get into art school.*

With the sounds of The City retaking dominance over the roar of the melee, I returned to the stoop. The street glistened from the freshly smashed Buick windows. It reminded me of diamonds. At that moment, I realized how tired I was. It was time to call it a night. I climbed the five flights to my new apartment. *well, new that it's mine.* I kicked off my Adidas country sneakers – classic white with green stripes – and lit the remnants of a joint in an ashtray. Grabbing a cold beer from the fridge, I flopped down onto the futon on the floor. *what a physical day. christ, who needs a gym?* I stared ahead at the Bahamian Cooler ceiling fan that my father had picked up for me at Macy's on the old charge card. Daddy showed up with two sixes of Bud, a sack of burgers from the Greek deli, the fan and a ladder. In a flash, he had it installed perfectly; he had been a master electrician at Con Edison for forty years, after all. We ate, drank and laughed under the new spinning fans. Since I was on the top floor, just underneath the roof (and heat rises), Daddy said he figured the fan would help me to keep cool. I still slept with all of the windows open at night to get a nice cross-breeze. Lost in thought about my father, I stared up at the blades keeping a steady circle.

But, as usual, my thoughts turned to Sandra. *i'd like to fix this place up a little. you know: paint, maybe some carpet. not too much furniture, though. i like the open space.* I also liked the idea of cooking, so I was determined to set up a nice kitchen as well. I'd always said that cooking was just good provisions, imagination and not too heavy with the spices, especially if you're entertaining. I loved watching Julia Child on Chanel 13 PBS. *that lady does mescaline, though, i'm positive. i should find out what sandra's favorite food is... probably italian by now.* The anger and frustration overcame me and I punched the futon. My mind drifted all over the place, but it was anchored by thoughts of Sandra. I allowed myself to fantasize about the night I'd invite her over. I planned to fill the whole apartment with flowers and candles. *maybe i'll even go to sam goody and ask that fag manager for some good, romantic music.* I drifted off to sleep with a smile on my face and my head flooded with thoughts and ideas.

---

my cock looks like it went through a meat grinder. holy shit! thanks a lot, ladies from the bay! The pressure from the hot water pouring from the shower head didn't help either. *better stop and get some neosporin at the pharmacy.* I had WNEW FM blasting, rock and roll at its best. That morning, they were doing a whole Rolling Stones set and "Under my Thumb" was shaking the walls of the apartment. Towel flung around my neck, I was swinging my hips like Mick Jagger, singing into a toothpaste tube and feeling really good. Soon I was heading over to the Cuban's for a toasted roll and a Cuban cafe con leche... mucho fuerta. The little lady with the gold teeth smiled at me when a car pulled up, hauling none other than Kelly the Mick and his sidekick, Colin Garvan. *great. i so wish i weren't here.*

Never one to miss the opportunity to be obnoxious, Kelly the Mick swaggered into the luncheonette, asking loudly, "Hey! You got any newspapers, señorita? I need to check the back for the number." The owner handed him a paper, to which Kelly added, "The usual... please." He added the nicety to the end as though she should be grateful for it. She wished they weren't there as much as I did. Garvan gave me a half-a-nod when Kelly the Mick wasn't looking. I just couldn't figure Colin out. He came from a nice family and was always a pretty good kid when we were younger. For Christ's sake, he was the head altar boy at Holy Cross, and he'd become a baby-faced killer, feared by pretty much everyone. *his poor parents.* Kelly the Mick, on the other hand, was your classic bully. His childhood had consisted of welfare cheese and peanut butter. With no father to speak of, his mother ran an after-hours joint and a bordello on Eleventh Ave. She'd died of a heroin overdose awhile back. This guy never had a chance either. I guess because his life was miserable, he was going to make sure everyone else's was too.

The gold tooth owner gave them two steaming plates with eggs, bacon, potatoes and white toast and cups of tea. *real micks.* They wouldn't lay off haranguing the lady: "More catsup," Garvan demanded.

"Any Tabasco?" from Kelly.

"Extra potatoes?"

"Is this butter?" The Spanish lady wanted to cry. She endured it, though. I made a mental note to learn a lesson from her. These two assholes were eating like they were heading for the chair. Spitting out bits of egg as he spoke, Kelly the Mick inquired, "What? Are you too cool to say hello, Doonan? Big shot, huh?"

"No, Kelly," came my reply. I didn't want any shit. "I was just day dreaming, that's all. Hey, Colin, how you doing?"

"Listen, Doonan, we're going to the Big "A" today. Why don't you take a ride, have some laughs? asked Kelly.

"I gotta pass. I have to work and then I've got some stuff to do."

"Well, I'm putting a crew together – strictly Irish, you know – like the Guineas don't let nobody in, well neither are we. Me and Colin here would love for you to go in with us. We're handpicking and you're on our wish list."

"How did I get so lucky?" I answered back.

Clearly Kelly didn't catch the sarcasm. "Well, you're neighborhood, you're Irish, you come from good people and you've always been stand-up. I also know you don't like Danny Albanese 'cause he's banging your girl. Plus, his old man has put a move down and took over the neighborhood. The old Irish let it go; they don't want to do it anymore. Well, fuck that. That's why we're gonna make a comeback. Fuck these wop pricks." Kelly's voice had grown beyond loud. The nice Spanish people working in the shop were terrified. Kelly and Colin stood up. The Mick gave me a hard stare and said in his most threatening voice, "Francis, let's go."

I didn't bat an eye. "No."

Kelly the Mick snarled back, "You're always going to be a cunt, Doonan, you know that? Why don'tcha go play with your flowers and hang out with those Jews and niggers you run with? We're gonna save and preserve this neighborhood without you." They started for the door and then turned. "You change your mind, you know where to find me. Gracias, señorita. Oh, and breakfast is on <u>him</u>," thrusting his finger in my direction. A few seconds later, I could hear the squeal of rubber coming from the street. *must've been kelly's testicles acting as good years, dragging along underneath his chevy impala.* I paid the Cuban lady and left her a good tip. She stroked the back of my hand and smiled. The danger was over, so I hit the streets again.

Blinded by the morning sun back out on the avenue, it was a Saturday and the building at 602 was jumping. Outside was a big moving truck sporting a yellow "W" and a big green shamrock on both sides. The Doonan Family Exodus was under way. Much of the community had turned out to help. They brought gifts, baked goods, cards and well wishes. It was truly a scene. Diana Nuñez, the matriarch of eight from the second floor, had difficulty holding back the tears because she "Would miss such a nice family." In broken Nuyorican, she proclaimed us Doonans "The nicest Irish peoples she ever knew." Seeing this outpouring of sorrow for my family's departure left me conflicted. I just didn't know how to feel. I found myself up on the roof of the building. I didn't feel like I was being abandoned. After all, I was seventeen. I'd have my own place. What <u>didn't</u> I have to feel good about? But what I felt was fear, the way a kid does in the night when he isn't feeling well and it's so dark. Maybe I was feeling lonely. Who knows. I pondered that word as I lit up a joint and inhaled deeply. To the east was the ass end of Broadway. Pigeons filled the air like in the movies. *who the fuck keeps feeding them? fucking rats with wings, if you ask me. it's the age-old question in hell's kitchen.* With the joint consumed and my medication administered, the loneliness lifted and my confidence was restored. *guess it's time to go help the family.*

I couldn't ever remember seeing Daddy and Mommy that excited. It was definitely a new start for them. They were moving to a place out on Long Island called Long Beach, bordered on one side by Lido Beach and bordered on the other by Atlantic Beach. Also known as the Irish Riviera (because it was where families like mine who had saved a couple of nickels relocated to live in "the suburbs"), it was home to a large, affluent Jewish community as well. My family's new house was only a block from the ocean, which was nice for them since our ancestors were all sea people. It would be especially great for my sisters. They were all pretty girls, and I'd never liked the idea of all the vultures in the neighborhood ogling them and trying to get in their pants.

Stepping into the apartment, Mommy was carefully removing the drawers from her prized china closet, the contents of which were as fragile as they were beautiful. Boasting such names as Waterford and Beleek, each piece had been handcrafted in Ireland. She looked up at me as I stood in the door frame, watching her back. She smiled bittersweetly, and gazed at me with a look that only a mother can perfect. Without saying a word, she opened her arms and I flew to her embrace. There was little question that she could smell the marijuana all over me, and although she made no mention of it, the fear washed all over me once again – I was going to be alone. I held on just a little bit longer than I normally would have, even in the face of all that sentimentality, and I think my mother needed it just as much as I did. As we broke our embrace, my mother snapped right back into "To Do" mode. "Listen. I'm going to leave you some dishes and silverware, as well as the big pot and some pans. There'll be plenty of sheets and towels on the shelf in the bathroom as well. And I won't hear a 'no' out of you. I'll be going shopping on Long Island and buying all new stuff, so that's that." A soft kiss on her forehead said "thank you" as loudly as my words would have.

Looking around the place, my whole family was either wrapping, lifting or staring at items, lost in memories. The air was filled with the rousing rhythm of the Furey Brothers' "The Reason I Left Mullingar." The sound of Irish music floated throughout our home, compliments of a radio in the corner and WFUV. Fordham's University's little station broadcast Irish music every Saturday and Sunday, and its notes were infectious. Daddy sat in that corner near the radio, Bud in hand and <u>beaming</u>, when his mouth opened and he spontaneously began to sing along: "To work till you're dead, for one room and a bed; it's not the reason I left Mullingar." We all cracked a smile, wondering if it was joy or the drink that made him sing. He was the captain of this voyage, and we were all along for the ride. Everyone bounced a knee or shook a hip, and even one of the movers stopped and did a bit of a jig. I daresay the movers had never had a better gig. Daddy had barely gotten a full breakfast down their gullets before he was taking their lunch orders, plying them with ice cold Budweiser the whole while.

While we were all occupied by the dancing and packing, and dancing and cleaning, and dancing and carrying, the door opened again, and in stepped Howie carrying a large, obviously heavy box. He gave me a quick nod and then headed straight for my mom and dad. He set the box on the table next to my mother, and although he had obviously rehearsed the speech over and over, Howie said something about, "This day is both a sad and joyous one... kind of like sweet and sour Chinese food." We'd all struggled to keep straight faces as Howie had tried to be as eloquent as he possibly could, but my father snickered under his breath and everyone howled in unison. Mommy kissed Howie on the cheek and began to open the box as the humor of the situation got the better of us and our laughter got deeper and louder. Mommy's gasp stopped all the merriment cold as everyone crowded around the table to peer into the box. The source of Mommy's astonishment was the most staggeringly gorgeous Waterford crystal chandelier any of us had ever seen.

Of course, my father chimed in to clip the wings of the moment. "Howie, my lad, you are going to make inventory day for some Bloomingdale's clerk a total nightmare this month." Even my mother joined in the giggling as my father offered Howie a beer. For half a second, Howie looked unsure, not sure if he was supposed to accept. He'd never been offered alcohol by my dad before. "Oh, go on and take it. It's fine. But if you don't want it, you might consider pouring it on that fancy glass lamp. This thing's so hot here, there's smoke billowing out of the box!" Another round of laughs followed, this time with Howie joining in, Bud in hand. "Now what would you like for lunch? Hot and sour soup from the Chinks?" *a jew eating pork on saturday; that's some funny shit. saturday! shit! i have to go to benny's to pick up my deliveries.* I excused myself, but Howie stayed. We never even gave it a second thought. He and I loved each other like brothers and the family was as much his as it was mine. Hell, we'd spent all of our time together growing up, so we might as well have been raised together.

On my way out the door, I took half a second to stop and take in the scene. Though happy and familial, there was still some realization under the surface of the impending loss everyone was feeling or would be soon. Bounding down the stairs and exploding through the front door of the building, I tore down the avenue. As soon as I rounded the corner onto 43rd, I lit up another joint and had to fight the temptation to stop back in at Show World and drop a quart. That bamboo escape between m'y ₗ helped distract me long enough to get past Show World. *fuck. i'm lovely. not so much walking now as floating.* In what seemed to simultaneously take no time and forever, I arrived in front of the flower shop to find that Benny had left a package with a note on it:

> Kid, meet me at Gino's Restaurant on Lex, btwn 61st & 62nd on Monday. 1:00 p.m. Don't be late. You'll love the joint. They've got zebras on the wall! Told Howie to pick you up a suit. 42 regular, right? He'll give it to you tomorrow. Tell him your shoe size. There's some Italians around somewhere. See you then.
>
> Ben

I couldn't do anything but stand there, staring at the note. Part of it was the weed, but part of it was my disbelief at how life was shaping up for me. It was almost like a movie. All of my contemplating and theorizing had started to round the edges on my buzz, though, and I knew it wouldn't be long before I'd need more, so I grabbed the package and headed back towards home.

I hung the right off of 43rd just in time to see my Uncle Patsy motioning to one of his workers who was tapping a keg in the adjoining lot. What had been organized chaos when I left was a full-fledged, three-ring circus now that Patsy had arrived. Shaded beneath his big, white Panama hat, my uncle looked distinctly like Burl Ives in "Cat on a Hot Tin Roof." In his own endearing New York-Irish brogue, Patsy proclaimed "I'm here to help me sweet sister move." But anyone could bet all they owned that Big Daddy would not be doing one ounce of labor that afternoon. People knew that was just Patsy.

Some typically Irish song about a rebel on the gallows telling the Brits to go fuck themselves cascaded down from my family's open window and flooded the canyons of Hell's Kitchen with its music and sentiment. I almost pissed myself laughing at a soused Diana Nuñez, trying to sing along without knowing hardly any English, let alone the lyrics to the song. A friendly slap on the back brought me back from the moment. "I'll be back, Francis. Gotta go to Brooks Brothers. It was a 42 regular, right?" Howie shot me one of his trademark half-grins. "Any preference in color? Nah, come to think of it. How about you just let me surprise you? Oh, and no sweat on the shoes. I got Nicky working on a pair, but no tassels. 'Tassels are for ass'els.'" He giggled at his creative, though hardly intellectual rhyming joke, then added, "Hey, let's go see what Sonny has on the menu later, huh? I got some extra cash and I'm always curious as to what the offering is." I nodded and Howie turned to bolt away, almost running into Sandra. While the two of them were tied up with apologies, I turned to leave.

"Francis, stop being a baby, would you? Come over here and talk to me." Her voice rang out in that seductively sweet, yet distinctly Hell's Kitchen manner that I just couldn't resist. I was putty. I turned back around with my best imitation of indifference, but that smile melted my posturing like an Italian ice on the Fourth. My eyes went immediately to the plate in her hand. She raised it to chest level proudly. "It's a Duncan Hines cake I baked for you and your family. See all the flowers on top? I did those with butter cream and food dye. I thought you'd like them, 'Frankie Flowers.'" Her eyes sparkled as they locked on mine, and it was everything I could do to keep from passing out. I obviously overcompensated, because her smile slipped into a playful pout. "It's my peace offering to you. I'm not the best baker; it's kind of hard, but I did it all by myself." She actually beamed more brightly than the sun, and her beauty was so intoxicating that I was struck dumb. Rather than risk forcing out a comment and sounding stupid, I grabbed the plate with a smile and ran the cake up to my mother. Without so much as an explanation of where it had come from, I barreled back down the stairs, three at a time.

Bursting back out onto Tenth Avenue, I expected to bask immediately in her presence, but was simply blinded by the sunlight. Using my hand as a visor, I scoured the sidewalk, Uptown and Down. She was gone. *how could this be? she was just here a second ago. surely she wouldn't leave.*

she must be talking to somebody. I started asking people at random if they'd seen her until I noticed my Uncle Patsy was staring directly at me with a knowing gaze. I didn't even have to ask. He knew the question. "She just drove away in the car with that no-good, little fecking zip. What's-his-name." I didn't even need to hear it. I knew already. *danny.* "Albanese's ugly kid." The rage and disappointment and embarrassment all welled up within me. *she's cruel. there's no other way of looking at it. she brought the cake as a "peace offering," my ass. she just wanted to fuck with me.*

Without wasting another second thinking about it, I dashed back up the stairs and into the crowded apartment, unnoticed. Snatching the cake adorned with butter cream flowers as though it were ticking, I slammed the door on my way back out of the apartment and shot up the short flight of stairs to the roof. Back into the blinding sunlight, I flung the cake off the top of the building like an Olympic discus-thrower, watching its entire descent into a million pieces all over the lot next door. Castillo, the super, stepped out from behind a chimney to watch it too and then just gave me a "You're fucking nuts" look and walked back in through the bulkhead, shaking his head. *i don't give a shit what him or anybody thinks.* I plopped down on the edge, just a shift in weight from going over. The position was not lost on me. *i ain't gonna jump. it's just indicative of how i feel right now. ...who am i reassuring?* Maybe in an effort to feel a little less crazy, I stopped talking to myself in my head, and started speaking out loud to Howie as if he were right there. "Howie, we are <u>definitely</u> going to Sonny's tonight. We're gonna get lit. Then we're gonna find some girls. And then we're gonna fuck the living shit out of them. Yep. That's the deal, my friend." *yeah. that's less crazy. howie's over on madison, rifling through summer-weight linen suits and i'm discussing our evening's game plan with him. fuck it.*

My sister's voice sliced through the noisy silence of the avenue below, "Francis, who are you talking to and why are you dangling from the roof?"

"What do you want, Philomena?" I snapped back, more embarrassed and surprised than angry.

"Mommy and Daddy sent me to get you. We're leaving." The guilt at having yelled at her flooded through me. *i wish i could tell you how much i love you right now, and that it's really sandra i'm mad at. ...but i won't. i will just sit here, silent, and pretend it didn't happen. as usual.* I was right. I just walked toward the door... but I held it for her... and we descended the stairs together. There was already a noticeable echo in the building from the vacant cavity that had housed the Doonans. Out on the stoop, Patsy was in the middle of one of his bombastic dissertations about the journey of the Irish and how "this family" represented some of the "great people" who built this country, the Irish.

My father decided he'd heard enough and interrupted. "Everyone," he started, "I want to thank you all for the kindness you've shown my wife and family. And I'd be grateful if you'd continue to keep an eye on Francis, to keep him in line. But I'm not pretending this will be a easy job!" A laugh emanated from the crowd as tears streamed down my face. I guess I was finally touched by the culmination of the day's events. Mommy grabbed my hand reassuringly from behind and pressed a handkerchief into it as the crowd lined up to hug my parents and sisters, one-by-one. Everyone was loaded up in more ways than one, so the goodbyes stretched on and on until the caravan began the trek eastward, led by the moving shamrock. Still pontificating about the Irish, Patsy hopped into the truck's cab as his crew loaded the keg into the back. Ironically, I could still hear the music from our radio... <u>my</u> radio... in the window, droning: "Only Her Rivers Run Free."

I only wanted to do one thing with my new freedom and in my new place: hang on <u>my</u> stoop. I walked to the corner to buy an icy six pack of Budweiser, and although the store was exactly four doors away, the return took me almost fifteen minutes. I had to stop and slap hands with Brian and Romeo T, out walking their German shepherds. Running to catch up with them, another member of the crew, Cal, asked, "Hey, hey! How's it hanging, Doonan?"

"To the left, of course," came my trademark response.

Bruno, the pizza guy, was handing a slice with extra hot peppers to Redbone, but stopped momentarily to say hello. "Hey, Francis, what? Did you stop eating pizza?" Bruno lived to break my stones. With his face full of mouth-scalding pie, Red gave a nod and scampered off after the guys.

I'd almost made it to the sanctuary of the stoop when the miniature Asian nightmare locked eyes with me just a few steps away That nightmare was a sixteen-year old girl named... something Chinese, but better known in the neighborhood as just Min... short for "I'm in," we all said, because whatever was going, she wanted to be a part of it, and whatever was good, she wanted to be in the thick of it. Plus, "Min" just sounded like a Chink name. She also happened to be a "gen-u-ine article" beggar, so I had my five-spot at the ready and just held it up in front of her face. She looked almost offended. "What? I wasn't gonna ask to borrow money from you. I just thought I'd say hello. Just talk, you know. Don't you want to talk?"

"Nope," I responded. "But now you owe me fifty bucks." For someone who didn't want to take my money, she sure managed a great impression of one. *that debt will never be paid.*

"Thanks, Francis. I owe you. I'll get it back to you next week." We both knew she didn't mean it. Settling into my captain's chair of the stoop, I popped two beers and guzzled them both, letting out a mighty belch and crushing the cans. *yeah. <u>that</u> was necessary. i'm a fucking caveman. i wonder how close the family is to landing. they're probably in that great prairie known* *as queens right about now. next stop, long island. i actually can't believe they're gone.* Almost as if to remind myself that they were no longer there, I reached over and rang the old family buzzer. No response, of course, so I started to play the buzzer keyboard... and like a pipe organ, multiple voices cursed back through the intercom. 602 was the kind of building and Hell's Kitchen was the kind of neighborhood that, unless someone inside was expecting you, you better not touch that bell. It wasn't long before Diana Nuñez sent down her son, Luis (who was in training for Rikers Island). He came through the door with a Louisville Slugger resting on his shoulder.

Choking back a laugh, I asked, "Hey, Luis, what up? You going to play ball?"

"No," said Luis. "Some motherfucker is playing 'In-a-Gada-da-Vida' on the motherfucking bells. You see anyone, Francis?"

I shook my head. "I just got here, man."

"Yo, Francis, you hear from your peeps yet?"

"Nimrod, they just left an hour ago," I replied.

"Yo! What up with the nimrod, you Irish fuck, don't you see I got a bat?"

"Yeah," I shot back playfully, "But I also know you love me."

Luis smiled and lowered the bat. "Lemme get one of those beers. I just woke up." I dangled a spare in front of him. He took it and took off. *breakfast of champions.* I stood there, tempted to try a new tune on keyboard, but decided I'd played enough. I felt a little sleepy. I felt a little restless. I really couldn't tell what I wanted to do. It was the allure of hanging out on the stoop. I leaned back to catch a little cat nap, knowing that the people scurrying to the theater must be thinking I was a bum since I was too healthy to be laying in a doorway.

It wasn't long before I was sawing wood and dreaming about Sandra. *big surprise.* Deep asleep, I didn't even feel it when a theatergoer walking past stopped long enough to tuck two dollars between my chest and arm. Min didn't miss it on her way back down the block, though, tiptoeing over to snatch the money. That stirred me just enough, so Min tried to cover her proximity to me with a warning. "Francis, wake up. Five-O is doing a sweep tonight. They just grabbed Milk and Vit both. That prick, Sgt. Hampton, is riding tonight. I think he's been to the movies too many times cuz I hear he's even looking for pearl-handled guns."

I rose and stretched like a fat girl's panties. *it's amazing what a little nap will do for you. more beer.* Just then, rounding the corner came a blue cruiser, driven by Sgt. Kevin Hampton, himself. Officer Raúl Negron was in the passenger's seat, turned around, saying something to Milk and another friend, Vittorio "Vit" di Cicco, who were in the back. Hampton cruised by real slowly like a hunter gloating over his bagged bucks. Milk caught my eye with the most annoyed look as Hampton gave me the "you're next, prick" glare. *don't think so, bull. i'm too smart for your civil service ass. besides, uncle patsy owns you.* Hampton owed my uncle over $1000 in unpaid bar tabs. I was so tempted to say, "Wanna beer? Thirsty, boy?" but I thought better of it. The cruiser sped up and sped away. I wasn't worried, though. They'd never get Milk or Vit on anything. There was no danger of them going into the system. *shit. i need more beer. fuck that. i need to get twisted.*

Howie finally arrived with a large duffel bag. He was about to explode with excitement. "Francis, I'm telling you. You're gonna look so fucking GQ. Wait 'til you see what I got you." He unzipped the long bag and took out an aquamarine linen/cashmere blend suit. "They say this cashmere comes from the pussy of a sheep," Howie added. "Feel this. Now that's a suit. Put the jacket on, Francis. I rose on shaky legs but slipped it on. Howie yelled out, "What a winner! You look like Nick Nolte in 'The Captains and the Kings.'" The pants looked like they were pretty long, and would probably have to be fixed, but he was right. It was fantastic. Howie took it a step further: "It's fantastic with your hair... and it really brings out your eyes...."

"Whoa!" I interrupted. "What? Did you jump to the other side in the last few hours? Now you're Mr. Fuckin' Blackwell all of a sudden?"

Howie knew I was just messing with him, but he went into his guilty act all the same. "Well, that's a fine way to pay back a friend who has risked life and limb for your wardrobe. I have been insulted in my life, but this takes the cake." He faked stuffing the suit back into the bag.

"Want a beer?" I asked him so he'd snap him out of it.

Quick as a wink, Howie fired back, "Yes. Now check out these shoes. Made from the finest leather in all of Milan. Nice, no? There's some shirts, belts, socks and a couple of silk ties."

"Lemme guess," I asked, "Made of the finest silk, straight from Iran."

"From Persia, actually, but you were close. Shows you know quality when you see it! But you're on your own with the underwear."

I couldn't tell if he'd gotten the joke or not, but I didn't care. I leaned over and pinched Howie's cheek. I couldn't have loved that kid more. I told him I'd be right back as I ducked into the building to squirrel the booty away upstairs. Howie gave me a nod and had just cracked open a beer as Sgt. Hampton's cruiser pulled up again. "Where's Doonan?" he snarled. Hardly looking up, Howie shrugged his shoulders. "Bullshit. He was just here."

Howie looked the sergeant square in the eyes this time and replied slowly and deliberately, "I ain't seen him."

"Yeah," the cop came back in obvious disbelief, "Well get your dumb fucking Irish ass off the stoop and put the beer away or I'll run you in." Howie broke a big smile as Hampton pulled away. He couldn't have known that nothing would've made Howie feel better than to publicly acknowledge him as Irish. Of course, his mother was probably shuddering blocks away in shul without the slightest idea why.

Sgt. Hampton had scarcely turned onto 45th before I pushed the door open onto the stoop to hear Howie report that our visitor in blue had been inquiring about my locale. He was sure to include Hampton's validation that others regarded Howie as Irish, and then added that he needed to run up to a rooftop over on 48th, where he had something stashed. I followed him over and waited on the building's stoop. I wasn't tremendously particular; a stoop was a stoop. Stoop mentality prevailed in that region, after all. Of course, I liked mine better; it was nice and simple. That one on 48th had too much wrought iron design bullshit on it. *the super here must be a crystal meth freak with a blow torch.* Howie came out moments later with a life-size wooden mannequin. My expression obviously screamed, "What the fuck?"

Howie was ready with an explanation. "Hey, Sonny said to bring some wood, and I was in Wallach's the other day when the prick was begging to be robbed... so I did. I can't wait to see Sonny's face." As we cut over to Eleventh Avenue and headed up, past where it became West End, a car was stopped at a light with its windows down, blaring the Beach Boys: "... catch a wave and you're sitting on top of the world...." It made me realize that Howie had been carrying the mannequin under his arm like surfers in Malibu carry their boards. *are we having our endless summer?*

The sun was dipping behind some taller buildings, but Sonny could still see us coming a mile away. He had been setting up shop, sweeping the perimeter of the can area, but he dropped the broom and hustled in our direction when he saw us. "What the fuck? You crazy Irish mo'fuckers carrying your victims around with you now?" His concern melted into amusement as he gave the mannequin's noggin a knock "This mo'fucker sure is stiff. What the fuck, Howie?"

"It's for the can, man." Howie beamed. "Pure pine. It'll even smell nice."

"Sorry, fellas. Not today." Sonny's gravelly voice replied. "We got a private party this evening."

"Whaddaya mean? You said we were always welcome here."

"Oh, you are, Francis, man. You are." Sonny wouldn't look me in the eye.

"Then what's the problem?" I continued. "We got money, we ain't never no trouble. We always kick to the offering, right?"

"Well, that's the problem," Sonny explained. "I got a shit load of Nicky Barnes' Red Star heroin on the menu for tonight and I don't want to be responsible for starting you guys on a losing journey."

Howie shot back immediately. "That's bullshit. We got free will. We get high, yeah? Nothin', but nothin's gonna grab a hold of us. We're tough. We're Hell's Kitchen, born and raised. No way a little dope can beat us."

I chimed in, "Besides, only niggers and Spics get hooked on that shit. Not us...." I caught myself too late. Realizing what I'd just said and starting to apologize immediately, Sonny cut me off with a glare that burned through his shades.

"Save the 'Blarney,' Irish. I've been hearing that same sack of shit for 50 years. Those lines roll off me like water off a duck's ass." I felt terrible. Here was a man who was basically a strung-out junkie, living on the wind, but trying to be human above all... and there I was, this know-nothing, ass-ignorant mick kid, who could only mock him. Embarrassed beyond measure, Howie and I had as little to say as the mannequin, so we all stood there in an awkward mute.

Sonny let the uncomfortability sink in, that unblinking glare still penetrating his tinted lenses. Finally, his acquiescence broke the silence: "Fuck it. Twenty dollar buy-in, and be ready 'cause tonight's gonna be crowded." I started in with a fresh attempt at an apology, but Sonny cut me off again. "Save it, Irish. Just help me straighten this place up." Sonny silently felt bad because he really liked us. Anyone who knew him also knew that Sonny didn't <u>do</u> compassion, but it ate at him that we were a couple of good kids, about to take a wrong turn on one of life's many highways and byways. We worked in silence until Sonny sent us over to Schwartz Liquor to pick up two cases of total rot gut wine, the owner's "offering" before joining the party himself in a few hours. As we slipped away into the darkness on our errand, Sonny was left alone, leaning on his broom and staring after us. He knew there was no way to keep us from heading down the path we'd chosen, but he felt bad all the same. "Come here, dead man," he croaked to the mannequin, grabbing it by one arm and stuffing it down into the center of the unlit can. Sonny continued to stare. "Your friends will be with you soon there, dead man."

Howie and I did our best "We own these streets" strut across 72nd, certain that we looked more like confident and tough city kids than the scared, confused and lonely little boys we really were. A perfect mimic, Howie would stop every female he passed with one accent or another. The Cockney always seemed to work best for telling girls we were lost, and asking if they knew how to get to the Empire State Building. The girls always fell for the accent since Howie sounded just like the Beatles when they landed at Idyllwild. It took everything I had, though, to keep from cracking up in the girls' faces. Howie was as good as Rich Little, and he could've just as easily been a stand-up comedian as he was a Tenth Avenue swag artist. For the non-Kitchen squares, that meant "stolen without a gun." Before you could say, "I surrender," Howie had pounced on a couple of girls from the Bronx with his best Frenchie accent... except there was no way they were buying it. In the face of their glares and a "Go fuck yourself," Howie pulled off his invisible beret and hung his head. I chimed into the girls that their disrespect wasn't right, but Howie knew I was going to have to break his balls all the same.

The defeat was hardly long-lived, though once the Gray's Papaya at 72nd and Broadway caught our eye. We were both starving, and since Gray's is a poor-man's staple in NYC, it was calling our names. It was usually calling the names of a whole lot of other people since there was a line out the door (most of them young girls), everyone waiting to pay a buck for two dogs and a drink. You just couldn't beat that kind of a deal. I could see it in Howie's eyes that he wanted to start again on his linguistic barrage, but I reminded him that we had to get the wine back to Sonny before it got too dark.

We took our food outside and hopped atop a couple of newspaper vending machines. It was one of those classic spring nights in The Capital of the World. The streets were packed and buzzing with hope; everything was going from bud to bloom. The long, dark winter was over, and there were lovers, hand-in-hand, families pushing their young in strollers, and runners wearing everything from ill-fitting sweat suits to professional marathon gear. And, of course... women. Thousands of them. We knew we'd have sore necks in the morning as much as our heads were swiveling.

Satiating our hunger with hot dogs and eye candy, we headed over to the liquor store on Amsterdam, and as soon as we passed through the door, the owner, a guy named Larry Schwartz, moved toward us quickly. He'd obviously figured us for a stick-up team, not so much because we looked like one, but probably because he was just incredibly paranoid... or at least acted that way. "What you guys want? You got proof of age? If not, then get the fuck out. I don't need no trouble."

He barely gave us a moment to breathe, much less speak, so just as he was about to usher us right back through the door, I spun around on my heel and barked, "Sonny sent us for the Wild Irish Rose."

Larry recoiled, looking back and forth over his shoulders through the corners of his eyes at the customers in his packed shop, gauging if any of them had overheard. He hissed, "Why didn't you say so?" He motioned to the big guy with no neck who'd been sitting next to the door.

"Like you gave us a fucking chance," countered Howie. Larry dispatched the big guy, who was obviously both the owner's security guard and lackey, down to the basement to get the cases. In no time, we were on our way back to The U.N. with the cases in tow. They were pretty heavy and Howie kept a running monologue about how "This is pretty cardiovascular, you know? A good work out."

I pretty much walked along in silence, carrying my case and ignoring how annoying Howie was getting. But I realized that the irritation was actually from me beginning to get a little edgy. It had been a long day, filled with emotion. In short, the real problem was that I was beginning to sober up. I needed to get high, plain and simple. Finally, my jones stopped me. "Howie, wait a minute. Hold on." I set down my case.

"What? Are you a pussy or something? You want me to carry both of them?"

I let the remark slide, ripping open the top of my box and removing a bottle. I spun off the top and guzzled half of the basement-temperature, rot gut, ghetto lemonade before I finally stopped to take a breath. Howie grabbed the bottle from my hand and finished it off before spinning around and launching it through the air into a corner trashcan.

By the time we'd arrived back at the spot, quite a few people had arrived. Howie saw his unscathed mannequin sitting in the can like some faceless bather and smiled. We set down the cases of booze as Sonny shuffled over to take a look. If he noticed the empty slot, he didn't acknowledge it. It was a weird-looking group of people, sort of a real-life "Night of the Living Dead." Chief among the strange that night was Sonny himself, who seemed uncharacteristically neither sunny nor blue. In fact, that night he seemed nothing short of tremendously unnerved. I chanced asking him if everything was okay, and he replied very matter-of-factly, "Listen, there's a lot of pressure on me tonight. To begin with, I'm holding a nice piece of heroin that's worth a lot of time inside if I get run with it. And you never know when the man is gonna sweep down on my spot. Plus, this stuff is ultra good; I can already tell by its color. See?" He pulled a tiny plastic bag filled with eggshell-colored powder out of his jacket pocket. "It's off-white, not actual, pale white. Pure white means it's cut, but this stuff is a killer. I don't want nobody dying... at least not here. And that especially means you two whitebread greenhorns. I really do want y'all to reconsider about taking a pass on this here tonight." We both shook our heads. We were invincible, after all. We knew what was best for us. "Well, it's your funeral. Don't say I didn't try."

Sonny shuffled over to the crates Howie and I had hauled over from Amsterdam and stepped on top of one. "Alright, lets begin the beguine. Listen here, motherfuckers, you know what time it is. Have your money ready. Take a bottle, and enjoy the ride. As usual, if the man comes, you're on your own. And I'll warn you that this shit is strong. "Mr. Untouchable" doesn't fuck around, so don't be stupid about your intake. Light up and have a good trip." Two or three dozen people hustled over, pushing their way past us. They were like a kind of Noah's Ark of Despair, one of every kind. I had a pang of conscience. *maybe sonny's right. we don't need to do this.* But my body and my brain weren't on speaking terms at that moment. As I snapped from my inner debate, I realized that I'd been moving forward on the line automatically, with Howie right behind. Sonny paused momentarily before he took my $20 bill and handed over a small bag of green plastic. Howie got a red one. *sonny looks like father healy handing out communion at holy cross. should i say amen?*

Howie and I were holding our red and green bags in sweaty palms, not entirely sure what to do. The rest of the crowd had each found little areas to rip this stuff up, so we followed suit. Sonny paused from counting his money to watch us sadly. Instructing a Spanish kid to stuff newspaper into the barrel and get the fire going, Sonny's eyes never left us. It was painfully obvious that we didn't know what we were doing, and perhaps Sonny Blue was hoping we would give up and change our minds. He certainly wouldn't be our tutor.

We stood with our backs together, trying to see in the dark what everyone else was doing. A Puerto Rican girl seemed to materialize before my eyes and I almost jumped out of my skin. "Hola, Papi. I'm Angel. You motherfuckers look lost." Not knowing whether we should admit to our ignorance… or whether this chick was even a cop, all I could manage was a gulp. "Well what have you got?" she asked. *fuck. she is a cop. where's sonny? i can't see him anywhere.* Before I could make a more concerted search for Sonny, Howie opened his hand and raised it to her eye level. *we're fucked.* "Damn! A twenty? That's way too much for cherries." Our blank stares betrayed our naïveté, so she continued, "Cherries? Virgins? Greenbacks? Newbies? All right here's the deal. You motherfuckers need less than a nickel bag, believe me – this shit is potent – which leaves you with fifteen. You give me a ten piece, which will leave you with five for tomorrow; you'll need it. We'll call it tuition, alright? I'll sort of be like your tour guide. You know what I'm saying?" We nodded. "All right, then. Give me your shit and let's go over there." My legs were shaking so much I could've been naked in the Arctic, but still we trudged after our tour guide. We huddled near some construction site debris and Angel asked, "You want to snort or main line?"

"No fucking needle's going in my arm!" blurted out Howie. "I can't stand them."

"Well that answer would be 'snort' then," Angel quipped sarcastically.

"Besides, I don't like pain," I contributed to Howie's justification.

"No shit?" asked Angel. "Now ain't that why you're here, my little brother?" She produced a tiny mirror from the pocket of her jean jacket as her grimy hands began tapping a tiny mound of powder onto the mirror. I could see that her hands were swollen and each fingernail bore a different pattern of old, chipped polish. She lined the dope up into little lines, bearing a resemblance to the grayish lines of snow on either side of an NYC sidewalk the day after a storm. Howie bent down as Angel joked, "Damn, homeboy, take it easy or you'll snort my mirror up too with that big ass nose you got there." We all laughed nervously. Howie bent in again and snorted loud and deep; the shit flew right into his system. The blood had all rushed to his head when he lifted his chin. He bobbed down again and filled his other nostril. He grabbed his nose and then shook his head. "Don't sneeze, motherfucker," Angel warned, "Or else you'll fuck up the passage." Like a freshly-raised zombie, Howie slowly stepped aside.

I stepped up to the plate... kicked the dirt... shrugged my shoulders... swiveled my head... and then submerged to the mirror. Strike one! I took a long, thick snort. Next pitch, right nostril. Strike two! I stood up. Game delay. I joined Howie on the side as Angel stood over us with a queer grin on her face. In a voice that didn't seem like it was hers, she said, "Just chill, fellas. I gots to get mines and then I'll catch up with y'all." She ripped off her jacket and both arms looked like an aerial view of the Amtrak railway system. If she caught our stares, she showed no sign of it. Angel had busied herself cooking up some dope in a bottle cap. Her lighter ironically charred the Coke logo into blackness, burning and turning the powder into what looked like thick, muddy coffee. She had already tied off her arm with the scarf from around her neck so deftly that I hadn't even seen it happen. In the glow of the butane and bubbling horse, she looked satanic. I wasn't sure I was feeling anything, but if I were, it had to have been fear. She took the needle that had been clenched between her teeth and drew up some of this bottle cap java. She flicked it with her finger to let all the air bubbles escape and then started slapping her arm to find what was left of a vein. More skilled than a surgeon, the syringe was guided in and the elixir let loose.

Her metamorphosis took place right in front of us. It was evilly reminiscent of Jerry Lewis' Nutty Professor. Angel looked at us warmly with a smirk that said she wanted to fuck us. Ironically, she just had. The rest of the dope got slopped back into her jacket pocket without Howie and I noticing at all. Somewhere in the night, I heard Howie tell me that he felt sick to his stomach, but then I didn't really hear it at all. I was only vaguely aware of him emptying his guts around our feet. *did he say "that's better?"* Howie was slumped at my feet, but that fact hadn't registered until I'd heaved Gray's Papaya all over my feet and his legs. I slumped down alongside him in a pool of vomit, higher than we had ever been in our lives. "This shit's nice," a voice that sounded like it could be Howie's said.

"Shit... nice...." I echoed involuntarily. Angel had slipped away into the night; mission accomplished. The last image I registered before passing out was that of the dead mannequin fully ablaze. Why, I did not know, but I tried in vain to climb through the putrid smell of vomit, towards its wooden head, engulfed in flames... and then all went black.

A chilly Sunday morning had broken as I watched the sun beginning to come up through the one eye that wasn't air-locked to the ground. *this place is a shit hole in the daylight.* The encampment was empty; the battle was over. Taking what seemed like an hour, I was able to swivel my head just enough to view my dearest friend in the world resting just feet from me. Suddenly my heart leapt into my throat and I broke into a clammy sweat. Howie was the color of a lunch bag and didn't seem to be moving.

With as much strength and speed as I could muster, and with Sonny's "This shit is lethal" warning echoing inside my cavern of a skull, I rose and stumbled to Howie's side. *no, god, please. why do i only acknowledge god when i need something? oh, god i really need you now.* I had stopped breathing completely, and managed to reach Howie in time only to collapse on top of him. "What the fuck?" Howie croaked weakly. *music to my ears.* But I had expended all of my energy and will to move those few feet to Howie's side. I couldn't budge another inch. "What time is it?" Howie croaked again.

I looked at my wrist to find that my watch was missing. Growing wise to what had happened, I numbly checked the pockets of my jacket and pants. Every single thing of value was gone. A slow, similar check of Howie garnered the same results. *especially no dope.* "That little fucking cunt," I grunted.

"Christ, not the fucking Sandra melodrama again," Howie replied.

"No, the P.R. chick who got us high."

"Angel," Howie added.

"Angel. Yeah. That was the bitch's name. We'll see her again. It's a small planet." We still couldn't move.

"Fuck, was I stoned," said Howie. "That was some night."

I replied, "Shit, I'm still stoned. I can feel that shit running through my system." Looking around, I added, "It's got to be at least 7 a.m."

"At least," croaked Howie. "Oy! This ground is hard." As best we could, we both helped each other up.

"I wish we had the rest of that dope."

Howie agreed, "I'm hip. So, now what?"

"Home, I guess." All around the spot were dozens of pools of puke. My stomach lurched again, but there was nothing in it but bile... and not even much of that. *i can almost hear the currents of the hudson.*

We stumbled away from The U.N. together, passing by the ice cold burning barrel. Glancing in, we could just make out what was the charred and disfigured remnants of the mannequin's head and arms. Howie managed a chuckle, "I know how you feel, pal."

As we trudged along 72nd, our clumsy gait became a bit more regular by the time we reached Columbus. Heading right, back towards Hell's Kitchen, there was no one out but churchgoers, people hustling to buy all the news that's fit to print, asshole dog walkers and runners. At just about the point we reached St. Paul the Apostle at 59th Street, it dawned on me that it was Palm Sunday and we were about to run into a lot of people we knew. *fucking great. all these catholics – most of whom only show up on holidays to show off their kids and clothes – are gonna be judging me hard. and howie gets a hall pass cause he's jewish.* But it was too late to change course.

Howie looked like he was sleepwalking, and began to obsess aloud about his mother, who was going to be having a bird about him not coming home last night. Since his father had never been around and it was just his mom and him, Mrs. Nesto worried like all Jewish mothers... and then some. Howie never seemed to mind too much about it. His mother was the salt of the Earth, dividing her time between working for UNICEF and helping out around the community. Through it all, her whole life was Howie, and she would pray every day that he'd straighten out. *god, if she could only see him now.*

Just as we reached the stairs of St. Paul's, the doors opened and the 7 a.m. mass let out. It was like church was bleeding pastel. All the fucking Easter and spring colors flooded out. The only thing they were missing was Judy Garland. My attempt to navigate the crowd quickly only resulted in leaving me smack dab in front of Det. and Mrs. O'Casey, the parents of none other than Scarlet O'Hara herself. Det. O'Casey looked right at me... right <u>through</u> me. He was a big, tough, well-known, Detective First Grade with the NYPD. His picture was always in the "Daily News." On his arm was

Mrs. O'Casey, one of the patron saints of the neighborhood. Fortunately, she was busy talking to another parishioner, and hadn't noticed me. But there was little doubt that sweet Sandra – looking every bit like Grace Kelly – had missed me from her vantage point on the church stairs. Howie and I picked up the pace, and I could feel Sandra's eyes on my back. She knew there was something wrong, but she didn't have a clue what to do. She could only bake so many cakes.

We had skated successfully away, ducking into Googie's coffee shop. I grabbed a *Daily News* to find out the latest with Dondie, Little Orphan Annie and Dick Tracy. Howie pulled out the sports section to find out what time the Knick game was on. They'd be playing the Philadelphia 76ers, and if the Knicks stunk up the joint, we'd at least have Dr. J to entertain and amaze. Googie interrupted the diner-library's silence. "What's it gonna be, boys?

Howie had his regular, "A number 1 with O.J. and coffee." I ordered the number 3 with tomato juice and coffee. We were both surprised not to be feeling much, much worse. Aside from a little stiffness from sleeping on the cold ground, we were both definitely still high.

Googie returned with the juice and coffees, throwing in a, "By the way, boys, you both look like shit."

"And a good day to you too," I countered. We slurped our hot coffee as the church crowd started to filter in for breakfast. *shit. we're trapped. nowhere to escape. this place ain't that big.* A little line had formed at the door, right in front of the counter. Googie was flipping out, cursing in Greek to the Spanish short order cook who looked as though he'd had too many cervezas last night. Howie could tell by the look on my face what was going through my head. "Fuck it," I said. "If anyone says anything, I'll tell them to mind their own business." The food came out, steaming hot and Googie refilled our coffee cups. "Just eat nice and slow. Who knows what's gonna happen. If you start to feel sick, just bolt for the door. I'll throw money down for the check. Ah, shit. We got no money. Fuck. Googie is gonna have a canary."

Howie had black ink from the sports pages all over his hands and egg yolk dripping down his chin as they finished their breakfast. I just decided to relax. Googie knew I was good for it. And, besides, Googie owes Uncle Patsy some money, so he'll be cool. After a quick conversation, some sighs and eye rolling, Googie just put the check up on the wall. I promised I'd come in during the week and take care of it. We got up to leave and Howie said, "Listen. I gotta hustle while I have this little bit of energy, okay? I'll call you tonight. You're alright, right?" I nodded and Howie bolted. I also felt a little surplus of energy, but really didn't feel like going home to crash yet. It was a nice day. I really wished I had a nice, fat dube.

Heading out of Googie's, I cut across 56th Street on my way over to Eighth Avenue and the Blarney Stone to visit Uncle Patsy. After my eyes adjusted to the dimness inside, I could see Pats at the end of the bar eating a huge steak, half a dozen eggs and a couple of big boiled potatoes, with a pitcher of German Dinkelacker at arm's length. He was in mid-lecture with one of the bus boys about the benefits of digestion. The purpose of the beer, he explained, was to wash everything out and aid in the digestive process. *ah, uncle patsy... the poster boy for good health.* He stopped, mid-advice, when he looked up and saw me. "Ah, my boy, Francis. Must be you're coming from mass. You could've dressed better." *the last time pats was in mass is when they were baptizing his fat head in, just as bald 50-odd years ago as it is today.* "Fancy a drink, Francis? By the looks of you, you need a shot of Bushmill's." *irish whiskey. big surprise there.* "Very medicinal, you know, Bushmill's." Patsy free-poured like a cowboy. *oh, fuck, that burns to the toes.* I gasped for air as my eyes teared up with great, glittering drops. But a nice, warm, even glow eventually overtook the burn, so I drained the glass. Without asking, Patsy obliged again. *thrown back... and all was well again. oh, how i wish i had that joint. fuck it. more whisky'll do.* After a couple more glasses of Bushmill's, I looked up and noticed that Uncle Patsy had Mutual

Life of Omaha on the TV. Two mountain rams were smashing their heads into one another. *the goat equivalent of me and howie.* I giggled in that way only drunkenness allows as Patsy looked over and added, "I know. This is great shit, right? Very educational."

The bar was beginning to fill with the mostly Irish locals, straight from the pews, so I thought it would be a good idea to beat the rush and get to the steam table lunch to coat my stomach and then begin the serious drinking. By the time the Knicks pre-game show started around noon, I was already pie-eyed and insulting Marv Albert's rug inside my head. I almost fell off of my stool, and tried to cover the misstep by acting like I was heading out. "See ya, Uncle Patsy," I slurred.

"Later, kid," he replied. "If you need anything, let me know." As if to accent his point, he tucked a folded up $50 bill into my hand. I looked up from my hand, gave a look to convey my thanks, and then staggered back out onto Eighth Ave. Although the day was warming up and the sun was high in the sky, I could feel it… especially since I was drunk: the loneliness was settling in and soon I'd be completely alone. *a familiar place.* Passing by the blur of closed shop fronts, I reached 58th Street and saw a jet black woman in red high heels, a leather mini skirt, a dark halter top and a little pink fur coat. Sporting one of the tightest hardbodies I'd seen in a long time, she looked just like Tina Turner in her prime. My personal radar equipment went to work automatically, pointing a growing hardon towards my Private Dancer. She took a few steps in my direction as my prick pulled me the rest of the way to her. "Hi, baby. You want a date?" She flashed the brightest and most intrigued smile my way.

In my brain's vain attempt to reassert control over "the little head," I brushed by her momentarily, but immediately pivoted back. "Maybe. What's it gonna cost?"

She already had me… and knew as much… but her professional instincts kicked in all the same. As if she could somehow see a badge number in my pupils, she stared deep into my eyes, lowered her voice and asked, "You a cop?"

"Fuck no. I'm no cop," I barked back. Without missing a beat, her hand shot down to my crotch and started kneading my straining erection. "What the fuck? Are you psycho or something? One second you're asking me if I'm a cop and then the next second you're giving me a hand job on the street!"

She pulled her hand away. "If you were a cop, you wouldn't let me do that." She put her hand back. "So you want to go out or not? You got some pretty blue eyes." That was my first chance to look back into hers. She was really very good looking and anything but old. I couldn't understand why she was walking the streets and not on the cover of "Ebony" magazine. She pulled me from the depths of her eyes with, "So, Irish, what's it gonna be?" It was then that I realized I'd been in a ten minute conversation with a hooker... in my own neighborhood... in broad daylight... on Palm Sunday. Guilt washed over me. She could obviously sense my hesitation, so her hand stroked up to my chest and she gave me a little peck on the cheek. "Listen," she cooed softly, "The name's Sticky. When you make up your mind, I'll be somewhere within a few blocks of here. As long as you're sure you ain't no cop, you come and find me, okay?"

As Sticky began to stroll away, I instinctively said, "Come here."

Without turning around, just to make sure that I was sure, she said, "The hotel is $50 and I gotta get at least $450 for a half-'n'-half." She finally turned around. "I usually don't do it like that, but you're young and kinda cute. Not like some of the fat, smelly, disgusting motherfuckers I usually get to deal with."

"I live a couple of blocks away," came my reply. "We can go to my apartment and I'll give you $50. That's all I've got." I pulled out the bill to show her.

"You ain't no freak, are you?" Sticky's questions indicated some hesitation, but the rest of her didn't seem to agree. My eyes and calmness answered her question. She smiled and presented her hand as if to say, "Well, lead the way."

I was glad there didn't seem to be many people I knew milling about the neighborhood. If Castillo, the super, hadn't been straightening up garbage cans when we entered the building, I wouldn't have seen a familiar face on the trip. "I live on the top floor, I'm afraid. And the elevator's been sent out for servicing." Castillo and I threw one another that "you piece of shit" look, but Sticky seemed to neither notice nor care. As she ascended the stairs, my gaze moved to her lovely round ass and the super's glare became filled with jealousy. *fuck you, you immigrant cocksucker. holy shit. she ain't got on no underwear. check out that bush. black as coal. fuck me. was that a shiny pink lip? i can feel that pussy from here. this is gonna be heaven.*

We reached the top, and as Sticky leaned against the wall to let me pass by with the keys, she said softly, in a little, winded voice, "You don't live with no one, right?" I shook my head, a little out of breath myself. "Good," she added. As we went through the front door, she looked around, kicked off her heels and then asked if she could use the bathroom. I opened the door for her and she slinked by, running her hand up my thigh and across my crotch on its way to the doorknob. I scurried around the apartment in an attempt to straighten up and to make sure I hadn't left anything "incriminating" out in full view. I used my foot to shove a pair of dirty underwear beneath the bed as Sticky emerged from the bathroom completely naked. I was literally paralyzed by awe at how gorgeous her body was. Extending her fingers, she said, "If you give me the money, we can get to it."

I fished in my pocket to place President Grant in Sticky's capable hand, and then managed to say, "I'd like to take a shower if that's okay."

"Sure," she responded. "And I'll hop in with you." *no argument from me.* My clothes were off in the blink of an eye as the caravan moved into the bathroom: I led Sticky, and my turgid member led us both. "You got a nice cock for a white boy," she moaned into my ear more than spoke. As if to emphasize her point, she took hold of it and pulled me underneath the cascade of warm water.

I wasn't sure if our time had already begun, and I was even less sure that I wanted the clock ticking just yet, so I grabbed the soap and started to lather up. She stood only half in the shower's stream, looking subtly amused. "What smells so good?" she asked.

"Dr. Bronner's Peppermint Soap," I answered, holding up the bar. "Would you like me to wash your back?" I could actually see her nipples stiffen as she nodded, lifted her hair, and turned around. *is she really getting turned on? that can't be the norm for a hooker, can it?* As I rubbed the minty lather all over her dark skin, she backed up slowly toward me until my erection was rubbing between her legs. If it were actually possible, my cock seemed to get harder. As the soap was running down her back and onto my dick, she suddenly turned around and crouched in the same motion, taking me into her mouth, Dr. Bronner's and all. *holy shit. i'm literally brushing her teeth with my cock.* The water continued to rain down on us while Sticky gave me one of the best blowjobs I'd ever experienced. I couldn't take it anymore, and since I didn't want to waste my orgasm without having a taste of what she'd given me a peek at on the way up the stairs, I stopped her and turned off the water. She stood up with a knowing smile as I quickly rinsed and toweled us both off, and practically carried her out to the futon.

Ever the professional, Sticky laid a hand softly on my chest as if to say, "Relax, Irish," and then lowered herself down onto the mattress. My dick was bucking and dripping like a rabid horse as I watched her two long, smooth mahogany legs open. Nestled away between them was the tiniest hint of glistening... pink... silky... Sticky. Dropping first to my knees, like slipping a belt through its loops, I instinctively slid inside her and felt the warmth from our bodies overwhelm me. A soft moan let me know she felt it too, so I started to pump harder. It wasn't long before the sensual gave way to the sexual and she began to tangle like a wildcat. "Give it to me, baby," she hissed. "Fuck that pussy. Come on, motherfucker!" Her outbursts took me completely by surprise, but couldn't have possibly turned me on more. By that point, I was humping her like a machine and she started screaming with both lungs: "Harder! Harder!" *poor rosie in the apartment below must be watching the plaster fly off of her walls and ceiling.* Flailing about, she grabbed both sides of my head and growled the commandment, "Now cum, white boy! Come on. Cum!" I managed between pants to say that I hadn't put on a rubber and asked if she was using anything. She screamed her reply, "Just cum, motherfucker! Cum!"

Thrusting all the way in as far as I could, I filled her insides, which just made me slide in more deeply. As if in reply, Sticky started cumming immediately, clawing my back. "Kiss me," she gasped. "Kiss me, Francis." Now, I didn't know much, but I did know that the number one rule for working girls was that kissing was a "no-no." She glared at me in an almost animalistically begging way. So, I did. She torpedoed her long, soft tongue into my mouth and traced the outline of my teeth before she found the tip of my tongue and we lay there, suspended, tasting one another. My dick started getting hard again. *and she's probably gonna go to the bathroom now and get ready to leave.* I was wrong.

She grabbed the back of my hair and growled through clenched teeth, "Fuck me again, white boy." Although my dick was willing, exhaustion had given the rest of my body a different idea... and it caught up to me as I felt myself hit a wall. Almost as soon as I started to hump, my body was straining for every motion, and my erection soon followed suit. I was on empty. I rolled off of her, spilling over with apologies. "It's cool, baby. You took care of me. That's all I can ask."

I laughed. "I thought it was supposed to be the other way around."

"Oh, it is, but you're nice. And I don't have a boyfriend right now... and, hey, I love to fuck. So what better profession, right? Actually, I'm only doing this to make extra money. I'm going to the Fashion Institute of Technology to be a designer. You know my clothes? I made all of them."

"Yeah, but isn't it dangerous out there? I mean, you're taking a big chance." I could hardly believe what she was telling me.

"I like it actually," replied Sticky. "It adds to the whole excitement aspect. I like to dance on the razor's edge."

"That makes two of us," I said. As much as it sounded like a quote from a movie, I'd never heard my need for all things extreme put so succinctly before. It was intriguing to meet someone else like me. We cuddled there in the quiet of my apartment, slowly drifting off to sleep. Sticky just smelled and felt good. I must've been so comfortable that I practically fell into a coma, because when I awoke at 6 p.m., Sticky was gone. On the bathroom mirror, she had written:

> "Irish, you're nice.
> Stay that way.
> Come and look for me sometime.
> Sticky xoxo"

After a moment of absorbing the note, I realized that I was staring at the words, but actually seeing my own reflection behind the prison bars of pink lipstick. It was such an odd feeling to go through the emotional ups and downs of feeling good... being truly content... and then feeling bad for myself... for Sticky. *and i don't know why.* I could feel tears making their way to the surface as I smeared the note into the mirror. Shuffling back to the futon, for the first time in a very long time, I cried myself to sleep. Oddly enough, I actually felt some relief. I slept soundly, awash in the smell of a hot fashion designer hooker and the sound of her tap dancing on that razor's edge.

I awoke the next morning without getting out of bed right away, choosing instead to lounge through that thoughtful period when a person runs down the list of all the things to be done and avoided during the day. *monday morning. great; everybody's favorite. oh, yeah. i have lunch with benny. shit! the suit pants have to be altered.* Jumping up and pausing only long enough to grab the suit pants and pull on a pair of sweats and a tee-shirt, I bounded down to Apt. 1RN. Everyone in the building knew that Diana Nuñez was a retired seamstress. I just hoped she was home. I rang her doorbell and could hear that familiar cough almost immediately. The door inched open cautiously, so I thought it'd be a good idea to greet her with sunshine. "Buenos dias, señorita."

"Good morning, Francisco," came her reply as the door swung open.

"I know it's very late notice, but is there any way you could alter the bottoms of these pants for me? I have to wear them at lunch and forgot they needed to be altered."

"Claro, niñito. Come on in. How are your parents doing?" I barely heard the question. *she must've been something not all that long ago.* The crew in Crotchville was already hard at work. *christ! stop for two seconds, will you? you know all her kids and she's watched you grow up.* But Diana had always given me sensual stares. It wasn't like those thoughts were coming out of nowhere. "Francisco? Tus padres?"

"Oh, sorry. Good, señora. Good. Sorry. I just got up."

"Bueno. Well tell them we said hello, won't you? Now, I can help you, but you need to get your dress shoes so I can measure them properly, okay?" After a quick dash up and down the stairs, I found myself in her bathroom, changing into the pants and dress shoes. When I came out, she had put her long black hair up on top of her head and had a mouth full of pins. She could still speak perfectly without moving her lips, though. "Okay, now stand straight up." The crew from Crotchville began to reawaken when she got down on her knees, but I forced that thought from my head as she began pinning the hem of my trousers. Spitting the extra pins back into her hand, she said, "Go back in there and take them off. Be careful not to stick yourself, and then come back in an hour." I headed for the bathroom as she said, "Those must be for a really nice suit, papi."

"Yeah, pretty nice," I replied through the door. "By the way, I was about to go get breakfast. Would you like anything from the store?"

"No, gracias. Just enjoy your breakfast."

Handing off the pants on my way out the door, I told her "Thank you. I'll be back by ten, okay?" Since I didn't have to meet Benny until 1 p.m., that gave me plenty of time. *didn't benny say there were supposed to be zebras on the wall at that joint he's taking me to? what kind of place is it anyway?* After a leisurely visit to eat breakfast, read all the papers and chat with Rohit, I headed over to the drug store to buy a box of Fanny Farmer chocolates for Diana Nuñez. I knew she wouldn't take any money, but my mother would've reached all the way from Long Island to slap me in the back of the head if I hadn't given her <u>something</u> to say thank you.

Diana came to the door with the pants hemmed and pressed. She had even put a French cuff on them for me. "They look fantastic. Thanks so much," I said, giving her the candy with a little peck on cheek.

"If I was younger, papi...." *i knew i was right!*

"Adios, Mrs. Nuñez, and thanks again!" Excited to see what the suit looked like on, I raced back up three flights to shave and shower in r my lunch meeting. My stereo was always on, but I decided

s "My Back Pages." Few songs spoke to me like that one. I put

and then slid into the pants. They were perfect. I sang along as

e belt and tied the tie, "...Lies that life is black and white spoke from my skull. I dreamed romantic facts of musketeers foundationed deep, somehow." And then slipping on the shoes and socks, I rejoined the lyrics, "Ah, but I was so much older then; I'm younger than that now." I caught a glimpse of myself in the full-length mirror as I donned the jacket. *wow. not too bad.* Brushing my teeth and slapping on some Old Spice were all that remained since I no longer had a watch to fasten. *that cunt, smiley. i'll hafta get howie to get me a new one.* With one last moment of admiration in front of the mirror, I headed out and over to Eighth Avenue.

Starting my journey Uptown, I looked around in hopes that I might see Sticky. But she was nowhere to be found. *probably in class learning about coco chanel or something.* I noticed a couple of people casting sideways glances as I passed. *this must be a really nice suit. it couldn't be me 'cause i'm a piece of shit. a joint would sure be nice for this walk. maybe i'll get a nickel bag if i see anyone.* Before long, I'd reached Columbus Circle and changed course along Central Park South. It was ironic that this was some of the priciest real estate in Manhattan, but the horse-drawn carriages that lined CPS made it smell of horseshit. *i bet the folks in essex house just love that.* It was one of those beautiful spring days that meteorologists called "one of the ten best of the year," and since it was lunchtime, many workers were sitting outside on the walls, the grass, the curbs. *i hope they've got a bar at this place, gino's. shit, they've gotta.* At Lex., I hung a left until I reached the green, yellow and red exterior of Gino's at 61st Street.

Just inside the restaurant, a squat Italian in a tight black suit greeted me, "Good afternoon, young man. Can I help you?"

More than a little out of my element, I replied nervously, "Yeah I'm looking for Benny Levine."

"Ah, yes, of course. Mr. Levine. He just called and said he'd be a few minutes late. Then you must be Mister Francis. Why don't you wait at the bar. Mr. Levine should be here any minute. I am Alberto if you should need anything." The invitation to sit at the bar was music to my ears. But the big Yugoslavian bartender didn't seem to want to cooperate, asking me if I was old enough to be sitting at bar. When he asked to see proof, I panicked, but the maître d' had overheard the question and stepped in, "It's okay. He's with Mr. Levine."

The Slav leaned in and said in broken English, "Yes. Now that I am getting good look at you, you are looking old enough. I am Sergio. What are you going to be having?"

Sighing with relief, I replied, "A Heineken, please." The bottle was ice cold and I inhaled the contents, asking Sergio for another.

Reaching into my pocket to pay for the beers, Alberto came over again and said, "Your money is no good here, Mr. Francis. It's on Mr. Levine's tab." Sitting back on the stool, I had a chance to relax and really take in the room. The restaurant was getting crowded with what appeared to be rather wealthy patrons. The waiters were all Italian, and all in grey cloth jackets. *and there are the zebras.* Sergio placed another Heineken in front of me.

While I was smile-flirting with the pretty lady in the coat check room, the door opened and Benny stepped into the restaurant. There were no two ways about it: he looked like a million bucks. Everything was custom, as usual. He kissed Alberto and palmed him some money. He kissed the coat check girl and palmed her some money. He shook hands with Sergio and palmed him some money. Without getting ten feet inside the door, Benny had already dropped half a yard. "There's my boy. Francis, you look great. Come on. Let's sit."

"Thank you, Sergio," I said, putting a fiver beneath my empty beer bottle in an attempt to emulate Benny's tipping style.

"Is already taken care," the Slav replied, tucking the bill into my breast pocket. "Enjoy you lunch."

Alberto led Benny and me through the dining area, where it seemed that almost everyone knew Benny, and vice versa. When we sat down, three waiters scurried over with cloth napkins and water, specials menus, and a beautiful floral arrangement for the table. Looking around the restaurant, all of the floral arrangements were similarly beautiful. That was when I realized that I had put most of them together. Benny took a seat and said, "Have whatever you want, kid. The food here's great. You look really sharp, my boy." Benny always had a way of making me feel good. Almost as quickly as he sat down, though, he got right back up and started to table hop like he was up for election, skating through the room to greet and shake hands with everyone.

I took the opportunity to appreciate the variety of the menu until our waiter came by to get my order. "Can I get a Gino's Chopped Salad without the anchovies?"

The waiter nodded. "What else would you like, my friend?"

"Oh, I was just asking. I'll wait for my friend to actually order."

"You mean Mr. Levine?" he asked with a widening grin of amusement. "He doesn't have to order, my friend. He eats here often, and we always know what he wants."

"Ah." *custom. everything custom.* "Of course. Well then, in that case, I'll have the linguine pesto."

"And still with the Chopped Salad, no anchovies?" added the waiter. I nodded. "Very good, sir."

As the waiter made his way to the back, I noticed that Benny and the three lovely, well-dressed ladies to whom he was talking were all looking over at me. I smiled and they returned the gesture. A few moments later, Benny returned to the table. "Sorry, kid, I had to schmooze a little. I do a lot of business in this room. So, you like this place, yeah? What's been going on, kid?"

"Not much, Benny," I replied. "My parents moved out to Long Beach this weekend."

"Well... nice place. We have a cabana at the beach club there, not too far from where I live." That made me feel good to know that my parents lived so close to the likes of Benny; they must be doing pretty well after all. "So what's happening to you?"

"My folks made arrangements for me to keep our old apartment in the building."

Benny furrowed his brow. "What are you... 17, kid?" I nodded. "That's how old I was when I left home. Are you going to school?"

"For what?" I demanded, a little more forcefully than I meant. "They teach me nothing I'm ever going to actually <u>need</u> in life."

Benny recalled that those were almost his exact words when he was 17, and they were words that broke the heart of his father, a fabric cutter in the Garment District. Benny had done alright with barely a high school diploma, but every hard-working immigrant always wanted a better life for his children. And, to them, education was the key to freedom. Benny was torn because he was strict with his own sons about education, but somehow he understood why things were completely different with me. Perhaps it was because I was a mirror image of him, immigrant parents and all.

Waiters arrived to snap Benny from his momentary reverie. Adding fresh pepper to my salad and placing what looked like a steaming hand grenade in front of Benny, he could doubtlessly tell by the look on my face that I was curious what he'd been served. "An artichoke, stuffed with cheese and bread crumbs," he offered. "You'll try some."

The waiter asked, "Will you have any wine today?"

"I'm Irish. What do you think?" came my reply before I realized that the question had been directed at Benny.

"Sure, Marco. Something nice for the meal."

"I know just the thing, Mr. Levine," Marco said before heading off.

Benny turned back to me. "Francis, those ladies I was talking to are going to join us for dessert, okay? They are all socialites, which means they marry well, tolerate their husbands, spend their money, shop, do lunch... and love to fuck. ...And not always in that order. But they also like to care for people." Benny responded to the puzzled look on my face by rubbing his index finger and thumb together, saying, "Cabbage. You fuck them good and they put you on scholarship. That's how I made my start-up money when I was younger." He added, whispering, "Thank God I have a strong back." Benny raised his glass to the gaggle of ladies and everyone smiled again. When Marco returned with the bottle of cabernet, Benny leaned into him. "The women over there... put her tab on my check. Also, those two guys at the table near the door, tell them, 'My compliments.'"

Marco nodded and slipped away. "So, Benny," I started, "Not that I'm complaining, but what's the reason for the lunch?"

"I wanted to introduce you to this kind of world. Look over there. You see that funny little guy with the glasses and hat? That's Woody Allen, one of the greatest American filmmakers; started as a comedian, you know. Everyone comes here: Kissinger, Sinatra, gangsters, big-time cops, politicians... a lot of call girls. There's lots of loot in this room, and then there's you and me, kid. And you're heading for all of this, Francis. So I wanted to give you the introduction." Benny was actually beaming. I suppose I was too. But our shining moment was short-lived as the ladies approached. Without taking his eyes off of our guests, Benny added softly, "Dessert's about to be served."

Benny stood and I followed suit. "Francis Doonan, say hello to Joy Sussman, Karen Winthrop and Svetlana Romanov."

I mustered all the politeness I could recall from my Catholic school-upbringing: "It is my distinct pleasure to meet you ladies." We exchanged polite handshakes, taking in one another subtly. They were all tanned, fit, beautiful and smiling. Benny pulled out the two chairs next to him to seat Joy and Karen while I did the same for the Russian lady. As I began to sit back down in my chair, Benny put his hand on my back and gently guided me to sit in his chair. He whispered softly in my ear, "Kid, lay off of Svetlana. That's me. The other two are fair game." I understood his meaning.

As the restaurant started to empty, waiters emerged with dessert trays, cups of espresso, and bottles of liqueurs and cordials. I sat back and listened as Benny held court. He oozed with charm, throwing out compliments and lines like a salesman with his business cards. Without any shortage of jokes or anecdotes, everyone at the table (myself included) was completely enraptured by our host. When a moment of silence finally did settle upon the table, the lady to my left said, "So, "Mr. Doonan," what about you? What's your story?"

Before I could even open my mouth to reply, Benny slid in and said, "Karen, my dear, if you want to know something about my protégée, you're just going to have to take him out." She smiled. I didn't know what to say (which was probably a good thing since I was plastered)... but knew well enough not to say a word all the same. Karen switched her glance to me and raised on eyebrow seductively. "Francis, give her your phone number. And treat him well, Winthrop." I smiled nervously now too, but scratched my number on the underside of a cocktail napkin with Benny's pen. Her eyes sparkled as I slid the napkin to her and watched her fold it once and tuck it into her cleavage.

Benny launched into another engrossing story that had all eyes glued on him... except for frequent, lengthy gazes between Karen and me. Benny couldn't have missed them, but it certainly escaped me when he called for the check. As if it were timed, the check dropped on the table just as Benny landed the punchline and everyone laughed while he signed the back of the check without even looking at it. *custom*. Rising to pull out Svetlana's chair, I followed Benny's lead again. But when he dropped a pair of Benjamin "Levines" on the table, all I could do was stand there and admire the master.

Karen gave me a soft peck on the cheek that said both, "Nice to meet you" and "We <u>will</u> talk later."

Benny shook my hand and pressed a twenty into it. "We're heading over the 59th Street Bridge, but here's a little something for a cab. I'll see you tomorrow at the shop." As usual, though, I pocketed the twenty and started the stagger home. As much as I'd had to drink, I figured the walk would do me good. Crossing over to Madison Avenue, I made a left and was bowled over by just how different this world was than the one I was used to. The sidewalks and streets were spotless, lined by beautiful stores, one after the other. Most of the windows looked like works of art and everything was expensive. By the time I reached 57th Street and took the right to head back over to the West Side, the autopilot could engage and I scarcely had a thought until I saw an old black guy on Ninth Avenue selling books. He was one of those homeless guys who packed and unpacked his goods every day into a dozen or more shopping carts, bound together like the Borax 20 Mule Team. I was fascinated by what a great selection he had. I pored over the thousands of books set out on the pavement and chose Jack London's "Call of the Wild," Alexandre Dumas' "The Three Musketeers" and "The Art Spirit" by Robert Henri. Although he was only asking a total of two bucks for the books, I dropped a five in his box and nodded when he gave me an acknowledging smile.

With the paperbacks tucked into various suit pockets, I ducked into the A&P to make use of their big, red coffee grinding machine. The powdery fragrance of the family favorite, Bokar Blend, filled my nostrils, making that aisle one of my favorite places in The City. Grabbing some other staples, I got back out onto the street just as night was beginning to fall.

Things had been going too well that day. My luck had to run out. And as I approached 52ⁿᵈ, it did. There on the bench in front of St. Clare's, I could see the black leather jackets of none other than Danny Albanese and three of his cronies looking like the retarded version of the Four Seasons. I was in no mood for their shit so I crossed to the east side of Ninth Avenue... and almost made it by unnoticed. I picked up the pace until I saw Danny's head swing around, flick his cigarette and hop off the top of the bench to start across the avenue. With those scumbags in tow, there was nowhere for me to go, so I stopped and set the grocery bag down. I was turning around when Danny approached with, "Hey, Flowers, what are you all dressed up for? You look like Little Lord Fauntleroy." His crew all cackled in unison, but I wasn't taking the bait.

"I had to go somewhere."

"Where?" he demanded.

"That's my business."

"Oh, really?" he continued. "Well, I want to know." Danny pushed the bag with his foot to see what was in it as he pulled the paperbacks out of my suit pockets and dropped them on the concrete. "What's this shit?"

"I'm just trying to expand my horizons," I replied, trying not to sound sarcastic. "Look, I gotta go. I'm meeting Howie."

Danny screwed his nose up in disgust. "What's going on with you, Doonan? You're like the neighborhood weirdo. You don't hang with nobody but that mopey kike. No one knows anything about you, and when we try to talk to you like civilized human beings, you come at us with some 'horizon' bullshit." I leaned down to retrieve my bag and books, but Danny snatched the front of my jacket roughly. "I'm talking to you, prick."

"I'm not in the fucking mood," I shot back.

"Well, how about I slap you into the mood?" He did just that with three hard slaps to my right cheek. I took them all with no reaction. His cronies started in with cackles and "oohs" as a crowd started to gather. The red handprint on my face and a death glare in my eyes were the only evidence I was giving that I'd been struck. Even Danny was stunned that I hadn't cried out or something. So I took advantage and began to walk away. Never one to leave well enough alone, though, Danny started grandstanding. "See? I told you he was cunt. All cunt, by the looks of it." His boys were dying with laughter and even most of the crowd was snickering and cutting their eyes at me. I hung my head and tried to leave again. "Where you going, Flowers? I didn't say you could leave. I'm not done with you yet." Grabbing me by the lapels again, he got so close to my face that I had to endure every bit of spittle and every whiff of his bad breath. "You know, Sandra is with me because you're all cunt and she knows it. Everybody knows it. Besides, you couldn't handle her hot little twat like...."

"Don't talk about her like that!" I interrupted. He finally had his rise out of me.

"What's wrong, Flower Book Boy? Did I hit a nerve?"

"I don't care what you say about me, but keep Sandra out of this."

"Why?" he continued, grabbing his crotch. "I didn't keep this out of Sandra." Clutching my face with his open hand, he added, "Can you still smell her pussy on my hands? I been fucking her all afternoon."

The crowd howled, but I heard none of it. My rage had shut down all of my senses and I just reacted. With one great burst of energy, I head-butted Danny's hand into his great, ugly face. Dropping the grocery bag and books, I started pumping a left jab piston-like at his nose. Danny fell back into a gated store front as I charged in and ripped three body shots into him, unleashing a series of vicious uppercuts before anyone could register what was happening. Danny was out on his feet and the crowd was stunned to silence. Everyone on the block could hear the thud of Danny Boy Albanese hitting the pavement. But unable to hear their jeers, I couldn't hear their silence either, and continued raging, screaming, "You want more, Danny? Get up, you Guinea sack of shit!" Turning my focus to his crew, I added, "Anybody want some of me? Here I am!" His cronies had disappeared into the crowd, which was beginning to disperse nervously itself. Uncomfortable that my fury had gotten the best of me, I cocked my head back and screamed, "FUCK!" as long and as loud as I could. It was then that I had noticed my gallon of milk had burst when I dropped the sack to attack Danny. Dumas, Henri and London were nothing but swollen honey- and oatmeal-covered blobs. As hard as I could, I kicked the pile, scuttling its contents into the gutter and middle of the street.

Stalking away from the still-prone Danny Albanese, I looked like a hurricane had hit me: hair all over the place, cheeks cherry red, hands bleeding from the imprints of Danny's teeth. I was more than a little bothered by my own rage. I'd never really fought like that before. *maybe i just remembered some of the moves i saw muhammad ali put together on "wide world of sports" and it was like instinct.* My whole body was trembling, so I ducked into Rudy's, the extremely packed, local, skeevy gin mill, for a few shot-'n'-beer chasers. Ironically, Rudy's famous jukebox was blasting Al Green's "Love and Happiness," and before he asked what I wanted, the bartender asked what had happened to me. "Nothing," I started my lame story. "I just fell is all. New fucking shoes. You know how slippery Guinea leather is."

"Bullshit," the bartender barks back. "I'm not buying it. I've been around the Wild West Side long enough to've seen everything, and you didn't slip on no shoes. Don't bring your shit in here, Doonan."

I figured that was as close to a bum's rush as I wanted to get at the moment, so I decided to leave on my own. By the time I got within sight of the stoop, I could see that there was a small crowd gathered out front. *shit. he followed me home.* But it wasn't the Retarded Four at all. Right out in front was Kelly the Mick and Colin Garvan. They greeted me like a war hero come home from overseas. "Frankie Flowers! Who the hell knew you had it in ya?!?" exalted Kelly. "I hear you smoked that little dago fuck. Now you gotta throw in with us. We'll fucking crush him and his old man!" Colin Garvan was clapping my shoulders like Angelo Dundee did Ali, but I pulled away.

"I'm still not interested. What's done is done. I didn't even want this," I said.

Kelly snarled, "Well, you got no choice now, daffodil, 'cause they're gonna be laying for you, and you can't take them all on." He thought better of his tone, and it softened notably. "Come on. This is the main problem with us Irish. If we can stick together, we can eliminate all them other groups. If the Irish truly united, we'd control the fucking world, right?"

I just wasn't interested in any frenzy-whipping that day so I stepped past Kelly the Mick up onto the stoop and fumbled in my pocket for my keys. "No, thanks, Kelly. That's your life, not mine. Danny and I had words and that's all. It's over."

Colin stopped the shoulder massage and Kelly spat on the sidewalk. Spinning around abruptly, they stormed to the car and got in. Before peeling away, Kelly screamed out the window, "I'll be sure to wear red at your fucking funeral, Doonan." Howie, Milk, Vit, Clayton, Redbone, Brian and Romeo T... my real friends since childhood... were left standing with me around the stoop.

Almost in unison, they chimed in a chorus of "We're here for you, homeboy. Don't worry. Don't sweat that shit. They're assholes." They were like my private army of bodyguards, and the stoop had suddenly turned into Fort Apache... except this general genuinely didn't want to fight. I appreciated the support from my friends... and it was even kind of nice being heralded as the day's local Michael Collins, but I was genuinely sad that things had gotten so out of hand. I always tried to avoid that kind of thing, and wondered if Sandra would've even cared that he had defended her honor. *it's her fault anyway. if she weren't fucking him....* But I couldn't even force myself to have a bad thought about her. So there we were on that spring night in NYC, eight childhood friends holding down the stoop, waiting for the inevitable war. Instead of doing what we should've been doing – homework, playing CYO basketball, practicing instruments, talking with our parents, whatever – there we were, standing with our shoulders hunched, hands deep in our pockets, glaring and spitting looks out onto the avenue for anything that wanted to ignite.

Clayton came running up, making an already jumpy crew even more so. He was beaming from ear to ear. You're becoming a little hero quick, Francis. Word all over the Kitchen is that you're "Dorothy," motherfucker. You killed the Wicked Witch's ass!" Everybody got a chuckle out of that except for me. The only way I felt like Dorothy was that we were both lost. Clayton's comment seemed to break the ice and someone felt it was safe to break out a spliff. The smell of marijuana soon enveloped the stoop. I grabbed the joint when it came my way and took a few deep drags on it. I just couldn't deal with what was going on. Wondering what was going to happen made me wish I were sleeping and that this was all a bad dream. I just checked out.

It was standing room only at 602 Tenth Avenue and all seemed quiet... or at least sedated... on the Western Stoop when the night's peace was broken by the squealing of a car's tires peeling off of 43rd Street. Screeching to a stop came a familiar site in the neighborhood: a cherry red Delta 88. Johnny Rugs Albanese had barely thrown the car into park before leaping out, and close on his heels was a menacingly large blonde stooge that stuck out from the rest of J.R.'s crew in that he was obviously not Italian. I could see Danny cowering through the rear side window, bookended by two more goons. J.R. made a beeline for me, yelling, "Come here, you little Irish prick faggot!" Not a soldier at Fort Apache moved an inch. They surrounded me like a suit of armor, which just infuriated J.R. even more. "Doonan! Come here! I wanna talk to you." *interesting choice of words.* He had literally started screaming and never let up.

Without breaking my gaze, I moved through the Kitchen Curtain. "It's cool, fellas," I said. Stepping down onto the sidewalk, I walked right up to J.R. "What do you need, Mr. Albanese?" I was always respectful, even to people I hated.

My politeness seemed to anger him even more than my friends' defiance. J.R. exploded. "Who the fuck are you to slap my boy? They were just having a little fun with you, and you had to sucker punch him like a *finoch*?!?"

"That's not what happened at all, Mr. Albanese. I wasn't looking for any trouble then, and I'm not looking for none now."

"Yeah? Well it's found you, you little mick cocksucker. Nobody hits my boy and gets away with it." Danny could only manage to glare at me from the back of his father's car, and I could tell, even with the distance and darkness, that his face was pretty lumped up.

Across the street, Kelly the Mick and Colin Garvan had crept up and were watching the scene from behind parked cars, each with a loaded .38. "I left the engine running. This is a perfect time to fucking whack these wop pricks," whispered Kelly.

"Doonan's got balls," added Colin. "He's standing up to Old Man Rugs pretty good."

"We'll get Doonan on our team yet."

J.R. began to notice the typical crowd gathering, frustrating and making him madder by the minute. "So you're telling me you <u>didn't</u> just haul off and hit Danny when he was asking you about some book you had?" I shook my head and looked right at Danny. *that's the best fucking lie you could come up with?*

"He's a fucking liar and a cheap shot artist!" Danny yelled from the safety of the Delta 88.

"My son is no liar, Irish. And if it had've been a fair fight, he'd've wiped the fucking floor with you."

Howie couldn't hold back anymore, stepping forward from his place in the Kitchen Curtain. "Your son is a punk bully with a big mouth. He got what was long overdue," he screamed. The enormous blonde stooge stepped in Howie's path. "What do you want, Blondie? Can't Dagwood fight his own battles?"

"Piss off, you hooknosed cunt!" he growled in a thick British accent, throwing Howie hard into the side of the building. The scene was getting more and more tense as traffic started to slow from the rubbernecking of drivers trying to see what was going on. Kelly the Mick and Colin were just waiting for an opening to blast away.

Looking over to see Howie straining to get back to his feet, I said, "Well, what are you going to do, Mr. Albanese? This is getting ridiculous. We're just kids. It was just a fight between two kids in the neighborhood."

"Alright, then," J.R. spit back. "Then I want you to fight Danny fair and square this time so he can kick your wise Irish ass real good and you won't have a chance to be dirty. You know where Gleason's Gym is at 31st, off of Eighth?" I nodded. "Well, be there tomorrow afternoon at three, and you and Danny will settle this in the ring. Then we'll see how tough you are."

I could barely believe what he was proposing. "Mr. Albanese, I would rather just shake Danny's hand and get on with my life."

"Spoken like a true faggot," he sneered.

"Alright," I replied. "If this is what you want, so be it."

Two police cruisers came screaming up from 42nd Street with lights flashing. The cops jumped out. "What's going on here? Come on break it up, you love birds. What, Albanese? You getting into young boys now?"

"There's no problem, officer," J.R. says through his teeth. "You've got it all wrong. We were just setting up a little boxing tournament. You know, the Irish against the Italians." Officer McLeary obviously didn't get the joke... and even more obviously didn't like J.R.

"Yeah, yeah, Albanese. Tell your story in that pimp-red niggermobile... driving away." With the introduction of the police into the scene, Kelly the Mick and Colin had decided it was best to slip away as the crowd dissipated. Before the Delta 88 pulled out, though, the Englishman pointed directly at Howie as if to say, "You're mine."

"Fuck you, Cro-Magnon face," came Howie's nervous response. "You look like something off the Darwin Chart."

The cops had no sooner followed J.R.'s lead than my friends' chorus began anew: "You'll do him again. That's all, just remember what you did today." For just a fleeting moment, I actually wished for the first time since they'd moved that I'd relocated to Long Beach with my family. But just as quickly, I knew that my love for this rock called Manhattan was way too deep... and I loved this particular rock known as the stoop just as much.

Brian came off of the stoop and started putting on a boxing clinic for me. "Francis, come on. Let's move a little. We gotta get you ready." I followed him down onto the concrete. I was sincerely paying attention... because I was sincerely scared. What had happened earlier that day was pure fury, pure instinctual reaction. I didn't know if I could replicate it. I didn't know if I wanted to. But Brian was pretty good; he had fought in the Golden Gloves. "Keep your hands up, Francis, and move. Stick him with your jab. You're a little taller than Danny, so you have a longer reach. Hit him as many times in his spaghetti box as you can. That'll make him drop his hands, then you target his puny fucking head. *i wish brian could just be my replacement for this fight.*

Howie chimed in, "I'll be working your corner no matter what. I won't leave your side, Francis. Nobody knows you like me." To hear Howie proclaim his loyalty like that allowed me to crack my first smile of the day. It was short-lived, though. Kelly the Mick and Colin Garvan had driven around the block and pulled up again.

Kelly shouted from his car, "We're gonna back you up in this thing. Way to go, Doonan."

"There ain't no 'thing,'" I retorted. "After tomorrow, it'll be over. I don't need your help." Refusing Kelly the Mick for a third time was not lost on anyone within earshot. Fuming, he threw the car into drive and sped uptown.

We all stood there in an uncomfortable silence for a moment until Howie broke the silence, "So who the fuck was that big, limey, Lurch-looking motherfucker with Johnny Rugs?"

Romeo T chimed in, "They call him The Duke. People say he was some sort of amateur boxing champ from the backstreets of London, but he killed somebody in the ring and had to hide out over here. I hear he's pretty dangerous."

"How dangerous can an Englishman be?" asked Howie.

"Yeah," added Romeo T, "for an Englishman."

"Fuck the English! Up the Irish!" Howie started chanting over and over. Everyone laughed. No one could resist loving Howie. Redbone came back from the store with a case of Budweiser while Clayton lit up another joint. "Yeah! Might as well keep the party going!" Howie broke his chant long enough to muse, adding, "But none of that for you, Francis. You're in training."

"Yeah, okay," I agreed. "It's time for me to turn in then. I still have to go to work tomorrow, but I'll talk to Benny about letting me out early. I'll see you guys tomorrow."

"Alright. We'll meet you in front of Gleason's at 2:30. Good night, champ," said Brian. "Oh, and don't jerk off tonight; save your energy."

I barely had the energy to flip him the bird as I disappeared into the building, much less climb the five flights to my apartment. When I reached the top floor, though, I decided to go up to the roof for a little pre-bed calming like only the night lights of Manhattan could provide. I could still hear the voices of my friends wafting up through the night air. Thoughts of the fight to come left me confused and frustrated. Fighting Danny Albanese was not what I wanted at all. I just wished I could leave all of that bullshit behind. I started to really miss my family. I started to feel like an 11-year old again. That was the age at which I remembered truly feeling carefree for the last time. At 17, I was just scared and lonely and hungry and angry and tired and confused... so confused. I kept looking down off of the roof into the empty parking lot below. *maybe i should just jump and make everyone happy. johnny rugs, kelly the mick, colin garvan, shit... even sandra?* But the thought of my mother and father made me step back from the edge. *i can't do that to them, especially now that they're so happy.* Alongside all of the morbid thoughts that were flooding my brain, I suddenly felt a mental presence... like an old friend that you know is no good to hang around. It was almost tangible. I just felt like I was in so much emotional pain that all I could think to do was wonder where I could score some heroin. But I didn't have the strength to do anything but collapse... which is precisely what I did... right there on the roof.

It wasn't until a flash of lightning illuminated the sky and I started getting pelted by the drops of a warm spring rain that I awoke to realize I was soaked and sleeping in my brand new suit. Although the suit was nothing but rags now, the rain still felt and smelled good. Trudging a dripping trail down to my apartment, I peeled off my clothes and sunk to my knees. I hadn't been in this position since I used to recite my bedtime prayers next to my father. But that night, I was a little boy again in more ways than one.

I was glad to be seeing Benny in the morning before the fight. He always had good advice to impart. As I nestled underneath the covers, my mind wondered what Danny was thinking at that moment... and whether he prayed that night too. Drifting off to sleep, the last thought I recalled was whether God would answer Danny's prayers... or mine.

"Walk like a man! Talk like a man!" blared from my alarm clock radio, beginning that daily negotiation between ears and brain. My eyes finally cracked open in time to hear Frankie fade out: "Walk like a man from you. I'll tell the world to forget about it, girl, and walk like a man from you...." Propping myself up on one arm, the radio continued, "Good morning, New York City. It's 7 am, here in a wet and rainy Big Apple. Keep your dial set to CBS-FM 101.1. We'll be back after these words from our sponsors."

Rolling out of bed, I plodded into the bathroom to turn the hot water on full-blast, and then called down to the deli to order my usual breakfast: two large coffees with four sugars in each and two egg, cheese and extra ketchup sandwiches. *man, i'm starving. today calls for a little of jimi's "machine gun" with the volume cranked. oh how my neighbors love me.* The door buzzer rang. *wow. that was quick for the delivery.* I pressed the button and waited with money in hand for the delivery guy to make it up the five flights. A few seconds later, the door opened, but it wasn't the food. "Morning, champ," Howie greeted me, opening the door himself. "I brought you some Tropicana. Just wanted to make sure you're okay."

"I'm fine," I replied, heading back into the bathroom to turn on the cold water and cut some of the steam.

Howie continued, "Listen. Just fuck Danny up like you did yesterday and it's history." *somehow i don't think its going to be that easy.* "I actually have to go right now, but I wanted to make sure you started off your day with some Vitamin C. I have to head over to Bergdorf's; the early bird gets the leathers, you know! But don't worry. I'll be there at 2:30, no matter what."

"Fuck! I love this part!" Trailing down the stairs, everyone for blocks could hear him scream off key, "...and let your bullets fly like rain, machine gun...."

Steadily draining the quart of O.J., a knock came at the door and I opened it in mid-swallow. Howie must've let in the delivery guy on his way out. I overtipped him a little bit and began eating my sandwiches nice and slow. The coffee helped immensely to clear out the cobwebs. *i obviously kind of know i can beat danny; shit, i did it before. but if i do, when will this shit end? what if i just let him beat me? it's not like it's really a big deal to me. i'm not worried about the macho thing. my friends will have more of a problem with it, but i'll explain it to them and, in time, they'll understand 'cuz we all love each other. that's what i'll do, then. i'll get on the ropes, let him tune me up a bit, and when the time is right, go down. that'll make his daddy happy and everything's back to normal.* Noticing the similarity between my apartment and London, the fog rolled in from my still-running shower, snapping me back home. I allowed myself the luxury of a half-hour shower, emerging refreshed and renewed. Coming up with a solution to the Albanese problem even allowed me a similarly fresh frame of mind.

Throwing on loose, comfortable clothing, I had just closed the door and put my key in the lock when I heard the phone ring. I just stood there for a second, letting the answering machine get it. I didn't feel like talking to anyone at the moment, but I thought to hang around for a second to make sure it wasn't someone I should talk to. "Good morning, Francis. This is Karen Winthrop calling. I hope it's not too early to ring you, but you wandered into my mind this morning. I'm going to be taking a ride up to the country on Friday and would love it if you could join me. My number is 212–" *"a ride up to the country." god, gotta love it.* "–9169. I hope to hear from you. Soon." *that'd be nice, to have a break from the neighborhood for a couple of days. if it weren't for this oscar-winning beating i hafta take, this would actually be shaping up to be a pretty good day.*

perhaps i spoke too soon. A torrential downpour stopped me short of stepping out onto the stoop, but it didn't take long to recognize the unmarked police car parked right out front. The window rolls down just enough to let a hand pass into the rain. One brisk jerk of the wrist motioned me to come. It wasn't until I'd gotten closer that I could see the face of Detective Jack O'Casey; his partner was in the driver's seat. He reached back to unlock the rear door and ordered me to "Get in." Wiping a faceful of water away with my sleeve, Det. O'Casey continued, "First off, Doonan, I want to apologize to you." *shit. i've never seen him like this. it's actually hard for him to say this.* "Sunday, when I saw you in front of St. Paul's, I intention-ally looked at you like you were a piece of shit... and I know you saw me. But... as it turns out..., I guess I'm wrong. I heard about what happened yes-terday, and what Albanese said about my Sandra. What you did, that's very honorable, and I sincerely thank you." I couldn't react at all. I just sat there, listening. "You know, she's my only child – my little girl – and it breaks her mother's and my hearts to think she keeps company with that piece of shit. This legendary New York cop was actually showing some genuine emotion; his voice cracked and the tone of the conversation shifted. "I want you to kick his Guinea ass good today, Doonan. My hands are tied. I just put in my retirement papers and I can't have anything jeopardize my pension. I worked hard for it a lot of years, and my family deserves it." He paused as if to accentuate the button: "So do that for me. Do that for Sandra."

I didn't really know how to react, so I just sat there until he broke the silence, all business. "You need a lift anywhere?"

"Yeah," I mutter. "27th and Sixth Avenue, if you don't mind. I have to go to work."

"Alright," said the detective as his driver pulled away. "I'm going to be sending Sandra Upstate to my sister's; the schools are better and this is just not a good element for her. She's far too beautiful and sweet for Hell's Kitchen." *i second that emotion!* I got lost in that thought for a moment, but said nothing as my heart also sank, thinking that my Sandra would be gone. I wondered how long I'd have to get in touch with her before she left. The car slid to a stop and O'Casey turned around and sincerely shook my hand like a man does with someone he sincerely respects. "If there's anything I can ever do for you, son, here's my card." He stuck it in my breast pocket and then suddenly grabbed me by the collar and pulled me a little closer, hissing: "And remember. Kick. His. Fucking. Ass. We'll keep at his father; he'll fuck up eventually, and we'll be there to get him."

I stepped out of the car into the rain, and on my dash to the shelter of the doorway, smelled something familiar wafting my way. My nose instinctively sought it out like a homing pigeon, and when my eyes caught up, I saw the great Chonley Diaz lean out of another doorway just long enough to smile and raise his eyebrows the same way he raised the baby banana-sized joint clutched in his fingers. "Eh, my little amigo, come join me for the morning ritual. This Jamaican dude around my way rolls them up and sells them; calls them 'spliffs.' He mixes in a bit of tobacco to give it an even burn. There's a small labor fee for rolling it, but this weed is primo." He handed it to me for a gargantuan inhale, and was he ever right about it being good weed. "Señor, what, are you fucking Humphrey Bogart?" We laughed, huddling from the rain in that doorway, two old friends stoned off our birds.

"So what brings you around, Chonley?"

"Well, Benny hired me back again for the thousandth time. He says he hopes this time it's for good. Me too. I'm getting tired of moving around.

I also used to have a little side gig from Benny. Now that was good dough. I hope to get that back." Knowing full well that he was referring to the job Benny had given me, I took a long hit and stood there in silence. "C'mon, it's time to go to work." We entered the store together to be greeted by Benny's beaming smile.

"Well if it ain't my two favorites: Fric and Frac... and on time, no less. Now that's what I call conscientious." *unconscious is more like it.* As we headed off to the locker room, Benny added, "Francis, in an hour, come to my office. I want to talk to you. Until then, you and Chonley start on the sunflowers; they're going to be a big number this season.

"Welcome back, Chonley."

"Thank you, Benny," he replied. "It's good to be back."

The next hour passed quickly. When I reached Benny's office, he was on the phone. He motioned to the coffee and box of Entenmann's coffee cake. I had a fierce case of the munchies, so I grabbed a huge piece; there was nothing like a good sugar rush. When Benny had finished his call, he looked up at me and said, "Let me take a quick piss." He left me there, gorging myself on sweet cake and looking at the picture on his desk of the Ice Queen and his two boys, awash in tons of paperwork. Mellow music played softly in the background as my eyes scanned the room, passing over the suits and sports coats hanging on hooks across the wall. His office looked more like a Barney's outlet. Realizing the front of my shirt was covered with crumbs and powdered sugar, I was making as graceful an attempt as a stoner can manage to dust it off as Benny returned and laughed at the sight. "You see? That's why I love you so much, kid." A little embarrassed, I stopped. "I heard about your problem with the Albaneses."

"How'd you find out?" I managed to ask.

"Francis, this is a small world and an even smaller planet. Good news travels quick, but bad news even quicker. That fucking Albanese is a fucking asshole; always was, always will be. I've known him since we were kids. I was with the Rivington Raiders back then and he was with the Tenth Street Boys; we were bitter enemies. If you look real close at his upper lip, there's a scar there that's from me. We had it out at a dance once. He was a loudmouth bully and tried to hit on my girl."

"That's just about what happened yesterday," I interjected.

"Well, the apple doesn't fall far from the tree. So, my boy what time is the duel?"

"Three p.m." I replied.

"Good. That'll give us time. We'll go over together." He could see the surprise in my face that Benny would find the time to come with me to settle a neighborhood squabble. "I swear to you I had to go over there anyway. My friend, Burt Sugar of 'Ring Magazine' fame called and told me Roberto Duran – you know, 'Manos de Piedre' – is working out there, and I should come watch him. They say he's like an unleashed panther. You ever see him fight, kid?"

"Yeah," came my reply. "His hair is even tough. But what does 'Monastery Pedro' mean, anyway?"

"'Manos de Piedre.' It's Spanish for 'Hands of Stone,' kid." I was hardly listening. I felt a little better that I was getting Benny's support. I just didn't know if Benny would approve of my plan. I turned to head back downstairs when Benny added, "Take it easy today, okay? You'll need your energy. Hey, one other thing. Was Danny Albanese a loud-talker? I mean in his manner. Yesterday?" I nodded. "Just like his old man. You know what that means, kid? The classic defense against fear is noise. Noisy pricks are just people that're afraid. That's all. And wherever Danny Albanese is today, I'll bet he's scared shitless of you. We'll leave at around two so we can walk over. It's close."

"Thanks, Benny," I said, exiting his office. He responded with one of his trademark winks and a nod.

Chonley was waiting for me when I got back. "What was that about?"

I lied. "Oh, something about a heather shipment I fucked up." Chonley could tell I was holding back... and I could tell he could tell. Out of respect, he kept quiet. In the midst of the disquieting silence, I became very aware of the big industrial clock on the wall. It sort of became a part of my afternoon the same way as the clock in "High Noon" became a part of Gary Cooper's. I hadn't wanted to let on to Chonley what was going to happen because he was a classic, high-strung, macho Latino, and his involvement might have ended up getting him hurt.

At 2 p.m. on the button, Benny was waiting by the door. Chonley slapped my hand as Benny turned and strode out, leading the way like Patton, straight across 27th Street toward Eighth Avenue. As we took the right toward 30th, Benny asked me, "You ever been in Gleason's, kid?" I shook my head. "Well, it smells like the inside of an old, sweaty jock strap. That's how you can tell it's a great gym." I could hear the words Benny was saying, but I wasn't really listening. My anatomy was like a pinball machine; everything was popping, flipping, jumping.

I snapped back when Benny mentioned that we were going to make a stop right around the corner from the gym. Entering a shop adorned with a sign that read "Colon's Cuban Seeds Cigars," the one old man within jumped up to greet him. "Mr. Benny! Mr. Benny! Long time."

I couldn't be certain, but I thought Benny greeted him back with a "Hiya, champ." They embraced before Benny turned, one arm still around the old, red-haired man's shoulders, and said, "Francis, say hello to Esteban Colón, former Bantam Weight Champion of the World. I noticed that the man barely used any force while shaking hands, a trait that I had learned all real fighters, surgeons and piano players possessed: you always protect the tools.

"Nice to meet you, young man. Any friend of Mr. Benny is a friend of mine." His voice was heavily accented, but brimmed with a self-assured calm. "Let me guess. You want five of my best." Benny smiled and nodded. As the shop owner walked over and sat behind a high table, he added, "What happened to you, Benny? You used to buy them 50 at a time!"

"Yeah, I know, but I gave them up," came Benny's response. "Gotta watch the ticker. Doctor's orders." Watching this artisan at work was a treat in itself. Carefully choosing several leaves, rolling them, cutting, trimming, forming; the precision with which he worked was Old World for sure. Within moments, sitting on the counter were five perfectly formed masterpieces of Cuba. *that's amazing.* Esteban smiled, seeming to hear my thoughts. Scooping up the five brown torpedoes and replacing them with a U.S. Grant, Benny added, "These are for Burt Sugar. I'm going over to see him. Duran's at Gleason's, you know." Without any visible reaction to the news, Esteban hugged his old friend and patted me on the shoulder.

Once we got back out onto the street, Benny continued without pause. "You should have seen him, Francis. He was beautiful; moved like a cat, thunder in both hands. Smart under pressure and a lot of class. He was one of the best. At the height of his career, though, he killed a young Mexican in a championship fight and walked away from the sport forever. He was never the same. Me and a bunch of guys helped set him up in that shop. Shit, it's been over 40 years." I was struggling to pay attention. I loved listening to Benny; I could do it all day... just not today.

We were a little more than 50 feet from Gleason's when I recognized that cherry red Delta 88 sitting in front of the gym. Not surprisingly, J.R. and Danny were inside, along with the Duke and two of Albanese's other gorillas. My stomach would have done a flip-flop had I not seen Vit, Brian, Milk, Redbone and Romeo T standing in front of the door. Of course, Howie was not among them... but he was famous for his punctuality problems. A big, crudely written sign on the door announced that the gym was closed for a private workout until 3 p.m. "...And that means you, moron" was its last line. A quick glance at my watch told me that we had about 15 minutes to wait. I took the opportunity to introduce Benny to all the boys. Benny passed around hellos and handshakes, adding, "You guys remind me of my own boyhood cronies." Clapping a hand on my shoulder, he continued, "Kid, let's go inside for a minute."

"But what about the sign?" I asked.

As if he didn't hear me at all, Benny rapped on the door. No answer. He rapped again. A voice that sounded much like a fork caught in a garbage disposal shot back from the other side of the door. "What are you? A fucking cretin, asshole? Can't you read? It's written in perfect English, you schmuck motherfucker." The metal door heaved and squeaked as it scraped an arc into the pavement. A weathered old ogre of a man, chomping on a cigar that looked like it was a part of his lip, stepped into the sunlight as though out of a Damon Runyon tale. His face was screwed up as if in preparation for beginning the verbal assault anew, but instantly softened and dropped when he saw who was standing outside the gym. "Benny! Bubeleh! What? Are you slumming?" Seamus Boylan was a Holocaust survivor and a product of the Lower East Side... but most importantly at that moment, he'd been a friend of Benny's for years.

True to form, Benny dangled one of the five Cuban masterpieces in front of his grizzled old friend. "Hello, Seamus. Have a fresh one and say hello to Francis." I shook his hand while trying to keep my eyes from wandering around the gym. It was like another world in there; hushed and reverent, almost like a church. But instead of priests, nuns, altar boys and parishioners, there were trainers, cutmen, racketeers, and wannabees... plenty of wannabees. But the main attraction was dancing in the main ring: "Manos de Piedre." Benny whispered to me to go stand by the ring apron to watch, maybe pick up a few tips. "Absorb, my boy. Absorb," he Obi-Wanned into my ear. I didn't need much prompting.

Almost as recognizable in boxing circles were the two men working Duran's corner: Freddie Brown and Ray Arcel. Although everything they said had to be repeated through an interpreter, the Hands of Stone themselves needed no translation. "One more, champ. You're looking good." Arcel yelled, "Bring in the dancer!" A new sparring partner began to make his way into the ring, looking like a Christian on "Double the Lions Night." The bell rang. Duran was a machine. His feet were firmly planted; legs like pillars; body toned and in perfect condition. His hair was jet black with a life all its own. Sweat glistened and ran over every part of him as he pounded on his sparring partner, stepping in with body shots that exploded in echoes through this cathedral of pain. His arms were like long, relentless jackhammers. *he looks kind of like a really pissed-off panamanian beetle.* They signaled the end of the round, and for half a second, panic and fear gripped me as Duran glanced my way while I wondered if I had thought that observation or spoken it aloud.

But I was literally saved by the bell; it rang and Duran turned that fiery focus back on his opponent. To his credit, the other guy moved much like Ali – real flashy, which I liked. But Duran stalked like a patient matador... and the ballerina's dance floor got smaller and smaller until he was in the corner and the ring was cut off. Without warning, Duran unleashed a barrage of three body shots, two left hooks to the head and a right uppercut. He shoved the hapless dancer to stand him up straight and then discharged three straight right hands to the head. Arcel barked suddenly, "Stop! That's it! What? Are you trying to kill him?" Duran growled, but like a predator tempered by pity, withdrew without waiting for the translation. Once his head gear had been removed, the champ immediately went over to his fallen, broken adversary and touched his face gently, following it with a kiss on the cheek.

Less than ten feet from me, I clearly heard him say, "Muchas gracias, amigo." A strikingly handsome Black fighter with tasseled shoes stood "on deck" near me. Staring through glazed eyes, he too could only look on in amazement through the shine of a baby Jheri curl.

Benny appeared at my side with another character for me to meet: Burt Sugar, sporting a Panama hat and a fresh Cuban. "So what do you think of that, kid? Francis, this is Burt. He says Duran's ready to face Leonard in Montreal, and if anyone should know, it's Burt Sugar."

"Of course, everyone thinks I'm crazy, but he'll destroy Sugar Ray. You'll see. Anyway, Benny told me about your fight with Albanese's boy. Good luck today. Remember what you saw just now. Maybe it'll come in handy. I gotta get running, Benny. Good to see you as always. And nice to meet you too, Irish." It seemed as though most of the gym's denizens cleared out along with Burt, leaving the hazy sunlight streaming through the open door to make the room reminiscent of a tomb. I just wanted to run for it and puke my guts out, but it was too late for that.

I could hear Seamus shout out the "One buck apiece!" admission price from the door, to which most of my crew immediately clamored in protest. "A buck apiece? Fuck that!" Milk chimed in.

"I don't want to hear nothing from you punks. A buck it is and that's that." My friends were still arguing and angling to get in, looking like Leo Gorcey, Huntz Hall and the Bowery Boys.

Benny noticed the row immediately and, in his typically smooth fashion, walked over and palmed the gatekeeper twenty bucks with the assurance, "It's on me, Seamus."

Looking almost as though he'd been chastised, Seamus replied, "But there's only six of them, Benny, and I ain't got no change."

"Keep it. Get some cigars." The boys charged in past Seamus' fat grin and ran straight to me, offering a hailstorm of advice and encouragement: "Francis in the house!" "Fuck him up, Irish; he's all yours." "We got your back, Doonan." One voice was noticeably absent from the din, though. I looked around for the clock on the wall. *3:15? that's late, even for howie.*

My train of thought jumped its track, though, as the Albaneses made their entrance and Danny sauntered right for the ring, climbing in with his trademark counterfeit bravado. Right on his heels, the Duke got in and started instructing him like some psychotic Ernie Fossey. I realized that Benny's eyes had been as subtly trained on Danny as had mine when his voice entered my ear quietly. "Listen, kid. You're smart, so use your intelligence with this Guinea. His father was never a candidate for Mensa, so chances are that neither is Junior. So stay on your toes. Stick, move, work off the jab. Conserve your energy because these will be the longest three minutes of your life. Seamus is refereeing and he just told me it's gonna be amateur style: three three-minute rounds." To allay my fears, he added a fatherly pinch-caress of my cheek and the encouragement, "You'll be fine, kid."

While Benny shook hands with acquaintances on the way to his ringside seat, the boys from the Kitchen headed my way to show their support. I actually had more on my mind than just the fight. When Howie said he was going to do something, he did... late, perhaps... but this was pushing it, even for him. "Where's Howie?" I asked Redbone.

"Dunno, Francis," came his reply. "He was supposed to meet us on the stoop. We all came over together. Maybe he got pinched boosting." I just shook my head. *howie's too good. something's not right.* I couldn't figure out what in the world (or whom) Howie had gotten himself into. It just wasn't like him.

The cacophony that vomited from the mouth of J.R. Albanese broke the anxious civility that had hung in the air... and set the tone for the event. "Well, well, well, if it ain't Benny the Kike. Good day to Jew, Mr. Levine."

Without so much as turning around, let alone giving Albanese the pleasure of seeing him annoyed, Benny shot back immediately, "If it isn't Johnny Rugs the Dago. Wop's new, Rugs?" J.R. was not quite so skilled at masking his rage, resorting to throwing one of those "old country" Italian "fuck you" gestures at Benny's back.

The place started to fill up quickly since half the neighborhood was there. Even women from the Kitchen sat ruddy faced and smileless in the gym. Mrs. Clancy waved an Irish flag and shouted, "Kick his arse, Doonan! Do it for your people!" The fight had taken on an international significance. I just wished I could disappear. Some of the focus was taken off of me, though, when Roberto Duran emerged from the locker room to leave. Much of the crowd was in tow, asking for autographs or just jockeying for a good vantage point to see the champ.

"Hey, Duran," yelled out one local tough named Ciaran Doherty. "Come to Ninth Ave. and I'll show you some hands of stone!" Duran stopped dead. *perhaps he understood more english than everyone realized.* He locked eyes with Ciaran for a fraction of a second before he broke the gaze and tried to cover it with a smart remark. Duran smirked still unblinkingly, and before continuing on towards the door, he looked in my direction and nodded, his smirk opening to a genuine smile. *yeah, he's gonna kill leonard.* Doherty decided to capitalize on the Champ's exit. "Everyone saw that, right? Me and Duran, man to man. Mutual respect. He didn't back down and I didn't back down. Shit, I love that fucking Mexican."

Seamus coughed, "He's from Panama, you fucking retard."

Doherty's retort served only to bolster Seamus' claim: "Panamanish, Mexican. What's the difference? They all eat beans." The crowd howled while Benny directed me to get in the ring. As I climbed through the ropes, an ancient fireplug of a man stepped in my direction.

"Chickie," he croaked, extending his hand. I was so nervous by that point that although I shook his hand, it never occurred to me to reply with my name. In one swift movement, Chickie had removed my shirt and turned me around to rub my shoulders and talk in my ear. "Just relax, kid. You're shakin' like a dog shittin' razor blades. You gotta calm down. Now

I'm gonna wrap your hands and put on your gloves; you ever wear gloves before?" A bit overwhelmed, I simply shook my head meekly. "Well, I'll take care of it. No worries. The key to life is relaxing." Again, with one swift movement, the old cornerman was in front of me with a roll of white tape. My arm was extended and Chickie swarmed around it with the tape like agitated wasps.

Breaking the trance of watching him work, I was able to take in his features up close for the first time. His face was as flat as that villain from Dick Tracy... what's his name... with a nose that almost seemed to be made of clay since it sloped sideways instead of jutting out from his face. Both ears were cauliflowered, and in truth, he looked more monster than man. Any guy named Chickie had doubtlessly seen his fair share of wars, but there was a calmness, a subtle confidence that radiated from him and did indeed help to relax me.

Before I knew it, I was sporting red, leather, 16-ounce Everlasts to complement my gray fleece sweat pants and white, high top Chuck Taylor's. During the brief glance I permitted myself at the opposing corner, I saw Danny in baby blue, nylon sweat pants and matching Chuck Taylor's. His father stood by his side, removing the four or five gold chains from around his son's neck. The Duke was massaging Danny's shoulders while the din from the crowd grew to a dull roar as more supporters flooded in for both sides. There were more than 100 redheaded and olive-toned people packed into the gym, but two or three scans of their faces convinced me that there was still no Howie.

My search was interrupted by Seamus' booming voice. "Everyone, quiet while I go over the rules!" Somber as a hangman, Chickie accompanied me to the middle of the ring with Benny discreetly nearby. We met Danny, J.R. and the Duke there. "Now, if there's any doubt, let's get it straight that I'm the fucking king of this castle and what I says goes. When I says, 'Break,' you break. I don't want no dirty shit, and if there is,

I'm stopping this. Gleason's don't usually do this kinda thing, and neither of you guys are fighters, so I'm not gonna see somebody killed. You all got that?" Danny and I just stood like lamp posts, glaring into each other's eyes. "Now go to your corners," Seamus continued, "And, at the bell, come out fighting." I used the brief moment in my corner to scan one last time for the still-absent Howie. *that's just not like him. what the hell?* The bell announced the beginning of round one.

Half-dancing, half-lumbering, I headed for the middle of the ring with the West Side crowd going nuts. Danny charged at me full speed, fists and arms straight in front of him. Without a punch thrown, Danny's semi-tackle left me looking up from the canvas through stars that resulted from my head slamming to the floor. Seamus instantly yelled Danny back into his corner, but I couldn't distinguish Albanese's laughing, snarling face from any of the others ringing the gym. Leaning down for a better look, Seamus asked, "Are you alright?" I managed a slow nod, so he continued. "Do you wanna keep going, kid?" I stood up immediately and grunted a "Yeah" through my mouthpiece. Turning back to Danny's corner, Seamus ordered, "Okay then. Touch 'em up and let's go." *time in. the battle resumes.*

Through the ringing in my ears, I could distinctly hear J.R. yelling at the top of his lungs. "Cripple him, Danny! Get him good!" As drunk on my feet as I felt, it was not difficult for Danny to circle me without much effort, jumping in periodically with wing punches. I did my best to respond with some flat-footed jabs, actually connecting with a few as a panicked Danny began to swing for his life. In a sudden switch, I went to the ropes with Danny hot on my heels, still flailing away. *i can almost feel benny's eyes on me. surely he recognizes that i'm not putting up much of a defense. it won't take him long to figure out what i'm doing; violence is just not in my nature.*

Danny's punches were beginning to add up; red marks were starting to blossom all over my body as I tried to take the most convincing beating I could. *i hope this is making the albaneses happy. i just wants this to be over.* At one point, I must've been strangely reminiscent of the Crucifixion, leaned back so far on the ropes with my arms outstretched, feeling forsaken. The bell ended both the round and – temporarily – my suffering. Full of unearned confidence, Danny stalked back to his corner on fire, met by the boisterous approval of his father and the Duke. The Italians in the crowd were sharing in the celebration and had begun to taunt and berate the Irish West Side spectators

Benny's calm, low voice sounded in my ear, "Listen to me, Francis. I know what you're doing. I understand, and it's very respectable, but you gotta protect yourself too. A punch is still a punch."

I could only stare back, just managing the words, "Did Howie make it?"

"I don't think so, kid. Not yet."

Ciaran Doherty butted into the conversation, literally and figuratively. "Hey, Doonan, you want I should trade places with you? I'll clean his greasy fucking clock. No? Well then come on! Don't disgrace your race and the neighborhood for fuck's sake!"

The bell to begin round two should've brought me out of the corner swinging, and had my heart been with the rest of me, I probably could've put Danny away anytime I felt like it. But as it was, he was fairly confident and fighting his heart out in case the bout went to the cards. And without sincere resistance, there was no denying that Danny was winning... in a big way.

Wherever my heart was laying low, my brain must've been by its side since I felt more preoccupied with where Howie was, rather than concentrating on the fight. I took advantage of a momentary break in the pummeling to scan the room. J.R. was beaming, and although Howie was still nowhere to be seen, Kelly the Mick and Colin Garvan were standing near the door, not far from a sour-faced Det. Jack O'Casey. I returned my gaze to Danny just in time for him to unload a barrage of blows, the first of which cut my right eyelid, sending blood streaming down my pink Irish frame and dripping onto my sweatpants. By the time the attack waned I was also bleeding from the mouth and could hear Rosie O'Brien from 48th Street scream out, "Get off the feckin' ropes and hit him, Francis... like this!" The crowd howled as she demonstrated a three-punch combo, but the Hell's Kitchen crew was clearly growing concerned that I was beginning to get hurt.

Seamus looked over at Benny with an appeal for direction. His eyes said, "I gotta stop this; the kid is getting murdered!" as clearly as his mouth could have done. Benny shook his head subtly. He knew that the assembled crowd would wreck the joint. A single finger went up from his hand discreetly, cuing Seamus to let it go only one more round. Several moments later, when the bell signaled the end of the round and I was approaching my corner, Seamus hissed, "Defend yourself, kid! Come on!"

Benny was waiting by my corner too, and although I could see that he felt bad for me, there was an air of understanding about him... an air of resolve that there was nothing he could say or do. I took a deep breath and shot Benny a half-shrug. He nodded slightly as I turned around to sit down and began rubbing my shoulders. I could see the crew out of the corner of my eye, heads hung. They certainly weren't considering leaving; they just didn't know what to think. Like mine, the boys' heads all snapped to the side as light streamed in from the gym's main door when it flung open and two silhouettes rushed through. *howie! thank god. i was getting worried.* But within seconds, I could tell that it was actually Clayton and Patty Boy rushing forward in a panic. I strained for a glimpse of Howie. *maybe he's behind them?* They made right for the crew, Clayton shooting me an uncomfortably telling glance. I instantly felt like I was going to retch. "What's wrong?" I demanded, shaking off Benny and almost upending Seamus as I leapt to the rope.

Choking back emotion, almost incapable of meeting my gaze, Patty Boy spoke in a monotone. "The cops found Howie on the railroad tracks next to Tenth Avenue, less than a block from the stoop, beaten to within an inch of his life. He's got a fractured skull, they said. They just left his mother at St. Luke's-Roosevelt. He's in surgery now to operate on his brain, I think. It looks bad, man. Really bad."

Clayton continued, "We're heading back, but we wanted you guys to know. Poor Mrs. Nesto is in tatters. I'm going home to get my mother to help her."

Det. O'Casey had approached when he saw Clayton and Patty Boy rush in, and Kelly the Mick and Colin were not far behind him. They all overheard what was said, but the bellowing from the Italians in the crowd eclipsed the ensuing conversation. "Finish it! Finish it! Come on! Ring the bell! Finish it!"

Benny had heard as much of the report as I did, stepping in front of me as I struggled to catch the follow-up. Putting a hand on my shoulder to keep me from coming through the ropes, he cautioned, "We will go to the hospital as soon as you finish the fight, Francis." He responded to my glare of disbelief. "You have to finish this, Francis. You must." Seamus was standing near the middle of the ring, stalling for the right time to resume. Ten million feelings surged through me at once like an emotional electrocution. *i'm so confused. i have to get out of this place! i don't want to be here. oh my god. my friend. my heart.*

The roar from both sides of the crowd had turned Gleason's into the Forum at The Garden. Through a kaleidoscope of tears, I looked across at the opposite corner, my eyes locking with the Duke's, who sort of cocked his head and shook briefly, almost imperceptibly, with a private laugh just for me. *that motherfucker. he did howie.*

The bell heralded Round Three and I might as well have been in the audience watching because something took control inside of me and

I could do little more than observe the beating that my rage doled out on Danny. Stepping in on him more quickly than anyone could've imagined – least of all myself – I started pumping jabs right into Danny's great dago gob, watching his confidence drain away alongside the blood streaming off his chin. I could tell from the dazed fear in his eyes that Danny knew as well as I that he was done. But I shoved him back onto the ropes all the same, unleashing a flurry of body shots that elicited gurgling, breathy squeals of pure pain with each blow. "Come on, Danny! What the fuck is wrong with you?!?" J.R. was standing on the side of the apron, practically leaning into the ring. Realizing he had little chance of willing a comeback from his son, J.R.'s glare turned to the Duke, knowing instinctively that this was somehow his fault.

With Danny trapped on the far post, I was as unmoved by mercy as I was by the insane cheering of Ciaran Doherty and the Tenth Avenue crowd. The beating my fury was dictating was clear-cut and unalterable as I rained shots from his belly to his head, punctuating the assault with a rapid-fire upper cut and a swift hook to the solar plexus. Literally, the only thing that was keeping Danny Albanese standing was the post. But even that proved little assistance when a right upper cut sent his mouthpiece airborne and the next uppercut pushed his teeth through his lip. Thoughts of Howie, near lifeless on an operating room table, head splayed open while his mother's heart shattered fueled the ire that left me pile-driving punches into Danny's face and head. We were both covered in blood, but it was no longer possible to distinguish his from mine. One thing was for certain, though: Danny had been out on his feet for some time before the bell finally rang and Seamus jumped in to save the battered teen.

At the same moment, J.R. leapt into the ring and charged straight for me, prompting a warning yell from Benny that spun me around, snapping a six-inch right hand – leveraged by all of my body weight – right onto the tip of the elder Albanese's chin. Like a felled cypress, J.R. was knocked out cold and literally crashed to the canvas from beneath his wig. In a matter of seconds, the scene screamed out of control as the Duke came through the ropes looking for me but was intercepted by Colin Garvan's .38 pointed right at the Brit's forehead. "Make one more move, motherfucker, and I'll blow your fucking head off." The Duke froze dead in his tracks, averting his gaze to take in the pride of "the Albanese Familia" laid out on the ground. Scattered scuffles had broken out among the denizens of the neighborhood.

Cooler heads were trying to prevail, as Seamus was shouting instructions to clear the gym. "We don't want a bloodbath in here! It was a fair fight!" Benny had quickly made his way over to Ciaran Doherty to solicit his help in dispersing the crowd, which he gladly provided.

Within the next several minutes, the Italian contingency had the Albaneses sitting up, tending to Danny's mangled lip and trying to calm a senseless J.R. who was screaming, "Where the fuck is my piece?" At least one person knew he wasn't talking about a gun; Ciaran Doherty had laughed himself into a coughing fit almost two blocks away after depositing Johnny's "Rug" into a sewer.

Kelly the Mick headed in my direction, but had scarcely gotten out, "Way to go, Doonan. You're one tough mother—" when I barreled past him on my way to ask Seamus if I could use the showers. *after everything else, mrs. nesto can't see me like this.*

"Sure, kid," came Seamus' reply. "I even have some extra sweat suits from the Olympic team kids I coached. I'll get one for you from my office." As I ran off to the locker room, Seamus headed into the back with Benny. "Bubeleh, I knew this kid was playing possum, but when he lit up! Holy shit! He was a wrecking crew! You know, with the proper guidance and training, this kid could go all the way. He can even take a punch!" Benny knew what was on Seamus' mind. Every old timer who'd ever trained or handled a fighter always wanted that one last shot with a promising up-and-comer. Seamus was no exception.

With the gym now almost completely empty and the din dying to an eerie silence, I stripped down and paused briefly to look at my white Converse high tops that now looked more like they had painted flames on them from all the blood. Even under the storm spitting down from the nozzle I could hear the echo of Det. O'Casey's voice. "Tell that kid he's a credit. I'll catch up with him soon."

"I'll tell him," echoed Benny's reply. Trudging damp footprints back through the locker room, I saw that Seamus had left a fresh new towel on the bench next to the promised sweat suit. A fresh towel was almost a thing of fable in any boxing gym, but I understood as I picked it up and noticed the name embroidered on its corner: "Roberto Duran."

"Come out when you're ready, kid. I'll be waiting." Dressing quickly, I only half-accidentally threw Duran's towel over my shoulder and headed out to the sidewalk. Benny was there with a cab waiting to whisk us away to St. Luke's on 59th Street. Danny Albanese was on his way to St. Vincent's, fortunately heading in the other direction. Most of the cab ride took place in silence, partly because I was beginning to realize the extent of the physical beating that I'd taken, but mostly because of the emotional toll and worry for Howie. I thumbed Duran's towel, praying silently until Benny held a silver flask stamped "Tiffany & Co." under my nose and dropped two Valiums into my cupped hand. "Kid, take these. It'll calm you down." I threw them to the back of my throat and chased them down with Benny's burning offering from the flask.

"Can you cut over to Tenth Avenue now?" I asked the cabbie. I wanted to pass by the stoop. *i don't know. maybe it'll all be a bad prank and howie'll be out there holding it down.* But no one was there. I had never seen it look quite so barren before.

As we were approaching 59th, Benny pulled out his wallet. "Francis, I'm embarrassed to admit that I don't know Mrs. Nesto, but I do know Howie. I'd appreciate it if you'd give her this for anything she might need."

He put five $100 bills in my hand and folded my fingers over Ben's face. "I'm sorry, but I can't go in with you. I just can't handle hospitals. I hope you understand.

"Now don't go doing anything stupid, kid, and call me tonight when you get home. I love you, Francis."

There was an unconditional sincerity to his words. My reply came out as easily as my name. "I love you too, Benny." As his cab pulled away, I could feel the combination of the Chivas Regal and Valium beginning to take effect. A wrapperless, lint-covered peppermint would have to do for covering up the alcohol on my breath. I didn't want Mrs. Nesto smelling it on my breath.

As soon as I stepped through the hospital's automatic doors, I could see the crew at the end of the hallway: Clayton, Brian, Red, Cal, Romeo T and Vit. Clayton's mother, Alice Brooks, was sitting next to Mrs. Nesto, holding her hand. Even at the distance, I could tell that they were both crying. All of the boys were sullen and somber, and their mood seeped into me more and more as I approached. I was almost afraid to approach Howie's mom. I suppose I felt guilty, like it was somehow my fault. I suddenly felt the strong desire to turn and bolt, but Mrs. Brooks spotted me first and brought my presence to Mrs. Nesto's attention. With a gulp and a deep breath, I walked the few remaining feet to Mrs. Nesto just in time for her to fall into my arms, "Oh, Francis, what am I going to do? My poor baby. What happened to my boy? He doesn't bother anybody. He's a good boy."

I couldn't tell if the trembling in her voice was a result of the rest of her body shaking, but she clung to me for dear life. I knew we had to sit down though. After the punishing couple of rounds I'd endured early in the fight, I barely had the strength to hold myself up, let alone Howie's mom. "Let's sit down, Mrs. Nesto." I led her back to the bench slowly as Clayton's mom directed the other boys outside to give us some privacy. "Do you know what happened, Mrs. Nesto?"

She rambled her reply between muffled sobs in an exhaustedly hollow, disembodied fashion. "I don't know, Francis. Howie left this morning in a great mood. I made him breakfast. We talked... laughed.... He told me he was meeting you this afternoon and that he would see me this evening. The next thing I know, I get a call at work from the police that he was in an accident, and could I get here as soon as possible. I didn't know what to think, what to do, so I rushed over as quickly as I could. But when I got here... I... I just couldn't believe what they told me. A homeless man found my Howie... my baby... my little boy... like a broken doll, thrown across the tracks. He told the police that if he hadn't found Howie when he did, he would have been run over by the afternoon Amtrak stock train run." The thought of this was too much for Mrs. Nesto to bear and her weeping intensified so that both her voice and breath seemed trapped in her throat. During that moment of awkward silence, her eyes registered the state I was in. "What happened to you, Francis? Do you know anything about this?"

The look on her face... not to mention the reality of the situation... broke my heart and I just couldn't tell her the truth. "Have you talked to the doctors," I asked in a clumsy attempt to change the subject.

She understandably didn't seem to notice. "I'm waiting for him now. Howie's surgery lasted more than three hours; they had to drill two holes into his head to relieve the pressure on his –" But Mrs. Nesto's voice faded to incoherence under the crashing of another wave of emotion. She completely broke down and began hyperventilating, prompting Mr. Brooks to return from down the hall.

"I'll be right back," I managed to stammer out, feeling the emotion overwhelming me too. I thought I should go outside to find the boys. They had set up a vigil up the block; beer and weed were plentiful.

"Francis, you gotta find out who did this and we'll pay it the fuck back in a giddy-up, son," proclaimed Redbone, who, despite being a tower of rock-hard muscle, very rarely got mad... and was even scaring us. When he did get pushed far enough to become angry, little could change his course.

"We have to stop whatever this is," I replied. "It's all about nothing. It's stupid. It's senseless, and someone's going to end up getting killed. The best thing we can do is pray for Howie and send him our best energy and thoughts." We were interrupted after a few moments by a security guard, who approached us and asked for me. I returned to find Howie's and Clayton's mothers waiting.

"The doctor is coming out soon, Francis," Mrs. Nesto said. "I wanted you to be present to hear what he has say." The three of us stood there, holding hands and one another until the door swung open and a surgeon in bloodstained scrubs approached us. The wait was too much for Mrs. Nesto. She took a few hesitant steps toward the doctor. "How's my boy? Can I see him now, doctor? I want to see my baby."

When the surgeon was within reach, she clutched his hands and looked up at him imploringly. The brief moment of silence seemed to stretch on eternally. I almost knew before he said the words. "I'm very sorry, ma'am. We did all we could. The trauma to his brain was just too extensive."

Mrs. Nesto didn't seem to understand or at least acknowledge what she had just been told. Mrs. Brooks tried to steady her physically. "What do you mean you did all you could?" I demanded.

The doctor stood up straight. "He's gone. I'm so very sorry for your loss." The words landed this time and I turned to help Howie's mother as a wail unlike anything I had ever heard from a human or animal pealed through the corridor. The doctor added one more "I'm sorry" and then turned to exit back through the swinging door. I could feel the wet, pit-like sensation building in the back of my throat, and would have vomited had it not been for keeping the fainted Mrs. Nesto from slamming to the floor.

Mrs. Brooks and I managed to get her over to the bench as the boys, who had been watching through the hospital's glass entrance gathered what was happening and came running. For the next several minutes, we became a mass of bodies, just weeping and holding on to one another, each expressing his shock and grief in a different way.

Staring blindly ahead in disbelief, I suddenly was filled with the need to leave... to find my friend... *i dunno... to see for myself.* Slipping through the same swinging door as the doctor, I found myself in the restricted area of the emergency room. It didn't take long to come across the macabre scene that I'd theretofore known only from the movies. There, motionless on the operating table was the covered body of my boyhood pal... my best friend, my right-hand man... my Howie. Taking as deep a breath as my lungs would permit, I pulled back the sheet and the bluish-purple color of his head bore witness to how much my friend had suffered. I couldn't bear to focus on the great incision that had exposed his brain to the surgeon, couldn't bear to notice the twisted and displaced mask of a face that Howie now wore. Although he scarcely still seemed to be the same friend I knew, my heart recognized him and I folded over his cool frame, covering him with my heaving torso. Great gulping sobs broke up my last address to him. "How could this happen, Howie? We had too many plans. You were going to be my best man and the godfather to all my children... and I for you."

I stood back up, taking his wrist, the frantic desperation painting my words. "Come on, Howie. Wake up. It's Francis. It's me." The silence of the room thundered in the hollow of my skull. "Come on, Howard Joel Nesto! I know you can come back." My plea almost took on the tone of a small child. "Come back for me, Howie. Please, Howie. Please, God!" I was practically convulsing from the sensory overload, feeling the heat drain from his body, taking in the blood on the sheet, the pile of crimson ribbons in the corner that had been his clothes... his wallet... his sneakers.

Lost in agony, logic left the room. I began trying to lift him up, willing him to rise. My voice began to rise as the frenzy heightened. "Come on, brother. Let's just walk around for a sec." I struggled on. "Come on! You're from Hell's Fucking Kitchen. Come on! You're Irish, right? We're tough, right, Howie?" Exhausted and beaten and delirious, I slumped to the floor, returning Howie's body to its prone position. "No!" I screamed over and over, getting louder and more insane with each outburst. "No!"

A solitary nurse looked through the small square window in the door and then vanished, reappearing moments later with two burly security guards. As they approached, someone else barged past them and a familiar voice commanded, "Don't touch him. He's alright. Just give him a second."

Both guards stopped dead in their tracks as I heard the voice say softly in my ear, "Francis, it's me." Benny had returned. Guilt and gut had made him turn the cab around. "Come on, kid. You shouldn't be in here. Come with me, Francis." Helping me to my feet, I felt like he was bearing all of my weight as I heard him reassure the guards, "He'll be alright. We're leaving."

Slowly walking me out of the building, I saw Benny motion "I got him" to the boys. Mrs. Brooks nodded knowingly, still embracing Mrs. Nesto. Outside, the air was fresher, but the moment was no less stale and oppressive. A cab was waiting with the meter running. "Get it out, kid. Get it out." Knowing it was finally okay to do so, I couldn't remember if I blacked out or just blocked out the outpouring of sadness and rage, but I released everything, body and mind, and slid into the cab. As it pulled away from the curb, the wind caught five bloody, crumpled $100 bills and left them strewn along 59th Street.

I don't know if it was more a result of the day's events or the Valium and scotch, but I remembered little about the ride before we stopped in front of a Fifth Avenue awning at 69th Street that read "The Noble." The doorman opened the cab as Benny exited, turning to help me get out. "Would you let Ms. Winthrop know she has visitors?"

"Right away, Mr. Levine," he replied. Eyeing us oddly as we entered the building, the doorman had already summoned the elevator and pushed "23" before we limped inside.

As the doors slid open, there stood Karen Winthrop, a vision in delicate early evening attire and matching slippers. Judging by the hand that shot to cover her mouth, I must have been some vision too. Benny threw her a look as if to say, "I'll explain everything; let's just get him inside," and the shock on Karen's face dissipated.

Karen stepped aside as Benny and I stumbled into the most gorgeously spacious apartment I had ever seen in person. The scent of eucalyptus broke past the smell of dried blood and antiseptic that had seemed to linger in my nose forever. It was a welcomingly soothing change. "Listen, kid, down the hall and on the left is the bathroom. Why don't you go take a long, hot shower and get yourself together? We'll dig up some clothes for you. It'll give me a chance to talk to Karen here."

She smiled at me with a genuine compassion I hadn't seen in some time. "Anything you want, Francis, please help yourself. My home is yours."

"Thanks," I answered back, the first word I'd uttered since the hospital. Flipping on the light, I could barely believe my eyes: her bathroom was massive; literally bigger than my entire apartment. Stripping off yet another pair of completely blood drenched clothes for the second time that day sent my thoughts back to Howie... a devastating nightmare that not even the water from four pulsing showerheads could massage into manageability. Wiping away tears to restore some clarity to my vision, I accidentally reopened the cut under my eye and it started to drip down onto the shower floor. It was then that I noticed the pale red whorl at my feet as the dried blood was freed from my arms and face. As each scarlet drop exploded into the whirlpool, I began to cry harder as I realized that my blood was mixing with that of Howie's... and both headed down the drain together. The metaphor was hardly lost on me.

Out in the living room, Benny explained the day's events to Karen, who was almost matching Francis tear for tear. "Oh my God, Benny. That poor kid. What can I do to help him?"

Benny touched her face softly. "I knew I could depend on you. I knew I wouldn't even have to ask."

Blotting her eyes to avoid smearing her mascara, Karen sniffed. "Anything you want, Benny. You have always been a mensch with me. Always very generous, so just say the word and consider it done." They both stopped speaking momentarily when they could hear soft sobbing in the shower.

"I'd like Francis to stay here with you for a few days if that's okay. I'll have Howie get some clothes for him. That's not a problem." The furrowed brow of confusion on Karen's face made Benny realize what he had just said. His bottom lip began to tremble slightly and water welled in his eyes, prompting Benny to grab for his handkerchief. Karen moved closer on the sofa and put her arm around his shoulders.

"Don't worry, Ben. I'll call my shopper at Bergdorf's in the morning and get him some clothes."

Benny cleared his throat and then replaced the hankie a moment later. "I have to leave in a minute, my shayna maideleh. I must go to the dead boy's mother to offer my help with the funeral arrangements. And then I should stop by Francis' building to talk with his friends and implore them to keep cool heads before I return home to Cedarhurst."

"Okay. I should get him a robe." Still expecting me to be in the shower, Karen opened the door slightly and caught me standing there naked, drying myself slowly. Interestingly enough, there was no awkwardness between us whatsoever. Without so much as the beginning of an uncomfortably stumbling apology, she said, "Try this on, sweetheart; it should fit. And when you're ready, come out and make yourself at home. I'll help you relax with a nice massage later on. You look like you need it."

"I'm done, thanks," I said, slipping into the soft embrace of the terry cloth robe. Following Karen into the living room, Benny rose to meet me. I walked over to him, only just able to meet his gaze. Everything in my body hurt except for the small area on my shoulder where Benny rested his hand. It was a reassuring touch for both of us.

"Okay. So let's get this straight," Karen chimed in, entering pointedly with an attitude of renewed optimism. "I'm the captain of this ship and what I say goes." Indicating the handful of pamphlets she was carrying, she continued, "These are menus from several close restaurants. I don't know what type of food you like to eat, but they're all very good, quality and variety." I opened my mouth to say I wasn't hungry, but her hand and stare stopped me. "You have two choices: either tell me what you want or I'll order for you." She punctuated the ultimatum with a sweetly sincere smile.

Although her optimism and generosity were clearly well-meaning and kind-hearted, Benny could tell that this was all a bit much for me. "That's a good idea, Karen. Why don't you go ahead and order something for him?" Adding in an intentionally audible whisper, "He likes Italian." With a nod of understanding and playful resolve, Karen disappeared into the kitchen as Benny turned back to me. "Listen, kid. I want you to stay here for the next couple of days, alright? Karen will take care of you. She mentioned that you already had plans to ride up to the country with her in a couple of days, yes? Well I think that's a great idea. Besides, I'd like the time to find out what the word on the street is about this whole situation.

I've got to find out if you're in any danger. After all, you decked a made man today... not just his son. Although you had every right, there's got to be ramifications for this. I want to try and smooth things out.

"I'd also like the time to find out the whole story behind what happened to Howie. Unfortunately, you are going to find out what it means to sit shiva a lot earlier than either one of us planned. I'll get all the info on the funeral and everything else. Don't leave here until you hear from me, alright? I'll work all of this out and then send a car for you when the time calls for it."

I just sat there, numb, hearing but unsure if I was listening. Way down deep in the basement of my soul, I could feel the demons beginning to shake the very flimsy metal gates of their incarceration. *i hope they don't get out. i want to bolt so bad across the park and find sonny; get so high i'll never have to come back. maybe the easiest way to join howie.* I knew Benny was talking to me; I could see his mouth move. I just couldn't force my ears to take in his words. 'Though my other senses were working: my eyes, obviously... and my nose was registering Karen's perfume and Benny's cologne. The flowers, the candles, the eucalyptus all filled my nasal passages while my taste buds tinged the aroma with the rusty iron of blood and the bitter bile of sick. *but my eardrums are blocking out all but the clanging of those fucking gates.*

Somehow the smell of steeping tea and the calm coo of Karen's speech silenced the demons. Entering with a tea pot and cups on a tray, she said, "This will soothe you, Francis. Do you take sugar? I'm guessing since you're Irish you take milk."

Karen's voice trailed off as Benny stood. "I need to get going, I'm afraid. Listen, Francis, I've been thinking about it and I don't think you should tell your parents just yet. It will be too upsetting and things are still too up in the air." I'd considered the same thing and gave a slight nod of agreement. Palming ten $100 bills into my hand, Benny added, "And I want you to take this. You may need it for a few things over the next couple of days."

I remembered the money from earlier, shoving my hands into pockets of pants I was no longer wearing. "Oh, shit! The $500 for Mrs. Nesto. Shit! Shit! Shit! I don't know what I did with that."

"It's only dirty paper, kid. Don't worry about it." Leaning in, he kissed my forehead as a father does a child, freshly roused from a nightmare. Turning to Karen, he added, "Take good care of my boy, Winthrop. This is a great man we see before us."

Karen walked Benny to the door, accepting an embrace and a lingering kiss on the cheek as they parted. When she stepped into the hallway to see Benny out, the doorman approached from the elevator with a large plastic bag of take-out food. After reimbursing him, Karen slid back inside and began removing the food from its cardboard and plastic containers, replating the contents onto the beautiful china she'd set on the table. My gaze alternated between the bottom of my teacup and the remarkable views of Central Park behind the living room's tall windows, but in just a few minutes, she invited me over.

"Thank you for the tea. It was delicious."

"My pleasure, Francis. Hope you're hungry. I wasn't sure what you'd want exactly, so I got a little bit of everything: spaghetti marinara, broccoli rabe, some garlic bread and salad...and I seem to remember your affinity for the stuffed artichoke at Gino's the day we met." I forced out a meek smile of appreciation. "Would you like some wine with your meal?"

Without waiting for my reply, the demons screamed, "Yes!"

Both Karen and I were a bit surprised at the insistence in my reply. "Wine it is then," she said, disappearing into the kitchen for a bottle. Left to my thoughts, they couldn't help but turn to memories with Howie until Karen returned and poured half a glass of the reddest, most sweet-smelling elixir my nose had ever consumed. With the first forkful of pasta past my teeth, I realized just how hungry I really was and began to swallow the rest of the fare more than chew it. My Upper East Side Angel began to rub my shoulders and neck while I ate in silence, consuming glass after glass of the 20-year old cabernet until all that remained on the table were dishes.

"More wine?" she asked, heading back for the kitchen.

I couldn't answer myself, so the demons did it for me.

Slipping into the glass some of the Valium that Benny had left and Karen had crushed up for me, she returned quickly. "Here you go, Francis. Why don't you go lay down while I straighten up?" The last of the wine vanished down my gullet as I nodded groggily. Shuffling into the large master bedroom, the wine and the sedative and the day did what Danny Albanese had been incapable of accomplishing.

On the other side of Central Park, near the Hudson, Sonny Blue was tidying up the U.N. in preparation for the night's fare. Wood for the burning barrel had seemed to be in short supply as of late, so he was adding "logs" of rolled up *Village Voices* to the pyre. On an otherwise freshly tidied clearing, a bit of debris blowing in the wind caught his eye. Halting its progress with his foot and then stooping to pick it up, Sonny immediately recognized it for what it was. "Now if that's not blood money, there ain't nothin' is." Dropping the stained $100 bill into the flames dancing up from the barrel, he added, "That much blood all over the face of an ol', white, dead man....? Hmm... well you sho can't be alone, Mr. Franklin." Taking a quick glance around at the surrounding grounds, he looked back at the bill curling and changing color from reddish-brown to black, and then added, "But your friends will be with you soon there, dead man."

As planned, Benny first paid a visit to Mrs. Nesto and then to the stoop to calm the growing hotheadedness among the boys from the neighborhood. They were like an Indian war party, occupied equally with notions of revenge and worry about Francis' whereabouts. Benny also took advantage of the opportunity to pass on the word that Mrs. Nesto was going to be having Howie's viewing at Buckley's Funeral Home the following day. They seemed to be pacified by learning they'd see Francis there at 1 p.m.

His errands complete, Benny arrived at his home on Long Island just after 2 a.m. and told the driver that he may as well hang close since he'd need to return to The City a couple of hours later. Palming the driver a $50 bill, he said, "There's a good all-night diner on Rockaway Boulevard. Why don't you go get something to eat and then come back. You can park in my driveway and catch a few Zs until I'm ready to return to Manhattan around 5:30. Of course, I'll pay you triple-rate for your time."

Without missing a beat, the driver replied, "I'm not worried, mister. You're one of the best customers I've ever had. Plus," he added, in a weak attempt to make a joke, "I know where you live." Benny neglected to parrot the driver's chuckle, but rather turned and walked toward his front door.

Entering his dark and still home gave Benny little distraction to stop thinking about Francis. Sitting alone with his meditations in a great leather chair inside a massive, unlit living room, Benny eventually drifted off to sleep, content at least that Francis was asleep next to Karen Winthrop in the protection of her Fifth Avenue home. A creature of habit, Esther Levine rose at 5 a.m. sharp to find Benny slumped in that same chair. "Darling, why didn't you come to bed?" As she had done many times before, she slipped the nearly empty glass of warm scotch from her husband's grip and kissed him on the forehead.

Rubbing the sleep from his eyes, Benny replied, "Good morning, my dear. I hope I didn't worry you. I was just too exhausted to climb the stairs when I got in."

"Ah," she said, taking in the scene and pausing to process its details. "Benny, why is that car in our driveway? And why is there a man in it with the motor running?"

"Oh, don't worry, Esther. That's just my car to take me back to The City. I still have to take a shower and get dressed. Would you make some coffee, please?" He was hoping she wouldn't persist with the questions. Benny had neither the time nor the inclination to explain what was going on.

"Okay, Benny. But I simply don't understand why you have to leave again already. You just came in at two." Benny silently recognized the hurt in his wife's voice, noting that she obviously knew when he got home and could have come down then if she had wanted to do so.

This was par for the course in the Levine Household. If Esther didn't ask, her husband didn't explain, so Benny continued, changing the subject before she had a chance to pry. "I have the Macy's Flower Show this week. And you know if I'm not there to watch those meshuganas, they'll put us in the poor house." He knew she was unlikely to raise any objections at that since it hit her right in the Chanel bag. Esther raised both eyebrows and sighed in agreement, turning to reach for the coffee canister.

Benny thought it best to take advantage of the momentary silence, so he went upstairs to shower and shave, picking out a dark suit and black tie to wear to the service. Figuring he would definitely need them later, he also grabbed a dark pair of sunglasses from his bureau drawer before heading back downstairs to pour cups of coffee for himself and for his driver. Esther stopped him on the way out the door. "Benjamin, where are you going with my coffee cups?"

Benny didn't want to argue and had become well-versed in the method of distracting and dodging his better half. "Honey," he practically purred. "I'd like you to go to Fortunoff's today to get some new kitchenware. I've really gotten weary of these. Alright?" He knew that giving Esther the opportunity to spend money would erase any itching for a confrontation she might have kicking around within. Benny took a step out the door, but was stopped by a thought. Almost without turning around, he added, "And, sweetheart, one more thing: please tell Eli and Ari that I love them very much. I'd like for us all to spend some time together as a family this weekend." Esther approached her husband slowly, the look on her face betraying her confusion, but something about the sincerity in Benny's tone kept her from following up his request with a question of her own. The mister kissed his missus on the cheek and exited into the damp, early-morning air.

Gently tapping on the limousine window to wake the driver, Benny handed him the coffee. "Take your time. I'm going to have a smoke." Benny Levine hadn't had a cigarette in over five years, but he was having one that day... despite the haranguing that was sure to come from his wife if she saw him. But he was no fool. He waited just long enough for Esther to climb back in bed and reset the clock for 9 a.m.; Fortunoff's opened at 10, after all.

They listened to sports radio during the ride into Manhattan. The only thing anyone was talking about was the upcoming fight between Roberto Duran and Sugar Ray Leonard. Like the airwave pundits, the

driver opined that "Leonard'll mop the floor with Duran. He's just a Baby
Ali."

Benny let him speak his piece before responding, "Listen, kid. I
don't know much, but I do know this: Leonard is no Ali. Don't get me
wrong. He's good; I'll give him that. And he seems like a nice enough guy,
but there is and will only ever be one Muhammad Ali. No way – unless it's
fixed – does Leonard beat Duran. No, this time the bull kills the matador.
You mark my words. And if you're a betting man, you work too hard for
your money to give it away on Sugar Ray. Duran will win – and Leonard's
going to catch a beating in the process – because Duran is already in
Leonard's head. You'll see.

"Now, kid, if you don't mind, I'm going to try to catch a few more
winks while you're battling the beginning of the morning rush. Wake me
when we get to my store at 27th and Sixth." The driver nodded to his passenger and turned the radio's volume down while Benny stretched out his
legs and reclined deeply into the leather upholstery.

Ruth Nesto shuffled aimlessly about Apt. 2RN after picking out her
shoes and ironing her dress. Although she was a fiercely independent
woman who had refused all offers of company from friends, she could
think of nothing else that needed to be done, so she wandered from room
to room, looking for... what, exactly, escaped her. She stopped in the
doorway of Howie's room, almost afraid to go in. Taking a few moments
to imagine how her son interacted with everything in the room, she
examined and touched everything as though it were a relic. Sitting down
on the bed, she leaned forward to bury her head in the pillow, drinking

up her child's scent, running her hand softly over the blanket as though it were Howie's soft hair. When she was finally able to focus on her son's face in the many photos around the room, she noticed that every one of them was also inhabited by a beaming Francis Doonan. "Poor child," she muttered, her voice breaking under the weight of the words. "He must be so torn apart." She knew that 453 West 43rd Street would never again see the laughter and silliness that those two brothers had shared since they were little boys.

As much to occupy her mind as her time, Mrs. Nesto forced herself to review the details of the funeral arrangements. With Mr. Levine's assistance, she'd written a numbered list on the back of his business card. She had okayed the Buckley Funeral Home because of Howie's affinity for the Irish. Mr. Levine agreed that there was no problem with that as long as a rabbi was there to say Kaddish. She was not the most religious person, but there were certain traditions from their faith that could not be overlooked.

Still, although Judaism frowned upon it (and many post-Holocaust Jews would consider it unthinkable), Ruth had decided to cremate Howie's remains. Without her son, she had no desire to remain in Hell's Kitchen and would be leaving as soon as possible to go live with her sister in Canada. The fact that she could transfer her job with UNICEF to the branch in Montreal made the decision even easier. Cremation gave her the option of taking her son's remains with her instead of returning to the painful memories in NYC when she wanted to visit Howie.

Despite her sister's request to come for the viewing and then help with the relocation to Québec, Ruth asked that she stay put. "I have plenty of support here already," she reasoned with her sibling over the phone. "The difficult period at a time like this isn't immediately after the loss; it's weeks later when everyone else has gone about their normal lives and routines. I'll need you rested and ready when I get there, I expect. I will almost certainly be coming to your home in pieces and, without my Howie, I'll need you to be the glue to hold me together." Ruth's sister found it difficult to disagree with that logic, and knew cooperation was more in order at the moment than an argument. Ruth's new home would be waiting for her when she was ready... with the open arms of the only family she had left.

Benny woke from his nap as the driver was pulling up in front of the store. Chonley Diaz and the other workers were hanging out in front of the entrance, and greeted the boss as he emerged from the limo. "Good morning, Chonley," he replied. "You and I have a very special project this morning." As Benny recounted to Chonley the details of all that had transpired the day before, his eyes turned red and froze into a blank stare. Chonley knew Howie almost as well as he knew Francis, and couldn't imagine that light being snuffed out so needlessly.

Chonley was at a loss for words. "Whatever you need, boss," he muttered, entering the shop behind Benny. The two old men set to work immediately. It had probably been more than ten years since Benny had handled flowers himself, but by the time they finished, there in the middle of the work area sat one of the most beautiful creations those two artisans had ever crafted... a giant floral shamrock funeral piece that read:

"Howie
Our Brother
Francis, Benny and the Boys"

With more effort than I could've possibly imagined it requiring, I managed to open my eyes just the tiniest bit as the sunlight assaulted my vision and made my head throb more intensely. My nose flooded with the stirring aroma of fresh-brewed coffee while every square inch of my body groaned in discomfort as it awoke, bit by bit. Rolling over before attempting to sit up, I found myself alone in a large bed within an even larger room, neither of which I recognized in the slightest. The last digit on the alarm clock next to me flipped over to read 8:03, and although the familiar drone of 1010 WINS was coming from somewhere beyond the doorway, I still didn't know where I was. Tiptoeing as quietly as my battered frame would allow, I followed the sound of the radio and some type of machinery through four palatial rooms, each luminous from the massive streams of morning sun pouring in through the windows. Stopping just outside the doorway to a large in-home gym, my memory started to return in fits and starts when I saw my Upper East Side Angel sweating profusely astride a stationary bicycle. Getting a glimpse of her in workout clothes made me realize just what phenomenal shape she was in. I was hesitant to speak or even make my presence known since I was having some trouble remembering her name, but it didn't take long for her to catch sight of me.

"Well, good morning, Francis. I didn't expect to see you before noon. I was actually kind of hoping you could sleep in." My meek smile must've given away the fact I couldn't place her name. "I'm Karen, remember? Karen Winthrop? Benny brought you here after the fight and... the hospital," she added, choosing her words carefully.

"Yeah, I remember," I lied clumsily. "Sorry. I'm just a little confused at the moment... maybe not quite awake yet." Stepping inside the room, I caught the first glimpse of myself in the floor-to-ceiling mirrors on the wall. As it became clearer just how much of a beating I'd sustained, the details of the fight came gushing back. Since my brain was straining to adjust, it took a few moments to realize that I was also standing in front of this relative stranger wearing only underwear that wasn't very successfully hiding my morning hardon.

Karen must've seen me blush and then make an awkward attempt at being distracted by something behind me because she dismounted the exercise bike and said, "Let me get your robe. Why don't you have a seat? I'll be right back."

Jumping at the chance to obscure my erection with my lap, I sat down on a weight bench a little too quickly and felt a bit of a head rush come on. As the stars assembled before my eyes momentarily, I ran fingers through my thick red hair. Maybe the head rush served to open the floodgates of my memory since the nightmare that was the previous day poured in like a deluge... one quickly matched by my tears.

Trying in vain to pull myself together when I heard Karen approaching, I was granted a momentary reprieve when the phone rang as she was steps from the doorway. I could make out most of the conversation by hearing only her end: "Hello, Benny. ...Yes, he slept like a baby. ...Well, I was going to make him some breakfast. ...Ah, okay. Well, hang on a second. Francis," she called out to me. "Francis? Benny's on the phone. He'd like to speak to you."

Rising more slowly than I'd sat down, it took me several seconds to reach her. "Thanks." She gave me the phone. "Hey, Benny."

"Good morning, Francis. You feeling okay, kid?" I paused. I didn't know quite what to say. "Well, as good as can be expected anyway?"

"Mm hmm," I managed.

"Good, good," came his reply. "Listen. I saw both Mrs. Nesto and the boys from the stoop yesterday. Everything is taken care of. I don't want you to worry about anything, okay? Now this is going to be one of the longest and most difficult days of your life, but I'll be there with you. We'll get you through it. Just continue to relax and make sure you eat. You might even try Karen's whirlpool. That should make you feel better... at least on the outside. I'll see you soon though, kid. Keep your chin up."

"'Kay, Benny. Thanks," was about all I could get out before handing the phone back to Karen and then shuffling off toward the living room.

She spoke for a few minutes more and then hung up, following me into the living room with a cup of coffee and a plated piece of crumb cake. "This should tide you over until I can whip up some breakfast. Is scrambled okay?" I nodded and she leaned in to kiss me softly on the cheek. "Be strong, sweetheart... because you are, you know." *whatever i did to deserve this angel and her kindnesses, i should've done more of it!* "While you're eating, I'm going to hop in the shower, and then we'll stop by Bergdorf's to pick up a few things we got for you. Any color in particular that you fancy?"

"Yeah," I replied, crumbs falling from my mouth. "Howie always talks about this one particular green. It's like London green or something? He says I look good in it." Realizing I couldn't use the present tense with Howie any longer, I got choked up and went silent.

Not surprisingly, Karen stepped in to cover. "Loden green, I think you mean. And Howie's right. You'll look great in it."

Matty O'Toole was well known by almost everyone in The Kitchen as the extremely talented undertaker at Buckley's Funeral Home. But to a certain smaller group, he was also known as a talented part-time booster. Howie Nesto had been a member of that certain small group... mostly because he had been an equally talented "professional peer." So, out of respect (and because Matty had known well what Howie looked like before his maiming), O'Toole had gone through the better part of

eight hours and a full bottle of Bushmill's Irish Whiskey while working ceaselessly to erase the damage done... or at least hide it enough for
Howie's mother and friends to look on him one last time. Dressed in a
freshly lifted suit, Matty was proud of the magic he'd been able to work on
Howie... especially considering what he'd looked like eight hours earlier.
That had been a task that came with a great deal of pressure since Howie
would be lying in Buckley's main room with the expectation that most of
the neighborhood would visit to pay respects. And as his special trib-
ute to a "fallen comrade," Matty had called his cousin, Desmond, of the
FDNY Emerald Society Band to bring three bagpipers, a tribute reserved
in ancient days for Irish royalty long before a pipe had ever sounded in
Scotland... and surely there had never been as princely an Irishman in
Hell's Kitchen as the Italian Jew named Howard Nesto.

Benny tucked a pair of $100 bills into Chonley's breast pocket with
instructions to drop the floral shamrock wreath off at Buckley's and then
to go home and change for the viewing. But although he knew the wreath
would be delivered, there was little guarantee that Chonley would show
up at the funeral home. After all, $200 and four hours to kill was quite a
lot of temptation for a man who had as many demons raging inside him
as Chonley Diaz did. When he was finally by himself in the flower shop,
Benny called Karen's apartment to check on Francis. "You'll be happy,
Ben," she reported. "We got him a gorgeous suit, shirt and tie, complete
with Italian leather shoes, of course. I even convinced the tailor to come
home with me for a few minutes so he could make everything just right."

"You could probably talk anyone into doing anything, my dear." The affection and gratitude in Benny's voice were clear. "I'll be sure to reimburse you when I arrive."

"Benjamin Aron Levine," she retorted without the slightest hint of sarcasm. "Don't insult me. I want to do this. That boy deserves a break for once in his life. If you watch him for awhile, you can see how sweet and sensitive he is underneath. I honestly don't know how he's managed to survive in that neighborhood for as long as he has."

"This kid's a fighter, Karen. If nothing else, that can't be denied."

"Oh, Benny," Karen interrupted. "That's the door. My stylist is making a house call to give Francis a trim just to clean him up a little."

"Okay, then. I'll see you soon. And Winthrop? You're one great fucking dame." Benny could hear Karen's smile through the phone before he replaced the handset and headed immediately for the car.

"Where to, Mr. Levine?" the driver asked.

"Ultimately 69th Street and Fifth Ave., but I need to stop by the Dante Social Club first. Head up to 39th, and then cut over to between Eighth and Ninth. You'll recognize it by the smattering of gorillas out front." Sure enough, from almost half a block away, the driver could see a handful of large, olive-skinned men in ridiculously ill-fitting Adidas sweat suits milling about on the sidewalk.

The car pulled over right next to them and Benny let himself out, striding past the menagerie without so much as a glance thrown their way, let alone a word. As he was about to step through the front door, the largest of the simians put his large, meaty paw up in Benny's path and grunted, "Whoa. And just where do you think you're going?"

Benny replied matter-of-factly, "I'm here to see Johnny." All eyes and ears were on the door. None of the Albanese thugs had ever heard the boss referred to as anything other than "J.R." or "Mr. Albanese."

"Ain't no 'Johnny' here, old man."

Without so much as adjusting his gaze, Benny pointed behind him at the cherry red Chevy Delta 88 parked by the curb. "Like hell there ain't," he started, brushing past the doorman. The goon made an attempt at grabbing Benny by the lapel, but he slipped aside much more deftly than anyone else would've expected, rewarding the effort with a swift slap in the face. Grabbing him roughly by the back of the neck and pulling him to Benny's ear level, the old man growled, "Listen, you cocksucker. I used to eat grease ball fucks like you for lunch. And although I'm trying for a healthier fare in my old age, I still get the appetite every now and again. Capisce?" He dug his perfectly manicured nails into the scruff of his neck for extra emphasis. "Now get Johnny for me."

Before the thug could give any thought to whether or not he could preserve his reputation in front of his cronies, the door opened and the rather intimidating bulk of J.R. Albanese filled the door frame. "What's all the racket out here? Ah. It's only the Jew."

"Good morning, Mr. Albanese." Benny's tone was cool, but respectfully conciliatory.

J.R. took a moment to assess the situation and then obviously decided to play nice. "Joey, step aside for Mr. Levine, will ya? Where's your manners?" The gorilla instantly regressed to a chimpanzee, moving away from the door as Benny nodded, smiled and entered the dark interior of the Dante Social Club. It was at least ten degrees cooler inside, and as Benny's eyes adjusted to the low light, he took in the décor that seemed pretty much standard for one of these places. An off-balance pool table sat in the middle of the large main room with an outdated jukebox and a handful of one-armed bandits along the walls. Assorted furniture was scattered about, overseen by the yellowed images of pin-up girls so old that they'd have to be in their 70s by now. A wiry troll of a man stood near the bar, producing way too much steam from what was clearly already an overworked espresso machine. The steam partially obscured the back shelf of the makeshift bar, which was overstocked with dozens of bottles of liquor. Almost the entire back wall seemed to be constructed from what had to be thousands of cartons of Marlboro cigarettes... all stolen, of course. The one section that stood out from the others was the immaculate table in the corner, made from some rich, dark wood and covered with a silk tablecloth. Two very comfortable-looking chairs stood on either side of it, lit by a Tiffany lamp overhead that still sported the price tag.

J.R. silently led Benny to that table and motioned for him to have a seat. "Carmine, two Chivas on the rocks." A young kid from the neighborhood, barely dropout age, who'd been sitting discreetly near the troll, sprang to his feet and headed for the liquor. "You still drink Chivas, right, Benny?" The semi-impressed smirk on Benny's face served as his reply as Albanese continued, "And bring over some cigarettes with an ashtray."

It was a ridiculous request since the wall next to them was completely made of Marlboro boxes; Benny was done being even slightly impressed. Despite whatever attempts at civility, the bully would always be the bully. J.R. was apparently an overachiever in this respect, adding, "And then go take my car to get it detailed... and no fucking lollygagging or I'll fucking strangle you." The boy brought over the drinks and cigarettes, and after scooping up Albanese's keys from the table, beat a hasty retreat into the sunlight.

"Salud," said J.R., raising his glass.

Benny would've preferred not to have to share a drink – much less a toast – with J.R., but on that day, he decided to let it pass. "La chaim," he answered back civilly, clinking glasses... although the sick, dangerous wheeze of a laugh that came from behind J.R.'s puffy lips did little to make observers think that this was a shared friendly sentiment. The two men sat silently for a moment, staring at one another. Benny noted peripherally that J.R.'s bottom lip was still quite swollen and his face sported a brown and violet bruise. Most entertaining was that the elder Albanese's wig had apparently never been "dredged up," so he had resorted to exposing his pate to the outside world. Benny just couldn't shake the mental comparison to a retarded Benito Mussolini.

J.R. sucked the scotch through his teeth noisily while Benny swallowed his glassful and then cleared his throat to speak. "Okay. So I'm sure you already know why I'm here."

Albanese pounced as though he'd been playing a high-stakes game of Chicken. "Of course I do, and the answer is 'Fuck you, fuck him, and fuck everyone in his drunken fucking mick family!'" He was practically out of breath from holding in that outburst for so long.

Benny could see that this was going to be more difficult than he thought, so he stood slowly, pushing the chair back with his calves. J.R. tensed up, questioning whether their confrontation was about to involve gunfire unexpectedly. More than one hand in the room disappeared into the inside of a jacket or the rear of a waistband. Benny acted as though he hadn't noticed, walking over to the bar and grabbing the bottle of Chivas Regal. Returning to the table as slowly as he'd left, he said, "I hope you don't mind, Johnny."

"I could give a fuck," Albanese snapped back, incensed at how Benny referred to him. "I got a whole truckload of this overpriced piss in the back."

Pouring himself another glass and then taking a long, languid sip to let J.R. calm down a bit, Benny continued. "Listen. We have to find a way to stop this thing before it spirals even further out of control. There's already a kid dead—"

"I ain't stupid!" J.R. interrupted, practically coming right out of his chair.

"Your kid's hurt. My kid's hurt. Hell, even you're hurt—"

"There it is!" J.R. interjected again, laughing soullessly. "You were just waiting for your angle to rub it the fuck in! Well you know what that means? It means that Jew boy won't be the only dead Heeb around here. You hear me?" Driving the point home by banging his fist into the table, sending his glass of liquor flying, he shouted, "Morto!"

Benny leapt to his feet, unsure if he wanted more to respond physically to the threat or remove himself from the presence of that ignorant Guinea. The couple of seconds that ticked by seemed to drag on forever. Even though no one had frisked him, Benny knew that there was no chance of popping Albanese and then escaping intact. More likely, he'd make the trip to Jersey's Great Swamp atop a Delta 88 spare in J.R.'s trunk. But leaving without some resolution defeated the purpose of going there in the first place. Benny took a deep breath, but his voice still betrayed the anger inside. "You know, Johnny—" Albanese grunted again. "I call you 'Johnny,' not out of disrespect, but to remind you of a time when that's how you were known to me. That was a long time ago, Johnny. We are grown fucking men now who have known each other for a long fucking time... through good times and, unfortunately, bad times. Right? Well, this is one of the bad times. Because no matter who likes who... no matter who is on whose side... violence unchecked leads to revenge... and that leads to <u>more</u> violence. And dead kids on both sides leave screaming parents... and politicians with axes to grind... and cops with hardons. And <u>that's</u> bad for business. And it doesn't matter – me or you, Irish or Italian, Jew or gentile – you narrow-minded, bigoted dago, when business suffers, we all suffer. Can you get <u>that</u> through your thick greaseball skull?"

No one in the room had failed to see how unglued the normally reserved older businessman had become... and how much sense his argument had made. J.R. almost seemed amused. "Alright, alright. You've made your point. Holy Christ. Sit down before you have a fucking stroke." Turning to his flunkies, he added, "Sheez! Who'd've thunk Hymie still had it in him?"

He shot Benny a quick look to see if he'd taken offense at the slur, but Benny had been goaded by better... and far smarter. He sat back down, tucking his silk tie inside his suit coat. Albanese poured two more glasses of Chivas and handed one to his old rival. Without taking his eyes off of his host, Benny continued, "Look, J.R., I'm here to vouch for this kid, Francis Doonan, too. He's a good kid, and he wanted no part of this. Let's be totally honest. Your son and his mini-crew started this ball rolling."

"Gimme a fucking break. You don't know what you're talking about, Levine. But I don't give a fuck about any of that. As you say, business is business... but how in the hell am I supposed to save face here?"

"What are you, Chinese all of a sudden?" Benny retorted. That was enough to break the ice as they both laughed. He knew he had Albanese. Reaching across the table to shake his old nemesis' hand, Benny continued, "Look, no one can deny that we've got history... and it wasn't all that long ago that we even used to be pretty good pals. But we've both got businesses to run and neither of us needs any childish distractions. True?"

"True," J.R. sighed. "Let me talk to Danny and square this whole thing. Maybe you'll bring this Doonan kid by here next week? We'll have a sit down and smooth things out."

"Sure," Benny replied, knowing full well that the event would never take place. But he also knew that if J.R. gave him his word, that would be good enough. Albanese may have lacked class, but he still knew the value of honor. They shook hands and kissed each other on the cheek. "Oh, yeah, and one more thing: this guy, this 'Duke,' tell him that what he did was not a nice thing." Benny could see in J.R.'s eyes that he hadn't completely backed the Brit's actions, but he'd never admit it. "You don't have to comment, but that kid he beat down was a good boy. It ain't right... and it almost put us all on the brink."

"I hear ya," was all J.R. managed to say until Benny rose to leave, when he added, "That Doonan... he's one tough cocksucker. What a pair of balls on that kid! I could use a kid like him on my team." Benny just nodded and exited the Dante Social Club.

As Benny's limo slid away from the curb, a cab pulled into the spot and let its fares out: the Duke and a stitched-up Danny Albanese, supporting his weight with a cane. As quickly as he could, Danny entered the club and went right to his father's side. "What the fuck did that Jewish piece of shit want?" he demanded.

Instantly, J.R. slapped his son squarely in the face. "Danny, it's about time I taught you some manners." Fearing that the elder Albanese's gaze would shift to him, the Duke turned his eyes to the linoleum tile and shrunk to the shadowy corner on the far side of the bar.

Karen and I had been getting to know one another in a strangely effective fashion. Our conversations were brief and infrequent since I didn't feel like talking a whole lot, and when I did, it was just in little spurts. But Karen was very respectful of that and could gather a great deal by being an amazing listener. *she must've had a lot of psychoanalysis; she's too calm to be a new yorker.* Karen had ordered a delectable feast for lunch – which had pretty much become par for the course in that castle in the sky – and I was making an attempt to help her clear the dishes and everything from the table despite her protests.

I'd been incredibly moved by the music that had been playing during lunch, and actually had to fight back another breakdown more than once when the swells of the music threatened to make my heart jump its banks. "I really like the music... what you've been playing, I mean. What is it?"

"That's Mozart. His 'Requiem,' actually. I became very interested in his music when I saw a play on Broadway a few years ago called 'Amadeus.' This particular piece was believed to have been written for his funeral."

"Very fitting for today...." my voice trailed off. She could see my eyes start to glisten. "So haunting."

Karen could see that she had inadvertently touched a nerve with her choice of music so she tried to change the subject without being too obvious about it. "It's actually a myth, though. It was a commission. In the play, you're led to believe that the man who commissioned the piece was actually Mozart's bitter rival, but that's a myth as well. It was commissioned by a wealthy businessman for his wife. He had intended to claim it as his own work, but even Mozart himself didn't write the whole thing, ironically. His wife had to hire someone else to complete the work secretly so she could get her husband's payment for it." She could tell by the look on my face that I was at least interested in what she'd said. Whatever the case, it'd momentarily gotten my mind off of the coming afternoon's events.

The phone rang. Karen went to answer it and then walked to the front door, calling out, "Benny's here."

A few moments later, in strode Benny, planting a soft peck on Karen's cheek. I stood up as he headed my way with a big smile and an embrace. "Let me get a look at you. Wow. Straight out of GQ, my boy. How you feeling?" I shrugged. He continued, "Understandable. Well, listen, I took care of your problem with the Albaneses. It's over... and you can take that to the bank, so put it out of your mind."

Benny didn't make those kind of statements lightly. I breathed a sigh of relief. "Thanks, Benny. Thanks a lot." *how many millions of times in my life will i say that to this man?*

"I'm afraid I'm not going to be joining you gentlemen today," Karen chimed in. "But, Francis, I expect to see you back here tonight. Don't make me come looking for you," she added with a smile. All the same, I knew she would make good on the threat. *the food is great, the digs are unbelievable and the company is first rate; it's just the day that's a motherfucker.*

We all exchanged pleasant goodbyes before Benny and I headed down to Fifth Avenue and into his car. A short while later, we were westbound on 43rd Street, but I was a little surprised when we drove right past Buckley's. Benny had a reason for it, though, as we took a right at the light and stopped halfway up the block. The stoop in front of the 602nd building on Tenth Avenue was standing room only. Most of the young people from the neighborhood were there for the departing of one of their own, all dressed respectably. The driver jumped out of the limo and stepped back to open my door before Benny's, a first for me. All of the familiar faces from The Kitchen were there, genuinely glad to see me. Benny stepped alongside me and pressed a pair of dark sunglasses into my hand. *limo, dark glasses? it's like i'm a movie star... unfortunately today's feature would be a tear jerker.*

The whole crew came up to meet me with a somber handshake or a gentle word: Vit, Cal, Redbone, Brian, Patty Boy, Clayton... even Min was there, and everyone was dressed in their Sunday best. It was a nice enough day with plenty of sun, but there was a threat of rain. Still, not even that would keep the neighborhood from turning out to pay its respects. We all began the short walk down the avenue and over towards Buckley's when I saw Mrs. Nesto and several of her friends from work approaching from the other direction. My mind scrambled to come up with something... anything to say to her, but the words just wouldn't come. Little did I know that she was having the same dilemma. I stood and waited for her to cross 43rd

Street, our eyes locked the whole way. When she was a few feet from me, she rushed into my arms, embracing me silently. The mother of my best friend took me by the hand... exactly as she would have done with her own son... leading me the rest of the way to the funeral home and then inside. Benny and everyone else followed us quietly.

Matty O'Toole took responsibility for leading Howie's mother and me to the back room for our first opportunity to see his body. The room was large and flowers adorned every possible inch not already occupied by a chair. Up front and near the head of the casket stood the largest floral shamrock I'd ever seen. I could read its sentiment from the back of the room and was able to produce a genuine smile through the Niagara Falls of tears that overtook me. Mrs. Nesto and I inched reluctantly closer to the casket while Matty tried to maintain his composure and make the moment easier by talking calmly to Howie's mom. "I did the very best that I could, ma'am. He was my buddy, after all. I hope you'll be pleased." *he's trying to hold it together too. you would think in his business he'd be used to these things, maybe even callous. i guess this one hit too close to home.*

Finally the moment couldn't be postponed any longer. Taking a deep, shuddering breath, Mrs. Nesto approached the casket fully and stood up on the kneeler to lean in over her boy. The room was so silent that even the white noise seemed to vanish. She suddenly cried out, "My sweet Howie. What have they done to you? Oh my God!" Benny and I grabbed on to either arm as she flung herself forward across her child's chest. The room could take no more. Every person present lost it with varying degrees of volume. It was doubtlessly one of the saddest scenes anyone there could ever remember witnessing... myself especially. *but i have to be strong for mrs. nesto; be the man in her life today.* Benny, too, was thinking about his own sons, and didn't know if he would've handled himself even as well as Howie's mom.

With help from Benny and me, Mrs. Nesto sat in the front row of chairs, her face buried in a handkerchief. Most eyes in the room were occupied with sorrow, but I clearly saw Kelly the Mick and Colin Garvan come straight down the middle aisle with a large funerary wreath that read "Hell's Kitchen Boy." *what phonies. at best, they barely gave howie the time of day; at worst, they were never at a loss for some bullshit anti-semitic remark.* But I softened for a minute. *well, at least they're here.* Not wanting to leave Mrs. Nesto's side just yet, I waited until I made eye contact with both men and gave a nod of appreciation to each. Kelly the Mick nodded back and Colin Garvan touched his heart to offer his condolences before the two headed to find a chair near the back of the room. *they are actually human for one moment.*

As my gaze shifted back to the casket and the line of mourners that was forming to pay respects to Howie's mom, I caught sight of Chonley Diaz approaching, tears streaming down his face. I was surprised that he'd showed up, and even more impressed at how moved he was by the event. I'd never seen that side of him before. He came to me while someone else was speaking to Mrs. Nesto, bent down, and kissed me on both cheeks. Too overwhelmed to speak coherently, Chonley just gripped my wrist tightly until Benny stood up by my side and offered his hand. "Good for you, old man. Good for you."

Stepping to the side, Chonley was able to reply, "It's just... you know... when it happens to the kids. And the parents. I mean, what's she to do? It's just...."

"I know, my friend," Benny answered. Hugging each other, the two old men wept silently.

Discreetly observing the exchange between these two men I respected so deeply, I took in an even more affecting sight out of the corner of my eye: practically the entire neighborhood had lined up to pay respects to Mrs. Nesto, one by one. About three-quarters of the way down the aisle, I even caught a glimpse of my own parents. *of course; uncle patsy must've called them. he's apparently not the only one; the line is filled with faces i haven't seen in awhile. jesus. the o'connors moved from the neighborhood at least five years ago.* It didn't take long for my mother and father to reach Mrs. Nesto and exchange those silent sentiments that can only pass between the parents of best friends.

When my mother released Howie's mom, I saw the briefest flash of both relief and guilt in her weathered Irish face... both relief and guilt that I wasn't the one in the casket. She clutched me in a way that made me wonder if she intended to release me. My father joined us a moment later and I was finally able to let go and cry in my mother's arms in a way I hadn't since my days at Holy Cross. *god, this feels good.* My father finally took the first step toward helping us regaining our composure. "The girls all wish they could've come, but they're busy with after-school activities and that sort of thing right now. They send you their condolences, of course."

"Yes, they wanted very much to be here, Francis." I smiled and she put her hand softly on my cheek in that mother's way of both consoling and assessing the condition of her child. "Poor Ruth. I'm going to go see if there's anything I can do."

A woman on a mission, that little Irish lady from County Leitrim marched right over to her friend's side to offer an ear and a shoulder as my father remarked, "Well, there's Pats." My uncle had arrived. Daddy and I both made the same observation simultaneously: Uncle Patsy was three sheets to the wind. "He's crazy," my father said, answering a question that hadn't been spoken aloud yet, "but he'll keep it together. He knows where he is and what his place should be."

The boys from the stoop were scattered all around the room, and I made a point to stop and take a moment with each one before returning to the side of Howie's mom. Benny busied himself by walking around to look at all of the flowers, and I saw him stop by a small arrangement of red roses.

The card read "From the Albanese Family." He wasn't sure what to make of it, so rather than creating any type of a stir, he just continued on his rounds. Mrs. Nesto saw him as well and made the comment that although the arrangements were all so lovely, she wished she'd have thought about asking people to donate to UNICEF in place of sending flowers. *she'll be surprised to know that the hat's been passed in the neighborhood already and she'll receive a large sum of money to do with whatever she likes... an old new york tradition to take care of your own despite all the rivalries, jealousies, egos and ethnicities.*

Father Joseph Healy entered the room and, bypassing the line, headed straight for Mrs. Nesto. Within feet of her, he seemed to have a change of heart and came in my direction instead. "Francis, may I have a moment of your time, son?" We stepped to the side. "I'm sorry to bother you with this, but I was wondering if you could tell me whether or not you think Mrs. Nesto would be offended if I said a few words and prayers for her son. I know they're a Jewish family, I mean."

"Absolutely not, Father," I replied. "I think it would mean a great deal to her if you would. She's got Howie's rabbi coming as well. Perhaps you could do something together." Fr. Healy raised his chin slightly in understanding, muttered a "Thanks," and then headed back towards Mrs. Nesto. Again, he changed directions; seeming to think my own mother would be easier to approach.

Benny had slipped outside with Uncle Patsy to have a smoke. *when you quit quitting, you might as well do it big! that'll mean a call to benny's therapist for sure.* "I've closed the Blarney Stone today," Uncle Patsy said. "After 4 p.m., we'll have food and spirits."

"Very nice. It'll be a big comfort station on Eighth Avenue," Benny mused. "Can I contribute to help with the cost?"

Patsy looked genuinely touched. "Thanks ever so much, Mr. Levine. You're indeed a gentleman, but I'll be taking care of it myself. I loved that knuckleheaded boy... and I'm doing it for my poor nephew too." Nothing more needed to be said. The sentiment hung in the air like the lingering smoke from their [Marlboros].

"Rabbi Singer," Benny said to the stocky, bearded man approaching Buckley's.

"Ah, good day, Mr. Levine. How is Esther? And the Rebbe?"

"Well, Rabbi. They're well. Thank you for asking."

"I'm sorry I can't chat, Benjamin, but I'm running a bit behind." Stepping headlong through the door, the rabbi and I practically ran into one another.

"Doonan!" Without even allowing me to get out a greeting to Benny or my uncle, Clayton stepped right in my path. The only time he ever called me by my last name was when he wanted to talk pills... which was often. After all, Clayton was what we called a drugstore cowboy; he worked as a stock clerk over at Leventhal's Pharmacy. "Today's score is Rorer 714 Quaaludes. Who's better than me? I sell a ton of these over at Studio. They're a hot number... great for fucking." Realizing where he'd just said what he'd just said, he added, "Oh, I'm sorry. Shit! My mouth. Sorry, Howie. Fuck! I mean... frig." He and I both broke an unexpected smile at the absurdity of his unintelligible rant. Dropping five of the pills into my hand, he said, "Here. Have a couple of these, but only take them one at a time, brother; they're potent! Oh, shit, and don't let Old Man Leventhal see you." Less than ten feet from us stood Louie Leventhal, Clayton's boss, still in his white pharmacy coat. He had snuck away from the store to pay his respects. Pocketing the large pills, I was sorely tempted to pop one, but I'd vowed to stay straight for the afternoon. Still, the demons were running loose in my body, and the best I could do to keep them at bay was to hold them down until Howie left for the crematorium. *all bets are off then.*

The sound of raised voices grabbed my attention so I stepped back inside to see about the commotion. Kelly the Mick was in the back, gripping a bouquet of red roses and talking animatedly with a handful of guys from the neighborhood. I asked a couple of times what was going on, but grew impatient with being talked over by Kelly. Since I could tell the issue had to do with the flower arrangement, I snatched the card from the Albaneses, turned to Redbone and barked, "Get that the fuck out of here! The Albaneses got some balls!"

Ripping the flowers from Kelly the Mick and then depositing them in Red's hands, Kelly the Mick didn't even seem to mind the bleeding cut the thorns had left behind. "That's my boy, Doonan," he said, clapping me on the back.

If he was looking for some type of reaction from me, I wasn't going to satisfy him. Looking up with icy cold eyes, so that no one would mistake my meaning, I said slowly and somberly, "I'm telling you all now if the Albaneses have the balls to show up, everyone is just going to leave it alone. Mrs. Nesto gets our full respect, and that's it. As far as I'm concerned, it's over."

Kelly the Mick sucked his teeth, but then put both hands up as if to say, "I won't be involved." I could tell, though, that the look in his eyes was really saying, "What a pussy." *i couldn't give a shit less.*

I pushed past Kelly the Mick to reenter the main room, and headed back to Mrs. Nesto's side. My mother could tell by the look on my face that something had transpired in the rear of the room and shot me a quizzical look. Trying to diffuse the situation further, I made an attempt to adjust my demeanor... but that was short lived once I saw Sandra and her family step into the room. Our eyes locked immediately and neither of us seemed to blink as she made a beeline right for me. I was a mixture of emotions as she approached. Bittersweet relief washed over me as she flung her arms around my neck and began nuzzling my chest. It was the only thing I'd wanted for so long, but I almost resented it coming now... at such an inappropriate moment. I snapped back from that thought when she whispered, "I'm so, so sorry, Francis. I would like to spend some time with you. Soon, okay? I'd like to talk; there is so much I want to say to you."

Again, the mixed feelings coursed through me. I was overcome by a heady, uncomfortable curiosity at what she wanted to say. At the same time, I was nervous because her father was standing only feet away and was completely aware of the exchange. But it either seemed like there was nothing he could do... or nothing he <u>wanted</u> to do as he put his hand on my shoulder and said, "Our condolences, Francis. If it's any consolation, I give you my word that the NYPD is working hard to find your friend's killer."

"Thanks, Detective," I stammered. Hearing Howie's mom call my name, I excused myself and the O'Casey Family walked back to take a seat.

"Francis, sweetheart," she said, "I'm sorry to take you away from your friends, but I'd like to ask you a favor. Would you mind saying a few words alongside Fr. Healy and Rabbi Singer? We all agree that it's best to keep the comments extremely brief. But I know it would've tickled Howie... and I'm certain it will help us all." Tears welled up in my eyes and a great stone in my throat kept me from responding so I just nodded. "Good," she replied, grabbing my hand and giving it a little squeeze.

Fr. Healy had already made his way to the front of the room before asking if we could all please sit down. Everyone took their seats and silence fell upon the room instantly. "I'm not going to stand here and say that our brother, Howie, is in a better place because I know it and you know it... and it's not really what you want to hear. In situations like this, it's difficult to deal with the anger at having our loved one taken from us so senselessly. But we are all God's children and all a part of His plan. So I am going to ask you all to pray for the soul of our dearly departed Howie in your own way... and also to pray for his murderer." An upset buzz began to sound from the mourners so the priest finished his thought quickly, "Because he is in a Hell on Earth this day, and while Howie's trials and tribulations have ended, they are only beginning for his killer." The buzz died down markedly. "Thank you, Mrs. Nesto. Rabbi Singer?" With that, Fr. Healy stepped to the side, near Howie's casket, and began to pray silently.

Rabbi Singer stood and approached the podium, stopping just a pace away. Turning to look straight at me, he smiled gently and said, "Francis, I think you should say something now. God is here and speaking to each of us in our own fashion. But just as much, we need to hear from those who knew and loved him best."

I'd almost been on the verge of retching ever since Howie's mom asked me to speak, but being put on the spot like that made it suddenly ten times worse. I instantly looked for Benny in the crowd, pulling courage from his gaze and simple smile. Walking to the front of the room, I wasn't sure if I would pass out or forget how to speak English or what, so I steadied myself with both hands on the podium and took a deep breath. "To be honest, I'm not the best public speaker and although I know what I feel right now, I'm not so sure I know how to say it. I hope I don't embarrass Mrs. Nesto and myself, but here goes."

My voice cracked, my mouth went dry and my speech plodded along just a little bit at a time, but every eye and ear was riveted on me. That made it even more nerve-wracking. "Well... you all know me and you all know how I felt about Howie. Nothing I could say now can change that or make anyone understand it clearer than just knowing it from knowing us. But I want you all to remember this: a man is only dead when he is forgotten, when nobody talks about him anymore. So don't ever forget Howie. He'll live on forever in our hearts and our minds and our stories. He deserves nothing less. God bless you, Mrs. Nesto." I took one last look into the faces of the people gathered there and saw and heard the outpouring of emotion over the loss of one of The Kitchen's faithful. "Thank you," I said, passing Rabbi Singer on the way back to my seat.

"I know from looking at the room," began the rabbi, "that there aren't a lot of other people of the Jewish faith here with us today, but we all pray to the same God... and we all loved Howie. And there are many hearts here today, Mrs. Nesto. That will help yours to beat stronger. Draw from them your consolation for the past, your comfort for the present and your hope for the future. At this point in the service, it is traditional among Jewish families to say Kaddish. Many commonly refer to this as the 'Prayer for the Dead,' but it is actually the 'Mourner's Prayer.' Kaddish does not mention death at all, in fact, but instead praises God Almighty... an important distinction that unites us. For those among you who know the words, I invite you to recite it with me. For those who don't, I hope you will listen and appreciate the poetry of our prayer. If you will bow your heads...."

goodbye, howie.

Mrs. Nesto and I had a quiet moment after the service, during which she told me that she wouldn't be going to The Blarney Stone with everyone else. In fact, I was a bit shocked to learn that she'd be leaving for Montreal in the morning, and would like to give me some of Howie's ashes when she returned. Of course, I told her that I would be honored and assured her that if there was anything she needed, all she had to do was ask.

Sitting at the end of the Blarney Stone's bar, packed in with what seemed like the whole neighborhood, I had to be the only sober person there. *i can hardly believe it myself. everyone else is putting it away like they're going to the chair.* Lost in thought, I reached into my pocket, fingering the Quaaludes that I'd gotten from Clayton earlier, but decided that that's where they should remain. Benny interrupted my "daymare" with a couple of steaming plates of corned beef, potatoes and cabbage. "I don't know, Francis. This is my second go-round, and I'm pretty sure that your Uncle Patsy and Leo Steiner over at The Carnegie are neck-and-neck in the corned beef race! I haven't seen you eat a thing since you got here. I haven't seen you drink anything, come to think of it. You've just sat over here by yourself and played pocket pool. What's the story?"

"Nothing, Benny," came my reply. "I'm just not hungry, I guess."

"Or thirsty."

"Or thirsty," I added. "Just a lot on my mind."

"I understand, kid. I'm just breaking your balls a little. Listen, I have to get going here in a minute and thought I'd offer you a ride up to Karen's place. I'm heading past there anyway." I nodded. "Well, let me tell your Uncle Patsy thanks. Why don't you say your goodbyes too."

"Nah," I replied. "I'm just gonna head out quietly. If I try to say goodbye to everyone, it'd take me an hour to get going... and, besides, I'm not in the mood for making a bunch of explanations."

"Suit yourself," said Benny, stepping onto the sidewalk and motioning for his car.

After Benny and I climbed into the back seat and the driver was given our first destination, I put my head back and took a couple of deep breaths. "You're burnt out, kid. This trip to the Upstate with Karen is going to be just what the doctor ordered for you. You just need some time to clear your head and recharge your batteries."

I remembered responding with an "Mmm hmm," but then I must've nodded off, because the next thing I knew, Benny was tapping me to tell me we'd arrived at The Noble. The driver opened my door, but before I exited, I was sure to look Benny squarely in the eye. "Thanks for everything, Benny. Seriously. For everything. You've been a real... I dunno. I couldn't have made it without you."

Benny flashed his patented grin. "Don't mention it, kid. Be in touch, okay?" I closed the door and watched as the car blended in with Downtown traffic. Benny turned briefly and gave me a quick wave. I returned it with one of my own and then headed toward the entrance to the building.

"Good evening, Mr. Doonan." The greeting from the doorman half-startled me. "Mrs. Winthrop told me to inform you that she will be home shortly. But she left you her keys and said that you should make yourself at home."

Dropping the keys into my hand as he pushed the elevator call button, I managed a quiet "Thank you" before the doors to the elevator closed and lifted me away from the lobby. After some fumbling with the keys in the lock, I reentered my little Castle in the Sky to see that Karen had left all of the lights on for me. In the middle of the coffee table was a note:

My dear Francis,

By now, you know where everything is. Will be back soon. If you're tired, feel free to get some sleep. Will catch up when I see you next.

Karen XO

I sat down on the sofa for a moment to gather my thoughts. I was really touched by how nice Karen was and how genuinely unconditional her generosity felt. But, at the same time, I was troubled; I barely knew her. *maybe i should just go home. but the thought of lying alone in my apartment... tonight... i dunno... frightens me somehow. fuck! the demons are blasting livewires to my brain: fuck it. fuck everything. time to get fucked up... to obliterate the pain... myself... the situation. i'll do anything to silence the demons.* Jamming a hand into my pocket, my fingertips seized two of the Rorers. Withdrawing and opening my hand to look at them, they were diamonds and sugar cubes and cyanide all at the same time. *don't think; do.* The demons rushed me into the kitchen before my brain could override them, popping the pills into my mouth, swinging open the refrigerator door and then guzzling half a pitcher of water. *won't be long. clayton said these things are powerful. how many was i supposed to take? fuck it. too late now.*

Standing in the middle of the kitchen, my eyes darted from one vaguely familiar, yet unsettlingly foreign object to another. I wasn't hungry. I wasn't tired. I guess I was... restless. So I headed back for the living room, flopping back down on the couch. I switched on Karen's enormous TV, flipping through the channels while waiting impatiently for my medicine to ring the doorbell. I was far too annoyingly distracted to be interested in anything on the tube, so I hit the power button and decided to give figuring out her stereo system a try. It was incredibly nice; unlike anything I'd ever seen before. I pushed the button marked "On/Off," and several component pieces lit up like a welfare mom's face on the first of the month. But for the muted fireworks, nothing happened; it didn't make a peep. So I started randomly flipping switches, pushing buttons and turning dials until the music blared out suddenly and surprised me so much that I stumbled back over a footstool and fell down into a low armchair. *fuck me! who am i? the guy from the maxell "blown away" ads? how do i turn this down? the music's fucking deafening.* I leapt back to my feet to turn every dial I could see until one almost instantly brought the music down out of the decibel stratosphere. The cassette tape of Mozart's "Requiem" was still in the deck and the measures came floating through the speakers.

that song.

The demons stopped momentarily to listen.

I stood in the middle of the floor, motionless... almost paralyzed... as feelings of guilt about the Quaaludes began to bubble up from my toes. I couldn't understand exactly why, but I was actually sorry that I'd taken them. *shit! i gotta get these out of my system.* No longer distracted, the demons raged in disapproval and convulsed the gates to rubble. I bolted up away from their torture and raced for the bathroom, starting to strip to the waist on the way. Slamming the door and flinging my clothes to the tile floor in one motion, I dropped to my knees in front of the toilet and jammed a quaking finger to the back of my throat. A torrent of sour sick gushed from my gullet, splashing against the back of the bowl and blighting my view of its bottom. I groped for the faucet with my clean hand to turn on the water so Karen couldn't hear me if she came home mid-puke. Steeling myself once more, I drove my index and middle fingers way past my tongue and spewed another stream of vile mess into the toilet. Rather than feeling some relief from all of this madness, I was still so dizzy that I barely realized where I was. Pulling myself up to stand, my reflection looked back from the mirror a violent shade of crimson with bulging eyes. *the goddamn bathroom is spinning now. i cant be fucking high yet, can i? i just took these motherfuckers ten minutes ago!* Surrendering to the inevitability of what I had to do, I genuflected again before the porcelain altar and began to rummage through its polluted waters, through its contents that had, only moments earlier, lived within my stomach. Only-just-recognizable chunks of corned beef mingled with strands of mucous and tattered pieces of cabbage covering hunks of potato... but no Quaaludes, not anywhere. *they're coming out if i have to yank them out!* Resolved to shoving my whole hand down through my esophagus, my entire body began to shake violently as it purged my system of all therein. Everything from head to toe splashed into the basin, including what I was certain had to be my heart and brain, gallons of brackish bile... and two small, bone-colored Quaalude lumps, stuck together and just beginning to disintegrate. I let out a grunt of relief and collapsed from exhaustion on the dirty toilet bowl rim just as I heard Karen's distant voice, "Francis? Where are you? Everything okay?"

I turned the faucet off hurriedly and grabbed a wad of toilet paper at the same time to wipe up the vomit splatters as I responded, "Yeah, I'm in here. I'm just going to take a shower. I'll be out soon." I flushed the toilet and opened the shower door.

"Oh, okay. Well, take your time."

I started the water flowing through Karen's four showerheads, and took the opportunity to grab a bottle of Listerine from the medicine cabinet while I was waiting for the shower to warm up. Swigging a big mouthful, the burn in my mouth and throat from the day's first drop of alcohol rewoke the demons; they were pissed and wanted the real shit. I stepped into the shower, still holding the liquid embers in my mouth for as long as I could bear in an attempt to sanitize my breath and silence the demons. Eventually, I spit out the mouthwash, confident that all remnants of my war with the Rorers had disappeared. I finished up my quick shower, wrapped a towel around my waist and stepped out of the steam filled bathroom.

Karen was sitting cross-legged on the couch in a pair of gym shorts and a tee shirt, her perfectly painted ruby red toenails flanking a quart of some pricey chocolate ice cream. Watching her pull an upside-down, half-eaten spoon of cold cocoa from between her lips in the most remarkably sensuous way, I never wanted to be a utensil so badly in my whole life. She swallowed, licked her lips slowly and said, "Sometimes you just have to be bad." All I could do was nod. "Want some?" she asked, patting the cushion next to her. I nodded again and sat down. "Open up," she ordered. I obeyed, feeling the soothing cold spread through my mouth as the sugar took away the lingering bitterness. One gulp and I felt the relief immediately as the creaminess coated my stomach. "How are you doing? I mean, how are you handling things?"

"I'm alright, I guess," I responded. "It's going to take some time."

"Of course. But you have plenty of that, handsome."

Another nod. Another mouthful of ice cream. During the brief silence, I was working up my nerve. "Karen, can I ask you a question?" She lowered the spoon. "I don't mean to seem ungrateful, but why are you doing all of this for me?"

Karen smirked pleasantly, licking off the spoon and depositing it back into the container. "Well, first off, I'm a friend of Benny's... and you're a friend of Benny's, so that makes us automatic friends. Plus, I could tell that you're genuinely nice, and that goes a long way with me." She brushed the towel off of my knee and stroked the exposed skin gently. "Besides, you turn me on. Plain and simple." My dick shot up through the widening gap in my damp towel like a crocus pushing through the early spring snow. I pulled her into me with one arm behind her back and kissed her deeply. She returned the kiss with equal passion, losing no time opening up the towel and pumping my throbbing cock with both hands. While I continued to chew lightly on her lips and tongue, I slipped my fingers up the leg of her gym shorts and straight into her dripping, steaming-wet pussy. She moaned softly into my mouth until I pulled back, still staring intensely into her eyes, withdrew my digits from her crotch and then shoved them entirely into my mouth. That drove Karen mad. She let out a heated groan of approval and dropped immediately into my lap, licking and sucking the length of my member until it pounded violently.

Without removing myself from the milking of her lips, I reclined next to her so that I was looking at two smooth, shapely legs. In one motion, I tore away the gym shorts and lifted her briefly to bring her lower body down squarely onto my face. Driving my mouth and lips as deeply inside her as I could, my tongue was pummeling her clitoris like a boxer beating a speed bag. My efforts grew even more ferociously uninhibited with each vacuum-like thrust of her mouth along my shaft. I slipped two fingers back inside her as the tip of my tongue continued to dart around her pink bud. But once I slid a finger on my other hand slowly but firmly inside her ass, she began bucking like an unbroken pony and screamed, "Oh, my God, Francis, I'm going to cum! Oh, my God!" Without any more notice than that, she actually ejaculated a clear, thick liquid, covering my face and practically smothering me with her orgasm.

As far as my penis was concerned, Karen's hands and mouth grew entirely still and I wondered selfishly for a moment if she'd run out of steam. *i wonder if i'm going to have to finish myself off.* Almost as if she heard my thoughts, Karen flipped up to a sitting position and growled, "Oh, we're not done. I want you to fuck me now. Fuck me as hard as you can and fill me with that thick, hot seed."

"But what about getting pregnant?" I asked, almost boyishly.

"I have an IUD. Now get that cock inside me... now!" Partly from lust and partly from intimidation, I gripped the base of my dick to steady it unnecessarily as she straddled me and slid down my length with ease. Both of our bodies were consumed with the warmth of sexual endorphins as our lovemaking grew more and more wild. After she came three more times, I finally shot my creamy rope deep within her and we collapsed together on the coffee table.

I don't know if we both passed out or I was just imagining having drifted off, but when I finally summoned the strength to open my eyes and lift my head, Karen was fast asleep, smiling sweetly. I lifted her gently and carried her into her bedroom. She never stirred as I removed her tee shirt and pulled the covers up over her nakedness. Returning to the living room, I opened up a window and looked out into Central Park, drinking up the sweet smell of the fresh air. *true, i'm happy now... but for how long?*

Sandra O'Casey had been tossing and turning in bed until well after four in the morning. She had gone by the stoop at 602 Tenth Avenue earlier... several times in the last two days, in fact, but it was always vacant.

That was a rarity; she couldn't remember the last time she'd walked by without seeing at least one of the guys out there. But it was Francis whom she was so desperate to see. They hadn't spoken since Howie's viewing, and Sandra couldn't get the feeling out of her soul that the whole situation was her fault. A couple of days ago, she'd been hopeful that they could talk, but he'd completely cut her off in the meantime. She felt that maybe she deserved it, but that thought didn't get her any closer to being okay with it.

Sitting up in bed, Sandra grabbed her princess phone and set it in her lap, absentmindedly stroking the top of the handset. She picked it up but kept her finger on one of the cradle's plungers. She thought about what she could possibly say to him... especially at 4:15 in the morning... and then hung up the phone. But just a few seconds later, she'd picked it up again and began fingering the dial. Almost without realizing she'd called, the line connected and she heard, "This is Francis Doonan. Please leave a message." At the beep, she took a deep breath and started, "Francis...?" and then hung up. "Ugh! I'm such a coward!" she screamed into her pillow before redialing the number.

Again she was greeted with "This is Francis Doonan. Please leave a message." Waiting through a series of short beeps, she spoke after the long one. "If you're there, please pick up. It's Sandra. I know it's like four in the morning, but I really have to talk to you. Please pick up, Francis." She stopped speaking momentarily, heard a beep through the receiver, and the line went dead.

Depressing the cradle plunger to reactivate the line, she redialed and heard Francis' now all-too-familiar outgoing message. After waiting even longer for her signal beep, Sandra blurted out, "Francis, I know you're probably very mad at me and maybe even hate me, but I really have to talk to you. Please. Won't you pick up... please? Okay, well maybe you're not there. Will you please call me when you get this at least? Hope you're okay." She hung up and replaced the phone on her bedside table. "Where is he? Is he monitoring his calls?" she asked herself. The idea of sneaking out crept into her head but exited just as quickly once she remembered that she would never be able to get past her father. Frustrated and unable to come up with any other approach, she laid her head back down on the pillow and continued staring at the shadows on the ceiling.

As the sun began to peek over the sad skyline that was Weehawken, New Jersey, Kelly the Mick and Colin Garvan were having a drunken breakfast at the Market Diner on Eleventh Avenue. Chewing a mouthful of Spanish omelet, Kelly decreed, "We've got to start some serious recruiting in this neighborhood again. It's time for these wop pricks to go." Colin nodded, sopping up more buttery syrup with his already saturated piece of pancake. "I just gotta figure out a way to get Doonan with us. He's becoming a regular little legend around here. If we get him now, a lot of people will follow after him."

"I known him a long time, Kelly. It ain't never gonna happen."

"Yeah?" replied Kelly. "Well, where there's a will, there's a way."

Colin swallowed hard, the remnants of a blueberry lodged between his front teeth. "Nah. Where there's a will, there's a <u>relative</u>."

Kelly was not in a comedic mood that morning. "Shut the fuck up."

Colin snorted. "You've got no sense of humor. Or maybe you're just not smart enough to get the joke."

"Think I'm smart enough to find your brain with a bullet?" It was scary how quickly things could turn lethal between those two.

"Keep your shirt on," Colin replied.

He continued, "I'll tell you one thing: that English cocksucker, the 'Duke' or whatever the fuck he calls himself, is mine. I don't know when or where yet, but his day's coming."

Kelly the Mick nodded, glaring through the starving eyes of a junk-yard dog. "Not soon enough."

I wasn't sure if my dream originally started at the beach or if Karen's bizarre alarm clock took my mind there. My ears were filled with the sounds of crashing surf and distant seagulls as I forced my eyes open into unwilling little slits. "Sorry, Francis," Karen said, standing over me. "You should go back to sleep. I'm just meeting friends at yoga class. I'll be back in a couple of hours so we can shoot for leaving around 11. Hopefully we'll miss all the traffic that way." She leaned down and kissed me, pulling the covers up to my chin. "And I plan on bragging to my girlfriends just how good you made me feel last night. I can feel you all through my system." The smile that came to my face was an easy one. *having a hot chick brag about your skills in bed and then get to roll over and sleep in? heaven.*

Karen slipped out of the apartment and I drifted back into a brief slumber. Waking a little more than an hour later, I took a quick shower and headed straight for the kitchen, a man on a mission. I'd decided to have breakfast ready for Karen when she got home from her yoga class, and thanks to the incredibly well-stocked kitchen, the food options were end-less. I started out grinding up some coffee beans, and once I had a big pot of wake-me-up boiling on the stove, assembled all of the ingredients to make a world-class omelet. I gave a quick call down to the doorman and asked if he'd do me the favor of giving me a heads-up when Karen came home so I'd know when to start cooking her food. He was more than happy to help.

Snacking on a couple of pieces of toast in the meantime, I figured that Mozart wasn't quite the mood I was looking for that morning, so I dropped a different cassette into the tape deck: The Beatles' "Abbey Road." *howie's favorite.* I rewound the second side to the beginning and pushed play. The words came blasting through the speakers like sunlight through the clouds. "Here comes the sun. Here comes the sun." Glancing around the apartment at the sun streaming through every window, I actually allowed myself to get caught up in the lyrics and started to sing, "Little darlin', it's been a long, cold, lonely winter. Little darlin', it feels like years since its been here." I began drumming with the whisk and knife, opening the refrigerator to take out stuff to make a couple of nice salads. I closed the door as the lyrics blared, "And I say, 'It's alright!'" The words hit me like an uppercut. They could've come straight from Howie's mouth. I suddenly felt overcome and empowered all at once, standing in the middle of the kitchen, clutching the lettuce and tomatoes, whirling like a dervish and shouting at the top of my lungs, "Sun, sun, sun, here it comes!" over and over. *it's so hard, howie. i know it's going to be alright, but it's so hard right now. i miss you, man. i miss my friend.*

I continued to stand there through "Because," moving to the counter to make the salads while singing along with "You Never Give Me Your Money." Towards the end of the song, I was convinced that Howie was there, talking to me. I finished chopping and the utter silence welcomed the words: "One sweet dream, pick up the bags and get in the limousine. Soon we'll be away from here. Step on the gas and wipe that tear away...."

Dancing around, setting the table to "The Sun King," the doorman rang up just as the music moved on to "Mean Mr. Mustard." *perfect.* Dropping the omelet mixture into the waiting Belgian pan, Karen came through the door, beaming at the smell. "Whatcha cookin', good lookin'?" she asked, planting a small kiss on my cheek.

"You'll see," I replied. "Sit down. I want to serve you." She smiled sweetly, clearly touched that I was making this effort for her. I brought in the toast and coffee as "Polythene Pam" and "She Came in Through the Bathroom Window" cycled through, even treating Karen to a little of my lyrical smarts. By the time "Golden slumbers fill your eyes, smiles await you when you rise. Sleep, pretty darling. Do not cry...." pealed through the apartment, I reemerged from the kitchen with a work of egg-art, served in a sizzling pan. It was hard to miss the emotion in Karen's eyes as we ate our breakfast slowly and contentedly.

I looked up when "Carry that Weight" began, singling along softly: "Boy, you're going to carry that weight; carry that weight a long time."

"You have a very nice voice, Francis. And I love that song," Karen commented.

"It was Howie's favorite," I replied.

"Album or song?" she asked.

"Both." I raised my coffee mug. "Here's to Howie."

She clinked her mug with mine. "To Howie," she echoed.

We finished our meal in silence, pausing to look at one another and smile at the lyrics "And in the end... the love you make is equal to the love you take." Karen reached across the table and took my hand.

"Let me get this stuff cleared away."

"Not on your life, Francis Doonan. You cooked. I clean up. And as soon as I grab a quick shower, we're out of here. A weekend in the country is just the answer. It's about a two-hour ride, though. Why don't you pick out some music? Your soundtrack choice for breakfast was stellar."

"Sounds like a deal," I replied. "But remember that I do need to stop by my place to grab some stuff before we go."

"You're the boss," she said, heading into the bathroom.

Perusing Karen's extensive music collection, I grabbed more than enough to fill two hours. There was just no way we could leave without some Dylan, some more of the Beatles, the Stones, the Kinks, Jimi, a little Credence Clearwater, some Temptations, some Smokey.... I felt like a kid in a candy store.

Karen was in and out of the shower quickly, and after only a brief call to the garage to have her car readied, we were headed out the door for our Upstate getaway in record time. Taking the elevator all the way down to the basement, the doors slid open and there was a gorgeous white BMW 320-I with a sun roof waiting for us with the driver's side door open. I didn't mind admitting that I was struck a little dumb by the sight of that unbelievably beautiful automobile, and Karen must've sensed that. Without moving a muscle, she let the keys dangle from her fingertip. "Do you drive, Francis?" she asked.

I knew exactly what she was offering, but I also knew that I'd better come clean all the same. "I do, but there's a problem. I never bothered getting a license."

I expected those keys to return to the cradle of Karen's palm, but instead she asked, "Do you know how to drive stick?"

I laughed. "At 15, the first car me and Howie ever stole was a stick." She deposited the keys into my hand. "But what if we get stopped?"

"We won't," she replied. "And if we do, who cares? You only live once."

We roared up the ramp and into the sunlight on Fifth Avenue with Dylan droning in the background. A short while later, we turned off of 43rd just as "Positively 4th Street" began. No matter how hard I tried, the lyrics made me think of Sandra: "You got a lotta of nerve to say you are my friend. When I was down, you just stood there grinning. You got a lotta nerve to say you got a helping hand to lend. You just want to be on the side that's winning." As we pulled up in front of the stoop, I said, "Hey, Karen, some night you gotta come hang out with me on my stoop; see what life looks like from here." She smiled and nodded as I got out of the Beemer and headed for the front door. I grabbed the mail and determined that they were just bills as I climbed the stairs to my place.

After stuffing a couple of shirts, some jeans, a sweatshirt and my toiletries into an Adidas bag, the blinking red light of the answering machine caught my eye as I was heading out the door. I hit play and waited long enough to hear the beginning of Sandra's voice. I don't know; maybe it was the Dylan, but I just didn't care what her message said. While she was still in mid-sentence, I closed and locked the door, bounding down the stairs and back out onto Tenth Ave.

I immediately ran into Clayton, leaning off of his bike in an attempt to catch a rap with Karen. Of all of my friends, Clayton was the biggest pussy hound, but he had no idea that Karen was with me. The amused look on her face gave me the idea to fuck with Clayton a bit so I walked right up to him and threw my arms around his neck. "Who's your lady friend, man?" I asked innocently.

"Francis! Hey, brother! Oh, this is Karen. I just met her. Karen, this is Francis."

"Pleased to meet you, Karen," I said, walking around to the driver's side of the BMW without missing a beat and getting in. "Thanks for the introduction, Clayton."

We slid into the traffic heading Uptown as Clayton stood there, mouth agape. "Damn. My man, Francis."

No sooner had Francis and Karen disappeared along 45th on their way to the West Side Highway, than Sandra O'Casey came into view, heading for the stoop. Clayton spotted her right away, and out of allegiance to Francis, he resolved to avoid making eye contact with her. Sandra had other ideas, though. "Hey, Clayton. What's up? You see Francis around?"

Clayton regrouped. "Nope, I ain't seen him for a few days now." He pulled a thick joint out of his cigarette pack and lit it to accentuate his disinterest.

"I'm worried about him. He doesn't answer his phone."

"Like I said, I ain't seen him, but I can tell you he's alright all the same. He doesn't need you to worry about him." Clayton's word choice was specific, and its effect was not lost on Sandra. He continued puffing, basically dismissing Sandra, who clearly wanted to give him a piece of her mind, but decided that would be pointless.

"Well, would you please tell him I was here?" Clayton responded with a thick plume of skunky smoke. "Thanks," she sighed, walking away.

A short trip down Ninth left her standing in front of one of Hell's Kitchen's landmarks, Calvecchio's Italian restaurant. The owner greeted her warmly. "Ah, Miss O'Casey! How are you? How're the folks? I have some delicious semolina rolls today. You must try one."

"Thanks, Giuseppe, but I'll just have a salad and a Coke."

"Coming right out," he responded, and in just a few moments, he brought over her food. "Mangia," he said, pinching her cheek with the huge sausage fingers that every girl in the neighborhood had felt at one point or another. Sandra began to pick at the salad, but stopped suddenly, standing up and asking Giuseppe if the payphone worked.

"Of course, of course. It's in the back."

Sandra headed into the back of the store where an ancient phone booth stood. Opening the door and sitting down, she was surprised to note that the fan actually worked inside. She dialed the Dante League Social Club, knowing that she'd have to listen to the customary dozen or so rings before someone answered since everyone there would be out front harassing the Spanish girls who worked in the millinery lofts and factories. Finally the receiver picked up and a man with an English accent barked, "I'm listening."

She knew it was the Duke. Although she wanted to hang up, she replied, "May I please speak to Danny Albanese?"

"Who wants him?" he fired back.

"Sandra. Sandra O'Casey."

"Hang on." Sandra could hear the handset bang against the wall as the Duke dropped it to dangle at the length of the cord.

A few minutes passed before she heard Danny's voice on the line. "Sandra, what did I fucking tell you about bothering me here? This is my place of work! What the fuck?!?"

Disgusted by his tone and vulgarity, Sandra wondered silently how she ever got mixed up with Danny. "He's an animal. He comes from animals and he's surrounded by animals," she thought to herself as she almost began crying. "And what does that make me?" Her thoughts turned to Francis as the silence on the line thundered.

"What? Did you call me to be silent?" Danny interrupted the quiet.

"No," she replied, regrouping and clearing her throat. "I'm sorry. I need to see you and talk."

He snapped back his reply, "Well, that's impossible. Right now we're very busy. I have to go make some pick-ups in a little while–"

Sandra talked right over him. "Please, Danny. It's important. I've never asked you for nothing, have I? I'm right around the corner at Calvecchio's. It won't take long. I promise."

Danny wheezed out an annoyed sigh. "Alright. I'll be over as soon as I can."

"Thanks," Sandra whispered. "I appreciate it."

"Yeah," he replied. "And tell Fat Giuseppe to make me an eggplant parm plate... and put some garlic on it. Just tell him I want the Danny Special."

Danny hung up the phone, leaving Sandra with the ringing from its loud click in her ear. She replaced the receiver and sat, frozen in place, enjoying the isolation of the phone booth and the comforting whir of the old fan. The minutes passed more quickly than Sandra realized, so she was a bit surprised to hear Danny's voice and the scrambling of the whole staff of Calvecchio's rushing about to kiss his ass. She quietly slipped out of the phone booth and returned to the dining room just as Giuseppe bellowed, "See? I told you the principesa was still here."

Danny was already in place across from where Sandra had been seated. He had pulled her salad across the table and was eating anything from it that wasn't green. "Yeah, yeah. I heard you. Just make sure there's plenty of gravy on my eggplant. You guys are getting cheap with the sauce lately." As Giuseppe's sons tripped over one another to get the plate, Danny looked Sandra up and down. She was obviously upset. He started, "This better be good, goddammit."

Although she felt the urge to puke lurking just on the other side of her throat, Sandra managed some Irish courage and snapped back, "Oh, yeah, it's real good, Danny. It's a doozy. Hell, it's going to make your day... no, your week—"

Danny's gaze of amazement at Sandra's unexpected bravado was broken when one of the sons interrupted her, setting down a steaming plate swimming in red sauce. "If, uh, there's anything I c-c-can ever do for you... or your f-father... any kind of job, ya know? I'm just not really cut out for this restaurant thing." His voice trailed off, almost as though he'd thought better of speaking after the fact.

Danny glared up at him, fork already cutting into the eggplant. "Yeah. I'll let you know," he replied dismissively.

As the waiter slunk away and the junior Albanese stuffed a dripping, oversized forkful of food into his face, Sandra stared at the oil and vinegar beginning to separate below the wilting leaves of lettuce on her plate in an attempt to drum up more courage. "There's no other way to put it, Danny," she started softly. "I'm pregnant."

Danny dropped his fork noisily, prompting every Calvecchio eye to turn towards booth three. "What did you just say?"

"I'm five weeks pregnant, Danny, and I'm freaking out."

"Whoa, whoa." His mind was racing, which was at a snail's pace for Danny. "How do you know it's mine?"

Tears welled in her eyes as Sandra looked like she'd been slapped in the face. "You fuck. How could you say that to me? You're the only guy I've ever been with and you know it!"

"I don't know anything," he replied, prompting Sandra to stand up abruptly to leave. Just as quickly, Danny snarled, "Sit the fuck down or I'll slap the shit out of you." Like chimpanzees watching visitors from their cages in the Bronx Zoo, the restaurant crew tried to watch, but as discreetly as possible.

"I have to go to the bathroom," she fired back. "Is that alright with you?" He shoveled another bite between his lips, shifting his focus back onto the plate of food as his reply.

Sandra entered the bathroom feeling trapped. She looked up at the only window in the room, a tiny, two-foot-square that she couldn't have possibly crawled through. Tears began streaming down her cheeks as it started to become increasingly difficult to breathe. Sandra sat down on the toilet to catch her breath. "Just relax," she told herself. "I don't know why I ever thought I'd get a different reply from that sonofabitch... but this still hurts." Taking a wad of toilet paper to wipe her eyes, she added, "I wish Francis were here right now; he would make everything okay." The thought only made her cry harder.

The son who had served Danny's food approached him again timidly. "Is everything to your liking, Mr. Albanese?"

"Which one are you again?" Danny demanded, barely looking up.

"Gino."

"Right. You know what? I might actually have a little job for you after all... sometime soon. If I call here for you and you're not here, I'll say that... um... Romano called. Alright? That way, you'll know to come see me."

Gino saw Sandra approaching and took the opportunity to try to impress the younger Albanese with his ability to be both committed and discreet. "Yes sir, Mr. Albanese. You can count on me," he said, slipping away as Sandra resumed her place in the booth.

Danny looked up briefly, staring her down. "So what are you going to do?"

"Well, I'm not going to have it if that's what you're asking."

"That's not what I'm saying at all. Jesus Christ! And I'm a devout Catholic anyway. I'd never even think to ask that," he replied.

Confused by Danny's answer and looking down at the remnants of his eggplant bathing in red sauce, Sandra suddenly envisioned the pamphlets they gave out before mass with the graphic pictures of aborted fetuses. It was more than she could bear. Springing up from her seat to make a mad dash back to the bathroom, she barely got the toilet seat up before emptying the meager contents of her stomach into the bowl. Shaking and dry heaving, Hell's Kitchen's own answer to Grace Kelly knelt there on the floor of a public restroom until she felt stable enough to stand.

Splashing some cold water on her face, Sandra headed back out into the dining area to find her booth empty. Assuming Danny was in the bathroom, she sat there for almost 15 minutes before spotting the faint blue lines among the meat sauce stains on the napkin tucked beneath her plate. She realized that they were the reverse lines of letters whose ink had bled through the thin paper. Pulling it out and opening it, Sandra recognized Danny's childish handwriting immediately.

Do what you gotta do.

Look under the plait.

She didn't know whether to laugh at his stupidity or cry at his predictability, but Sandra already knew what would be waiting for her under the dish. Three green bills were folded in half and resting under her salad plate. She sat there in disgust for a second, finally standing and hustling out of the restaurant, forgetting to pay her check despite the $300 clutched in her fist.

As soon as the fresh air outside hit her face, the tears returned and all Sandra could think to do was run west, toward the river. She was terrified and didn't know what to do. She couldn't tell her parents; her mother would have a heart attack and her father would kill her. Even the girls from the neighborhood would eventually tell someone and the nuns from St. Agnes would either make her have the baby or see her banished to Hell. Arriving at the railing marking the water's edge, Sandra leaned over, staring at the Hudson. The notion of jumping in grabbed hold of her momentarily, but it scared her so much that she stepped back, buried her face in her hands and screamed, "Francis, where are you?"

It felt strange for the crew to hang on the stoop without Francis and Howie. But they were in the midst of a unique time in their young lives and they were hurting; being together was the only thing that made that better. Despite Benny's appeals, there was no denying that they wanted revenge for what was done to Howie. Patty Boy was the first to put it to words. "Yo, why don't we just go over there and fuck them Albaneses up Hell's Kitchen style? Right now. Broad daylight. Who's gonna say anything? We know everybody. Shit, we'll even be doing the cops a favor. My moms is dating a cop from North and he says they all fucking hate the Albaneses as much as we do. Let's just get good and fired up and go do this."

Redbone and Clayton both chimed in their agreement when Brian said, "Let's go get some bats from the HKYO gym. I got the keys."

Cal supplied the lone, momentary voice of reason. "Hold up. First off, we ain't doing nothing without Francis. When's he coming back anyway? Clayton, you were the last one to see him. Didn't he say anything?"

"I told y'all. He didn't say shit, yo. He just split with that fine mami."

Redbone weighed in. "Alright. We'll wait for Francis, but we're gonna do this no matter what. Agreed?" Nods and fist pounds went all around.

"Now who's got the fucking herb?" Patty Boy asked.

At that moment, Romeo T rounded the corner with a million dollar smile, which only meant one of two things: either he just got laid or he was holding killer weed. Fortunately for the boys, it was the latter. Cannabis sativa lit up the stoop while two police officers sat across the street in a custom surveillance van with tinted windows.

After the second joint had made a complete revolution, Castillo, the building super, came through the front door. "You kids go somewhere else. I getting complaint. This is no a hang out."

The boys were in no frame of mind to listen to reason. Squaring off with him, Brian replied, "Listen, you fucking beaner, when you were pulling the hairs offa coconuts, we were on this stoop, and we'll still be on this stoop when they deport you... or bury you. Now go fuck yourself if you know what's good for you."

Castillo was accustomed to playing "macho papi" with his wife and kids, but he knew that wouldn't fly here. "They no pay me enough to deal with you kids' shit." To a handful of threatening glares, he turned and went back inside just as one of the tenants threw a pair of eggs down at them.

The guys scattered momentarily as the eggs smashed on the pavement. Clayton looked up and yelled, "Hey, bitch, how about some bacon too?" They all howled. "We got the munchies, you motherfucker!"

J.R. Albanese sat at his pristine table in the social club, trying to absorb Machiavelli's "The Prince" with a dictionary at arm's length. The Duke was in the backroom, pounding on the heavy bag with a force that was simply unnerving. It was not difficult to see how Howie could've ended up looking the way he did before he died. Danny sat at the bar, cleaning three of his new "weapon of choice," a 9 mm pistol: one for him, one for his father, and one for The Duke. Danny hadn't given a second thought to Sandra or her news with the exception that, when she inevitably asked him to go with her for the abortion, he could send that tool, Gino.

It actually worked out well that there were people in the neighborhood seeking to become soldiers for the family. J.R. didn't agree with the "old guard," so he was preparing himself to make a move beyond the neighborhood. Although he was really nothing more than a low-level bully in the grand scheme of things, J.R. had experienced his own modest level of success through force and intimidation, so like Kelly the Mick, the elder Albanese was in the recruiting process. To make such an ambitious statement would require plenty of firepower, and he wouldn't have minded having the Irish West Siders on the payroll. He'd said many times that they were vicious and nuts... and would eventually end up killing one another, but he knew that Kelly the Mick would never stand by and watch that happen. So, J.R. thought, if he couldn't have them, he'd have to neutralize them. And there was no better way than by flooding the neighborhood with drugs. He could make a profit while burning out their brain cells and eliminating any competition. "Machiavelli would be proud," he told himself.

Just under two hours had passed when Karen and I got off at the Kingston Exit on our way to her country house in West Hurley. When she told me that we would be stopping in Woodstock to get groceries, I naturally assumed that it was the same place where they'd had the legendary music festival, but she told me that the actual location was a little further up, in the town of Bethel. *you'd never know there was a difference, though. everyone in town looks like they just settled here after the concert.* It was really kind of cool, though. The quaint, country town was sort of a hippie land where all the people were smiling, something people in The City rarely saw or did. Plus, the air there was fresh and brisk. *makes me feel hungry.* Karen must've read my mind because she said, "Hey, let's get something to eat before it gets too dark. There's a neat little restaurant on the other side of town called Joyous Lake. They've got fantastic food and a lot of local musicians hang around there." It didn't take long after we entered the restaurant to realize that Karen hadn't read my mind at all; stopping there had been a planned event. As soon as I sat down, I could see two men huddled at a table in the corner, two men who were recognizable from coast to coast: the one man wrote... Rick Danko, and the other man talked... Bob Dylan himself. Karen looked into my eyes until I smiled, which was precisely the reaction she had been hoping for. She had succeeded in impressing me.

After a pleasant meal and an even more mellow trip the rest of the way to Karen's house, I got out of the car and stretched. Leaning back and taking in the sky, I was struck by just how many millions of stars there were and how bright they seemed. Then it dawned on me that I could probably count on both hands the number of times I'd actually seen the stars in my 17 years on the planet. It was amazing. Karen was just looking at me from the porch as I stared up at the Heavens. "You okay?" she asked quietly. I looked at her for a moment, nodded, and tilted my head back again. "I have to make a couple of phone calls to take care of some business back in The City before it gets too late. I'll probably be awhile, I'm afraid. Can I get you anything?"

"Nah," I replied. "I'm just going to hang out here for a little while if that's okay. Maybe explore a bit."

"Okay." She smiled and headed inside. It was so dark there that, when Karen flipped on the lights in the entryway and front room, it seemed to burn as brightly as the sun. *i guess when you're not used to darkness and total quiet, the tiniest bit of light or noise seems gigantic.* I had the impulse to walk into the woods a short way to reach a point where I could neither see nor hear anything man-made. I'd heard that there were places in Central Park where you could do the same thing, but I'd certainly never been able to find them. The illumination from the stars and the moon seemed plenty to navigate at least a little adventure so I headed off in a direction parallel to the road. It was so quiet that a cricket's chirp and the wind blowing through the trees seemed as loud as the cabs racing up Tenth Ave. *the long, gray winter is over and everything is coming alive again.*

It didn't take long before I could neither see nor hear anything but nature. But, as a result, everything started to look the same and soon I couldn't be sure which direction I'd come from or where I was supposed to go to get back to Karen's. I couldn't honestly say how long I'd been walking, for that matter. As anxiety and panic started to rise up inside of me, I realized that the demons had come North in the car with us. My mind started to flash with images about Howie while my mouth and gut craved a drink. Little by little, I started moving more rapidly, cutting in and out of the trees and bushes, my heart pounding like a jackhammer. I didn't know if I was distracted by its beating up in my ears, but I panicked at the realization that I couldn't really feel my legs moving along underneath me. My breathing became labored as rivulets of clammy sweat stung my eyes and soaked my shirt. *with all this fresh air, i can barely get a breath! what the fuck am i feeling? is this howie? are you doing this, howie?* The fear made me move along even more quickly, my body spasming and quivering. Since I wasn't used to being sober, I didn't recognize the signs of withdrawal. *fuck! i haven't had a drink in over a day. i sure hope karen's got some booze at the house.* Jonesing for a drink made me remember the Quaaludes in my jacket pocket, and the thought instantly calmed down the demons. *but that's back in the car. well, adventure's over. i gotta go back. but fuck! there's no point kidding myself; i'm lost. i don't even know which direction i went originally. i sure as shit don't know which direction to go now. if i just turn around, i've got at least a two-in-three chance of either getting back to the house or reaching the road.*

The woods around me were darker than anything I could've imagined, and almost by instinct, I found myself running faster in the direction I'd chosen randomly. I held my hands up loosely in front of my face, sure that I'd either run into a tree or lose an eye to a low-hanging branch. Of course, it was a root that felled me as I tripped and went down hard on my left knee with all of my weight. My heart was bouncing in my chest enough that my shirtfront had to be moving with the beat. Exhausted and panting, I took a moment to make sure my leg wasn't broken or bleeding. Without any good idea of what to do next, I sat there beneath a large tree to rest for a second and gather my thoughts. Eventually, those thoughts turned to Howie and I began to have what I suppose must've appeared to be a one-sided conversation with him. But it wasn't a conversation in the conventional sense. Although I spoke aloud at times, it didn't involve words so much as it involved thoughts and feelings and fleeting images. I wondered more than once if I were breaking down again. I missed my friend more than I knew how to handle.

As the night air in the countryside of Upstate New York began to turn colder, my body began to tremble. I wasn't positive if it was because of the temperature or my frantic pace... or a lack of rest and emotional stress. Actually, although I didn't realize it at the time, the DTs had set in. I closed my eyes for a second. Maybe it was to slow the images... to keep the dark from playing tricks on me... or maybe I had intended to pray. *god, i know i'm not a saint, and i know i do a lot of stuff i'm not supposed to do. i know that you see all of it, but please help me. i can't promise that i'm going to become perfect or anything like that. i dunno. i heard that you help those who help themselves... well, i can't. i'm just being honest. but i need your help. please be good to my friend, howie. please....* My voice – or perhaps it was my inner voice – trailed off as I succumbed to the overwhelming frustration and futility of my situation. *what the fuck am i doing here?*

Karen glanced at her watch after finishing the last of her phone calls and saw that almost two hours had passed. Figuring he must've come inside and gone to bed without her hearing him, she walked to the bedroom and throughout the house, but found it empty. Stepping outside, she expected to find Francis on the porch, but he was not there either. She called to him, but when he didn't respond, she sat down to wait for him. Glancing at her watch again, she said to herself, "Where the hell could he be? The car's still in the driveway, so he has to be close... but where?" She was a little worried. After all, he was on shaky ground to put it mildly. Karen knew that she wasn't going to call the state troopers or anything, but she resolved to wait another five minutes before going to look for him. Thoughts filled her mind of the time she foolishly brought her friend's poodle to the country for the weekend, and all that she found of the poor little thing was its paw; the country vermin had a field day. Half-frightened and half-pissed, she went to the garage to get the big flashlight she'd last used in her vain search for Sprinkles.

Starting into the woods, Karen was petrified. Things were moving all around her even though the strong beam of light cut through the darkness of the woods like a razor blade. "Francis! Francis, can you hear me?"

Probably because of both physical and mental exhaustion, I'd nodded off, leaning up against the tree. I had no idea how long I'd been out, but I stirred when I heard Karen's voice faintly calling my name. Standing up, the woods appeared to be slightly less dark and foreboding. I began calling out, "Karen! Over here! I'm over here!" A dot of light turned in my direction, getting larger and larger by the second. In just a few minutes, it backlit the woods as Karen stood in front of me.

There was not even a hint of a smile on her face; just concern. "There you are. I was worried sick," she said. "Why would you wander off this far and this long at night?" Silently, she thought to herself, "Maybe I shouldn't have brought him up here. I don't even really know him."

"I didn't mean to," I replied. "I guess I got lost." *maybe i shouldn't have come here. i don't know this lady if i'm being truthful... and i'd rather be home with my boys anyway.* We suffered through an uncomfortable moment before I said softly, "Sorry." We embraced, both looking off in separate directions.

Without saying a word, Karen turned and I followed her. We walked silently and awkwardly back to the house, clutching one another's hands. The night had gotten truly cold, but the dead air between us made it seem like snow was falling. Arriving back at the house, I immediately went to the car to get my suit jacket, and Karen's annoyance at even that little detour was obvious. Grabbing one of the Quaaludes, I swallowed it dry. *this one is staying down.*

Karen walked on into the house and I followed after, heading for the comfort of the living room. She entered a moment later with a bottle of Jack Daniels. The demons were on their feet with approval. *relief is on the way, irish boy.* Karen handed me the bottle and a couple of glasses before going over to start a fire. I knew that it was probably the polite thing to offer to do it for her, but the demons would suffer no more delays. I sat back in the chair, poured four fingers of Jack and downed it straight. *patsy would be proud. the meltdown of the rorer 714 has started; the eagle has landed.*

Using one of those chemical fire-starter logs, Karen needed only a minute to get the flames twisting and leaping beneath the mantle. Turning around for a sip of whiskey, she noticed immediately that her glass was still empty and that I was far, far away. Without saying a word (and sure that I wouldn't even notice), she slipped out of the room and up to her bedroom to stare at the ceiling. She was correct that my powers of perception were on par with my appropriateness, but the demons weren't letting me give a shit that night. I downed another glassful of whiskey, staring glass-eyed, straight ahead into the flames. The opiates had met the elixirs.

Colin Garvan inspected his old Cagneyesque Tommy Gun as the '76 Impala carrying him and Kelly the Mick cut slowly across 39th Street. As the car slowed to a crawl in front of the Dante League Social Club and both headlights went black, Colin leaned halfway out of the passenger's side window and pulled the trigger, spewing flames from the barrel. The bullets engraved a zipper whose teeth were suddenly ripped open across the club's windows, bursting them and exploding shards of glass everywhere. His Chicago Typewriter continued clacking until the ammunition expired and the Dante League Social Club signs had all but disappeared, leaving the vanished windows looking like a jagged-toothed silent scream. Without uttering a word, Colin withdrew back into the car while the pair sped off, but their message had been clear: The war had begun.

Kelly the Mick was clipping along the West Side Highway toward the George Washington Bridge, still careful to maintain a legal speed; he couldn't chance getting stopped. The smell of cordite and gun smoke had filled the car and neither he nor Colin could've possibly hidden the adrenaline that was pumping through their systems. After only five silent minutes, Kelly turned the radio on and the weather report from 1010 WINS came through the car speakers. "Weather! All these cocksuckers ever talk about is the fucking weather!"

Colin began to feel overwhelmed... perhaps by the smell of the fumes, perhaps by the painful cut on his right index finger from pulling on the trigger so hard... but most certainly by the seriousness of what they'd just done. "I almost burned my hand on that fucking muzzle! Did you see it? It was cherry-red it was so hot!" he blurted out over the report of tomorrow's temperature in Bloomfield. Another infinite moment of silence passed between them. "You know? Maybe we should pull over before we hit the Bronx and stash it in the trunk. Just in case we get stopped or whatever." Kelly nodded his agreement and stopped a few minutes later on a dim, deserted cul de sac in Upstate Manhattan.

By the time they climbed back into car, the Tommy Gun was safely inside a duffle bag, which was, itself, inside an opaque plastic bag, resting beneath two spare tires and a ton of miscellaneous shit in the trunk. The ignition turned over as the radio was in the midst of delivering the news for which they'd been waiting so impatiently: "... details are sparse at the moment, but we can confirm that, a short while ago, automatic gunfire ripped through the Dante League Social Club, reputed to be the Hell's Kitchen hangout of alleged mobster, Johnny "J.R." Albanese, and his crew. No word on casualties as of yet. The area has been restricted to police and emergency services units only, but we are still trying to put together more details. We will keep you updated as more information becomes available."

Kelly shouted, "Woo hoo!" and drummed the steering wheel with his hands as though he'd just won the lottery, making the car swerve within its lane violently.

Remembering their need to maintain a low profile while the gun was in the car, Kelly gripped the wheel at ten and two, dropping any sign of celebration from his face. In a soft, introspective voice, Colin said, "I actually have an erection."

Allowing one another the luxury of an exchanged look and chuckle, Kelly asked, "So where's Murphy's retirement party?"

"Over on Brain-Dead Ave."

"Bainbridge Avenue it is, then," Kelly replied. "That'll be the perfect alibi."

Striking a mocking tone, Colin continued, "Jeez, Detectives, as much as we'd like to shake the hand of whoever done it, we couldn'ta been involved. We was miles away, helping a fellow Son of Erin celebrate his retirement from the Sand Hogs Union.

"And if the drink doesn't make the exact time hazy enough, Murph'll be happy to back us up when we give him the machine gun as a retirement gift. He's an avid hunter, right? Well there's no way in hell he can miss with this!"

"Yeah," Kelly added. "And hopefully it'll be cooled down enough by the time we arrive to get it out of the car."

Traffic into New Jersey through the Lincoln Tunnel was at a stand-still as rubberneckers joined the majority of the neighborhood in gawking near 39th Street and Ninth Avenue. Red, Vit, Patty Boy, Clayton, Brian and Milk had abandoned the stoop in favor of a better vantage point atop a building on 40th Street. Knowing the "Tar Beach" rooftop maze of Hell's Kitchen was one of the perks of being a native. Clayton voiced what most of the boys were thinking. "Do you guys think Francis had anything to do with this shit?"

"Nah." Red provided the epiphany for the group. "This is that psycho, Kelly the Mick. I know it. I can feel it."

Thanks to a tip from his guy at the Daily News, First Grade Detective Jack O'Casey arrived at the scene of what was left of the Dante League Social Club less than five minutes after the crew from the stoop. As he stretched the yellow tape barricade over his head to pass by, two reporters, Michael Doyle and Ian Middleton, approached him. "So what's the skinny, Danny?"

"Don't know yet, boys. Let me check it out and I'll get back to you." Pausing for a second thought, he added, "Don't worry. I'll guarantee an exclusive. Are there any photographers here?" Middleton knew this was typical, Irish-dick egoism: exchanging the exclusive for getting his picture in the paper... yet again.

Doyle took the bait first, though, motioning his photographer to come over. "I'll get one, O'Casey." He waited for the detective to strike an appropriate, bogusly candid pose and then snapped the photo with the Albanese's shot-up storefront as the background.

Pivoting back to the crime scene, Det. O'Casey approached the uniformed Lt. Sullivan. "So what've we got, Kevin?"

"A regular fucking Vietnam. Looks like a large caliber gun. Forensics is on it now, but c'mere; I gotta show you something." He led the detective past a couple of uniformed cops searching a cherry-red Delta 88 and into the social club, glass crunching underfoot. To the right of the entrance, another detective was talking to J.R. Albanese and his son.

"Hey, McCann, keep them here," O'Casey said to the other detective. The first casualty to catch his eye was an espresso machine behind the bar. Riddled with holes, cloudy water dripped from its base as a faint plume of steam rose from its dome. Thousands of cigarette and gold-and-white cardboard pieces littered the floor. Intentionally grabbing a carton from a section untouched by bullets, a portion of the Marlboro wall came crashing down. O'Casey shot a menacing smile back in the direction of J.R., removed and opened a full pack, and then lit a cigarette while following Lt. Sullivan into the darkened far end of the room. There, the detective found the oddest thing he'd ever seen. An 80-pound Everlast punching heavy bag looked almost as though it had been sawed in half, with the top portion left dangling from a chain and the remainder mixed in with something on the ground that he had to turn his head and use his imagination to identify. It was a human body, largely in two pieces and bisected at the waist. Still attached to the bare-chested torso was a big, bald head and two arms sporting a pair of red boxing gloves. The twisted remainder was identifiable by a tattered pair of trunks and Everlast shoes laced up on the feet. The red and orange guts of both the boxer and the boxing bag blanketed the scene like a grotesque Shake-n-Bake chicken coating.

Lt. Sullivan mused, "The deceased probably should've taken an eight-count. The M.E.'s on the way. We're still trying to I.D. him since, naturally, our poor Italian 'victims' have contracted amnesia about him... despite the fact he was training inside their establishment."

"I know who he is," O'Casey replied. "Well, I know his street name, anyway. They call him 'The Duke.' He's from somewhere in England, as I understand it. Some sort of amateur boxing champ. Works muscle for Johnny Rugs... and he also happens to be the main suspect in that Nesto killing. We can probably consider that case closed now." The detective knew exactly who separated The Duke's upper half from his lower half, but truthfully couldn't have given a fuck less.

Someone from outside called for the lieutenant and he excused himself, leaving O'Casey alone with the body. He looked around discreetly to ensure that no one was watching, and then leaned down to spit right in the corpse's grimacing face. "You fucking English cunt!" he hissed, spinning on his heel to walk back to where Det. McCann was continuing to question the Albaneses. "What we got, Connor?"

"Oh, you know, Jack, the usual. Mr. Albanese, Senior, here claims that he was home with his wife and a bowl of spaghetti, getting ready to say the Rosary and head to bed. Albanese, Junior, meanwhile, claims that he was already asleep due to the pain medication he's on."

"Yeah," O'Casey snorted, heading back for the street. "We won't get any more out of them. Go ahead and let them go."

J.R. raised his voice at the detective's back, "Hey, O'Casey, what about my place? And my guy! They killed my guy, you prick!"

O'Casey spun around and charged right back at the elder Albanese, grabbing him by the arm to drag him to the side in a decisively old-school, blackjack-mentality manner. Danny Albanese immediately started whining, "Hey! Police brutality! He's harassing my father!"

McCann delivered a sharp elbow inconspicuously into Danny's ribs and then leaned in to say softly, "Shut the fuck up, zip," following it with a more boisterous, "Wow. Are you okay, sir? You got gas?" Truthfully, neither the discretion nor the softspeak were necessary. The mostly Irish crowd wouldn't have said a word, much less thought to intervene.

"What about your place?!? What about your guy?!?" O'Casey spit the words sarcastically into J.R.'s face. "You're in one piece. So you've got proof now that at least God doesn't hate you Guinea motherfuckers as much as the rest of us do. Go home. Get on your knees. Tell Him thanks." Releasing his death grip on the mobster's arm, Det. O'Casey turned and strode away. As furious as the mobster was and as much as he wanted to shoot... a gun... his mouth... whatever, there was absolutely nothing he could do safely, so he grabbed his still-winded son and hustled him out the door and into the Delta 88.

Det. O'Casey paused only briefly to watch out of the corner of his eye as Danny and J.R. Albanese loaded themselves into his car and drove away, signaling his approval for them to pass through the barricade. Michael Doyle had seen the detective exit the Dante League Social Club and was standing at the ready with a photographer at his side in an effort to remind O'Casey about his promised exclusive. Beaten to the punch again, Ian Middleton remarked to one of his colleagues under his breath, "Jack O'Casey is the biggest camera whore I ever saw. He'd pose taking a dump if he thought someone'd take his picture doing it."

Stepping in to be included in a shot, McCann posed with O'Casey as he began to tell Doyle what he felt before what he knew. "This is off the record, but what you see here is only the beginning. A turf war is about to take place. More bullets are going to fly if steps aren't taken to calm this situation now. Everybody from this area needs to be careful or we're going to see innocent civilians hurt. Truthfully, I think this is probably retribution for the killing of a neighborhood kid, Howie Nesto, earlier this week. But time will tell on that one. As of right now, there are no suspects, but plenty of 'persons of interest.'"

The detective's statement was interrupted by an overzealous patrolman who approached, herding the boys from the stoop before him. They'd been rousted by uniform cops from the roof and led downstairs. "We may have something here."

O'Casey noticed immediately that these friends of his daughter were all sporting bloodshot eyes, stoned out of their minds. Momentarily buoyed by the surprising fact that Francis Doonan was not among them, he looked down at the patrolman's nametag and said, "No, Officer Hawkins. I've known them all forever. They grew up with my little girl. Trust me. They're good kids... just nosy."

Hawkins let them go reluctantly, handing the detective a sheet from his notebook. "You're the boss, but I was sure to take all of their names down first." Even the quickest glance was enough for O'Casey to note that every last one of them had given a false name. He knew they were doubtlessly laughing all the way back to that stoop over on Tenth Ave.

For the umpteenth time in my life, I needed a few minutes to figure out where I was when I awoke in a leather chair, swimming in the stale smell of Jack Daniels. It didn't help, of course, that Karen's country house had been set up almost identically to her apartment in The City. But, then again, had I been in NYC, I couldn't have seen the three breathtaking deer that were nibbling on a tree branch just on the other side of the sliding glass door. I made my way over, quietly but dizzily, to watch them more closely until I heard Karen say, "Well, good morning. I'm surprised to see you awake," and the deer bolted into the woods.

"Morning," I mumbled back through cotton-mouthed lips, unable to tell if she was mad at me or not. Feeling more than a little uncomfortable, I shuffled into the kitchen to make coffee. *ah, fuck. it's been a long week. i hope she understands, but if not, i'll just leave. she can drive me to the bus; no big deal.* As the rejuvenating scent of coffee filled the air, I thought I should make an attempt at breaking the tension... if there was any. "Listen, I'm sorry about last night."

"Don't be ridiculous, Francis. You're only human. How much can you take without a little release, right?" I thought I could see sincerity in her eyes and it made me breathe more deeply. "Besides," she continued. "That was yesterday and this is today. Let's enjoy it. It's why we came up here, isn't it?

"Now take your mug up into the shower with you and then let's go into town for breakfast. We can just... play and do some fun things later on. It's going to be a beautiful day." I appreciated how effortlessly she had cleared the air, so I responded by walking over and kissing her on the forehead before heading into the bathroom.

Karen waited to hear the bathroom door close and the water surge through the pipes before walking to the kitchen and picking up the phone, dialing the number for Benny's private answering machine at the store. Its usual purpose was for receiving messages discreetly from his lady friends, but this wasn't going to qualify as "the usual." When the machine's greeting ended, she started in immediately.

"Good morning, Benny. It's Karen. We're up at the country house. Don't worry; everything's alright.... I mean... basically... alright.

No, no. Everything's fine, Ben.

...I just don't know whether I'm doing the right thing here or not, but this kid needs professional help. I mean, well... you said that he's not dangerous or anything, right?

No, of course not, Karen. That's silly.

...Well, I hope not, anyway.

He's just....

I just... don't... know if the way I can help him is the *kind* of help he needs, you know?

Ah, shit. I'm rambling.

Sorry, Benny. I just needed to say all this, I guess, and I can't say it to him. And it's just the two of us, after all.

Jesus. I'll stop with the pity party routine now.

Sorry, Ben. I'll see you when we get back. Bye, babe."

Karen was hanging up the phone as I walked in behind her, causing her to spin around. I couldn't tell if that was something to hide or surprise on her face, but I offered instinctively, "Sorry to interrupt, but I realized that I left my clothes in the car."

"Oh, it's not a problem," she replied calmly. "Believe it or not, when the weather gets nice this time of year, you have to call to make breakfast reservations. You're just in a towel, though, and it's pretty chilly out. Would you like me to go out and get your clothes from the car for you?" I smiled and shook my head while opening the front door. She semi-shouted after me, "Okay, then. Hop to it and I'll fix a couple of coffees-to-go for the ride."

Reaching into the car and grabbing my suit jacket, I instantly felt the two remaining Quaaludes behind the cloth of the pocket. Without a second's hesitation, I drew them out with two fingers and threw them as far as I could into the woods. *a couple of poor little west hurley woodland creatures will soon get an introduction to rorer 714s... and they won't know what hit 'em!*

In short order, Karen and I were enjoying the ride into town with Leonard Cohen streaming through the car speakers, whizzing past real country farms, cows, tractors... people who actually wave at you when you drive by. It was exhilarating. She turned out to be absolutely correct: the restaurant was packed. I decided not to question why we were waiting on line, though, if she had made reservations before we left. Out of the corner of my eye, the cover of the Daily News' national edition screamed "Hell's Kitchen War Erupts. One Dead. Michael Doyle. Page 3!" My mind went racing as my eyes searched for a phone. "I'll be back in a sec. Gonna make a quick call," I mumbled to Karen, almost absentmindedly.

Pumping coins into the pay phone outside, the line rang ten times before Clayton finally picked it up, pulling the receiver across what sounded like an ocean of crumpled paper before croaking a deep "Hello," as though his mouth were filled with golf balls.

"Clayton! What's up?"

"Yo! Francis! You missed it, man! They got that motherfucking English dude. Cut him right in half. Prick got what he deserved."

"Cut him in half?" I asked?

"Machine gunned that motherfucker!"

"And what about the Albaneses?"

"Ah, they weren't there. Too bad, right?"

I half-chuckled into the phone and continued, "Are the boys alright?"

Clayton came back reassuringly, "Oh, yeah. We were lighting up the stoop last night. Half the fucking neighborhood was there... and everyone was asking for you."

"Well, don't worry. I'll be back Monday morning. I'm gonna chill out up here. It's really nice and I really need a break."

"Oh, and Francis, Sandra O'Casey has been looking for you... hard, yo. She's asking all over. I've been stonewallin' her, but what should I tell her? Anything?"

"Just go ahead and tell her I'll be back Monday. I'll have to see her eventually." Hanging up the phone and opening the paper to page three, Det. O'Casey's big moon face beamed right out from in front of the Dante League Social Club. I crumpled up the paper, wondering why Sandra was looking for me so intently. *probably wants something. there's the rage rumbling.* I glanced in the window and saw Karen waving at me from the table. It wasn't difficult to get my mind to refocus on coffee and blueberry pancakes.

An attendant at Bellevue Hospital pulled open one of the scores of refrigerated drawers in the basement wall to slide out the frozen pieces of the corpse therein. Double-checking that the tag on its toe read "John Doe, a.k.a. The Duke," he compared the I.D. numbers and then made a brief note on its accompanying paperwork that the body was unidentified and unclaimed. Since the Albaneses had not been forthcoming with any information, the attendant ticked the box on his clipboard for "Potters Field." Shaking his head, the morgue worker thought aloud, "That big, lonely field out on Roosevelt Island is hardly fit for nobility, but if no one over in England is even wondering about ya, you must not be much of a 'duke,' yer majesty."

As the refrigerated body drawer slid shut, J.R. found himself in front of the remains of his club, near the squad car of two rookies who'd been sitting watch there all night. Yellow police tape had the majority of the sidewalk cordoned off, and kept Albanese from the front door, trying to pry information from the pair of sleepy cops. "Yes, sir. The body was removed more than three hours ago. It was taken to the City Morgue, but that's as much as I can tell anyone who ain't next of kin."

"Well, this is my fucking establishment, you jerk off!" J.R. fired back. "And I want to go inside and assess the damage. I'm the fucking victim here!" The cops stood motionless and silent with a "We have our orders" look on their faces.

Just as J.R. was weighing whether he wanted to upgrade the situation to a real problem, Albanese's Delta 88 pulled up and Danny leaned out the window. "Pop, let's go. Don't get your pressure up." J.R. could scarcely pull himself away from the grandstanding, but finally satisfied himself with spitting on the ground before he gave up and got in the car. Waiting for a moment for a note of thanks from his father, Danny was unsurprisingly disappointed before eventually asking, "Where to, Pop?"

"Arthur Avenue," the elder Albanese shot back. He was steaming mad, and was more thinking out loud than talking to his son. "We're going to see that fat fuck, your Uncle Nicky. No one is gonna fuck with me like this."

Danny chanced a question. "What about the Duke, the poor sonofabitch...?"

Seeming almost offended, J.R. spit out an interruption, "Yeah? And what about him? Fuck him! He's dead. End of story. I never fucking liked that tea-swilling cunt anyway. I only kept him around to babysit you, if you wanna know the real truth." Danny wasn't sure if the tears forming in his eyes were from biting his own lip or the usual slap in the face from his old man. Danny hated it when his father talked to him like that, but at least this time was a rarity: he hadn't done it in front of everyone else.

The rest of the ride to Armando's in The Bronx took place in dead silence. J.R. had gone there to talk with Nicky Derienzo, something of a big name in the world of hitmen. His thing was to bring stone-cold killers over from Sicily and put them to work in construction until he needed them." In as low of a voice as Johnny Rugs could muster at the moment, he provided Nicky a basic recount of what had happened, finishing with, "I want the ten baddest motherfuckers you got! Expense is no issue."

Nicky swallowed and adjusted his 300-pound frame before dabbing at his lips with the great, stained napkin tucked in between chins four and five. "Done," he replied. "You should try the calamari." Nicky also had a reputation as a man of few words, which usually were limited to: "fuck you," "pay me," "yes," "no" and "done." Everything else out of his mouth pertained to what went in it.

The wind was unusually still atop Kelly the Mick's roof as he exhaled a chest full of weed smoke and watched it hang like wet laundry inside his pigeon coop. Keeping pigeons was a tradition in Hell's Kitchen, and feeding them seemed to keep Kelly calm, something with which he needed a great deal of help while he waited for Colin Garvan to arrive. Kelly felt like a million dollars in the knowledge that he had sent a unmistakably major message to the Albaneses. His thoughts shifted to what his next move should be as Colin burst through the bulkhead door and out onto the soft tar with *The Daily News*, *The Post* and *The Times* in hand. The front pages of all three heralded their handiwork. Too excited even to speak, they embraced briefly and did a heavy-footed little jig in time to their own hoots and chuckles.

Back to business, Kelly the Mick stopped suddenly and grabbed his friend by the front of his collar. "Now we gotta build an army, and today is recruiting day."

"Goddamn! I feel like Uncle Sam!" Colin replied.

Kelly continued thumbing through the pages of the newspapers until he was satisfied that all was as he planned, and then he took out a pocket knife and cut out the front page picture of *The Daily News*. He put it up on the wall of his pigeon coop and gave it an affectionate little tap before stepping back to admire his new bit of artwork. "We need to head out to Woodside and The Leitrim House later on."

Colin looked confused. "The joint where Declan Owens hangs out? I thought they were all IRA out there. We're gonna get recruits from those guys?"

"Fuck yeah," Kelly snapped back. "The battle lines are being drawn and it's gonna be true Irish versus the wops. You can't get much truer than IRA, and if they ain't real soldiers, I don't know who the fuck are, right?" Colin Garvan nodded in silent agreement. "In the meantime, though, let's start right here at home and see what we can rustle up. We just gotta cruise the neighborhood and find the boys from the stoop by the parking lot."

"I know just where a some of them are right now," Colin added. Heading directly for the Hell's Kitchen Park, they found a handful of the crew playing roller hockey. As Kelly the Mick's car slid to a halt next to the fence, a couple of old timers were sitting on a nearby bench, remarking about how Brian, Clayton, Patty Boy... and especially Redbone in the net were wasting a lot of athletic talent on drugs and other bullshit.

"Stay with the car, Colin," Kelly the Mick ordered. "The Albaneses may be scum, but they aren't stupid. We leave nothing unwatched." Walking through the gate and right into the middle of the rink, Kelly motioned everyone to him. When the last guy had skated over, he began, "First off, where's Doonan?"

Without thinking, Brian replied, "He went away for the weekend. He said he's coming back Monday." Clayton sucked his teeth quietly and Brian shrunk at his lack of discretion.

Kelly the Mick continued, "Alright, well here's the deal. You all know exactly what's going on around here, and as I look at all of you guys' faces, I realize that you were all born here. Christ, most of your parents and grandparents were born here. Well, this neighborhood is up for grabs now. The docks shut down and a shitload of jobs were lost, but there's still a lot of action here. I know for a fact that the city planners have big changes in store for Hell's Kitchen. Hell, they even want to give it another name."

"Fuck that," Patty Boy retorted. "It's always going to be Hell's Kitchen." The rest of the boys grumbled their agreement in unison.

"Which is exactly my point," Kelly said. "We've got to protect and preserve our turf, and so I'm asking you guys to throw in with me. Otherwise the dagos will be pushing your folks and neighbors around... and eventually pushing them out. Well, that's not going to happen as long as I'm alive."

Although they weren't exactly moved to a frenzied bloodlust, Kelly the Mick's speech had nonetheless whipped up their senses of honor and loyalty... and their testosterone. "We're down," announced Redbone.

"You can count on us," Brian chimed in.

"Yeah, we're all down," came the general consensus from the crew.

"Great. Now you just need to convince Doonan. He's a tough little prick."

"Technically," Romeo T countered, "he was born in the South Bronx."

Without missing a beat, Kelly snarled back, "What the fuck does that matter? Where is he receiving mail, you dumb motherfucker?" He could tell by the look on Romeo's face, like a puppy who'd been swatted *almost* one time too many, that he needed to calm down and back off.

"You gotta fight for your territory... where you live now, right? Look, here's some money." Kelly tossed three $20 bills onto the surface of the roller rink. "You guys have lunch on me. I'll be in touch. ...And I can count on you, right?" Milk nodded as he stepped forward to gather up the money and Kelly the Mick smiled and returned to his car.

Milk smiled, "Let's get some weed first off, and then let's get some gyros."

"I'll grab the beer," Clayton added, "and then we'll meet at the stoop in half an hour to figure all this out."

The blueberries in our pancakes exploded like sweet water balloons, dyeing our mouths blue. The tension of the previous night seemed to melt away more and more with each consecutive time we giggled childishly while making comments under our breaths about felating Smurfs and showing one another our tongues. I had just retracted mine when a couple stopped next to our table while on the way to theirs. "Karen Winthrop? Is that you? It's me, Nancy. Nancy and Stuart Kirsch? Remember us? We're friends of your husband."

Karen looked up as gracefully as an indigo tongue would allow. "Nancy and Stuart. Of course. How are you, my dear?"

"Oh, we're splendid, thanks. I was just telling Stuart that I was positive it was you. Did John come up too?" Nancy asked, eyeing me suspiciously.

"Oh, no. He stayed in The City this weekend. He's been swamped with work; so many skiing injuries from this past winter. I'm afraid he's been non-stop in surgery."

"Well, he did a great job on my leg," Stuart remarked.

"Gosh, I'm sorry. Where are my manners? Nancy, Stuart, this is my little brother, Francis. He's visiting from California." Nancy's lips pursed into a little, wrinkled smile as she extended the fingers of her right hand to me. I shook it a little harder than I probably needed to as Karen continued. "I'm so proud of him. He just won the National AAU Golden Gloves."

Stuart chimed in again, "Say! The Great White Hope! You look to be a middleweight, Francis. Are you going pro?"

"I doubt it," I replied. "It would get in the way of my career as a gigolo."

Karen smiled, first at me and then at the Kirsches. The flat silence seemed to build until she offered, "You don't even have to go to school for that."

Not to be outdone, Nancy replied, "Do you have a card? One never knows when your services might be needed." Returning her plastic gaze to Karen as Nancy and Stuart continued on to their table, she finished, "All the best to John."

Karen chuckled without any reproach in her eyes, "Never a dull moment, Francis." All I could do was laugh. We paid the check and then stepped outside into the fresh country morning. "Let's take a walk. I want to show you something."

As we strolled up a hilly incline, I could tell Karen had something she wanted to say, and I had a pretty good idea what it was. She finally broke the silence. "Listen, Francis, let me explain."

"You don't have to," I interrupted.

"But I want to. You see, my husband is a very well-known orthopedic surgeon, and my mother thought that marrying him would be an ideal situation for me. So, she got together with his mother and arranged the whole thing. The truth is: John and I are actually great friends, but we haven't been a couple for a long, long time. We don't dissolve the marriage for tax reasons; there's a <u>lot</u> of money involved. And to be honest, believe it or not, John is gay." The look on my face betrayed my shock and confusion. "Yes, gay. I mean, he's never actually said the words or anything, but I've always known it. I've been his beard for years...."

"His what?" I asked.

"His beard. You know, that thing that makes him appear to be a man... or at least more manly; his front. It's better socially and professionally if John is perceived to be straight, and I don't have a problem with helping out. I'm certainly compensated well enough. John and I are <u>very</u> sexual... just not with each other... or not for many years, at least."

Karen suddenly seemed a bit uncomfortable with the topic so she changed it. "This is what I wanted you to see. Isn't it beautiful?" Near the top of the hill sat the charred remains of a monastery. It felt really... I dunno... holy up there. It was so quiet. I just felt compelled to keep trudging forward towards its stone arch. Karen wandered off near the line of the iron gate to the left, smelling flowers. I stepped inside and saw what was left of a prayer kneeler. Almost instinctually, I knelt down. I hadn't formally prayed like that in forever, but it seemed so appropriate... so necessary at that moment. My prayers began, and came rushing out like a torrent: prayers for my family, for Benny, for the boys, for Karen. *thank you, god for her!* And finally I prayed for Howie and Mrs. Nesto. When I'd finished, I stayed in position for a little while, knowing I'd have to go back home in a couple of days, knowing the heartache that would be waiting for me.

A little mist had started to fall through the missing roof of the monastery, and as I angled my face up to the sky, I saw Karen sitting silently and watching me, almost as though she were meditating. I finally shattered the quiet. "Whatcha thinking?"

Her eyes took me in for one more second before she responded, "That I hope you're going to fuck me again, Francis."

Signing the cross, I stood up and said "Race you to the bottom."

Sandra O'Casey was usually at her happiest working the serving line at the soup kitchen in the basement of St. Paul the Apostle Church. But that Saturday morning found her melancholy and withdrawn, preoccupied with thoughts of her situation and what the coming weeks were to bring. Overwhelmed with feelings of loneliness and despair at having no one to talk with, she looked up briefly to see another girl about her age staring back, a smile on her lips. Sandra noticed instantly that she was pregnant too. Her heart leapt at this unspoken bond with the girl until their moment was broken by a wail from one of the two other children the girl had in tow and then the stern voice of Sister Evangelista, who oversaw the line like a guard from the movie "Brute Force." Like a rusty gate swinging open, she squawked, "Miss O'Casey, are you unwell? Your heart does not seem to be in your duties this morning. Service to the Lord and His flock requires your full devotion. I'm going to have one of the other ladies take over for you so you can go home and tend to what ails you." Sister Evangelista turned and swept through the door to the kitchen without giving Sandra the slightest chance to respond. But rather than argue with the sister, Sandra piled as much food as the pregnant girl's tray could hold and then began removing her apron.

The walk back home was a short one, and as soon as the door swung open, she knew something was different. Her senses were over-loaded with two of her favorite scents: her father's Old Spice and her mother's White Shoulders perfume. She had barely made it into her very girly bedroom, packed with all of the unnecessary trappings a spoiled only-child could want when her father's voice rang out from down the hall. "Princess, is that you? Your mom and I were just getting ready to head out for that Knights of Columbus weekend up in the Catskills. Are you sure you won't change your mind and go with us? It's going to be fun. We can wait for you. There's still time."

"No, thank you, Daddy. I'm kind of over that whole thing. Besides, I'm really tired. I think I'm just going to take it easy and catch up on my reading this weekend."

"Jack, leave her alone. She already said she didn't want to go. She's old enough." Sandra's mother stepped into the bedroom and bent down to give her daughter a kiss. "Now, there's plenty of food in the fridge, and if anything goes wrong, call your Auntie Maggie. I left some money on the coffee table inside the *Redbook* in case you want to do something fun. I love you, pet."

"I love you too, Mommy."

Her father replaced his wife for a turn at saying goodbye. He was a strikingly handsome and masculine man when he wasn't having to wear the NYPD hard-ass persona. :We'll be back on Monday morning, angel.

You know I can't handle that Sunday night traffic. If you need to, call Aunt Maggie."

"Mom already gave me the speech."

"Well, if anything goes <u>really</u> wrong, you can always call the precinct. Betcha she didn't say that one." Sandra forced a smile and offered her forehead for a kiss. "Be a good girl. I know you will... 'cause that's what you are." He winked as the guilt from this harmless phrase that she'd heard a million times before knotted up Sandra's stomach. The detective planted a soft kiss just above her eyebrow and then took her hand to add an extra kiss. He slipped a $100 bill into her palm and wrapped her fingers over it, landing a couple of pecks on her knuckles. "Get yourself some sweets or something," he whispered. "I love you."

"I love you too, Daddy." She sat motionless until the front door closed and both locks clicked loudly. Throwing herself back into the arms of her mattress, she grabbed a down pillow and wailed into it like a wounded animal. Sapped of all her energy, Sandra couldn't even raise the mask, choosing instead to cry herself to sleep.

Several hours later, she was awakened by the horn and siren from a Rescue One fire engine racing by. As she blinked the sleep from her eyes, she could tell that dusk had set in and, rolling over, saw that it was almost 7 o'clock. Reclaiming her senses from the Sandman little by little, Sandra contemplated filling the rest of her night with muffled sobs in the dark... since part of her felt like that's what she ought to do. "Fuck that," she said aloud. "It's Saturday night in the Big Apple and I'm gonna have some fucking fun!"

Seemingly committed to shredding, more than shedding, the Catholic school, good-girl uniform, she sprang from her bed and flung open the doors of her closet on the hunt for something funky and sexy. It would've had to have been a hunt since most of her clothes were childish, but there was one form-fitting black dress and a pair of heels that

Danny had requested, but that she'd never had the courage to wear out of the house. Tossing them onto the bed, she strutted into the bathroom to turn on the shower as Donna Summer wailed through the air. Sandra was committed to doing something that night that she'd never done before: go out alone. Knowing that the shower would take a few minutes to warm up, she danced to the coffee table in the living room and found the $50 her mother had left in the pages of the magazine. With the hundred from her father and another hundred of her own, she knew she'd have enough to have a good time, even in the city where it cost money to breathe.

Sandra probably would not have gone prancing back through the apartment with such naked abandon had she known that Mr. Krause, a neighbor from across the street, had held vigil in his window every day for months, hoping this moment would arrive. With the corner of a pillow stuffed in his mouth and a hand stuffed down his pants, the old pervert was finally getting to worship his blonde goddess personally.

In what seemed like no time, Sandra had sung and danced her way into and out of the shower, and found herself standing like a dream in the midst of her own hazy, foggy world, dripping dry in front of a full-length mirror. For a moment... and for the first time... even she was taken by her own vision. Her fingers traced the reflection of her outline, skating over her glistening, porcelain skin... down past her small, firm ski slopes from which two erect cherries leapt... down to the light dusting of golden fleece that met at the intersection of two perfectly smooth legs that seemed to go on forever. Sandra allowed herself a devilish smile as she involuntarily stroked her taut skin. "Maybe I'll just go out like this. Wouldn't that be fun?"

Mr. Krause may have very well died of a coronary had it not been for the clouded-over windows in the O'Casey's apartment. Even his imagination couldn't have topped the reality behind the steam. With a newfound lean towards naughtiness, coupled with gazing at her own nakedness and letting her fingertips graze sensually over that form, there was little point in denying that Sandra was becoming more and more aroused. Even as she shook her hair to and fro to the music's beat and enjoyed the warmth from the blow drier on her upper body, her erect nipples echoed the tingling of her gooseflesh. Wiping a streaking swath from the mirror, she found it increasingly difficult to focus as she applied the very little makeup that her perfect complexion required. She added a final stroke of rouge and leaned back to admire her effort more completely, barely realizing that the makeup brush handle was snaking downward, passing between her breasts and over her stomach on its way to her womanhood. Her vagina was slick with moisture and provided very little resistance as the probe slid inside her. She moaned softly, almost leaning against the mirror while her increasingly frequent breath added steamy flames to an already re-clouding reflection.

Sandra rocked back and forth on her heels and tiptoes as the handle repeatedly penetrated and retreated from her quivering folds. With a great, shivering sigh, she removed the brush and dropped it, reinserting all of the fingers on her right hand except for the pinky, while her thumb massaged and stroked her clitoris. Her moaning and breathing grew more and more rapid as each digit flailed about less controllably and her left hand kneaded her chest. Finally, with a breathy grunt and a softly vibrating moan, her body shook like a leaf in a windstorm as orgasm overcame her. She panted and cracked open one eye, staring directly at her own gaze, allowing a mimicked smile that glittered like a secret-for-two in her reflection's eye. Although slightly lightheaded when she resumed standing up straight, Sandra felt amazing and slowly withdrew her gleaming fingers, thinking for a moment before rubbing them on her neck and wrists, touching a moist fingertip behind each ear.

In a matter of minutes, she had donned her dress and heels, adding a gold anklet and a black clutch to her armor. Three cabs screeched to a halt when she stepped onto the sidewalk and raised her arm. "Where is the lucky guy waiting that I'm taking you to see, gorgeous?" the driver asked as Sandra scooted into the backseat of one of the taxis.

"Ha!" she scoffed. "No guys."

"So you're just out for a night on the town, then? Did you call the fire department and warn them?" he replied jokingly.

"You're so sweet," Sandra said with a smile. "Yes, I'm going out, but I haven't yet decided on where. Any suggestions?"

"Well, looking like that, there's only one place that deserves you tonight:
Regine's, over on Park."

"Regine's it is, then." She sat back in the car seat with her clutch purse on her lap, and in a matter of minutes, they had pulled up in front of the carnival atmosphere outside of Regine's. The domino-like line of black and white limousines, one after the next, stretched for blocks along the curb. It was matched in length only by the crowd of partiers blocking the front entrance, each with the hope of getting in.

Without any idea about how to get past the half-a-fag doorman with the bottle blonde hair and bright red suit, Sandra just took a deep breath and strutted right up to him confidently. Before she could even open her mouth to try bullshitting her way inside, he lifted the velvet rope and said, "Welcome back, baby. Nice to see you again."

Afraid she'd be unmasked if she looked back, Sandra could feel the onlookers leaning in and gawking, trying to figure out who she was. One man said audibly, "I think that's Margaux Hemingway!" while she passed by the doorman and stroked his chest in appreciation just as she imagined movie stars doing. No one seemed to figure out that she wasn't... whomever they thought she was as one doorman after the next waved her through. The darkened club was even more outrageous inside than it was outside. Navigating the Eurotrash that Regine must've brought with her from Paris, the music was pounding almost as much as Sandra's heart. She didn't know if it was from fear, nerves or just plain adrenaline, but the sign for the ladies' room caught her eye and she headed in that direction to gather her bearings. Stepping inside, two very friendly girls were leaned over, snorting cocaine off of the sink counter. Just as she caught herself staring, one of the ladies noticed her. "Want some?"

Still afraid that someone might figure out she was an impostor, Sandra blurted out, "Sure." Painfully aware that she had no idea how she was supposed to do whatever they'd offered, she walked toward the sink and took the straw from the incredibly beautiful Latina lady. Attempting to do the same thing she'd seen them do, Sandra bent over, making her blonde hair cascade onto the counter.

"Let me help, baby," the other lady, an equally beautiful black woman, offered, gathering Sandra's hair into a pony tail. She was grateful for the assistance because the lady held the hair tightly and sort of controlled Sandra's head. Before she knew it, four lines were up her nose and she rose almost instinctively to look into the mirror. As she grabbed and pinched her nose, she watched the reflection of the two women tongue-kissing one another. Although Sandra had never seen anything like that before, somehow they seemed perfect together in that place and at that moment. So she bent back down and inhaled a couple more lines of blow before popping back up again, screaming silently within, "Wow! I'm so high!"

Looking again into the mirror, unsure whether they were darting or dragging, Sandra's eyes shone like disco balls in the middle of the dance floor. A voice broke her hypnosis. "I'm Monique," said the black girl."

"And I'm Carmen. That dress is fabuloso, mami," added the Latina.

Sandra could do little more than smile, pinch her nose and sniff. The two ladies had stepped closely to either side of her. Finally, her voice spoke as if on its own, "Thanks. I'm Sandra. It's really nice to meet you both. And thanks for the... stuff."

The two women exchanged an amused glance. "Stuff!?!" Monique shrieked. "Girl, you know how good that 'stuff' is? Calling it 'stuff' is an insult! This is <u>shit</u>, girl!"

Sandra couldn't keep herself from bursting out with a full-bodied guffaw. Carmen started laughing along too, resting her hand on Sandra's hip. "And I have all the 'stuff' you want, baby." Noticing that Monique had a thin line of blood turning the white residue on her upper lip a dark pink, Carmen wet a tissue and handed it to her. "Come on. Get it together, Moni. The night hasn't even begun." Carmen definitely seemed to be in charge.

"So who are you here with, sweetie?" she asked Sandra.

"Oh, no one," came the reply.

"Perfect! Now you are! Hang out with us and have a little fun." Sandra registered that Carmen brushed back her hair and licked the side of her neck... but she just couldn't get herself to care. "Ai! I love the taste of vanilla."

Throwing the wadded tissue into the sink pointedly, Monique snapped, "So, what? That means you're tired of chocolate? I'm sick of this bullshit!" she added as she stormed out the bathroom door.

"Never mind her," Carmen reassured Sandra unnecessarily. "She's just a little bit temperamental; that time of the month, you know." Sandra quietly wished to herself that she could say the same thing. Carmen handed her a Quaalude, saying, "You did a lot of coke. You better take this when we get to the table, okay, mami?"

Carmen led Sandra through the sea of bodies to a table in what appeared to be an exclusive section in the very center of the club, where Monique was already seated, watching a waiter pour glasses of Dom Perignon. Carmen slid in next to Monique, followed by Sandra, but the African beauty slid a few inches away from the Latina. "You're not going to stay mad at me all night, are you, Moni?" Carmen shouted above the pounding music.

"You hear that?" Monique shouted back, glaring. "Gloria Gaynor. 'I Will Survive.' And I will."

Carmen pursed her lips into a playful pout and gave Monique a little shove. "Ai, that was good, mami. But you know this is my song. So gimme a smile and bring yo survivin' little ass on. Let's show these tourists how to dance!" Pushing her friend out of the circular table, she grabbed her hand and dragged her onto the floor.

For the moment, Sandra was content to sit at the table since she had been replaying Carmen's instructions over and over since the bathroom. Popping the Quaalude into her mouth, she chased it with a flute of champagne that tasted like gold ginger ale. She poured another glass and realized that her horniness was returning with each abdomen-thumping pound of the sound system. Grateful that she'd worn no panties, Sandra's fingers were buried inside of herself again in moments until her pussy was dripping onto the vinyl cushioned seat.

Carmen returned to find Sandra slumped at the table with her eyes rolled back. "Oh, chica, was that Rorer too much? Monique is back in the bathroom with some more blow if you want some of that."

Sandra's attention snapped immediately back to Carmen. Withdrawing her hand from her crotch, she stuck both fingers into Carmen's mouth, and the Latina knew instantly what she smelled and tasted. She grabbed Sandra and started kissing her passionately. While their mouths explored one another's lips, faces and necks, their hands did likewise all over each other's bodies. In short order, a small crowd started to gather and watch.

At some point Sandra snapped back to her senses for a moment and half-heartedly questioned what she was doing. She had never been that high before; she didn't know if she could stop... or if she wanted to stop. Before she could think about the answer, though, the scene was interrupted by Regine herself, who had made her way over to the table to see what the commotion was about. "This is a respectable establishment, ladies," she said jokingly. Sandra and Carmen stopped, looking almost like chastised schoolgirls. "Oh, I'm only teasing. I just wanted to introduce myself. I am Regine. It is my name on the door."

"Sorry. It's nice to meet you. I'm Sandra."

"Enchantée, cheri. I know you, don't I? You are with Ford Models, oui?"

Sandra lied instantly. "Yes."

"I knew this. You have the classic 'American blonde' look that Eileen loves so much. Has she introduced you to Ralph Lauren yet?"

Sandra didn't know how deeply she had already dug herself into a hole, so she went with the truth. "No." She didn't even know who he was.

"Oh, she will. He will love you, cheri. Well, I must get back, but I wanted to see what was so interesting over here. And now I have! Au revoir. You two have a good time, oui? It's my pleasure to have you here."

"Oh, thank you very much. Mine is the... all... pleasure," Sandra stumbled, but Regine had already made her way out of sight.

"Mami, you are too funny!" Carmen said. Her mind was racing with thoughts about what a moneymaking thoroughbred Sandra would be if only Carmen could keep the scumbags away long enough to introduce her to the Arabs. She knew they'd pay big money... and it wouldn't be long before they got there. "You know what? We should have some dinner; its going to be a long night. We've gotta pace ourselves. Drink this," she added, sliding a glass of water towards Sandra. "I'm going to order us some food."

Sandra watched and listened carefully to everything Carmen did and said, and was extremely impressed to hear her order from the waiter in French. So that, when Carmen asked her age, Sandra snapped back, "Seventeen," before even considering whether she should lie.

"Perfect," Carmen replied.

"Why's that perfect?" Sandra asked immediately.

Deciding that she needed to change the subject quickly, Carmen continued, "So tell me about yourself, Sandra. What kinds of things do you like? What do you want to do once you're all grown up, corazón?"

"Oh, I love reading and writing. I think maybe I'd like to be a journalist or something because the thing I'd like to do most of all is travel."

"Bingo!" Carmen thought to herself. Monique returned to the table, interrupting their brief talk. She was so stoned that she was practically glowing in the dark. Sitting in the booth like a zombie, her eyes looked like closed galls windows. An awkward silence fell on the table, but it was made less noticeable by the heavy bass in the music that continued to pound through the club and all of its patrons. By the time the food began to arrive, Sandra's high had leveled off a little bit. She didn't know if it was the coke or the Quaalude, but she had gotten her wish for the night: she definitely felt more numb.

Ruth Nesto had been met by her sister in Queen Victoria Station the day she arrived in Montreal, and was finally able to let down her guard and grieve for her son. Howie had made the trip with her too, and his ashes went everywhere with her as she explored the streets of her new hometown. Turning onto St. Lawrence Street during the first Sunday after her arrival, Ruth was delighted to learn that they had a weekly craft fair there that boasted some really unique and gorgeous items. She had decided long ago to purchase something very special, and just knew that the St. Lawrence Street Fair was where she was going to find it. After a short while of browsing, she found herself standing in front of a color-ful stall, convinced that it was the place she'd find the small container in which to send Francis some of Howie's remains. She only wondered if they'd have it in Francis' favorite color. Ruth described what she had in mind to the lovely Indian lady behind the counter. Preeti smiled and said that she had just the thing... and in purple too. She dug through a few boxes near the back of the stall and turned around with the perfect purple bottle in hand, complete with a pewter top that looked like the Queen's crown. She even slipped it inside a little, purple, cloth bag and exchanged it with Ruth for five U.S. dollars.

With her find in hand, Ruth next went in search of a café to have some tea and toast. Although the snooty waiter seemed less than thrilled to have to serve an "Englishwoman," Ruth was unfazed, and simply laid out an array of things that she'd brought with her. Removing the jar from her pocket, she used the teaspoon resting on the table to pour some of Howie's ashes into her new purchase. She replaced the pewter top, dropped the bottle into the purple bag, and then put that inside a padded, manila mailing envelope. Pulling a pen from her purse, she thought for a minute and began to write.

My dear Francis,

Please find enclosed this purple bottle. In it is a part of Howie for you. I'm sure you alone know where he would have liked to have his remains scattered. But I hope you will keep a little for yourself too so you boys will always be together. I guess that's why I bought you this little bottle in your favorite color. I also thought you and the other boys might like to have some things of Howie's to remember him by. So, I've enclosed the key to our apartment. If you and Howie's friends would empty it for me and take whatever you want and then give the rest of it to the Salvation Army, I would be very grateful. I just can't do it. And I just can't imagine living there without my boy. I hope you understand. I will miss you, Francis, and will always think of you as my second son. I know that the two of you were brothers in every sense and how much you loved each other. So please take care of yourself and remember Howie in your prayers.

With love,

Ruth Nesto

As Ruth was paying for her breakfast, she asked for directions to the Montreal General Post Office, which, like the GPO on Eighth Avenue in NYC, never closed. She had included her letter before sealing the package and told the clerk that she wanted to mail her parcel to the U.S., to be delivered the next day. "I'm sorry, madame," he told her, "but Tuesday is the earliest it can get there."

"That will be fine," Ruth replied. "How much do you need?"

"Ten dollars, please," the clerk said, filling out the paperwork and stamping the package in all the necessary places. Ruth handed over the money and the package, letting her hand linger on the envelope for one last moment. The clerk took the envelope and tossed it into the mail bin as it rolled by. "Will there be anything else, madame?" She just shook her head and he returned the gesture with a smile. Ruth turned and walked slowly over to the heavy brass door. With a labored shove, she was through the door and back into the sunlight... in an attempt to continue on with her life.

I had never eaten a meal in my entire life that required three hours to consume. Not counting the ones that my mother had fixed for the family, I'd never had a meal that was entirely made to order either. Then again, like myself, I doubted my mother had ever heard of "Pheasant Under Glass," much less eaten it. Benny had been absolutely right about the Reservoir Inn restaurant, and it seemed like we were going to be there another hour at least since Karen and I had just ordered complimentary after-dinner drinks of crème de menthe and Drambuie. The great, rustic fireplaces in every room had given a warm and peaceful feeling to the evening and allowed for some very easy conversation between the two of us. "It's hard to believe that's where the water in The City comes from," I said, looking out at the reservoir through the bay window by our table.

"They go to great lengths to protect it. I know from personal experience that you can get a ticket for skinny dipping in it." We both laughed. "So I shared a bit of a secret with you. Your turn."

I thought for a moment. "I feel guilty a lot of the time because I'm my parents' only son, and I'm afraid I disappoint them."

"Well, that's a very human thing to feel. I think everyone feels that. But you've been through a lot, Francis. Don't you think maybe you're being hard on yourself?"

I didn't really feel like continuing our discussion in that direction, so I changed gears a bit. "You know? I've always had this dream about being a florist ever since my parents took me to the Botanical Gardens in the Bronx."

"So that's how you got to know Benny?" Karen asked.

"Yeah. I saw an ad in 'The Voice,' looking for a part time florist. It wasn't exactly the most manly pursuit, so I kept it to myself that I wanted to go. And since the address was in my neighborhood, I waited until the last second to head over for the interview. When I get there, 20 or 30 people are already in this, like, crowdish line. I figure my chances are for shit, and I'm a little nervous about standing there forever where everyone could see me. But then Benny comes out, walks down the row, looking everybody over. I have no idea why, but when he reaches me, he points me in the direction of his office and asks me to go wait for him there. As I'm walking away, I hear him telling all the other applicants, 'Thank you for coming and good luck in your search for work.' There are all these groans until they notice that he's also passing out ten dollar bills and shaking hands with everyone in line. He was saying things like, 'Thanks for your time,' and 'Have breakfast on me.' Stuff like that.

"So I'm standing in his office, wondering what's going to happen, wondering if he's a fruitcake or something with a taste for Irish boys." Karen laughed, eyes sparkling. "Well, he was a florist, remember?" I added as justification. "Anyway, he walks in right past me and I hand him my application. He just takes it, wads it up into a ball and drops it into the trash. My head's spinning; I have no idea what's going on or what his deal is. I think maybe he's just fucking with me, but he asks my name and I tell him. Can't hurt, right? Well, he shakes my hand and says, 'Benny Levine. You start Monday, right after school. You are in school, right?' I nod... totally clueless. 'Good. Three p.m., then, and don't be late. Now here's twenty bucks. I've got a lot to do, so go have lunch on me.'

"I started to walk out, not knowing what had just hit me, but I turned back for a second. 'Sir, may I ask you a question?'

"'I've only got time for one, so let me guess: Why'd I pick you without an interview, application, nothing. Right?'

"I respond, 'Well, I don't want to seem ungrateful or anything, but yeah. You don't know anything about me.'

"Benny leaned in with that million dollar smile and said, 'Son, I'm from the neighborhood too. I know all about the Doonans, and so I know all about your integrity and work ethic. Besides, I've only gotten to where I am through gut feelings, and you're not going to prove my gut wrong, are you?' He gives me a wink and I'm speechless. 'Now, like I said, I've got a full plate today, so you introduce yourself to Chonley on the way out and we'll see you on Monday.'

"Of course, I hadn't worked there long before I found out about the answering machine and Benny's 'lady friends,' so it was laughable once I realized that he was about as queer as Warren Beatty."

"Well," started Karen, "as one of those 'lady friends,' I can truly vouch for Benny's taste in sexual partners."

We both chuckled a bit and I said, "I kind of wondered, but I didn't want to get into your business."

"Oh, it's not a problem. In fact, I'm very proud to say that I regarded Benny and myself as lovers once."

"Well, we both know that Benny has superb taste," I replied.

She stroked my cheek. "Aw, you're sweet, Francis. We met when I was in college... when I was working at Gino's, as a matter of fact. I couldn't take my eyes off of him. He was just so elegant and charming. Everyone loved him. Anyway, he was a regular and he sent me a note on the back of his monogrammed handkerchief one day, inviting me out for dessert. A couple of my girlfriends who also worked there giggled and called me 'Daddy's Girl' and things like that, but I knew that this was a man who was going to teach me things, so I walked over to his table and told him that I'd love to have dessert with him... and that I'd be keeping the handkerchief. Well, that dessert lasted for almost three years. And I knew from the beginning about his wife... and I even knew about the answering machine and his thing for taking Spanish ladies to the 'Me Tarzan, You Jane' room at the Skyline Hotel on Tenth. But I didn't see the need to let him know that I knew. Benny gave me something that went so far beyond sex that it didn't matter. It's why we remained so close after we stopped sleeping together. Benny and I are like soul mates in a special way and probably always will be."

"I know exactly what you mean," I replied.

———————————— ✣ ————————————

By the time Sandra was tapping at the surface of the oval-shaped dish that had been placed before her, Monique seemed to have returned from the land of the zombies. "You never had crème brûlée before, mami?"

"But mine's like a rock. Won't this crack my teeth?"

Carmen smiled. "Only the top is that way. It's like hard candy. It's what happens when you burn sugar. That's what crème brûlée means: burnt cream. Just crack through the top and it's a sweet custard underneath. Try it. No one does it like Regine's. Here," she continued, "this will make you like anything." She poured Sandra another full glass of Dom Perignon; the table was on its fourth bottle.

"If only Francis could see me now," Sandra said to herself, thinking at the same time that it was weird for her to be thinking about him when she was out on the greatest night of her life, living like royalty must. Pausing momentarily to keep the bubbles in the champagne from making her sneeze, Sandra watched as three men approached their table. For a second, she wondered if the drugs and champagne were making her imagine it. They all looked as though they'd stepped out of "Lawrence of Arabia," wearing sheet-like robes with smaller versions on their heads, bound by black bands. They were all dark-skinned and very good looking. Carmen obviously knew them, because as they stopped next to the table, she addressed them.

"Just in time for dessert, gentlemen."

"Carmen, you're so silly. We just finished it," Sandra giggled.

"They're having something else for dessert, little mami." She turned back to the Arabs and stood. "Your Highness, may I have the pleasure of introducing to you my good friend, Sandra?"

"It looks as if the pleasure will be all ours," one of the men said, reaching his hand out toward Sandra.

"Sandra, this is His Royal Highness, Crown Prince Mansour bin Asad. His Royal Highness, Prince Ali... and His Royal Highness, Prince Omar." Each man offered his hand in succession, planting a light kiss on the back of Sandra's.

Still clearly altered, Monique stood and offered her hand. "Your Majesties, it's an honor to see you all again." In an unmistakably cold manner, only one of the three men looked at Monique and offered a simple, curt nod. The other two had their gazes transfixed on Sandra.

"May we sit with you, Carmen, habibi?" Mansour crooned.

"By all means, Majesty." Carmen stepped aside so that Prince Mansour could sit next to Sandra. Had she been slightly less affected, it would have unnerved her the way he inspected her for several long, awkward moments... as though she were a racehorse. When Sandra finally noticed and a self-conscious look fell over her face, he even offered her a sugar cube of sorts. Reaching beneath his robes, his hand emerged with a large, solitary diamond, from which hung a thick gold chain.

"May I?" he asked, draping the chain on Sandra's shoulder, near her neck. "I was trying to determine what was missing from such a visage of perfection, and I have found it. Please accept this small tribute to your beauty."

"I don't know what to say," Sandra exclaimed.

"Say yes, baby," Monique interjected, reaching for the necklace. "Turn around and I'll put it on you." Seeming more an attempt at staying in the picture than being helpful, Monique's eyes could barely contain their jealousy.

The prince stood. "A word, habibi?" Carmen followed Mansour to the bar as Sandra, almost too excited to believe this was all happening to her began pelting Princes Ali and Omar with questions.

"Is this for real or are you guys playing a joke on me?"

"I assure you this is no joke," Ali replied.

"And you three guys are seriously princes?" she continued.

"Ali and I are," Omar responded. "But His Highness, Prince Mansour is actually a <u>Crown</u> Prince. That means that he rules our nation in the place of the ailing king."

"What nation is that?" Sandra fired back.

"It is in the Middle East, but Americans find it very difficult to pronounce... correctly." Without absorbing the insult, Sandra sat staring in amazement, stroking the chain and fingering its diamond. From the weight of the necklace alone, there was no question that it was real. "You would like our country. It is very beautiful."

"Isn't it mostly sand?" Monique asked, handing Sandra what appeared to be a tube of lipstick and tapping her nose discreetly.

She nodded in understanding as Ali turned his attention briefly to Monique. "Well, yes, there is a great desert region, painted with sand as beautiful and golden as Sandra's hair. We have nothing as tedious and unappealing as <u>jungles</u>." He accentuated the word pointedly to drive home the racial insult, watching as Sandra tried to inconspicuously snort more cocaine from the bullet she'd been passed.

Carmen, meanwhile, had dropped her air of deference and was negotiating hard over her new thoroughbred. "Majesty, I can honestly say that I've never come across a girl so perfect. She's what we call here in America 'Grade A,' and there has been a lot of interest in the room for her tonight. I saved her for you specifically, but you're going to have to make it worth my while. After all, how often do you find a perfect, blonde virgin who wants nothing more than to travel... to see the world... all lands, far and exotic?"

"So she would be willing to come back with me?" Mansour asked.

"She told me earlier tonight that it's what she wants more than anything. But a certain Swiss businessman was asking me only an hour ago if I thought she'd like to see Europe... with her own apartment in Geneva." Carmen could see that her lie had gotten the wheels spinning in the prince's head. "She's definitely a girl who is looking to get ahead and wants to take the best opportunity available to her."

"Alright," he responded. "I'll return in a moment."

Slipping away into the bathroom, Mansour was annoyed that he had to wait for a stall to open up as the room was filled with the loud sounds of snorting and sniffing. At last, when a door swung open and two men stumbled out in a scene that looked like OPEC fused with disco chic, he entered, closed the door behind him, and put his left foot up on the toilet seat. Lifting up his robe and pant leg, he unzipped the holster on his calf and pulled out a pad of $100 bills. Counting out more than a hundred of them, he put himself back in order and exited the bathroom, dropping one of the bills into the attendant's plate.

Carmen remained by the bar, her smile growing as Mansour approached. "Ten thousand blessings for you, my friend," he said, kissing her on each cheek and slipping the folded cash into her hand. "And you will receive fifty times as many blessings if you can see the golden child safely to her final destination. ...So I trust that when we return to the table, you will demonstrate your friendship by persuading the girl where her best opportunity rests?"

"Of course," Carmen replied, sliding the money into her clutch. "What are friends for, after all?"

"You will share this evening with the girl and us, of course?"

"Yes, of course, Highness. Whatever you desire."

"But the abedin... she will be too busy, yes?"

"The 'abedin,' Majesty?"

"I believe you call them 'niggers' over here," he replied colorlessly, lifting her drink and setting it down on top of five freshly drawn $100 bills.

Sweeping up the money and draining her glass in one motion, Carmen smiled, winked at Mansour and replied, "As I said, Majesty, whatever you desire."

As the prince turned to drain the remnants of his glass, Carmen headed immediately for the table. It had been clear that Mansour wanted Monique gone before he returned.

Observing discreetly, Mansour watched as Carmen slid into the booth, took Monique's hand and whispered to her. Monique pulled away slightly as though Carmen had nibbled on her ear, looked down into her palm and then laughed a little more loudly than she would have had she been clean and sober. She fixed a broad smile on her face that hardly agreed with her eyes while draining the last of the bottle of Dom Perignon that had been sitting in the middle of the table, and then stood abruptly and stormed away into the crowd.

Carmen raised her glass in the direction of Mansour, only to see that he had been approaching during the exchange and was just a few feet away. Ali and Omar had noticed the crown prince's approach as well, and left the booth to allow Mansour to resume his place next to Sandra. "Forgive my absence, habibi."

"Habibi?" Sandra asked. "I don't know what that means."

"Oh, it is simple. It sort of means 'My dear' or 'My love.' It is a term of affection. That is all."

"It's pretty," Sandra commented. She'd never met anyone as suave and charming as this prince. And no one in Hell's Kitchen bore any resemblance to his sculpted good looks... his olive skin and jet black hair. Mansour continued to fascinate Sandra, answering her every question about his family and his childhood, his culture and his country. "Why, though," she finally inquired, "do you wear your robes over here too? I mean, I assume you wear them there because it's so hot, but it's much colder here. Aren't you uncomfortable?"

"It is just our custom. We wear Western clothing beneath our robes," he replied, pulling at one of the folds of cloth to reveal a lapel.

"Ah, I get it. Sorry. I'm so stupid. I thought that cologne you were wearing smelled familiar too. It's Hai Karate, right? No, you'd probably wear something more expensive, like Gucci or Royal Copenhagen or something."

Mansour leaned back and let out a great belly laugh. "No, it's called 'Mansour.'"

"Oh. Like your name. That must be why you buy it."

"Not exactly," he replied with a big smile. "It's an aroma of Sicilian limes that I have made exclusively for me. That's why they named it after me."

"You're pulling my leg."

Sandra's innocence only seemed to arouse the prince more. "I assure you I am not... unless you would enjoy me pulling on it." He put his hand on her knee and rubbed softly. She didn't seem to mind. "If you'd like, I will show you the bottle. I have one in my suite at the Plaza."

She hadn't seemed to take the hint. "Carmen, did you hear that? Mansour actually has his own cologne! They named it after him." Noticing that the two of them and the three princes had been sitting at the table by themselves for quite some time, Sandra added, "Hey, where did Monique go?"

Carmen wondered if Mansour's patience was wearing thin. "Um, she had to go meet up with some other friends, but we may see her later."

"I hope so," Sandra said, putting the lipstick bullet in Carmen's hand with a wink. "I forgot to give her this."

"No, that's yours, mami. Monique wanted you to have it." Sandra looked confused. "As a matter of fact, let me fill it up for you."

Watching Sandra's eyes pulse as she stared at the pouring cocaine, Mansour said, "It is a shame that all of those people on the dance floor are being denied the presence of two women as beautiful as yourselves. Why don't you join them?"

"Ooh!" Sandra squealed, taking Carmen's hand as she passed the bullet back. "Great idea! And this is 'Night Fever!' I fucking love the Bee Gees! C'mon!" Pulling the Latina behind her, they morphed into the being that occupied the dance floor, moving and flowing between one another and the people around them. Carmen was a fantastic dancer in her own right, but she could barely keep up with Sandra. Soon, the whole club seemed to be watching the pretty young Irish girl from the West Side and Carmen didn't know which of the two of them she liked the attention on more.

"You have no idea just how lucky you were to meet me tonight, corazón. You hit the lottery."

"What do you mean?" Sandra asked, almost breathless.

"Mansour... the prince? He is one of the wealthiest men in the whole world, mami. Not just America. The whole world. His family's money comes from oil. Black gold. You know, like J.R. Ewing? Only a million times more than that! And he has his sights set on you! That's bingo, baby! You got all the numbers!"

"Wow. Well, he's really nice. I never met anyone like him before."

"Of course not, mami. Not many sheikhs make it up to Inwood."

"I'm not from Inwood," Sandra snapped back, suddenly remembering that she was an impostor. "I'm from the Hamptons."

"Oh, yeah? Which one?" Sandra stopped moving altogether and just stood, unsure of what to say. "That's what I thought." Carmen smiled. "Bullshit. I know a homegirl when I see one. You can drop the act. It's okay, mami. You're in. That's the hard part. Now it's all about where you go from here, you know? Where are you really from?"

"I said. I'm from the Hamptons." Sandra walked off toward the front entrance, but Carmen was right on her heels.

"Sandra, it's okay. I'm your friend. You can trust me. I'm just trying to help you. Look. Me? I'm from Spanish Harlem. Yep. 113th and Pleasant Ave. I even went to Catholic school just like you... right?"

Sandra looked into Carmen's eyes warily. It was working. "Right. Holy Cross."

"Holy Cross?" Carmen asked. "Where's that? Up by the bridge?"

"43rd Street."

"Oh, shit! You're from the Kitchen, mami! You're just an around the way girl."

Sandra allowed herself a big grin. "But I can't believe you're from Spanish Harlem! You seem so international... like you're from somewhere else. What are you? Dominican?"

"Ai, no, baby. Nuyorican, tried and true. All twenty years en el barrio."

"Twenty years?" Sandra repeated in disbelief. "You're only twenty?"

"If I didn't know any better, I'd be insulted, but I think I know what you're saying, so I'll take it as a compliment. Yes, I'm only twenty, but I've lived well beyond my years."

"Wow. I don't know that I'll ever be as sophisticated and worldly as you if I live to a hundred!" Sandra exclaimed. The paranoia returned suddenly, though, once she remembered that she'd been unmasked. "So what now? Are you pissed that I'm not a model like everyone thought? I've got a couple hundred bucks I could give you for the food and champagne and all. I didn't mean to deceive anyone. I just wanted one night of something different than Hell's Kitchen."

"Sandra, stop," came Carmen's reply. "I told you. We're homegirls. And it ain't where you're from. It's where you're going. The princes are going to pick up the tab anyway. And this is just the beginning. He gave you that necklace, didn't he?"

"I get to keep this?" Sandra asked.

"You're so green, mami!" Carmen said, laughing. "I told you. It's only the beginning." She slipped nine or ten $100 bills into Sandra's hand. It was more than she'd ever touched before all at one time. "Here. I want you to have this." Before Sandra could reply, Carmen just kissed her deeply.

"But... but, why?"

"Because it's always my job to make other people feel good, but I like you and you make me feel good. Now, the real question is whether you want this to be the starting gate... or the finish line. It's up to you."

"I want it to be the starting gate," Sandra said without hesitation.

"Good. But you're seventeen, right? You live with your parents, right?" Sandra nodded. "What time do you have to be home? Or can you call them and say you're staying with a friend?"

"Oh, I don't have to be home at any certain time tonight... or tomorrow night either. My parents are away until Monday."

Carmen almost yelped with glee. "Well, mami, since this is only Saturday, prepare to have the two greatest days of your life."

"Really?"

"Would I lie to you?"

"It's so tempting." Sandra seemed poised to wiggle from the hook for a moment, just as Carmen caught glimpse of Omar, sent to see what had happened to the prince's investment.

"You like Mansour, right? You said he was nice."

"Yeah, he's real nice."

"And it doesn't cost you anything to hang out and have fun, right?" Sandra nodded. "Then don't let nothing stand in your way, baby!"

"Fuck yeah," came the reply.

"Let's celebrate with a little Vitamin C, mami." Pulling out the lipstick bullet again and looking around, they both snorted deeply, and with a hoot, Sandra waved her hands above her head and danced back toward the lights and music.

As the night had progressed and the club had become more and more crowded, Regine's started to look like something out of a Fellini film about Sodom and Gomorrah. In an "anything goes" world, boys were girls and girls were boys; everyone was doing everyone and everything else. After several more lipstick "touchups" and Dom Perignon, Sandra was practically giving Prince Mansour lap dances in the middle of the club. When the musical entertainment started up, Sandra froze and seemed transfixed by the singer. "Carmen... Carmen.... I don't feel good."

Panic rushed through the Latina briefly. She was worried that Sandra had overdone it. "What's wrong? You need some air?"

"Well, I'm a little woozy, but I think I'm seeing things. There looks like there's a naked, black giant screaming up there... and he's got boobs."

Carmen turned to see what Sandra was talking about. "You're so stupid, girl," she laughed. "That's Grace Jones, not a hallucination. She's just funky."

"Yeah, well she could play center for the Knicks."

Carmen laughed again. "Well, don't worry about it. We're going to leave pretty soon anyway."

"You mean it's over? I thought you said two days."

"No, Sandra. You've heard of Page Six?"

"From *The Post?*"

"Well, yeah, but there's also this groovy after-hours club Downtown called Page Six. You're going to love it more than this place!"

Sandra seemed to perk up. "That's good. The walls in here are starting to move closer and closer in... and we probably shouldn't be here when they reach the dance floor."

Cruising up Tenth Avenue in his father's car, Danny Albanese readied himself for the reaction he was sure to get once he crossed 43rd Street.
In the distance, he could clearly make out most of Francis' crew hanging
out on the stoop, blasting a boom box to add to the regular Saturday night
din. Although he had no love for Doonan, even the younger Albanese
could see how noticeably absent Francis and Howie were. The boys
were not alone in struggling to digest the feelings of loss they were all
experiencing. Danny, too, was a bit out of his element... scared, even, by
the hatred that was roiling in the neighborhood and the death that had
started to become commonplace. But that was a feeling he'd kept to himself. The son of J.R. Albanese didn't think things like that.

"Get the fuck out of here, you faggot!" Milk's voice pealed through
the night. "Go back to where you belong! You ain't shit!" Danny refused
to give them the satisfaction of looking over, but he was anything but
unaffected. He remembered clearly how he used to be best friends with
Milk when they played on the same little league team together years
ago. Lifting his arm and raising a solitary middle finger, Danny just kept
driving as far up Tenth as he could before making the right to head back
down Ninth to the only place he might find the respect he deserved: the
remnants of the Dante League Social Club. And even at that, he'd only
find respect there because his father was currently gone, holding court
downtown in Little Italy.

"I'm telling you: Hell's Kitchen is open prairie if we can bust some
heads and put ourselves where we need to be." Surrounded by career
criminals and killers, Johnny "Rugs" Albanese was making his move by
laying out his own map for taking crime in The City to new places and
new levels. "First, gambling. We can control that quickly. Those micks

are worse than the Spics; they'll bet on anything. And when they've run through what little scratch they've got, we run the shylocking too. Shakespeare even proved that it's second only to whoring as the oldest profession in the world. It's a fucking no-lose scenario." The colorfully named goons around the table seemed impressed with Albanese's forward-thinking, but it still remained to be seen whether it would produce profits. Johnny could indeed be a genius, but how smart was he really if he was a <u>broke</u> egghead?

Albanese read the skepticism in their faces, but he was prepared. "But this is the capper, my friends. And now, for the *piece de resistance....*" He removed a small glass bottle from his jacket pocket and set it on the table for all the men to see.

"What's that? Your nitro pills?" one man asked.

"No, Arturo, my friend. This is the future." He opened the bottle and shook its contents onto the table: three little, dull-white rocks."

"What the fuck is that? It just looks like street salt," Arturo questioned again.

"I'm sure you've all heard of free-basing?" They nodded in unison. "Well, this is the poor man's free-basing. They're calling it crack cocaine on the streets, and I've got a chemist out in Queens who cooks this shit up 24 hours a day. You won't believe how much of this shit we can produce from the smallest amount of the pure. The niggers concocted it in the first place from sheer greed, trying to stretch what little shit they could afford, and now it's their new slave chain. But it's going to be a fucking fortune for us. Not only is it cheap and easy to make, but once one of these moolies starts, they can't stop. We've got customers for life... customers who will do anything for more of it. Fuck, that goes for everyone. Those Irish Cocksuckers too. If we start giving this to our crews to hit the clubs and after hours joints with, we can make more money than you could imagine

AND get rid of all these fucking niggers and Spics and micks. It's a win-win, and there's no way this doesn't work."

J.R. could see by the changed looks on his colleagues' faces that they now saw the potential in the plan. One raised his glass. "To Johnny Albanese."

"Ah, salud!" they all chimed in.

The dark stretch limousine pulled away from the curb with Sandra, Carmen and the princes within. As it slithered on its way downtown, Sandra had spent more time looking at the inside of the car than most people spent looking at a whole car that they were interested in buying! It was nicer than most of the apartments that she'd ever visited. "I love your car," she said finally, her voice tinged with intoxication and flirtation.

"Well, thank you, habibi. I have one just like it in my own country, but I come here to New York so often that I leave this one here."

Sandra wasn't sure she understood. "You mean you own this? It's not a rental from one of those places in Jersey or out on Long Island?"

The prince seemed genuinely amused. "Oh, no. It is mine... just like the driver." Sandra shot a glance over her shoulder, but could not see beyond the tinted divider. "His name is Ivan. He is a very useful man. Do you know what a Swiss Guard is?"

"Aren't they the men who protect the Pope," Sandra ventured a guess. "And they're the ones who wear the colorful costumes, right?"

"Very good!" Mansour exclaimed. "Both smart and beautiful. Yes. Ivan used to be a Swiss Guard, but I required his special talents more than the Holy Father."

"Aw, c'mon," she replied "Don't those guys go through years of training and have to be specially picked and all? He would rather be a driver than guarding the Pope?"

"Well, he also assures the safety of my family and me... and anyone I care for." The prince stroked Sandra's cheek as she broke a grand, impressed smile. In reality, Ivan was nothing short of lethal. And he had found many other ways to be useful to the Crown Prince... for which he was richly rewarded.

"Here, honey," interrupted Carmen. "Let's not bother the prince about his employees anymore, okay? Let's just have fun." With that, she handed Sandra a glass of Dom Perignon.

She gulped a mouthful of the elixir and then turned back to the prince. "Sorry, Mansour. I didn't mean to be a nuisance."

"You're not, child. You're not," he responded, patting her on the head like a pet.

"Would you like some of this?" she asked, offering the bullet to Mansour.

He chuckled. "Oh, no, habibi. You are most kind, but I have never partaken of such substances. Islam forbids it." He could see that she was hypnotized by his every word. "I also do not drink. It would displease Allah.

"But...," he continued, "I would like to give you something." The prince produced an intricately designed gold ring from beneath his robes and slipped it onto Sandra's finger.

Her voice colored with insincere surprise and modesty, Sandra asked, "What is this for?"

"It makes me feel good to lavish someone that I like with gifts, habibi."

"But you already gave me this beautiful necklace," She replied, stroking the length of the chain before ending with the diamond, twisting it between her fingertips like a child with a marble.

"And it looks enchanting on you. You like these presents I give you, don't you?"

She wondered to herself how anybody could <u>not</u> like the more than $20,000 worth of jewelry she was wearing. "Of course, but...."

"But you just enjoy yourself, my dear," he interjected. "I am truly touched that you would think of my enjoyment in the midst of your own." Sandra's willingness to serve him aroused the prince a great deal, and his hand slipped behind his robes to stroke a growing erection through the material of his pants. But Mansour didn't want his masturbatory soundtrack to be muted just yet. The sound of Carmen and Sandra giggling and snorting and kissing and moaning only served to make his hard on throb more intensely. Hitting a button and speaking into the intercom, the prince said, "Ivan, why don't we turn around and ride through Central Park before heading downtown? It should be beautiful at this time of the morning."

Sandra squealed with excitement. "I've always wanted to ride through the park in a limo. This guy, Danny, once took me in a limo to the circus and I begged him to go through the park, but he wouldn't. He wanted to act all macho, like his father. They're mafia," she tried to whisper, a difficult thing when babbling on at a million miles a minute.

Ever the good businesswoman, Carmen decided that she needed to calm Sandra down before it annoyed the prince, so she put a Quaalude into her own mouth and grabbed Sandra to kiss her. With her tongue, Carmen transferred the Rorer into Sandra's mouth and then sensually poured champagne down her throat to ensure the sedation would be only moments away.

As the sun began to peek out from behind the Manhattan skyline, Ivan spoke through the intercom for the first time, "Page Six, your Majesty." Deep in the heart of Greenwich Village, the prince and his court stepped out of the car and disappeared inside the building just as quickly. They filed through the three stories of an even more uninhibited, "anything-goes" world than Regine's, past the packed bars and occupied pool tables of the first floor, through the massive dance floor of the second floor, and between the pair of icebox-sized security men guarding the dozen or so steps that led to the private lounge on the third floor. This was the V.I.P. room, where no one but celebrities and their whores and dealers were permitted. At 6:30 a.m. – and in the state in which the entourage found itself – those twelve steps up to the lounge felt like scaling Mt. McKinley. But when they arrived into their own individualized area, each partitioned off by plastic palm trees and velvet ropes, the group flopped down onto the leather couches and began tapping out lines onto the large, mirror-top table. Each area had its own private waitress, truly stunning women who were easily among the most beautiful looking creatures in Manhattan. Sandra thought to herself that, for someone so gorgeous, the waitress was remarkably inconspicuous, and had taken the group's drink order and disappeared in the blink of an eye.

"Your Highness!" A remarkably good-looking blonde emerged from the darkness and began walking toward the table.

Ivan stepped quickly into her path, but then retreated just as rapidly when the prince responded, "Eve! How fortunate for us that you are here! It has been a very long time, habibi." Carmen was watching this intruder carefully as well, but was certain not to lose her cool. "Omar, give me something appropriate to say hello to our old friend."

Prince Omar slipped his hand beneath his robes and pulled out what looked to be a sparkling ladies' watch. "Well, let me say hello appropriately then too." Eve sat on the very edge of the couch, across from the prince, and put both feet on the mirrored table. Her hands vanished below her skirt line, and it wasn't long before she was moaning and writhing. All three of the princes stared at her perfectly shaved pussy, watching reflections of her fingers violate and molest it over and over.

"Oh my God," said Sandra. "I can't believe she's doing that. Right her and out in the open. Who is that?"

"Competition, mami," came Carmen's response without ever looking at either Sandra or Eve. "But be careful. She's a friend of the prince."

Sandra failed to adopt Carmen's tone of discretion. "I can't believe the waitresses would allow that."

This amused Carmen, so she ventured a glance over. "Allow it? They wish they could do it." Judging by the look on her face, Sandra had clearly not understood the intention. "Honey, didn't you realize the waitresses are men?"

Sandra's eyes snapped immediately to the nearest waitress, probing her breasts and crotch. "No way," she exhaled incredulously.

"Little mami, look at their throats. Why do you think they call it an Adam's Apple? Only men have it."

Sandra didn't want to look more unworldly than she already did. "I can't believe I couldn't tell!"

"Most people can't. Look at that fat guy over there. See him? That's Tony Rocks. Big time mobster. He's in here almost every night and drops tons of cash on Therese over there," Carmen pointed to a tall, lean dream waiting at the bar. "He tries to get her to do shots with him, let him touch her booty, whatever. He just loves that she plays hard to get... and it keeps him coming back, truthfully. Only thing is, he doesn't realize that Therese is actually Terrence. But it's a dangerous game. The day he figures it out, they'll find Terrence on the bottom of the East River, filled up with rocks to weigh him down." Carmen raised both eyebrows, taking another drink of Dom Perignon. "That's where Tony Rocks gets the name, after all."

Their own waitress returned with three bottles of champagne and a tray full of glasses. "Here you are, your Majesty," she said, setting the last bottle on the table between Eve's open legs. Raising her voice slightly to make it over the loud disco music the DJ was blasting, she added, "Better make sure this doesn't slip in there, honey."

With her competitive streak up and seeing the opportunity to move with the prince's attention somewhere other than on Eve, Sandra took a deep snort from the bullet and stepped over to straddle the prince. "Time for something new," she cooed.

He seemed a bit surprised, but not unhappy, replying, "Meaning unused?" It was clear just how into here he was.

"Meaning untested," Eve interjected from over Sandra's shoulder.

"Meaning not old," Carmen added, grabbing Eve's arm as she began to step toward Sandra. "He's into her, honey. Just let it play out and ride along to take the scraps. Start a fight and we're all gone." She stuffed a couple of $100 bills down Eve's bust line. Eve was a business woman too... and just because she was blonde didn't mean she was stupid. To punctuate the deal, she began kissing Carmen while they each started rubbing the crotches of Princes Omar and Ali.

Sandra continued gyrating and nuzzling... and eventually kissing the prince, and whenever there was a break in the action, Carmen made sure that Sandra kept it up by keeping her filled with alcohol and coke. Everyone came and went... and came some more... over and over. Page Six seemed to be able to preserve the night; it was even darker inside than outside. After a few hours, Sandra was completely chemically altered in every way, and wouldn't have even been able to stay sitting up if it hadn't been for the back of the couch. In fact, if she had been able to move from where she sat, she would have noticed the large blood stain on the cushion beneath her.

As the waitress delivered the latest bottles of champagne in the early hours of the afternoon, Eve came charging back into the lounge, clutching the hand of an exceptionally large bodybuilder. "Prince Mansour, I'd like you to meet Lefty. He's got something you've just go to see!"

Lefty nodded a hello to the group as he sat down and started to take stuff out of his pockets while everyone watched closely. He had an odd-shaped glass tube, into which he put a little screen before adding what looked like a pebble-sized piece of Ivory soap. Tipping the tube up so that the rock rested against the screen, he put the tube in Eve's mouth and flicked a lighter, sending a large butane flame to dance near the top of the glass tube. Eve sucked in deeply, almost seeming to extinguish the flame with her breath. Smoke filled the glass tube before shooting down her throat. She partially moaned and partially exhaled a long "Whoa!" before dropping the red-hot pipe that had burned her fingertips.

She seemed to sink into oblivion as Lefty looked up and asked, "Who's next?" Carmen pushed Sandra forward before trying it herself, with a new glass pipe and screen emerging each time.

While more and more people gather around to smell the strange scent coming from the little rocks and watch this brand new method of getting high, the prince motioned to Ivan. "I am uncomfortable with this invasion of our gathering. Would you please clear our area... but procure some of this man's goods all the same?"

Ivan tapped Lefty on the shoulder and asked how much the drug cost. "I've got $25 pieces, Col. Klink. You want to try?"

"No thank you," came the response. "Just buy. I'll take ten of them."

"Well, do you want me to show you how to do it?" It wasn't clear if Lefty was more elated by the buy or intimated by the buyer.

"That's not necessary. I assume I can purchase the pipes and screens from you as well?"

"Of course," he replied. "The rock is $250, and the equipment is $25." Taking the items that Lefty handed over, Ivan slipped them into his coat pockets and handed back $300. You can keep the change." Lefty shook Ivan's hand before he added, "Now have a good evening."

"What? I ain't leaving. I came up here to talk to the blonde chick." He pointed over to where Eve, Carmen and Sandra were huddled together, cracked up like Burrow's Turkish Taffy.

"She's with us. You're not."

"Well, now I am."

Ivan demonstrated his expertise at keeping his cool. "This is a private party, hosted by my client over there, and you weren't invited. So now we're asking you to leave." He calmly but forcefully put a hand on Lefty's chest and started to walk him back toward the door.

"Get your fuckin' hands off me, Adolf," the irate dealer exploded. "Look, I don't know where you're from, ace, but I'll tell you where you're at. This is the United Fucking States of America, so you and your little camel jockey friend over there can just settle the fuck down and get the fuck out of my face. Unless you want me to do it for you."

This was no small threat coming from a man Lefty's size, but no sooner had the last word floated into the air than Ivan dropped and spun on his left foot to sweep his right leg around and leave Lefty on his back, beyond the ropes and plastic palm trees. Stepping towards the still-stunned bodybuilder, Ivan lifted him by his black leather jacket and dragged him to the lounge's stairs, tossing him headfirst down to the second level, where the two security guards gathered Lefty up and removed him from the club. Ivan began replacing the palm trees and velvet ropes.

Uncomfortable again with all of the unwelcome stares, the prince nodded to Carmen that he wanted to be entertained. Even as high as she was, Carmen was still a working woman, so she started to stroke Eve's breasts and kiss Sandra. In their state, the two women didn't need much more prompting than that. Soon, all of the focus was on Sandra as Carmen kissed and sucked her pale, exposed breasts, stroking her thighs and taking turns with Eve fingering the Irish girl's dripping vagina. Eve continued to shoot seductive glances at the prince while she kissed Sandra and pulled her fingers out only long enough to lick her fingers, unaware that they were coated with the miscarrying child of Danny Albanese.

I awoke from a deep and heavy sleep to the smell of bacon and the sound of pouring rain. My soul was sated from the intense and passionate love Karen and I made the previous night, but the effort my body had given left it hesitant to leave regeneration mode. I could hear Karen tooling around in the kitchen. *how funny. i love to cook to joan armatrading too. she's even got on "down to zero." i need some extra-sweet coffee; the demons are on hiatus, but they're not gone altogether.*

As I trudged into the kitchen and went straight to the coffee pot, Karen looked up. "Good morning, handsome." Although my eyes were fixed on the pouring coffee, the rest of my face acknowledged and returned the greeting. "And thanks for the good night too," she added with a mischievous smile. "You know, I was thinking that, since it's raining, maybe we should go home later this afternoon. The radio says that it's not supposed to stop until midnight, so there's no real point to staying until the morning. But, if we leave here by 5 p.m., we'll miss the traffic getting back into The City; it should be smooth sailing all the way home."

"Works for me," I replied. "Besides, I love driving while the windshield wipers slap away at the rain."

"Oh, good, because it puts me right to sleep. I hope you don't mind driving back again, then."

"Not at all. Holy shit. Is it really two o'clock? I didn't realize I'd slept that late."

"You obviously needed that sleep, sweetheart," Karen said. "You've been burning the candle at both ends and you'll see that getting back to The City is going to be a shock on your system. Now eat before it gets cold."

I consumed less of a breakfast than I normally would have since I decided to go for a run in the rain. It required far more of an effort than normal. *my emotions and body are colliding. a little scary. i just wish i knew what i was going back to; it'll be all-new ground. there's something to be said for routine... for the regular. i really miss my mother and father... hell, even my sisters. as soon as i can, i'm going out to visit them in long beach.* I didn't know if the running was flushing something from my body or if the rain was washing something from my soul, but a feeling began to overtake me... the realization that my life would never be what it was again. *perhaps this is what growing up feels like... becoming a man... not just sticking your pecker in a girl. life is all about change, and change is good but that doesn't make it any less intimidating. after all, the demons are only under a momentary cease-fire.*

I stood in a great, empty field for awhile, allowing the cool rain to pour over me, leaving a shiny coating on my face and hair like the sheen covering the soft green carpet of grass that stretched out ahead. That bit of soul-searching provided me with the added energy to start a full-out sprint back towards Karen's place. As it came into view and I saw her on the porch, waiting for me with one of those enormous terry cloth towels that only the rich seem to know where to buy, I was struck by a feeling I hadn't known in some time: that I was running toward something instead of away.

It was typical for Romeo T to walk the streets and avenues of Hell's Kitchen at a clip, but seeing something that stopped him dead in his tracks was anything but typical. In the parking lot next to Francis' building, a creepy little guy climbed out of a truck looking like he'd just slept in it. He was wearing a pair of black jeans and a white tee shirt, both of which were far too tight for him, and he rode, more than walked, in an oversized pair of cowboy boots that matched his enormous "The King" belt buckle. Because of the rain that was falling, it was easy to see the box of Camel cigarettes through the rolled-up material of his right sleeve, and only an unhealthy amount of Brylcreem could've maintained the perfect duck's ass hairstyle he was sporting in the back. Before moving on, Romeo took a second to chuckle at how comical the guy looked, wondering if he'd stepped out of a time warp or if he was an extra on "West Side Story." Little did he know, though, that that creepy little guy was there to provide gasoline to throw on the fire that had been sparked recently in Hell's Kitchen. If Romeo would've looked more closely at the truck, he would've noticed that it had Florida plates, and if he could've peeked beneath the tarp in the back, he would've seen that it was full of guns and explosive material. And as if to punctuate the creepy little man's indiscretion about his payload, he had been asleep in the cab of the truck since he'd arrived from Miami early that morning... and was late meeting his buyers.

Everyone in McHale's Bar and Grill noticed its newest patron as soon as he stepped through the door, but only Kelly the Mick and Colin Garvan were there to meet with the miniature Elvis wannabe. They'd already had a burger and several rounds apiece by the time the man known only to them as the King walked up and said in an unmistakable Southern drawl, "My apologies to y'all for the lateness. I nodded off in my truck."

Everybody shook hands while Colin Garvan broke the ice, "It's not a problem. We were just checking out the game. You want a beer? A burger? They've got the best in The City here."

The King's eyes were darting back and forth to take in the place. He had obviously been in the same situation a thousand times before, but the fact that he had a perfectly clean record was why he was here. "Yeah, thanks. A Bud Draft, please."

As soon as the barmaid had brought a new round of beers, Kelly the Mick got right down to business. "So you have what we need?"

The hillbilly nodded while he drained his mug with a big grin. "Oh, yeah. All you boys need." He stood up and started to walk to the bar, apparently unwilling to wait for the raspy-voiced barmaid to return. The Wurlitzer jukebox caught his eye, though, and he made a detour to punch in an array of Hank Williams songs. As he continued on to the bar and his first song selection began to whir to life, Jimmy McHale, who'd been going over receipts near the back of the bar, took great enjoyment in hitting the jukebox's eject button. The King turned as the song stopped abruptly and said in his best Southern gentleman voice, "'Scuse me there, sir, but I just put that on."

Jimmy kept his poker face and pointed to a sign beneath the TV: "There will be no music during sporting events." He flicked a quarter in the King's direction and added, "And if I ever get the notion to enforce it, I'm gonna make a rule about no talking either."

The whole bar began to laugh as the King abandoned his empty mug and returned to the table. "Let's finish things up and get on out of here." Colin Garvan put some money down on the table and the three men moved toward the door.

"Welcome to New York City, Elvis." Jimmy McHale's thick New York accent sounded. "Y'all come back now, ya hear?"

The King led Kelly the Mick and Colin Garvan through the rain towards the parking lot where he'd left their merchandise. As they approached the truck, Kelly the Mick asked, "Are you taking us to where you stored the stuff?"

"What do you mean?" the King responded. "It's right here."

"Under that fucking tarp?" The King nodded. "What are you, a fucking imbecile? You left the stuff under a fucking tarp... unprotected... in this neighborhood... while you went to meet us? What the fuck's wrong with you?"

It was clear that the Southerner wasn't following why Kelly the Mick was so upset. "It's right there, just like I left it."

"You better fucking hope it is," Kelly the Mick shot back. "And where exactly are we supposed to check it out? Did you notice the traffic going up Tenth Avenue? Did it occur to you that we're out in the fucking open?"

"I didn't think it would be a problem," the King replied meekly.

"Well, it fucking is. Now shut your fucking mouth while I think."

"I need to get going, though."

"You'll leave when I'm done with you, you fucking yahoo." The King could tell by the look in Kelly the Mick's eyes that this was not a rational man, and although he'd dealt with plenty of violent people in his life, this was the first one that he was confident would shoot him just to see what color his blood was. Kelly the Mick turned to Colin. "Call Brian and tell him to come over here. We'll do the inspection and drop-off both at the same time. It's Sunday, so there shouldn't be a problem with wandering eyes." Colin darted across Tenth to place the call.

"Can I at least get out of the rain? Sit inside the truck, I mean?"

"I want to take a look real quick... just to see what we've got here." The King walked back and lifted one end of the tarp so Kelly the Mick could take a peek. He saw what appeared to be MAC-10 machine guns, .45 and 9mm pistols, hand grenades and plastic explosives. It was all better than he'd expected. He saw Colin heading back across Tenth Avenue. "Give me the keys to the truck and then hop in the cab. We'll be with you in a second." The King did as he was told. He just wanted to get his money and get the hell away from those Yankees.

Colin walked up, delivering news with a chuckle. "Brian's on his way. I had to talk to his fucking mother first, though. She was 'monitoring his goings-on since the Nesto boy died.' I said that we were making a donation of sporting goods to the Hell's Kitchen Youth Organization and she swallowed. Hysterical." He pointed to the back of the truck. "I saw you take a look. Everything cool? What's the plan?"

"We wait for the kid, take these over to the HKYO and then unload them under the tarp. We inspect everything there, and if everything's on the up, I pay this hillbilly cocksucker the ten grand and we head for The Freedom Pub."

"What are we going to the Bronx for?" Colin asked.

"Yours truly has already cut a deal with the Sinn Fein boys to sell them exactly half of this shipment for the bargain price of only ten thousand smackers. They ship their half of the haul over to be used against the

English; we keep the other half right here to be used against the Italians. And the IRA foots the whole bill."

"That's fucking genius, Kelly," came the reply. "But why don't we just whack this Blue Suede cocksucker, keep the cash and be ahead the ten grand. We could disassemble his truck and he'd just disappear."

"Nah," Kelly the Mick responded as if he'd already thought of that idea. "We might need the redneck again before it's all over. The dagoes aren't gonna just roll over and play dead." With that, the two friends walked to the driver's side door and opened it. "Scoot over," Kelly ordered. Colin slid in as Kelly the Mick climbed behind the wheel. He pulled out a small pipe and began to pack it with black tar hash.

"What's that?" the King asked with disapproval in his voice.

"Oh, this? It's just a little bit of none-o'-yo'-fucking-business," Kelly snapped back, putting the pipe in his mouth and taking a long puff. He passed the pipe to Colin as the cab began to take on the aroma of a Moroccan backroom. "Just hold your horses, chief. We'll be out of here as soon as our friend arrives." In just a few minutes, Brian rounded the corner and spotted the King's truck immediately. "You brought the key?"

"Yep," Brian replied.

"Cool. Get in." The King scooted over again as Brian squeezed into the cab and gave the stranger a quizzical look. "He's nobody. Hurry up. Let's get up to the HKYO." Just as Kelly the Mick had planned, it took the four of them no time to unload the truck discreetly and look over its contents. Brian unlocked the sports closet for them and made sure that everything fit inside before recovering it with the tarp.

Up on the street, Kelly the Mick was handing the King an envelope. "Nice doing business with you." He gripped the envelope. "But next time, don't leave us standing there like a couple of jerk-offs, alright?"

"Sorry about that," the King responded. "Can you point the way to the tunnel? I really need to get out of here."

Kelly pointed, saying, "Just head down Ninth Avenue and follow the signs." He reentered the Hell's Kitchen Youth Organization as the King sped away. Colin Garvan and Brian were just heading out. "Now, under no circumstances does anyone get into the sports closet, right?" Kelly the Mick said to him.

"Of course not, boss" Brian replied. Kelly the Mick liked that he already had a loyal foot soldier "I've got the only key, but I'll get another one made for you guys."

Drawing a $50 bill from the wad in his pocket, Colin Garvan tucked it into Brian's shirt pocket. "Here's a little something for you. We appreciate the help. Maybe you could let Doonan know that we ain't such bad guys... that he could even make a little something from being loyal to his own kind?" Brian nodded and headed home.

A few minutes before 2:30 that Sunday afternoon, Prince Mansour finally signaled Ivan that he was ready to depart for the Plaza Hotel. As the three ladies and their regal escorts made their way toward the front door, they saw a man selling sunglasses just inside the club. Anyone who had been to Page Six before knew that the glasses were a must when leaving that cavern. The real light of day would be blinding. Ivan approached the vendor. "How much for the sunglasses, sir?"

"Two dollars a pair, my man," came the reply. Handing over a twenty, Ivan recovered seven pairs of glasses and handed them to Carmen while keeping his own set for the trip to retrieve the car. Stopping at the coat check window, he handed over a stub to retrieve his two guns that had to be checked on the way in. Replacing his pristine, top-of-the-line 9mm pistols in their double shoulder holsters, he stepped out into the daylight and returned with the limousine in a matter of minutes.

It was a shame that Sandra was in no shape to appreciate how truly palatial The Plaza Hotel was. After the steady stream of intoxicants she'd been administered for the last several hours, as well as her miscarriage and the sexual thrashing she'd participated in at the club, Ivan and Carmen practically had to carry her to the private elevator that led to the penthouse. With the princes in their own rooms and the girls crashed out in the guest suite, Ivan drew heavy, velvet curtains across the most magnificent view of Central Park to induce the night's calm embrace once again.

Ivan kept watch over the hibernating inhabitants of the penthouse as he half-slept in the living room, waiting for his services to be required by the prince. Sandra suddenly bolted straight up in bed, gasping for air much like a drowning woman who'd just broken the surface. She saw that the clock read 7:30 p.m., but that was the extent of the things she knew for sure. Still high, she started into a panic that awoke Carmen: "Where am I? What day is it? How did I get here? Who are you?"

"I'm Carmen, remember, mami? From last night? We all met at Regine's? Remember? We had a great time. Just relax, baby. Everything is alright." Even though she was still high too, that was not the first time Carmen had been in such a situation and the business woman had to eclipse the party girl.

Sandra began to calm down a little bit as the previous evening came back to her in pieces. Only four hours of sleep had charged her young batteries, but her mind still needed to play a little catch-up. Although the tumult had roused Carmen and earned a peek through a cracked door by Ivan, Eve had remained motionless throughout. "Shit," Carmen thought.

"Please don't make me have to deal with another stupid O.D. bitch." She crept slowly across the bed until her cheek was near Eve's mouth. She couldn't detect any breath. "Fuck me," Carmen said aloud softly.

"I'd love to!" Eve said, jolting awake and leaning up to kiss the Nuyorican beauty. "Morning, mami. Evie's hungry, so if I'm not eating some caramel pussy, can I settle for breakfast?" Carmen giggled with relief as Eve spotted Sandra and continued, grabbing Sandra's leg and exposing her crotch, "Or I'll have some Irish breakfast too. Mmm."

Sandra recoiled a bit from the pain coming from her vagina. "Excuse me a minute." Eve and Carmen watched as Sandra walked, still dressed in her black dress from the night before, into the bathroom. "Oh shit!" she exclaimed when she saw that she had been bleeding.

Carmen tiptoed to the bathroom door, knocked softly and opened it. "Everything okay, little mami?" She saw the blood. "Oh, sorry. Your time?"

Sandra looked up with tears in her eyes. "It shouldn't be. I'm pregnant."

Carmen took a second before replying. "Well, you're not anymore, corazón. Isn't that a good thing?"

Sandra hung her head for a second to take everything in through a clouded mind. "Yeah, I guess. But I'm bleeding a lot."

"Well it'll stop, Sandra. We can get you something from downstairs if you didn't bring anything. It'll all be fine. You'll see." She walked over to the shower and started it, filling the room with steam quickly. "I'll get you a robe and some pads. Take a hot, hot shower. You'll feel worlds better."

Sandra stepped into the massive shower and let the water pour down over her, washing the sweat and blood from her body. There was a knock on the glass. "Room for two?" Eve asked with a sweet smile. Sandra nodded and stepped aside. Eve took her place in the stream of water and started shampooing Sandra's long, golden hair. "I heard, sweetie. Should I say sorry or congratulations?"

"It's fine. It just hurts a little."

Carmen had stepped into the bathroom with three robes and looked at the thick, red clots in the toilet bowl. She wondered to herself if Sandra should be bleeding as much as she was, if she should still be hurting. "Maybe one of us cut her inside with a fingernail or something last night." Carmen's mind wandered to an even worse scenario before she decided to herself, "I just gotta see her through this thing with the prince. Get paid, and I'm out." She flushed the toilet.

"Well, hello," Eve greeted her as the shower door swung open.

"Alright, so I'm in charge now, ladies. We are all going to shower, see to it that little Sandra feels all better, and then we're going to order room service, eat like pigs and enjoy this palace!" Eve let out a brief whoop while even Sandra forced a little smile. She thought she was indeed feeling better... in more ways than one.

Carmen finished showering quickly and then stepped out to open the drapes and drink in that million-dollar view. As soon as they followed suit, Sandra and Eve stared in wonderment as well while Carmen got her phone book from her purse to look for a name. She dialed a number, waited for a voice prompt and then typed in "5-0-Q" on the phone pad before speaking: "Plaza Hotel. Ask for Ivan in the Penthouse."

As the three beauties glided into the living room area, visions even in white terry cloth bathrobes, the princes and Ivan were already wide awake and cleaned up. "My princesses," Mansour greeted them. "I have taken the liberty of ordering some food. I hope this is acceptable."

"Of course, your majesty. You must have been reading our minds," Carmen responded. "Ivan, may I speak with you for a moment?"

The two stepped to the side as the prince returned his focus to Sandra. "How did you sleep, habibi? Well, I hope."

The response was interrupted by the ring of a doorbell. Ivan nodded at whatever Carmen had been telling him and then opened the door. Two hotel employees entered, pushing carts overloaded with trays of food: bacon, sausages, eggs, fruit, French toast, pancakes, all sorts of pastries and bread, as well as pitchers of freshly squeezed orange juice and Bloody Marys, pots of coffee and tea... and, of course, two bottles of Dom Perignon champagne. Ivan signed the check as the entourage fell on the carts like vultures and retreated to whatever luxurious sitting spots each liked to wolf down the food. After he saw the room service employees out, Ivan picked up a phone on the bar and dialed the front desk. "Hello. This is the penthouse. An associate is going to be stopping by shortly named Clayton. When he asks for Ivan, please call and then send him right up. Thank you."

Ivan returned to a stool at the bar, sharpening the gravity knife that had been strapped to his ankle while the prince took small bites of a plain piece of toast and skimmed through the Business Section of the Sunday *NY Times*. Sandra took her plate of eggs and fresh fruit and went over to sit next to him. "Your majesty, I hope I'm not interrupting." He put down the paper and smiled at her with his mouth and eyes. "I just want to thank you for everything. The great time at Regine's and the other club last night, the jewelry of course, letting me stay here.... It's just all been really incredible and I wanted to say thanks."

"Well it is not over yet, habibi. I hope you will be with us for awhile yet."

Carmen overheard the conversation and stepped in quickly, "Of course you're coming back out with us, right, Sandra? We've all been invited personally by Steve Rubell and Ian Schrager to Studio tonight. Truman Capote is hosting a private party for Liza Minelli, and anybody who's anybody is going to be there."

"You mean Studio 54?" Sandra asked in disbelief. "Everyone I've ever known hasn't been able to get past the doormen. They always get turned away."

"Well, not tonight, mami," Carmen beamed back.

"But what will I wear? I can't wear the dress I wore last night." Sandra shot Carmen a knowing glance. Carmen couldn't have set the situation up more perfectly herself.

"My princesses, never you fret. Just go down to the hotel lobby. There is a superb little French boutique there named *Je T'aime*. Ivan, call the manager to have it closed for our friends... so they can go down and shop as they are." Carmen began a half-hearted protest until the prince raised his hand. "I want you all to look spectacular. I haven't seen Liza in some time."

Clayton had just been getting out of the shower when his beeper went off, so it only took a few minutes for him to gather up 50 Rorers 714s and head out for the Plaza. He locked his bicycle near the hotel's water fountain among the hustle and bustle of horse carriages, cabs, limos and the *noblesse oblige* before striding right up to the front desk in the main lobby and asking for Ivan in the penthouse. Moments later, he was speeding up in the private elevator to the top of the hotel. When the doors opened, Ivan was there to greet him with a handshake and a "Clayton, right? I'm Ivan," as three white robed ladies shuffled by him onto the elevator.

Clayton hadn't even had the time to notice that he knew two of the three women who'd just brushed past him. "Yeah, Clayton. Good to meet you."

"I can't believe we're going on a shopping spree at the Plaza," said Eve.

"This is like a dream," echoed Sandra as the elevator doors slid shut, prompting Clayton to spin suddenly when he thought he recognized the voice.

"Is everything alright?" Ivan asked.

"Yeah. I just thought I recognized that voice."

"Oh, that was Carmen. She's just going down to get something for tonight." Clayton accepted his explanation, but the voice he'd heard somehow didn't sound like Carmen's.

"Yeah, that must've been it. Anyway, here's your stuff. Fifty, like you ordered. You can count them if you like."

"I trust you," Ivan replied, pushing the elevator call button and handing Clayton three $100 bills. "Brand new," he joked, "but be careful. The ink may still be wet on them."

Clayton smirked, "Excuse me, but it's only $250. They're five bucks a pop."

"See? I knew I should trust you. You're an honest businessman. The rest is a tip for coming so quickly... and in the rain."

Like a polite, little, Catholic school boy, Clayton folded up the money and replied, "Thanks very much, sir."

"No problem." The elevator doors opened and Clayton stepped onboard.

Sandra was feeling slightly better, amazed and amused to be walking around an expensive clothing store with just a robe and a glass of champagne. But that didn't entirely mask the fact that she was still a bit nervous and intimidated in such strange surroundings. Still, she rationalized to herself that she'd taken the ride that far, so she might as well see it out. Carmen flashed her a smile and a wink as she was talking to Lauren, the petite French woman who ran the extremely high-end couture dress shop. Eve just looked like a child inside Willy Wonka's factory, running around unfocused and completely incapable of looking at any one dress for more than a few moments.

Clayton had made it all the way back to his bike with the familiar voice running through his head. He just couldn't place it, but one thing was for certain: it wasn't Carmen's voice. Curiosity started to get the better of him as he began wondering if that Ivan guy was lying about Carmen. "That's really not like her to be here," Clayton thought. "She's a party girl, not a whore. There's no way she could afford a stay here... and she damn sure couldn't afford to go dress shopping in a Plaza boutique." Finally, he turned around and headed back into the hotel, wandering around the ground floor until he saw Carmen through the store window in *Je T'aime*. Stranger still, though, was that he thought he caught a glimpse of someone who looked exactly like Sandra O'Casey. "What the fuck?" he said aloud after he replayed the voice from the elevator in his mind's ear. It was Sandra O'Casey.

Ignoring the large "Closed" sign on the shop's front door, Clayton entered and walked immediately up to Sandra. "What's up, Sandra?"

"Clayton! You two know each other?" Carmen looked confused.

"Young man," the store manager interjected, "the store is closed for a private event."

"It's okay," Carmen interceded. "He's with us." She was still trying to get a grasp on the situation... and determine if she should be concerned.

Clayton kept a set of disbelieving, judgmental eyes on Sandra at all time. "Yeah, we know each other. We grew up together."

Sandra was still too high to wonder if she should be embarrassed. "Hey, Clayton," she replied. "Have you seen Francis yet?"

Carmen decided to move fast. "Oh, then you're from Hell's Kitchen too? I never knew. Sandra and I are old, old friends. We met a long time ago at a church thing. I go to St. Ann's and Sandra was Holy Cross."

"Really?" Clayton inquired, keeping his eyes locked with Sandra's. He knew that was a lie; everyone associated with his crew knew everybody else... and everyone they knew. What he couldn't figure out was what Sandra was doing with a drug demon, party girl like Carmen... and what they were both doing spending time with the Richie Rich European dude in the penthouse. "Then you know her father, the Detective?"

Carmen was growing more uncomfortable. "Oh, of course. I mean, I've met him and all, but we usually hang out at my place so I haven't really spent any time around him."

"Strange joint to be dress shopping. Kind of far from Eighth Avenue... or 125th Street." Clayton continued to pry.

"Oh, well, we got invited to a party at Studio 54 tonight by my friend."

"Ivan?"

"Yeah, Ivan. And it's kind of a dressy affair, and he wanted us to look good, so he surprised us by getting us clothes for tonight."

"And who's this?" Clayton continued relentlessly, pointing to the blonde who was still overwhelmed with oompa-loompa fascination. "She one of your friends from St. Ann's?"

"What? Oh, no. This is Eve. She's a friend of Ivan's. Listen, Clayton, we really have to pick out what we're wearing and go get ready, but it was great seeing you... oh, and thanks for taking care of that thing for me." Carmen grew even more nervous. She'd forgotten about the Quaaludes, and finding out that Sandra's father was NYPD put a whole new spin on things.

He turned back to Sandra and lifted her chin. "And you're going along too, Sandra." She nodded her head and smiled absentmindedly.

"Why don't you join us?" Carmen offered in an attempt to make things seem on the up-and-up. "I'll just put your name on the list."

The offer intrigued Clayton. He knew he had Carmen squirming on the line, but he couldn't figure out exactly what was going on. Meeting up with them later would give him some more time to figure things out. Plus, he rationalized, what idiot turns down an invitation to a Studio 54 party? "Alright, cool. You can put my name down on the list as 'Clayton Q, plus three.'"

"No problem, papi." She was clearly relieved. "We'll see you tonight." Clayton headed for the door slowly, never taking his eyes off of Sandra. When he'd finally gone, Carmen turned to the store manager and added, "Alright. Let's get these dresses and get back upstairs."

A short while later, as Sandra, Carmen and Eve were returning from *Je T'aime*, each with a large bag dangling from her fingertips, Ivan opened the door on his way out to gas up the limo. "Your Highness," he bellowed, "will you require anything else while I'm out?"

Stepping into the living room to respond, and seeing the three ladies already changing clothes to give him a private fashion show, he responded with a wide grin, "No, my friend. It seems I have all I need right here."

Sandra slipped into her $8,000 pink Calvin Klein outfit and matching Italian leather pumps first, stepping up onto a marble coffee table, where she began twirling like a ballerina. The prince was mesmerized and slipped his hand beneath his robes to stroke his growing erection. He never even looked over at Carmen or Eve when they emerged in their new outfits, so Carmen thought it time to escalate the intensity of the performance. "Majesty, why don't you come sit over here?" She led him to a large leather chair that sat in the middle of a double doorway where he would have the best view of the sunken lounge and couches.

Carmen and Eve got on their knees on either side of Sandra, an act that made her stop spinning. Starting with each pink "fuck-me" pump, they began licking their way up, tracing every inch of Sandra's skin with their tongues while Sandra began to pull at the skirt of her outfit with arousal. Carmen had made sure that Sandra was chemically altered enough to go with the flow, and the girl wasn't disappointing her mentor. In a well-orchestrated move, Carmen and Eve simultaneously braced Sandra's back and swept her legs out from underneath her at the knees. Cradling a surprised Sandra, they swung her over to the couch and spread her legs open wide. One woman kissed the inside of Sandra's thighs while the other sat below her on the floor and leaned backwards, using her tongue to paint Sandra's entire genital region. The three women cooed and moaned over and over, switching positions to vary who was performing cunnilingus on whom. Sandra's body began to quiver as the first wave of orgasm swept over her. There was no question that she was enjoying her sex play with the other two. Grabbing Carmen and standing her up on the couch before her, the prince was treated to viewing Sandra's first time ever pleasuring another woman. She nibbled her way up Carmen's legs, stroking and penetrating her from the front, removing her moist fingers from Carmen's vagina and competing with Eve's tongue by using them to rub her own clitoris. By the time she'd flipped Eve onto her back and had straddled her on all fours, the prince was ready to explode. But it was Sandra who moaned and writhed in ecstasy as Carmen added her fingers to Eve's inside of the seventeen year-old before using her tongue to perform analingus on Sandra while riding a rainbow colored dildo.

Somewhere in the midst of this mini-orgy, Ivan returned to the penthouse to find it filled with sounds that might have been heard in a barn. He saw the back of the prince's head in the doorway and the briefest glimpse of the floor show he was watching. But knowing better than to interrupt, he slipped into the bathroom to get dressed himself and prepare for yet another long night.

As the clouds and the George Washington Bridge shrunk in my rear view mirror, Karen sat up straight in her seat and stretched as best as she could. "Oh my God, are we on the West Side Highway already?" she asked.

"Yep, sleepyhead. You were out the entire way, but at least your prediction about the traffic was spot on."

"Where are you going?" she asked as I got into the left lane in preparation to turn and go across the park.

"I was just going to get out at your house and probably walk home."

"Absolutely not," she demanded. "Francis, I would feel so much better if I saw you enter your building safely with my own two eyes."

"But what about all the stuff in the trunk?" I asked. "Chivalry's not completely dead, you know."

"That's sweet, but part of that giant maintenance fee we pay each month includes a little curb service from the doormen. Besides, they'd appreciate the extra cash... and I never tip small."

I laughed. "Okay, okay. I give in." Pulling the BMW up in front of my building, the stoop was there waiting for me, washed clean by all the rain. *how can i ever thank this woman enough for everything she's done for me?*

I turned to begin thanking Karen profusely, but she put two fingers on my lips to stop me. "Don't scare me, okay? We're going to be good friends and see one another again, right?" I took her hand from my lips and kissed her open palm. "Then just say good night, sweet heart." My blue eyes gleamed with large, clear tears as the rain began to fall again softly. I leaned over and kissed Karen gently and then hopped out of the car, scurrying around to the passenger's side door. I looked down the avenue at the traffic light on 43rd Street, waited until it turned red, took off my jacket to shield Karen from the rain and then hustled her back over to the driver's side. She lowered the window a bit and said, "No, chivalry is definitely not dead. Be in touch, handsome."

I opened the door to my apartment and immediately noticed the blinking red "12" on my answering machine. Six of them alone were from Sandra, each more cryptic than the last. One was from my sweet mother, another from Benny, and although I could hear nothing but grunts on three more, I knew they were from my Uncle Patsy, checking up on me. The last message was a pleasant surprise: Seamus Boylan, the old guy from Gleason's Gym was clearly uncomfortable with the whole concept of speaking to someone who was not there, but he left a message all the same, "Kid, I hope this is you. Um... well, anyway, listen. I been thinking and I just can't get your fury and heart outta my head, so come around and see me some time. Alright? What? Do I say goodbye to this damn thing? Argh. Call me." Seamus' message made me smile. *and who knows, i might actually call him back. right now, though, i'm hungry as fuck. time for a trip to the deli.*

Stepping back out onto the street, the energy from The City seemed to course up through my legs, energizing me, but bringing back the stress Karen had predicted. "My nigga!" I heard that familiar voice well before Clayton reached me on his bicycle. Leaping from the seat with a big grin and a hug, he sent me through the whole series of Hell's Kitchen handshakes. *god damn! it's good to see this man!* I could tell he felt the same. Outside of Howie, Clayton was my closest friend. "A little 'welcome back' spliff," he added, pulling a fat joint out of his pocket and lighting it up. I hadn't been high in more than two days, and although there was a brief temptation to decline, the demons revolted in unison. *and that weed smells so good.*

"You do know how to welcome a man back to the stoop." I took the joint and inhaled deeply, holding it for as long as my lungs could bear. Finally, I exhaled, and for a moment, my head was lost in the clouds.

"Yo, I gotta tell you something." I could tell that something was on his mind. "When you pulled off the other day, Sandra O'Casey was right on your heels, looking for your ass."

"Yeah, she left me a million bizarre messages on my machine while I was gone."

"Well, I barely gave her the time of day; you know, after dissing you and hooking up with that shitbag, Danny, I just don't give a fuck about her. But I gotta say that she looked freaked out. Crazy, yo." He took the joint from me and hit it deeply, passing it back before he continued. "There's something else, though, that'll blow your mind."

"What, man? You're killing me here... and I'm starving, so just spit it out."

"There's a bit to tell. Why don't we go over to the Kraft so we can talk and eat."

As we were stepping down off of the stoop, Milk skated towards us on his board. "Look at this," I said. "The streets are nearly flooded and there's Milk on a skateboard. And you know this nigga never falls."

"He just got it like that," Clayton added.

"Yo! There he is! What's up, Francis? Clayton tell you about the shooting?"

"I saw it in the *Daily News.*"

"And you know who did it, right?" I nodded. "Well, they been looking for you hard."

"Oh, yeah? Have they stepped to anyone else?" I asked.

"Shit, yeah. Everybody: Vit, Brian and Redbone have already thrown in with them," Clayton said.

I looked Milk dead in the eye. "And what about you, man? What are you gonna do?"

"Well, to be totally honest with you, I was thinking about it. You know I'm down for defending mines. And they really did do us a favor icing that English motherfucker, but I wanted to wait for you. So far it's you, me and Clayton holding out... oh, yeah, and I think Patty Boy too. Although Patty Boy ain't too swift."

"Listen," I said. "We were just on our way over to the diner. You want to come?"

"Nah, man," Milk responded. "I'm meeting this little cutie I was talking to down in the Village. I'm hoping to sink the little man in the boat."

"Typical," Clayton said with a laugh.

"Fuck you, man," came Milk's reply. "But we'll talk tomorrow."

As Milk skated away, Clayton and I walked the block and change to the Kraft. "So it's like that, huh? They've got everybody on the block except me, you and Milk?"

"From what I hear," Clayton said, holding the door for me.

"Grab that booth all the way in the back, near the exit door. I'm gonna take a piss and then you can fill me in on this Sandra shit." Rohit, the best diner waiter in all of NYC, came over with menus, took our order, and slid hot food in front of us in record time. Clayton filled me in on everything he'd seen at the Plaza and everything he knew about this Carmen chick. I sat there and listened for over an hour, but I didn't know what to make of the story. *i don't really owe sandra anything... but how did she get to the penthouse of the plaza hotel? something just isn't right.*

Clayton grabbed the check... *a first...* and said while we were heading back for the stoop, "I think we should go over there to Studio 54 tonight and check this situation out."

"I was just really hoping to come home and get some rest. You know, say goodbye to a hellacious week... and get ready for a new one."

"Well, I don't know, man, It's up to you... but if it turns out there's nothing to it, we're still in a Studio party, right? And I've got some lovely new Thai stick weed and a bag of Rorers with your name on them."

"Damn, yo, you don't fight fair, do you?"

"All's fair in love and pussy, Francis, my man." We both laughed. "But if you're coming, you have to put on your freshest gear. You know I'm gonna be funky in that 50s, vintage, red sharkskin suit with just the black tee and my brand new white Adidas Stan Smith's."

"You don't have to worry about me, man. I can hold my own. Just be sure you've got the Rorers and the bud."

"Oh, no doubt, Francis," Clayton replied. "Moms is rolling me a hundred joints of that Thai and some Colombian as we speak."

"No one rolls a fatty better than yo momma," I joked.

"If it weren't true, you ignorant motherfucker, I might think that was a slam. But I tell you what. Keep my moms outta this, and I'll keep <u>this</u>," he said as he grabbed his crotch, "outta yo moms."

I had to laugh. "Now that was good. I'm gonna give you that one." We were already at the stoop. "Alright. How can I say no? I'm gonna go up and crash for a few hours. Why don't you wake me up at eleven and we can hit Studio 54 by midnight?" Another run-through of the handshakes of Hell's Kitchen and I was on my way to La-La-Land. As I was right on the verge of slipping into a dream state, my mind instinctively turned to Sonny Blue and the can. *i'll visit there soon.* The demons were in control of my sleep, and I knew they'd leave me no choice.

J.R. Albanese returned to Leone's Italian Ristorante and walked back through a dining room full of customers who were enjoying the eatery's specialty, brick oven pizza. Heading through the kitchen and into a little backroom that was situated just next to the building's alleyway, he greeted the associates who had gathered that Sunday night for his weekly poker game. They were already well into the play, and the stakes had climbed higher than normal. J.R. was keeping an eye on the game as usual, but he was still distracted by thoughts of the following day. The Sicilian crew was due to arrive at the Dante League Social Club to begin repairing the damage. It would come in handy that the only thing they were better at doing than construction was killing. He was also concerned about his son. With the climate being as sensitive as it was, he couldn't afford Danny becoming a loose cannon... especially since J.R. planned to escalate the conflict with his Sicilians.

J.R. was brought back from his daydream by a strange tapping coming from the wall. He tried to concentrate on the sound, but the noise from the kitchen and voices from the game made it difficult. Just as he was about to silence everyone, he heard it again, but it was decisively more intentional that time. There was no way it could be random. "Jimmy!" he finally said. "What's that sound?"

Jimmy paused for a minute, unsure that he'd even heard anything. "Oh, it's nothing, J.R.," he responded.

"Bullshit it's nothing," the elder Albanese fired back. "That fucking tapping ain't nothing. What? Do you have fucking gnomes living in the walls or something?"

The old owner put his cards down and feigned listening... this time, more seriously. He thought he might've heard a knock. "Oh, oh, that. It's just the old pizza ovens cooling down. You know, the change in temperature. It makes them knock. It's nothing."

"Nothing my ass, you prick. I just walked through the dining room and you've got every moron on 56th Street out there. Those pizza ovens are still going, not cooling down."

"It's just tapping, J.R. What do you want me to tell you? This is New York. It makes sounds! Why are you breaking balls?"

"I'll break more than balls, you stupid old fuck. What's on the other side of this wall?"

"It's just the alleyway where we keep the garbage. Maybe it's rats."

"You've got rats?" J.R. fired back.

"No, J.R., no. Maybe they're trying to get in is all I'm saying."

"And they thought they'd get the job done faster with pickaxes? Take me out there. Now."

Jimmy cursed in Italian under his breath. "But, J.R., you have to go all the way around on the other..."

"Now," J.R. repeated. "Where does that big gray door in the kitchen lead to? The one with the bolt lock."

Jimmy realized that he was pushing his luck. Even though he was up in the card game and he didn't want to move for fear of altering his luck, not moving would've definitely brought down the wrath of Johnny Rugs. "Okay, okay, my friend. I will show you." He threw his cards in and stood up.

"Jimmy will be right back, fellas. Don't nobody move." The tone in J.R.'s voice left everyone in the room feeling like they'd do best to take his instructions literally.

The restaurateur led Johnny through a short storage hallway that was stacked from floor to ceiling with bags of flour and cans of tomato sauce until they reached a large, gray door secured with five old bolts. Jimmy opened them all as J.R. drew a little .22 caliber Saturday Night Special that he carried with him all the time. As soon as the door ground open, he pushed Jimmy out into the alley and told him to look around.

"What am I looking for?" the elderly Italian asked. "It's not that big of an alley. There's nothing really out here besides trash bags, an old chair and a couple of milk crates."

J.R. stepped out into the alleyway with his gun still in hand. He put a finger up to his mouth to silence Jimmy, walking slowly along the perimeter with his head cocked to the side as though he were listening for something. He did this for several minutes as Jimmy looked at him with confusion. "Can you hear anything?"

"No, Johnny. I don't hear nothing except the sounds from the street and the racket in the kitchen. What am I supposed to be hearing? You still hearing that tapping?" J.R. put his gun away and started to pull at the bags against the wall, lifting the milk crates and brushing at the pavement with his foot as if checking for anything loose. "J.R., are you alright? What are you looking for?"

"An associate of mine tipped me off that some of those Irish cock-suckers have been on the lookout for explosives lately. That's what those drunken micks use over there against the British. It's the true mark of a coward, Jimbo, somebody who's afraid to look their enemy in the eye. They kill from afar, you know, and they don't care if it's man, woman or child. They're animals. And they already got my guy, The Duke. They're not going to stop until they either get me or I get them."

"So, what? You think they're trying to blow you up?"

"Well, it wouldn't take much digging to find out that this is where I am every Sunday night, right? I hear tapping out here, like a hammer or a shovel, and couldn't it be one of those gutless pricks planting something to get us all through the wall?"

"Sweet Mary, do you think they'd do that?"

"That's what I was listening for: ticking or some kind of countdown mechanism." J.R. had continued to lift trash bags. A newly concerned Jimmy added to the effort. After several minutes, they stopped. "Well, it must've been nothing."

"But you can't be too careful," Jimmy added. "It's a good thing you've got people looking out for you."

"I've got ears everywhere. No one pulls something over on an Albanese without him knowing it. I didn't get to where I am by being stupid."

"That's clear. Must be a nightmare having to watch your back all the time like that. You want me to have one of my dishwashers hang out here in the alley to make sure everything's okay?"

"Yeah, why don't you do that... and then let's get back in there to the game. You've got money to lose." Obviously relieved, J.R. let out a big belly laugh and slapped Jimmy on the back as he went through the door. "Jennifer!" Albanese blustered to the owner's wife on his way through the kitchen. "Is it possible that you've actually gotten lovelier? How'd this cigar-chomping sonofabitch manage to find a woman who can cook the way you do... and is actually quite the piece of ass? Huh? Tell me that!" He let out another great laugh of self-congratulation at this imagined compliment while Jimmy's wife took a long drag on her cigarette, conjured up an insincere death-smile and made a mental note to ash in J.R. Albanese's gravy on his next visit.

A few moments later, they reentered the little backroom to find all five of their card-playing associates seated at the table, bound and gagged with duct tape. "What the fuck!?!" Johnny roared. Only two of the men at the table were even semi-conscious. J.R. grabbed the tape covering the mouth of one and ripped it off, taking more than half of his moustache with it. The pain jolted the man back to lucidity. "What the fuck happened? Who did this?"

"Three guys... ski masks. All of them about the same height. They had guns. Came in and put them to our heads. The biggest one told us if we made a sound, we were dead. The skinny one had a roll of tape. He went around taping us to the chairs. They were in and out in no time. They got everything off the table, plus they shook us down. Wallets, watches, rings, you name it. Before they bolted out the door, they gave us each a smack in the head with their pieces."

J.R. noticed the green cardboard shamrock that had been left in the middle of an otherwise barren playing table and began to turn his rage on Jimmy. "Those motherfuckers! And those fucking wetbacks in the kitchen... they saw nothing? Where's your hostess?"

"Oh God...." Jimmy hustled into the dining room area, clearly worried. The tables were still filled with unaware customers, but the hostess was nowhere to be found. Jimmy looked behind the counter and then in the bathroom before he found Marie, cowering on the toilet, shaking. "Marie! Marie! Are you alright?" the shop owner asked.

She turned to look at him, tears streaming down her face. "They're gone?"

"Si, si, they're gone. What happened?"

"I don't know, Mr. Jimmy. One man was having a calzone and he got up to use the bathroom. I didn't really look at his face. A few seconds later, two other men came in and went right toward the back. I thought they were here for Mr. Albanese's game, so I didn't say anything to them. A few minutes later, I feel something in my back and a man's voice tells me not to say a word or he'll kill me. Tells me to open up the cash register and hand him the drawer. Then he has me step backwards through the curtain. I couldn't see any of their faces, but there were three of them. The one with the gun walks me to the bathroom, opens the door and pushes me inside. He said that if I stepped out of the bathroom before they left, he'd shoot me." Marie's emotions overwhelmed her and she started sobbing, burying her face in Jimmy's vest. J.R. tore through the dining room and out onto the sidewalk, searching both ways for anything out of the ordinary.

But Patty Boy had already had the car running at 57th and Ninth, and sped off as soon as Kelly the Mick, Colin Garvan and Brian hopped inside.

"Alright, Kelly. You want a war. You got one." J.R. shouted, stalking toward his car before thinking better of doing that alone, pulling his gun and heading back inside to call some of the crew.

"Holy fuck! My heart's still pounding like it's going to explode!" Patty Boy said, turning onto 42nd Street on his way to the West Side Highway. "But I'm so fucking pumped! That worked like clockwork."

"I told you it would," Kelly the Mick grinned, dropping his ski mask into the takeout bag that contained their haul.

"Unbelievable!" Brian shouted, laughing hysterically and pounding on Kelly the Mick's headrest. "What was it like, Patty Boy? What happened back there?"

"It was just like you said, Kelly. I hopped the gate and went back behind the restaurant. I counted six paces back from the door and then just started tapping on the wall with the pipe. As soon as I heard the creak of the first bolt on the door move, I boogied back here and started up the car. What I don't get, though, is how did you know Rugs would come out to look for himself?"

"I know this guy," Kelly the Mick started, "named Richie Carrociolo. Works over on that Citibank jobsite on the East Side. He doesn't think I know that he's one of the sad goodfella wannabes sucking on Albanese's Italian sausage. So I go to him – real hush-hush like – and ask him if he can get me any explosives off the site... that I need it kept under wraps and I need to get them from somewhere out of the Kitchen. I tell him I have to have them for a job this weekend. He asked me a bunch of questions about what I needed it for and then finally told me he couldn't get them, but I said it was no matter; that I knew somewhere else to try. Well, of course I knew that cocksucker would go running to Albanese. It's what I wanted him to do. J.R. thought he was all smart, but I knew it'd put him on the look out and get him paranoid."

"We've tried to break in to Leone's so many times, we knew all about the door to the kitchen and the little backroom where Rugs has his game," Colin added. "Kelly was confident there'd be plenty of time for Patty Boy to get out of there safely... and with Brian in the back by the bathroom, all he had to do was wait for Albanese to come by. When we saw Patty Boy come out of the alley, in we went."

Kelly the Mick looked back at Brian and Patty Boy. "But most important, men, is that you're now in. The both of you."

As Carmen, Eve and Sandra walked back into the living room, dressed to the nines, the prince looked up and smiled broadly. The sight of his three princesses, radiant and glamorous, pleased him greatly. "Allah has smiled on me, and never more so than this day. You are all visions... oases in the desert, and I am blessed to have been able to drink when I was thirsty. But I am a man who is thankful for his good fortune, and I wish to express that gratitude to you. You all look so beautiful tonight that there is only one thing that can make you truly transcendent." Ivan came around the side of the girls with a tray, upon which three leather boxes rested. "Because you give me such joy and pleasure, I wish to return the favor." He walked up to Sandra and opened the box, revealing a stunning pair of earrings that were made of both white and black diamonds. All three of the ladies gasped as the prince handed them each a box in turn. "Now your loveliness is perfection. Now we are ready to see Liza." Everyone giggled as they headed out the door and piled into the elevator.

Specifically to please Sandra, the prince directed Ivan to drive them through the park again. "My habibi should have whatever her heart desires," Mansour oozed. Although she was still extremely inebriated from the champagne, Carmen's candy and the endorphins that raged through her body from their sexual escapades, Sandra was still able to appreciate the detour. When the limo turned off of Eighth Avenue and onto 54th Street, they instantly saw the hundreds of people who were standing outside the club's large glass doors, all held at bay by the infamous Marc Benecke.

As the limo rolled to a stop and Ivan got out to open the prince's door, Carmen said to Sandra. "Stay close to the prince or the doorman... that cunt-fag of cunt-fags... might not let us in. Don't even talk to him if you can avoid it. He's the most arrogant prick you'll ever meet... so much so that he's been threatened, punched and shot at more than most mob bosses. He even had the balls to keep Sinatra out one night!"

Benecke spotted the prince and immediately lifted the rope, brushing a couple of bare-chested blonde boys aside. "Your Highness, how are you this evening? It's wonderful to see you again." The prince raised both hands, almost as if he were blessing the doorman, nodded slightly and walked past. Once the ladies were through as well, Ivan shook Benecke's hand and palmed him a couple of hundred bucks.

As they passed through a second set of glass doors, an extraordinarily thin woman with a clipboard approached them. "Good evening, your Majesty. We're so thrilled to have you here tonight. I'm going to show you to our V.I.P. section as soon as you're ready. Since it's a closed party, we've moved that section upstairs from the basement just for the evening. Did you have any names that you needed to add to the guest list?

Carmen stepped up immediately, "Yes, please. A Mr. Clayton Q, plus three."

The woman's eyes flashed to the prince for confirmation. "It is as she says. Where is Liza?"

"Oh, she's up in the DJ booth with Truman. John McEnroe is also here somewhere. I last saw him talking with Margaret Trudeau, and I believe Keith Richards is up in the balcony with Mick and Bianca. I thought I heard that Calvin might be joining us later, but I'm afraid Michael Jackson has already departed for the evening." Turning to another, even thinner girl, the hostess said, "Tell Mr. Rubell and Mr. Schrager that His Highness, Crown Prince Mansour bin Asad has arrived."

Sandra had wandered away for a moment, looking out at the dance floor and marveling at the infamous "Man in the Moon with his Cocaine Spoon." The Stone's "Emotional Rescue" was thumping through every speaker and she could see at least one couple over near the staircase fucking in beat with the music. Eve came running by, screaming with glee. Carmen grabbed Sandra. "Come on, mami! Let's dance!"

"How I love coming here! It is like the Sodom and Gomorrah! Champagne for all!" spouted the prince. "Please. I would like to buy a glass of champagne for everyone."

"As you wish, your Highness."

"Mansour!" Steve Rubell slurred coming up to the prince and first shaking his hand and then turning it into a semi-hug. Ivan stood like a cat waiting to pounce as Ian Schrager broke himself away from his balding associate to come and say hello. "You just couldn't keep away from all this American split-tail, could you?"

"It's a pleasure as always, Prince Mansour. May I introduce our attorney, Roy Cohn?" The prince stuck out his hand.

"We've actually met before, Prince. It was a conference in Washington. I was with Senator McCarthy's team."

"Yes, of course, Mr. Cohn. That has been some time. You have an excellent memory. Shall we go and say hello to Liza?"

Just feet away, Clayton was growing more and more agitated with the charming Marc Benecke. "My name is on the list, dude," Clayton insisted, tapping the clipboard forcefully.

"Well, unless it's written in disappearing ink, I don't see it, 'Clayton Q.'"

"Oh, did you already get the addition, then?" the too-thin hostess asked, stepping outside. "Clayton Q, plus three? You got it already?"

Marc glared at the hostess and then back at a grinning Clayton. "No. No one told me anything."

"Well, you need to add him. Steve's orders. He's part of the prince's group. 'Clayton Q, plus three.'" She scampered back inside.

"But you said it was just the two of you," he argued, shooting me a condescending glance. "This is for 'Clayton Q, plus <u>three</u>.'"

Clayton didn't skip a beat as we passed by. "Two and three are in our pants."

"Oh, really?" the doorman countered. "So what's the 'Q' stand for then?"

"'Queer,' of course... sailor."

Clayton threw Marc a kiss as everyone on line cracked up. "Think that was funny, did you, you cunts?" he asked the crowd. "Well none of you are getting in now no matter what... so you might as well all go home. Good night, cunts. Good night."

Studio 54 was an all-out assault on my senses. Every kind of perfume and cologne filled the air... all kinds of smoke, sweat, alcohol, puke, shit, whatever. Flashing lights and a thumping bass line threatened to hypnotize us, but I snapped back into the moment when I noticed the homos eyeballing the fresh meat. "I'll be right back," Clayton said as he headed off for the bathroom. "I've got some business to tend to in my office." I couldn't tell if he had to go sell some of his stash or take a shit, but I saw a bar, and that was all I needed.

this place is fucking amazing. everyone here seems to be dancing and drinking and partying like it's their last night on earth. "Hey, honey. What'll you have?" The shirtless bartender had rested his hand on mine. I ripped it away.

"A Bacardi and Coke." *fag.*

"Excuse me, Mary," he responded with an eye roll. "One Butch-cardi and Coke, coming up." I put my money on the bar and looked out over the dance floor. I spotted Sandra right away. *my god, she shines brighter than those light towers and that enormous fucking disco bal, combined. i wonder who those other women are, though. she's clearly dancing with them. one of them must be the lady clayton told me that he sells to.*

"Take one of these; I just did," Clayton said, putting a Quaalude in my hand. My drink arrived and I asked for two more, popping the pill into my mouth and washing it down with the bittersweet liquid. We stood there for a little while when Clayton suddenly chimed in, "Hey! There she is. See her? That's Sandra down there, near the speakers."

"I saw her," I replied in a subdued fashion.

"Well why don't we go down there and see her? Talk to her? You'll see with your own two eyes what I was trying to tell you before."

I was too nervous. "Just hold on a second, will you? Let's have another drink or two." *after all, this is sandra o'casey, the girl who makes me breathe like i'm underwater. and bacardi builds courage.* I downed the remainder of my second drink and ordered two more.

"I've barely started this one. I don't need another," Clayton complained.

"It's not for you." We just stood silently, watching the three ladies dance while I waited for my drinks. The Rorer was coming on and a couple more drinks would make everything just right. I downed my third rum and Coke and took a healthy swig from my fourth."

"Ready now, you little bitch?" I shot Clayton a glance to get him to back off, but then returned my gaze solidly on Sandra.

Although the girls had stopped dancing, Sandra's head kept spinning. Eve and Carmen helped her get over to the roped off V.I.P. area that had been sent up for Mansour and his entourage. Carmen thought it was the perfect time to talk to Sandra. "So, what do you have to do tomorrow?"

"Ohmygosh," Sandra slurred. "I have to go to school. As a matter of fact I can't hang out too late tonight because I still have some things to do."

"What a shame," replied Carmen. "You know what I think? I think you should relax a little, live it up! The prince wants to take us to Miami for a few days. He's got a huge mansion right on the beach. Doesn't lounging in the sand and getting some color sound good? Ooh, mami, I'll bet you get golden, don't you?"

Sandra didn't want to seem rude or ungrateful. "It's very tempting, but I just can't. My parents are coming home tomorrow and I have to see them. I haven't talked to my mom in days and I'm going to have to come up with a good story as it is."

"You can't be serious. What are you, a mommy's girl? You don't make decisions for yourself?" Carmen chided.

Sandra didn't care if she seemed rude or ungrateful anymore. The champagne was talking. "I said no and that's it. That's my decision. Good enough?"

The smile dropped from both Carmen's face and voice at the same time. The look she gave Sandra nearly became demonic. "After everything he's done for you? After everything he's given you? He's a king, for Christ's sake, mami. Wake the fuck up. If you were in his country, they'd cut that pretty blonde head off. But you'd spit on him like this? When he's just offering you a little relaxation on a trip you could never possibly afford on your own? You'd just turn down his generosity and ruin it for fucking all of us, you ungrateful white trash!?!" She spit the words into the poor girl's face with a growing intensity and volume.

"What?" Sandra tried to protest. "Wait a minute. I don't owe him anything. I don't owe you anything either. I thought we were just having fun."

"You think someone just gives you jewelry and diamonds and thousand-dollar dresses because you make him laugh? You drank his champagne, ate his food, snorted his blow... sucked his dick! You ate our pussies for him to watch, Little Miss McInnocent."

"I'm no whore! I was just going with things. Experimenting."

"You're no whore, huh? Well look at that ring. It might as well have a price tag on it with a picture of your open mouth, because the tag on that necklace sure had your tiny little tits and even tinier ass on it. And look at these earrings, baby. That price tag has a picture of your worn-out, bloody snatch! So you're no whore, huh? I've got news for you, bitch! He's got the receipt... and he's taking his property to Miami!"

"Fuck this and fuck you! If he wants all this shit back, he can have it. I'm making a return...." Sandra tore off each item of jewelry and stuck it into her nearly empty clutch purse, jutting it into Carmen's face. "...With or without the receipt! I'm out of here, you crazy fucking spic!"

Carmen stepped in front of Sandra and grabbed her wrist with alarming strength, shooting Eve a look that clearly meant, "Move in." With lightning-fast dexterity, Carmen spun Sandra's weakened form around, squeezing with her right arm to restrain the terrified teenager and force the breath from her lungs simultaneously. Eve stepped forward with a crack pipe at the ready and slid the tube right into Sandra's mouth as Carmen relaxed her clutch on Sandra's ribcage and pinched her nose closed with her free left hand. "You're not trying to be a party pooper, are you, honey?" Eve asked sarcastically, flicking the lighter as Sandra inhaled deeply and instinctually in an attempt to catch her breath. As the smoke took over Sandra's body, Carmen held her up and feigned dancing with her to cover up the appearance of an argument.

"Do they look like they're fighting to you? ....What the fuck kind of pipe is that?" I demanded, slamming Clayton's arm with my own.

"Ow! Shit! That's for smoking this new kind of cocaine. It's the latest rage because it's cheaper. They say the high is more intense, but it doesn't last as long."

"Cocaine? But Sandra doesn't do coke."

"Well, she does now. See what I was saying before? You can see from here. Her eyes aren't even blue anymore. They're like that cloudy gray. See what I mean?"

"Let's get over there, man," I insisted.

Ivan had spotted Clayton much earlier, and noticed our approach then. He casually intercepted us as though we were long lost friends. "Well, my young businessman friend, we meet again so soon."

"Oh, yeah. This is that European dude, Francis," Clayton said.

I wouldn't be deterred, though, and kept walking. Ivan stepped directly in front of me and put his hand on my chest. It was like an anchor on the ocean's floor. "Sorry. This is my client's private party, gentlemen."

"Fine," I responded, "but that's my friend, Sandra, and we want to talk to her."

"Well, she's busy right now. You'll have to talk to her some other time."

"So, wait a minute," Clayton interjected, "Carmen and Sandra aren't even with you? Who are they with?"

"Just head back to where you came from. You can talk to your friends later."

"Oh, they're with the dude wearing his bed sheets? Aw, hell naw."

I was looking directly at Sandra, and I was almost positive that she'd looked right at me, but didn't seem to recognize me at all. I had never seen her that messed up before in my whole life. I waved at her, but she didn't wave back. She just sat there as though she were wilting. "Okay, sir, no problem," I said. "Let's just go back to the bar, Clayton." I turned and walked away.

"What the fuck? I was about to jump that dude," Clayton insisted, hot on my heels.

"You didn't see the guns he had inside his jacket." Clayton was struck dumb. "We're not gonna do nothing just yet. I have to think for a second what to do. I don't like the way she looks. I don't think she knows what she's doing." I ordered two more drinks.

Clayton said, "Listen. You don't owe Sandra anything, Francis. She fucked you over with Danny. That alone should tell you what she is."

I stopped him short. "Clayton, we grew up with her. We know her parents. She's from the neighborhood. She's in trouble, serious trouble, and we've got to do something about it."

"I think we just have to wait out tonight and look for an opening to get her away from those people if she keeps hanging out with them in the future."

"I don't know, Clayton," I said. "Something is just too wrong. That's not her. Something about the way she's acting, the way she looks, tells me that tonight is the only chance we have."

"Fuck this. I know that bitch, Carmen. I'm just going to go over there."

"And do what?" I asked. "We tried that already, remember? We don't want the Nazi doing something stupid and drawing one of those pieces. We have no idea what he'll do to us... or to Sandra."

"True," Clayton agreed, the wind taken out of his sails. We watched as the girls led Sandra to a chair in the V.I.P. area and sat down on either side of her. "I got it!" Clayton almost shouted. He turned around to one of the cocktail waitresses standing at the bar. "Can I borrow a pen from you?" She eyed Clayton up and down and then handed over the pen seductively. He scribbled a note on a napkin, folded it in half, and then turned back to the waitress as she was loading up her tray with drinks. "Can I talk to you for a second?"

"What are we talking about here, cutie?" she asked. "I've got a job to do."

"I need a favor... but I can make it worth your while." He deposited ten Quaaludes on her tray. "The girl with the long, blonde hair down there, in the section you're serving?"

"The prince? Yeah?"

"Well, she's a friend of ours and we've been trying to get a message to her all night, but we can't let the guy she's with see us."

"What kind of note?" the waitress asked skeptically.

I was amazed at how well Clayton could sling bullshit. I almost believed him myself. "We're trying to warn her," he started. "Her boyfriend is out in the line. He's about to come in, and he's going to start some serious shit if he sees her with him. He's fucked in the head. He'll probably beat her up." The waitress was glued to Clayton's every word. "We just want to give her the heads up to avoid any trouble. Can you get this note to her without anyone else seeing?"

"Sure," she replied, scooping up the Rorers and slipping them into a pocket. "I have to bring these to another section, but I can get it to her in a few minutes."

"Thanks, baby. You're the best."

"I don't know if this is going to work, Clayton. Those other two women are practically on top of her." I hadn't taken my eyes off of Sandra's face.

"Well, the blonde one's distracted... and I know how to get Carmen away." Clayton walked over, near the wall, and started waving his arms to get Carmen's attention. She finally looked at him and he waved her over.

Just as Carmen stood up and walked out of the section, the waitress entered. She set down a bottle of Dom Perignon on ice and several more glasses, as well as a couple of other drinks, hoping that Eve would look away long enough for her to deliver the note. She didn't have to wait long. Within seconds of Carmen's departure, Eve had her leg up on the chair, diddling with her vagina to the beat and "beep beep" of Donna Summer's "Bad Girl" for Prince Mansour's entertainment. The waitress saw her chance and took it. Reaching next to Sandra to get an empty glass, she dropped the napkin on the table and looked right into Sandra's face. "Blondie. Blondie!" Sandra looked up groggily. "You hear me?" Sandra nodded slightly. "The napkin on the table. See it? It's a note from your friends. Your boyfriend is here. You have to read the note and get out of here right away. But don't let anybody see you do it. Got it?"

"Danny?" Sandra managed to slur out a name.

"Yeah, whoever. Just read the note." A little more loudly, she asked, "Do you need anything else, sweetheart?" She turned to the rest of the group. "Anything else I can get you, your Highness?" He smiled and shook his head.

Sandra was confused, but she was at least able to put it together that she needed to read the note. She tried to do just that when she took the napkin and acted like she was blotting her lip gloss with it. But the lights were too dim in the section to make out the blue ink scribbling.

"Clayton, hey, papi. You made it," Carmen said, approaching Clayton and giving him a kiss on the cheek.

"Yeah, girl. Thanks for getting us in."

"No problem, J. You hook me up, I hook you up."

"Listen, I wanted to say thanks for throwing me that business earlier. Your man tipped me huge on top of it. So I wanted to show my appreciation." Clayton palmed twenty joints from his pocket and tucked them into Carmen's hand, curling her fingers over them. He never liked to be too conspicuous about his business dealings.

Carmen respected that, so she peeked at the contents of her hand as discreetly as she possibly could. "Oh my God, thank you, Clayton! You don't have to do this. It's only business, you know, but that's really sweet of you."

"It's nothing. Like you said, you scratch my back, I scratch yours."

Sandra had made at least a dozen attempts to read the note inconspicuously... and in her fucked-up state, but was never able to make out more than her name. Carmen had made her way back to their section and rolled her eyes at Eve's activities before sitting down in the chair next to Sandra with the lipstick bullet in hand. "Listen, mami, I'm real sorry...." Carmen started before Sandra stood straight up from her chair.

"I have to go to the bathroom," she announced, grasping at her stomach. She didn't know if it was Carmen's death clutch or the miscarriage... or actually having to go to the bathroom, but an abdominal cramp practically had her doubled over. The prince nodded and then jerked his head at Carmen to go along. Sandra's legs were like foam rubber as she made her way towards the bathroom with great effort. She managed to make it into a stall before Carmen came tearing through the bathroom door. Sandra pulled down her panties and sat down, but her body was so dehydrated that there was nothing in it to come out.

She recognized Carmen's voice immediately. "Mami? You okay? ...Sandra?"

Sandra managed a few words through her cottonmouth. "Can't I take a shit without the escort?" The bathroom attendant snickered audibly. Carmen leaned up against the sink and lit a cigarette, ashing in the basin as payback for the attendant's snicker.

Sandra read the note.

Sandra, me and Francis are up by the main bar. You gotta get away from these assholes. There reel bad news. Shake them and meet us so we can get you home. Hurry.

Clayton

P.S. Be careful cuz that guy Ivan has guns

"Francis is here," she whispered to herself. She read the note again two more times before dropping it in the toilet and flushing it.

"You okay in there?" Carmen asked again.

"I'll be right out," came Sandra's reply. She rose from the toilet seat the way a fighter with two closed eyes gets off the stool for the last rounds. With her equilibrium completely off, she exited the stall and staggered to the sink. With Carmen looming over her, Sandra leaned over the sink, too high to even focus on her own reflection. She started to pass out on her feet.

"She's been in there forever," I said to Clayton. "Are you sure she got the note?"

"My girl said she gave it to her with no problem. She said Sandra understood what it was."

"Maybe she went in the bathroom to try to ditch them and get to us."

"But that was Carmen who went in there with her. They're on her like stink on shit." Clayton replied.

"We'll wait here for a little while and see if she can break away. If she can't, I have a plan for going to them."

"What about the nutty German dude who's packing?"

"My plan doesn't quite cover that yet, but I'm thinking." I ordered another rum and Coke.

"Wake up, Sandra. You can pass out when we get back to the couch. Here. Have some of this." Carmen leaned in next to Sandra with the crack pipe, waiting for her to turn. But when she finally did, Sandra had called upon the last remnants of depleted energy in her body, and spun around into Carmen full-force. Caught off guard, the Latina stumbled backwards on her heels, allowing Sandra to push past her and make a break for the door. Sandra flung the door open and ran out into the club with Carmen in hot pursuit. Sandra was so disoriented, though. The whole place was spinning and she was unable to focus so she just went tearing up the aisle, away from the bathrooms as quickly as her rubbery legs would carry her.

"Oh, fuck. That's her," I said, catching a glimpse through the crowd of Sandra staggering towards us. Carmen came tearing out of the bathroom seconds later, running into a group of women and sending drinks flying. I sprinted in her direction, reaching her at the same time as Ivan and Carmen did.

"Francis," she gasped, collapsing in my arms as Carmen grabbed her wrist.

"Where are you going, you cunt?" she hissed.

"She's going with me, you cunt!" I barked back. Clayton had hung back to see if I was going to need him to jump in, partially from the fear of losing a customer as big as Carmen, and partially because he saw Ivan coming with his hand slipped inside his jacket.

"And who the fuck are you?" Carmen snapped back.

"I'm her friend."

Ivan intervened. "And didn't I tell you, friend, that you could talk to her later? That she was part of my client's private gathering? You have some difficulty grasping the concept of 'Fuck off?'" He snatched her arm and jerked her like a rag doll, trying to tear her away from my grip. I suppose he didn't realize that I was supporting all of her weight. She barreled into Carmen, sending her spilling onto her backside and I had to go down to one knee to keep Sandra from falling flat on her face. Ivan refused to release his grip.

"Leave her alone!" A lady's voice rang out above the fracas.

"Mind your business, bitch," Ivan snapped back, still struggling to get Sandra from me.

"Buddy, you better watch your mouth," another man's voice added.

Ivan looked up at the man and woman and released his grip, causing me to look up as well. "Diana, habibi! How is the most stunning woman in the United States this evening?" The prince had walked over personally to keep his henchman from causing a scene in front of Diana Ross and Reggie Jackson.

"Oh, Mansour. Does this attack dog belong to you?" She offered her hand and the prince took it, kissing it gently three times.

"Alas, yes, habibi. Sometimes my security detail gets a little overzealous."

"Well he damn near knocked that poor girl out. What is she? An assassin or something?" Diana Ross joked in a matter-of-factly way.

"No, no. This is all just a misunderstanding, yes, Ivan? Help the girl to her feet." He did as he was ordered.

"Have you met the prince, Reggie?"

"I don't think I've had the pleasure," Mr. October responded.

"Oh my goodness! Mansour, you're not the only royalty here tonight. Crown Prince Mansour, meet the New York Yankees' 'Sultan of Swat!'"

"Well, that was actually Babe Ruth's nickname," Jackson mused, taking the prince's hand, "but I'll take it as a compliment all the same."

"You two are easy to confuse. You both have candy bars named after you," Ms. Ross added.

"Well, the Baby Ruth wasn't actually named after him either, I'm afraid," Jackson laughed. "You're batting oh and two."

"Oh, shut up. You two are making me strain my voice before I have to sing."

"We wouldn't want to do that, Diana," Mansour said. "It is an immense pleasure meeting you, Mr. Jackson."

"The same here, your Highness."

"I have to go backstage, but I'll come over for a cocktail afterwards, alright?" She began to walk away with Reggie Jackson, tossing over her shoulder "And keep your dog on a leash, for Heaven's sake!"

Prince Mansour kept the same smile on his face as he waved good-bye to Diana Ross. Without looking at me, he asked, "What do you think you're doing, young man?"

"I'm taking my friend home, sir. I think she's had enough."

"Are you her guardian?" he asked.

"No, just her friend. That's all."

"Well, I'm not through with her," the prince replied, dropping the smile and looking at me for the first time.

his arrogance is amazing. "What do you mean you're not through with her?" I snapped back. "She ain't no rental unit, you asshole."

Ivan reached down and grabbed the back of my collar, but the prince raised his hand. Above all else, he did not want a scene. "She might as well be. I've paid for her."

i'm done with this sand nigger. "Let me tell you something. This girl's father is a First Grade Detective with the NYPD, and his precinct is less than a block away from here. I could be there and back in 30 seconds with a hundred officers. I don't know who you are or what you're about, but Sandra is underage, drunk, drugged... and since you bunch of fuckers won't let her go, that makes you kidnappers too. So if you want to fuck with me, let's go." The prince stared directly into my eyes as I was bluffing. "I already told the cops your whereabouts: Plaza Hotel, Penthouse. If I don't come out of this club with her, your Arab ass is in a lot of trouble. I don't give a fuck how many stars you know or how much money you have. This is America, asshole."

A thin smile grew on the prince's face as Ivan stood next to him, frozen like a German shepherd, suspended in mid-air and waiting to pounce. "I like you. You have a lot of balls, boy. I respect that. But let us suppose for a moment that you are not lying. You have no idea who I am. Have you ever heard of diplomatic immunity? You could come in here with a hundred <u>thousand</u> policemen, and they could do nothing to me."

I gulped. "Well you have no idea who <u>I</u> am. You have no idea who I work for. My boss' best friend is one of the editors over at *The New York Times*. Needless to say, her name ends with '-berg.' And if my memory is right, the Jews and you camel jockeys aren't exactly friends. You might keep handcuffs off your wrists, but she'll put so much shit on your name that you'll never be able to show your face in this country again, let alone this little shit hole club." *there are ways to punish someone beyond the law.*

The smile disappeared from Mansour's face. "Let them go," he commanded.

"But what about her..." Carmen started, pointing at the small purse Sandra still had clutched in her hand.

"Don't speak," the prince interrupted. "Ivan, get the car. The party is over. We will be leaving for home directly. I will have you take care of all of our things." Without another word, the prince stormed toward the door, leaving Carmen and Eve by themselves.

"What do we do now?" Eve asked.

"I saw some Frenchmen on the dance floor in Brooks' Brothers suits. Maybe they'll work. If I can only find another golden girl." Her voice trailed off as she disappeared into the throng of partiers.

Clayton stepped in to help me lift Sandra. "Yo, Francis...." he started. "Save it," I replied. "We just need to get her into a cab and home."

As soon as we were safely in a cab and turning onto Eighth Avenue, I tried to wake Sandra. I asked the driver to turn on the dome light. When he had, I immediately saw that she was blue in the face. "Sandra! Sandra!" I said, tapping her on the face. I couldn't get her to come around. "Take us to St. Clare's Hospital over on 52nd and Ninth." Sandra's skin was ice cold. *oh my god. she's not breathing.* I laid her back onto Clayton's lap and cleared her mouth. I wasn't entirely sure what I was doing, but I started trying to administer CPR. *i've always wanted to kiss these sweet lips... but not like this! not when they're blue.* The car screeched to a halt as Clayton jumped out of the cab and raced through the emergency entrance to get help. I tried to lift her, but she was completely dead weight. As I began to slide out of the car to attempt lifting her from another angle, I noticed blood all over my arm. From the way I'd been cradling her, she had to have been bleeding from her crotch.

After what seemed an eternity, Clayton led two nurses out through the door with a stretcher. They began examining Sandra even as she was being taken through the doors. I rushed in alongside her as Clayton stayed behind to pay the cab driver. One nurse turned and stopped me as order-lies wheeled her stretcher behind some curtains. "You can't go any further, sir. You'll just have to wait. What's her name?" I told her. "Okay. Just wait. Don't go anywhere. We'll need to ask for some more information." The nurse disappeared.

Tears started to pour from my eyes as Clayton came and put an arm around me. We just stood there in silence. *what if she dies? her father will go crazy. he'll think we had something to do with it. i wish i was home in bed and this was just a nightmare. at least i could wake up from it.* Finally I spoke. "We gotta call Father Healy. He'll know what to do."

After a tension- and tear-filled several minutes, Father Joseph Healy finally stepped into the E.R. waiting room at St. Clare's Hospital. After a hug for both Clayton and me, we went through the process of trying to get him caught up on Sandra's situation. At first, I grappled with whether or not I should leave out some of the more hardcore elements, but decided in the end to tell him everything. He didn't look pleased, but he also didn't look disappointed. He took it all in at face value without judgment, the way those priests who actually matter in a person's life are able to do. Fr. Healy got extremely quiet and stared at the floor with his index finger crooked over, resting between his nose and his top lip. Finally, he spoke, "Well, the first thing we have to do is figure out a way to get in touch with her parents. You say you think they went away for the weekend... but you have tried to call them, haven't you?"

Clayton and I exchanged a nervous look. "Father, you can't do that."

"What?" the priest replied.

"Well, that's why we called you first. Sandra's parents can't know about this. It would kill them... and that would kill Sandra."

"Don't be absurd, Francis. She's a child. They're her parents. They have a right to know."

"I'm serious, Father," I pleaded. "You don't realize the kind of relationship she has with them, especially her father. Disappointing him like this would send him into a blind rage... and send her over the edge. You see how frail she is already."

Fr. Healy's hooked finger returned to its place above his top lip as he fell deep into thought again. Jack O'Casey was indeed a high-strung and volatile man. The tales of "above the law" things the detective had done to enforce the law were legendary in the neighborhood. And the pontiff had always been concerned about the overly fragile side to Sandra's personality that he'd noticed lurking just under the surface.

"Well, let me go talk to the doctors and see what's going on. I'd like to talk with Sandra too, if possible. But it may all be for nothing. For all we know, her parents are home by now and worried sick about where their little girl is. Det. O'Casey may already be in contact with the officers at the precinct and come walking through that door any second."

father is right, of course. i hadn't thought about any of that. Sandra's life was in the balance in more ways than one. Clayton and I went back to our seats, flipping through torn copies of *Life* magazine without really absorbing any of the words we were reading. All that remained was to wait.

Every time something appeared in the door frame of the waiting room, my eyes darted over with every expectation of seeing Det. O'Casey standing there, gun drawn. After what felt like days, Fr. Healy emerged with an extremely serious look on his face. I'd always been terrible at poker, but I was trying to read whether it was bad news about Sandra all the same. "I've prayed about this, and the Lord has told me to help you children, so I'm going to go out on a limb and try." I leapt up and gripped Fr. Healy's neck like a little boy. "I know Sandra and her family very well, and I agree with your assessment of her situation. One of the perks of being a member of the clergy within the walls of a hospital is that you are able to ask for a person's trust... and for special favors, so I have asked that she be listed as Jane Doe and a Ward of the Church. I am still waiting for the doctor to give me his assessment. We'll figure out where to go at that point."

Clayton had fallen asleep in his chair, so I returned to the seat next to him and closed my eyes. I could hardly believe that I was completely sobered up. With all of the Quaaludes I'd taken and all of the drinks I'd had at Studio, I should've been finding it difficult to say my own name. But nerves and adrenaline were surging through my body, and although it was almost 3 a.m., I felt like it was noon. *shit! i have to meet benny in just a couple of hours. i'm never going to make it.* I went out to the pay phone in the hall. After I'd left a message on Benny's answering machine, I replaced the receiver and paused as I began to turn around. I thought for a minute and then dropped more change into the machine. I dialed Sandra's home number and waited with my hand over the mouthpiece. It rang and rang and rang. Sixteen times in all, I counted. Finally I hung up the phone, content that at least her parents weren't home yet. I returned to the waiting room to pace while Sandra O'Casey, the Jewel of Tenth Avenue, lay in her room like a broken glass doll.

On what had to be my 500th time around the room, I heard Fr. Healy's voice. "She was suffering from acute dehydration and has lost an enormous amount of blood. But she has also overdosed from the intake of a variety of drugs... nearly to the point of expiring. I stood in there while they worked frantically to stabilize her, and all I could think of was her first Holy Communion. In short, Sandra has been worked over pretty good. It definitely seems to be a criminal matter... quite brutal, painful and, I imagine, very embarrassing. They're still looking into a couple of things, but we'll see what's going to happen."

I took in the news. "I tried calling her apartment from the pay phone. It rang a bunch of times, but no one ever picked up."

"Okay. Well, we can safely assume, then, that her parents are not there. That buys us some time."

"Father Healy?" A short, bespectacled woman in a long, white coat had stepped into the room. "Can we talk outside for a moment?" After he'd followed her out into the hall, I walked over and sat as close as possible to the door to try to overhear. "Jane is stabilized now and resting. We pumped her stomach to evacuate the intoxicants and have replenished her blood and fluids with I.V.s. We had to do some stitching on her vaginal walls as well. It seems clear that she was sexually assaulted, although we found no presence of semen. There appeared to be several deep abrasions, probably caused by fingernails or some other sort of foreign object. They were responsible for some, but not all of her bleeding. Were you aware that she had recently been pregnant?"

"No, I wasn't," he replied.

"Well, it was very early in the first term. Based on her age, it is entirely possible that she wasn't aware either... nor would she have been aware of the miscarriage."

"A miscarriage? I see. Well, I can ask her and find out."

"We should let her rest for right now, but when she wakes up, we can ask her some more questions then. For now, though, she's out of the woods, but she's going to need at least a couple of days of rest."

"Alright. Thank you, Dr. Burke."

"Oh, and Fr. Healy? I forgot to give you this." She handed him Sandra's clutch purse. When she was in and out of consciousness, one of the nurses tried to ask her what she wanted done with it, and Jane said she wanted it away from her, that she never wanted to see it again."

"Right. Thanks." Fr. Healy returned to the waiting room as I made an attempt to dash back to my seat by Clayton's side. "So you heard all of that, Mr. Doonan?" I nodded. "Were you aware of her pregnancy?"

I shook my head. "In the cab, she was bleeding from down there but I didn't know why. There's only one person she's been seeing for awhile now. Danny Albanese. The baby would have to be his."

"J.R. Albanese's son? I wonder if he knew. Well, when she wakes up, I can talk to her about it more then."

The priest opened Sandra's clutch and was startled by its contents just as Clayton's snore woke him up. He cracked an eye long enough to make out Fr. Healy and me. "Oh, hey, Father. Any news on Sandra?"

"She's on the mend, but she still needs a good deal of rest." He turned to me. "Do you know anything about these?" Fr. Healy pulled out a couple of very expensive-looking pieces of jewelry.

"I've never seen her wear anything like that before," I replied.

"I have," Clayton chimed in. "At least the necklace. When I saw her with Carmen at the dress store in The Plaza, that was the only other thing she was wearing besides a big white robe. That sheikh guy from Studio 54 must've given it to her. Cats like that are famous for giving pretty young things like Sandra jewelry and watches and cars and shit... I mean stuff to keep them hanging around. I guess he gave her that other stuff too."

Fr. Healy put it back in the clutch and resecured the clasp. "She told the doctor she didn't want to see it again. That would make sense if it came from her attacker. I'm going to go in and sit with her until she wakes up. Why don't you boys go get some coffee and I'll meet you back here in an hour?"

Clayton and I headed over to one of the 24-hour joints on Ninth. "Yo, this is fucked up," Clayton said. "This is definitely not how I thought I'd be spending my Sunday night."

"Yeah, me neither. You still have any of those Rorers with you?"

"Am I ever unprepared?" he responded, pulling out his bag of pills and giving me one, tossing another to the back of his throat and chasing it with a swig of coffee. "Better still," he added, pulling out a joint and a lighter, "pure Thai stick, baby!" We continued to walk the streets of the Kitchen, smoking a joint and waiting for the Quaalude to kick in. "So she was really pregnant? For real?"

"That's what that lady doctor said." I could already feel the effects of the drugs.

"Ooh. Nasty. Imagine. A littler Danny Albanese. If they get dumber with each generation, think of how retarded that little baby would be."

"Yeah, but how beautiful with Sandra as its mother," I replied wistfully. *i still love her so much. i just wish that little one would've been mine.*

"You'll just never learn, man. Sad."

Fr. Healy had gone in with Sandra and pulled up a chair next to her bed. Just before the sun began to rise, Sandra's eyelids fluttered and, although she was barely conscious, she recognized Father right away. She tried to lean up on her elbows, but couldn't. "Relax. Don't try to move just yet, child."

She smacked her lips a couple of times in an attempt to talk, so Fr. Healy poured some water in an avocado-colored plastic cup and oriented the straw to reach her mouth. She drank and then croaked, "Father, am I in the hospital? How did i get here?"

"You were brought here by Francis Doonan and Clayton Brooks. They rescued you, in fact, and probably saved your life."

"Francis and Clayton? Really? I don't even remember seeing them."

"At the big discotheque on 54ᵗʰ Street, I believe," the priest offered.

The details, though foggy, came flooding back. "Oh, my God. I remember now." She suddenly became panic stricken. "What day is it? Are my parents here? Jesus, they're going to kill me."

"Just calm down, child. The sun's just risen on Monday morning, but we haven't been able to get ahold of them yet."

"You can't," she blurted out. "I have to get out of here. I have to get home."

"Relax, Sandra. We've taken no steps to notify them yet. I wanted to talk to you first. I'm aware of your situation, and I wanted to try to help. When are your parents expected?"

"Later this morning. Sometime before noon, I think." Great tears welled up in her eyes. "You can't tell them where I was. You can't tell them what I was doing, Father. You can't. They'll kill me."

"I understand, dear. I understand. But, Sandra, there's another thing I have to ask you. Were you aware that you were pregnant?" He could tell the answer instantly from the look on her face. She slowly and shamefully nodded yes. "And the baby? It was Danny Albanese's child."

"How...?" she started, realizing that Clayton and Francis had rescued her. She nodded again.

"Did he know?" Sandra nodded once again, burying her face in her hands and sending down a torrent of tears.

"Well, I'm sorry to tell you, child, that you lost your baby." Sandra continued to weep, but was silently and deeply relieved. Although she tried to hide it from Fr. Healy, he could still sense it, and so he decided not to ask whether she was already aware of the miscarriage. "You have been through a tremendous ordeal, Sandra. Your doctor has said that you've also been drugged and severely abused... sexually."

"Oh, no. Doctor Parker knows? He's been friends with my father since elementary school. He'll tell for sure."

"No, your attending physician, Dr. Julie Burke, here at St. Clare's. She's advised me that this is a criminal matter, that you should really talk to the police."

Sandra began crying harder. "I wasn't raped. I guess... I guess I went along with it. I don't know why. Oh, my God. Father, what you must think of me."

"It's alright, child. Christ died for our sins, remember? I'm just thankful that you're still alive. I want to help. I want to help with the trouble in your soul. And if I do, you just have to promise me that you will get some professional help for the trouble in your mind and body. Agreed?" Sandra nodded and reached over, grasping Fr. Healy's hand, giving it an appreciative squeeze.

A nurse stepped from behind the curtain. "Well, there she is. Good morning, sweetheart. Feeling better?"

"Nurse," Fr. Healy asked, "would you be so kind as to get the two boys in the waiting room so they can come in and say hello?" She smiled and exited.

In a matter of moments, Clayton and I stepped sheepishly into view, paranoid and a little sluggish from being stoned. "I'm going to go talk to the doctor and see about getting Sandra released into my care with enough medicine and whatever else she needs for the rest of the week. But in the meantime, there are things that you each need to do." He pulled a small notebook and pen out of his jacket pocket and put them on her tray, pushing the button to raise the head of her bed so she could sit up. "You need to write a note to your parents to tell them that you and I have gone to the Holy Cross Retreat Center in Mahopac. You're there to help prepare it for it's season opening... and we invited along young Francis to provide him with company while he grieves the loss of Howie Nesto. We'll tell them that you'll call after they're home, and that you'll be staying a couple of nights." Sandra began writing the note, but soon looked up at the priest, confused and unable to remember what to write. "Don't worry, dear. I'll help you."

Looking sternly at Clayton and me, he said, "Francis, you're to go get three coffees and bring them back. Clayton, behind the rectory is my old station wagon. Here are the keys. Get it and come back here as fast as you can." We started to head out on our errands until he stopped us. "And... give me whatever it is the two of you took. I'm not stupid. This poor girl almost lost her life because of that garbage and the two of you are partying it up like morons." Clayton and I just looked at each other and almost laughed until Fr. Healy barked, "Give it to me!" Clayton reached in his pockets and handed over the bag of joints and the bag of pills. "Now go. And be quick about it."

I returned before Clayton like a little boy who'd just received a spanking. Fr. Healy made no more mention of it. Sandra was sitting up and had some color back in her cheeks. She even attempted flashing me a smile. Fr. Healy just put a folded-up piece of paper in my hand and held out a set of keys. "Okay, now these are the keys to the O'Casey's apartment. Call from a payphone first to make sure they're not home, and then slip inside with the keys to put this note under the purple dolphin magnet on the refrigerator. Do you have that, Francis? It's very important. It's the only place that she leaves notes for them."

"Purple dolphin magnet," I repeated.

"Good. Go. By the time you return, we should be ready to leave for Mahopac." I saw Clayton pulling up in the old station wagon as I ran out of the hospital.

Sure enough, as soon as I'd returned and gave the good father a nod to say that the deed was done, Sandra was already in a wheelchair. We all pitched in to move her into the station wagon and did our best to make her comfortable. Fr. Healy spoke to us before we got in the car. Francis, you're coming up with me to help with Sandra. Clayton, I'll need you to do something for me first and then take the bus up afterwards." He handed Sandra's clutch purse to Clayton. "She's confirmed that the items in this handbag were from the Arabic man, and that she doesn't want them anymore. I've gotten the hospital to designate her a Ward of the Church in order to get her released to my care. That also means that the hospital bill will come to the church. I need you to take the contents of this bag and use whatever means you have with whatever contacts you have to get the most that you can for them. With Howie gone, from what I've heard, I know I've picked the right man for this job." Clayton and I both smiled like guilty men. "God be with you, son."

"And also with you, Father," Clayton replied as we pulled away towards the West Side Highway.

———————— ∭ ————————

Dorothy O'Casey practically leapt from the car before it even stopped in front of their building. Fumbling with her purse for the keys, she was so worried that she dared not speak for fear of screaming or crying. She walked along the building's main hallway, nodding civilly to one of their neighbors, but refusing to be taken in by any attempts at small talk. She turned the corner and grabbed the handrail, taking the stairs two at a time, up one flight after another until she'd reached their floor in the tenement. She had her keys in hand that time, though, and had scarcely cracked the door before she started to call out Sandra's name. The door to her daughter's room was closed, but she refused to bother with knocking. She flung the door open, but saw no trace of her little girl. She walked into the living room and flipped through the *Redbook* quickly, but didn't find the money she'd left there. Nothing else seemed to be out of place. Nothing was out of the ordinary... except she was missing her baby! More frantically, she stormed into the kitchen and immediately saw a note beneath the purple dolphin magnet on the refrigerator. Just as she had ripped the paper down and began reading it, her husband kicked the door open, both hands carrying luggage. "Boy, some people will do anything to get out of carrying up their own bags." Dorothy burst into tears. "Oh, I'm sorry," Det. O'Casey offered. "I was only kidding."

"No, it isn't that," his wife replied, smiling through the tears of relief. She handed him the note as the purple dolphin got replaced on the refrigerator door.

"You see? I told you she was fine. She was just missing our phone calls. That's all." He read some more. "Aw, what a good little girl she is." He kissed her on the head. "She takes after you, honey. Who else would give up a little freedom, away from their old parents, to cheer up a friend and be with a priest, doing charity work for the church? You know, you should trust her a little more and worry a little less."

Dorothy sighed. "God is good."

Fr. Healy pulled the station wagon up to the retreat house. I stirred from my nap in the front seat while Sandra still seemed to be sleeping peacefully in the back. *i think i'm still high… but that's definitely a hangover. fuck i wish i had a drink or some weed or something to stop this trembling.* Sister Mary Margaret, who had the shape of a fire hydrant, heard the car approach and stepped out onto the porch, ready to jump to duty. Fr. Healy and she were old friends, and there was a bedroom already made up once the three of us managed to get Sandra inside. Fr. Healy began filling the sister in on the situation, handing her the clipboard with all of Sandra's case history from the hospital. "Poor child," was the only comment the nun made.

"Sister," Fr. Healy replied, "what are we going to need for provisions?"

"Just about everything," Mary Margaret replied. "We were only just preparing for the season, Father."

"Okay, then, you've got it: food for five for… maybe a week?"

"Five? We're only four here, Father. We'll be expecting more to come, then?" she said, more than asked, in a lilting Irish brogue. "'Tis no matter. I'm going to stay with her right in that chair at the end of the bed with me new book, 'Trinity,' by a Mr. Leon Uris." She held the book up for us to see, flashing a great, ruddy faced Irish grin.

"Right, then," Father replied. "In the meantime, Francis and I are going to go over to the local Grand Union." We drove a short while until we pulled up in front of a typical supermarket. He parked and said, "Why don't you grab one of those carts over there, Francis?" I could see Fr. Healy looking in his wallet before he even got out of the car.

"If you're opening up next week anyway, Father, maybe we should stock up now and save time."

Fr. Healy chuckled. "Yes, that would be an ideal plan, my boy, but we'll have to wait for some money. You see, when the parishioners come, they pay the weekend fee and <u>then</u> we shop. We don't really have a reserve. In fact, we're going to be stretching things a little thin for this week. A priest's wallet is more likely to come apart because of moths than stress on the seams."

"Well, then," I started, "I'd like to make a donation, if I could. I mean, it's my fault you're involved in all of this. You shouldn't have to spend what little you've got. I'd really like you to take this." I handed him $600, adding, "I hope this will be enough for the week, as well as stocking up for some of the season."

Fr. Healy looked at me with disbelief. "I can't accept this, Francis. That's just too much."

"But you're only here because of me," I replied.

"Where on Earth did you come up with so much money?" He stopped himself short, putting up a hand. "Don't answer that. I've had my daily fill of surprises about the lives of you children. Well, if you're certain you can spare it, Francis, thank you. This will definitely fill the cupboards and then some! ...And in this event, you'd better get another cart."

We entered the supermarket and began to walk through each aisle, filling the two shopping carts with everything imaginable. "You know, this reminds me of when I was a boy. Every Wednesday night was A&P

night. We'd all go grocery shopping together. Anyway, one night it was me, Philomena and Bernadette – Charlotte hadn't been born yet – with my parents at the A&P. I wanted to get some candy so bad, but I knew my mother would never say yes. So... I have no idea why I did it... but I stole a big Tootsie Roll candy bar and figured that I could just eat the evidence as we walked around the store. But Tootsie Rolls don't exactly melt in your mouth, so hiding the chewing and the dark, sticky chunks stuck to the sides of my mouth from my parents and sisters was a real job. I was still at a loss for a good place to stash the wrapper, though, and just thought I was a genius when I stuck it behind some canned peas that were three deep. I looked around and, as I was swallowing the last bit of chocolate cement, just <u>knew</u> I'd gotten away with it. We got in line and my mother was looking through her coupons as my father was licking away to put the plaid stamps into the prize book with my sisters. It was my job to go into the line just before the cart so I could unload it onto the conveyor belt. When I finished and turned around to see the store manager at the end of the aisle, glaring at me, I knew I had nowhere to go. He just stood there, staring, until our food was almost all rung up and we were about to leave the store. I couldn't tell if I was just being paranoid until he tapped my father on the shoulder and whispered in his ear. My dad turned back around and put a crumpled Tootsie Roll wrapper on the conveyor belt with the rest of the food. It got rung up and bagged, but he never looked at me, never spoke a word. As soon as we got to the car, he hit me like he was Rocky Praziano. If it wasn't for the family Plymouth, I would've gone straight down."

"And what did you learn from that, Francis?" Fr. Healy asked.

"Oh, I know you're waiting for me to quote a commandment." The Father broke up laughing. "But sincerely, Father, that moment stopped me from ever even considering becoming a thief. It was the only time my father ever hit me."

"Well, that makes me feel a lot better about the $600 in my pocket," the priest mused.

"What? I can't have a job or nothing?" I asked.

"Oh, please, Francis. Don't try to put on that halo and wings just yet. I know a story or two about you and your friends that gives me ample reason to wonder. Or do you think I don't know about Howie – God rest his soul – and the London broil?" Fr. Healy asked.

"The London broil?" I questioned.

"It was a few years ago, but I know all about the time the two of you were in the grocery and Mr. Nesto stuffed a huge London broil down the front of his light-colored, corduroy pants. When the security guard stopped him and asked if it was his 'time of the month,' Howie replied something about it being a <u>hell</u> of a month right before you rammed into the guard's back and the two of you went scampering out of the store."

I just stood there with my mouth wide open. "How did you know about that?"

"You were neighborhood kids, Francis. They knew who you were… and I knew what you were made of. Who do you think paid Mr. Manzetto for those three pounds of meat… and then talked him out of pressing charges?" The priest tossed a bag of mini Tootsie Rolls into the cart.

After the men had left and Leon Uris' writing had just enough time to make Sister Mary Margaret's eyelids heavy, she was awakened by the sound of Sandra dry-heaving. There was little more than bile in her stomach to come up, but the sister grabbed the trash bucket all the same. "Those demons aren't happy about being chased away, are they darling?" Sandra's body almost began to convulse as her breathing approached hyperventilation. But the nun steadied her by literally laying on top of the girl, making sure to keep the golden locked head aimed away. When Sandra's breathing resumed a slower pace and the nun was confident that she'd drifted back to sleep, Mary Margaret lifted herself off the bed and sat back down in her chair with "Trinity."

Less than an hour later, the sister was standing above Sandra, dabbing at her brow, when she awoke with a great gasp. "You'll be wondering who I am," the nun said. "I'm Sister Mary Margaret, a friend of Fr. Healy's, and you're in Mahopac at the Holy Cross Retreat House." Sandra nodded, producing a weak smile. "I hope I didn't frighten you when you opened your eyes. It's just that you started breathing funny and I came over to be at the ready. Open your mouth, dear heart." The nun lifted Sandra's head slightly and administered a few pills with a small glass of water, gently returning her to the pillow. Content that Sandra was now well and truly on the road to recovery, the good sister headed back to her book, as a gentle breeze wafted in through the sunlit window and cooled the room.

Fr. Healy and I pulled up in the driveway, singing along to the Beatles "She's Got a Ticket to Ride" at full, off-key voice. I actually felt good and hadn't craved a drink or a drug in a couple of hours. "I'll start bringing the stuff in, Father. Why don't you go check on Sandra?" *i really like being helpful, being useful.*

After the last bag was unloaded and Fr. Healy had gotten a report on Sandra's condition, he looked at me and said, "I don't know about you, but I'm starving. Let's offer to trade duties with the sister so she can make us some lunch."

"No, that's okay," I replied. "I love cooking. I'd be happy to make something."

The priest made the sign of the cross. "Well, let me go see what Mary Margaret thinks would be best for the patient to try eating at this point. She might just still be giving her water."

———————————— ❦ ————————————

Clayton was able to catch a little sleep before leaving his apartment in the late morning. There was only one person he knew who could access the type of money he was looking for. Lucky had been a bookie in the neighborhood for more than fifty years. At noon each day, he'd drag an old metal kitchen chair out of the hardware store near Ninth and 48th Street, sitting there for hours to do his "special work." People of every walk and want would visit as though Lucky were the Pope. That Monday, Clayton rounded the corner for his audience with the Kitchen's Unholy Father.

"I've got something for you, man. They're diamonds, Lucky. For real." Clayton got straight to business; no conversation.

"You're standing in my sunlight, kid," the old bookie croaked. "I just got back from Florida the other day and I'm trying to keep this tan going. Can't you see your shadow? C'mon! Move a little to the left... your left." Lucky was one of those control-freak types who liked to make people think that he wasn't interested in what they had to sell when, in fact, he usually was.

"C'mon, man. If you're not interested, I've got a Jewish dude over on 46th who's waiting for me to bring this stuff by. I'm only here because you're closer."

"Alright, kid. Let's go inside before you piss yourself." They stepped into Lucky's showroom. The hardware store was just a front. Of course, they sold tools and that sort of thing there, but barely enough to keep the lights on. Lucky owned it primarily as a place to house boosted merchandise. Clayton had already transferred the contents of Sandra's clutch to another small, cloth bag, leaving her lip gloss, chewing gum and some cash in the purse, so he followed Lucky back to the "Employees Only" area behind an unusually thick steel Dutch door, and poured the jewelry from the bag onto a large silver tray that had seen its engraving freshly buffed away. There were three pieces: a sizable diamond on a heavy, gold rope, an intricately detailed gold ring and a pair of stunning circular earrings that were covered entirely with black and white diamonds. "You weren't joking, kid." Lucky couldn't disguise his interest while Clayton just beamed. "Where the fuck did you get this?"

"You should know better than to ask that," Clayton replied. "But if you're concerned that it's stolen, it's not. That's why, if you try to Jew me on the price, I'm going to take it to an actual Jew. Nobody's gonna be looking for this stuff. Promise."

"Alright. I got you. But diamonds really aren't my thing." Clayton started to scoop up the jewelry. "Wait a minute! I'm not saying I don't want them. It's just that my brother, Gino, is the jewelry expert. He'll want these. I'm sure of it. Come back in two hours and we'll have something for you."

Clayton headed home for another quick cat nap, but he still woke up with time to kill, so he decided to stop in at the Galaxy Diner for a quick sandwich. Romeo T was already there, nursing the tiniest bit of soda and pushing around the remnants of a plate of French fries. "To-nay!" Clayton greeted his friend.

"Hey! When'd you get out of Riker's, you moolie?" Romeo shot back.

"Fuck you," Clayton responded. "I'm too pretty to get caught. What're you doing here with all your friends?" He motioned around at the empty diner.

"Waiting for Vit, actually. We were supposed to be doing something, but he's late as usual. What are you up to?"

"Just have a little business to take care of. I'd tell ya, but I'd hafta kill ya," he joked.

"Yeah. 'Business.' Selling some weed ain't 'business.' It's just selling some weed." Vit entered with a mouthful of apologies. "Save it, man. You make being late an art form. I thought it was the jigs who were always late."

"Right," said Clayton. "It's you dagoes who are the ones that only bathe in cologne."

"Shut up, you fucks," Vit said. "I really do have a reason for being late this time. I just saw my cousin, Carmella. She said that she ran into J.R. Albanese at a christening yesterday and he told her to have me come down there and see him today."

"For real? What for?" Romeo asked.

"I don't know, but she said he was nice and shit. I wonder if there's some money in it somewhere. You guys wanna come with me? I don't wanna go alone."

"Man, count me out," Clayton said. "I wouldn't trust Johnny Rugs to lick my asshole."

"Yeah, Clayton's got 'business' up here." Romeo T laughed. "I'll go with you, though. What's the worst that could happen? People know that we're going to be there."

Romeo and Vit said their farewells and headed out of the diner and down Ninth Avenue. Clayton finished his turkey club and went in the opposite direction. He found Lucky sitting with Gino in front of the store. "Good morning, young man. I have an envelope here with $10,000 in it. Why don't we go in and take a look at your merchandise? If it's as good as my brother says it is, you can have this envelope." He grunted as he wedged himself out of the folding chair. "And believe me, young man, that's the best you're going to get. Certainly better than a Jew would give you." Clayton knew the stuff was probably worth four or five times that amount, but he wasn't going to argue. He disappeared inside the shop with Gino and reemerged a few minutes later.

Angelo looked up as Clayton passed by and said, "Don't you spend that all in one place." The two brothers laughed in unison as Clayton walked away, waving.

Vit and Romeo T got to what was left of the Dante League Social Club as the Sicilian crew was erecting a scaffold on the outside. Dodging a remnant of police barricade tape, Vit ducked under the scaffold. "Bad luck, man," said Romeo.

"Don't be an asshole," Vit fired back. "You don't really believe in that shit do you?" Romeo didn't respond, even though he kind of did believe in that shit.

The pair found J.R. inside, sitting down to lunch with his son. "Welcome, boys, you want we should get another couple of plates?"

"Sure," Vit replied.

"I'm actually not that hungry, Mr. Albanese. I just ate," Romeo said.

"Suit y'self," J.R. said, handing Vit a menu. "Take a look and order whatever you want. Luigi will go get it for you." Luigi looked like he'd just been paroled from San Quentin... but not for good behavior.

Vit looked up at Luigi and said, "I'll just have the same as them."

Danny hadn't taken his eyes off of the pair of friends since they'd entered, his face frozen in a look of disgust. "What are they doing here?" he whispered. "They're on the other team, pop."

"Don't be rude, Daniel. I asked this young man to come.... but I am thrilled that... what's your name son?"

"Tony, um Anthony, sir."

"...Anthony came along too. We're all Italian, right? Well, in the spirit of reconciliation, I thought that maybe they would grab the olive branch if it were offered to them... especially since even they can see that they're up to their asses in quicksand. *Capisce?*" Vit looked anxious, and even though Romeo would've really rather left, he figured he would at least hear J.R. out. Albanese continued, "Listen, I'm not going to sugar-coat this. I need you guys to be with me. We're all *fratelli, familia* here, right? And you need to be with your own people. Things are about to get very ugly around here with that Kelly the Mick recruiting up half the West Side. You both know that those micks fucked up my club... gunned down my guy... stuck up my game.... What am I? A fucking jerk-off here? I'm just supposed to sit back and let these guys shit on me? No. I didn't want this. I'm a peaceful businessman, but they won't leave me and mine alone... so you have to get in with your own. And I wouldn't want to see two of my own kind get mixed up on the wrong side and get hurt, right?"

Luigi came back into the room with three heroes rolled up in white paper. He set the bag down in the middle of the table and said, "That guy with the thing wanted you to call him, boss."

"*Mangia*, fellas," J.R. said. "We'll finish after you eat. I'll be right back."

Vit unwrapped his sandwich and dug in. Romeo and Danny were left staring at one another in total silence. Vit thought he'd try to break the ice. "So how's everything been, Danny?"

Danny glared at him with genuine hatred. "Fuck you," he said, getting up and walking away.

Romeo turned immediately to his friend. "Vit, what? Are you fucking crazy coming here? You think this sonofabitch means a word he's saying?"

"You're right," Vit replied, taking a final bite of his sandwich. "I'm just going to hit the john and we'll get out of here, alright?"

J.R. returned to the table while Vit was in the bathroom. Romeo sat nervously as Albanese unwrapped his hero and dug in. Vit came back moments later. "Mr. Albanese, thanks very much for the invite and the sandwich and all, but we're going to have to pass." Vit stuck his hand out to shake with J.R.

A piece of eggplant dropped out of his mouth, making a loud splat on the white paper. He looked up at Vit incredulously. "Oh, yeah?" Then he looked down at the teen's outstretched offering. He wiped his own hand with a napkin and then shook with Vit. "Well, I sure hope you washed your hands!" he roared, laughing. "Okay, boys. No hard feelings. You take care of yourselves, and lemme know if you change your minds."

Romeo T hung his head as he and Vit walked out. As soon as they'd stepped back out onto the street, Romeo said, "Fucking Christ, Vit! You could've got us fucking killed."

"Jesus Christ, Rome, I'm sorry. But I didn't know what he wanted to talk about. What was I going to do? Say no? We came and now we're going. We don't have to do it again. Relax."

Inside the Dante League Social Club, Danny chanced approaching his father. "I told you, pop. They're a couple of shitbags."

Danny was amazed that, instead of a sock in the gut, he actually got an apology. "You know what, son? I'm sorry for inviting those guys here. I don't know what I was thinking about."

Danny was taken aback. "You don't have to apologize or anything. I just know not to trust those guys. That's all." He snatched up the rest of Vit's sandwich and paper and stormed off to the trash can while J.R. snuck a peek downward to look at the note Vit had slipped him on a paper towel:

I'm in. I'll come back alone to talk to you later.

J.R. had gotten himself a spy.

Just as Kelly the Mick, Colin Garvan, Milk, Brian and Patty Boy entered the Blarney Stone, Patsy slammed down the phone after trying to reach Francis for the "900th time," pissed that he kept getting "that fecking answering contraption." The men sat at the table furthest from the door as Patsy muttered indiscreetly, "And what the feck is this?" Kelly the Mick looked over in Patsy's direction and gave him a jerk of the head. Patsy snorted, but didn't otherwise budge. He was unimpressed with Kelly the Mick's version of holding court. As the gangster droned on about his plans and perceived successes, the young boys listened intently. Patsy had three glasses of Hennessy while keeping an eye and an ear on the boasting before making his way over to the table with menus.

The boys, including Colin Garvan all said, "Hello, Mr. Doonan," one by one.

Kelly the Mick said instead, "Hey there, Pats. How are you today?"

Patsy ignored him. "What's it going to be, boys?" He took their orders and then finally came around to Kelly the Mick. "And what'll you be having?"

"Corned beef, cabbage, a couple of spuds and a stein of Heineken." Patsy nodded and turned to walk away. "Say, Pats," Kelly the Mick continued, "where's Francis hiding these days?"

Patsy pivoted back around and replied, "Well, for one, he ain't hiding. And for two, if he was, it would probably be from a little shite-eater like yourself." The elder Doonan continued to the steam table, but Kelly was infuriated by his behavior, so he got up and stalked after the bar owner. Everyone else at the table was silent and kept their gaze averted; they didn't know how to behave or react. Patsy handed their order to an employee at the steam table and said, "Make this nice for the boys over there," and proceeded behind the bar to pull beer.

Kelly the Mick stopped right in front of him on the other side of the bar. "Hey, Patsy, I don't like the way you just talked to me."

"Well, most people don't like the way I talk to them, so you're not alone. And if I had any friends, I'd tell you that only my friends call me 'Patsy...' so don't." He had six steins in his hand, beer flowing into all of them in turn.

Kelly was flustered. "You know, ...Patsy, I get a lot of respect around here these days."

Patsy looked up and flashed him a condescending smile. "Well, isn't that nice for ya? So why don't you sit down and wait for your food with all that respect? Or better yet, if you don't like it, why don't you just get out of my fecking bar? Go to McHale's. Play 'tough-guy cocksucker' with all the other tough-guys... sucking... cock." He glared right through Kelly the Mick as he gripped the edge of the bar so hard his knuckles turned white. Patsy just kept pouring beers, never taking his eyes off of the gangster.

"You're lucky, Doonan. That's all I can say."

"Oh?" Patsy said. "Lucky how?"

"You're lucky I don't kick the living shit out of you and then shake you down," Kelly the Mick snarled.

"You know what?" Patsy began quietly. "Handling this sort of thing in public like this is just no good for my business. If you want to continue this discussion, though, let me drop off the drinks and we can have a word back in my office."

"By all means," he snapped back, fuming.

Patsy took the drinks to the table. This one's on me. *Sliante*, laddies." Patsy turned back to Kelly the Mick. "This way, gent."

"What the fuck did he just call us?" Milk inquired.

"Slouchin' ladies? Who the fuck knows." Patty Boy answered back, taking a long drink of his beer.

Patsy led Kelly the Mick through a small maze of stacked beer boxes, back into the office where he turned on a light and waited for Kelly the Mick to pass by so the old man could close the door. He shut the door, spun around, and pulled a military-issue .45 that he'd taken as payment for a bar tab from a sailor not too long ago. Kelly the Mick didn't move a muscle. "Now let me tell you the rule here. You feck with me and I will blow your fecking head clean off. And what's more, I'll get away with it. Scott free. And before you mistake that for a bluff, you should know that I have cops, FBI, Secret Service and every other kind of law enforcement drinking in my bar. They'll fix it all for me. And you know why? Because they all know you're a fecking scumbag. As a matter of fact, you're a worse scumbag than your pathetic father was. We even called him 'Trojan' because of it. Your grandfather, on the other hand... now <u>he</u> was a gentleman, but your father must have birthed you right out of his arse. Oh, and another thing, you stay away from my nephew, Francis. He'd kick the shite out of you anyway."

Kelly glared daggers into the old man and started to fidget as though he were considering lashing out. Patsy just pulled the hammer back on his huge cannon of a gun. "Try me, boy-o. <u>Please</u> call me bluff."

Kelly the Mick looked solidly at the old Irishman before sending up the white flag in his own eyes. Patsy took a deep sniff. "Now go wipe the shite that's dripping out of your arse, eat your food and get the feck out of my establishment."

The two walked back through the beer maze and parted company on the other side of the door. Kelly headed directly for the bathroom while Patsy puts the .45 under his apron and headed back behind the bar, leaving his gun where he could grab at it anytime. While Kelly the Mick was in the bathroom, dealing with a lethal combination of rage and shit, he hated himself; he couldn't even bring himself to look in the mirror. He flushed his soiled underpants down the toilet, washed his hands, and headed back out into the barroom, only to find Patsy at the table with the boys. "Lunch is on me today, fellas," Patsy said when Kelly the Mick sat down. "And if anyone sees Francis, tell him I need to see him." Kelly just stared straight ahead. "Come on, then. Your food is getting cold.

"Well, I'm off to check me ponies, then," Patsy said, returning to his place at the end of the bar with a fresh glass of Hennessy and about a hundred OTB slips.

Kelly the Mick never touched a scrap of his food, but waited with Colin Garvan nonetheless until the boys went off to the HKYO to play basketball. They stood up in preparation to leave but Kelly stood a little while longer, just glaring at Patsy. The old man stared back for a minute and then waved goodbye to the men. Kelly the Mick turned and walked out the door. Once they were outside, Colin finally dared to ask what had happened in the back of the bar. Kelly didn't want to talk about it. He simply said, "I don't know who the fuck they think they are, but the Doonans are going to have their comeuppance real soon... all of them." Patsy had enraged Kelly, not so much by insulting his father, but by bringing him up at all. He hadn't thought about him in a very long while, for just those very reasons. Kelly the Mick decided that someone was going to pay. "I need to lay a beating into somebody. Who owes us money?"

"Well, Gerry Murphy does," Colin responded. "He'd probably be over at McHale's about now.

"Let's go," Kelly growled back.

Father Healy, Sister Mary Margaret and I were sitting in the sun-drenched backyard of the retreat house, eating burgers, baked potatoes and salad. The sister had judged that Sandra was still a little too shaky for solid food, so she was still resting in bed. "I think, Francis," Fr. Healy said, "that it would be a good idea if we stayed up here the whole week so that Sandra can rest fully and have the best chance of making sure that she goes home as good as new."

I agreed. "I can just call Benny at the flower shop. It shouldn't be a problem."

The priest turned back to Mary Margaret. "How soon can we get Sandra up, Sister? Because, after I stretch the truth with her parents by stretching her stay, they're going to have to hear her voice."

"She should have some strength by around four or five this afternoon," the nun replied. I went to the grill for another burger, so she whispered, "I'm just not comfortable with this, Father. Are you sure that lying to the girl's parents is wise?"

Fr. Healy took a deep breath and looked very pensive. "I've prayed on it, Mary Margaret. I don't know if I'm doing the right thing, honestly. But I believe I'm doing the Lord's work ultimately... and if I must do that for which I am not proud in order to save one of His flock, then that is what I shall do." I walked back within earshot. "Oh, Francis, you should call Clayton and tell him to come up here now. I can give you the directions from Grand Central or the Port Authority."

"Consider it done," I replied, biting into my third hamburger.

A few hours later, Sister Mary Margaret was spoon feeding Sandra some chicken noodle soup to give her a little strength for what was to follow as Fr. Healy brought the phone over to her bed. "Now take care to not to say anything that will make them suspicious, but you need to ask permission to stay the week. Say that you're having a great time, but there's a lot to be done. Still, say how tired you are from painting all day. That'll allow you to keep the conversation short." Sandra nodded. "Are you ready for this?"

"Yes, Father, and thank you. I'll be fine," she said. "Where's Francis? I thought I heard his voice earlier."

"Oh, that you did. He's gone in the station wagon to pick up Clayton from the train depot. He should be back shortly. Now would you mind dialing your home number for me?" He held onto the receiver while she dialed. Sandra's mother answered on the first ring. "Oh, hello, Mrs. O'Casey. It's Fr. Healy... from Holy Cross? Yes, God bless you too, dear. Oh, Sandra? Yes, yes, she's doing great. What a worker you have there, ma'am. Well, the Doonan boy has been having a difficult time with the loss of his friend, so we thought it might be good to get him up here and away from The City to help repaint the building and get his mind off of things. Oh, she and Francis have been extremely helpful, but I think they've overdone it for today. They're both dog tired. I'm sure they'll sleep tonight! Oh, of course. I'll get Sandra for you. Just one minute."

Fr. Healy handed the phone to Sandra. "Hello, mommy."

As I pulled the old station wagon alongside the railroad platform and honked the horn, Clayton was already there, waiting with the biggest cat-who-ate-the-canary smile I'd ever seen. I got out of the car and gave him the biggest hug. "Yo," he said, "I can't fucking wait to show you and Fr. Healy all the dough I got for that shit in Sandra's purse."

"Was it a grand?" I asked.

"Higher," he responded.

"Five grand?" He just screwed up his face and pointed upwards. "No fucking way."

"You'll see, yo. You'll see." As we got back in the car, he was clutching an envelope that was drenched from the sweat of his hands. "That trip was for shit, Francis. The train's air conditioner was broken and the humidity was killer."

I could see the brick of bills under the wet paper. "Damn, can I just hold it?" He put it in my hands as I was waiting to turn out of the train depot. "Oh, shit! That's some serious weight."

"Fucking-A it's some serious weight!" Clayton shouted. "It's ten motherfucking thousand dollars of weight, yo!"

"Get the fuck outta here," I shouted back. We both started hooting and dancing in our seats. "I can't wait for Fr. Healy to get a load of this!" I practically flew back to the retreat house, finding the priest out on the porch waiting for us as we pulled up.

"Clayton, I'm so happy to see you, son. I hope you got here okay."

"Oh, yeah. The trip sucked, but I've got something that's going to make you dance." Clayton was so excited to show Father what he'd brought.

"Well, don't keep me in suspense." Clayton tore the envelope paper away from the stack of bills and handed it to Fr. Healy. He flipped through the stack. "You got all of this?"

"Ten thousand bucks, Father. Can you believe it?"

"Well, as a man who took a vow of poverty, I'd have to say no. I never ever believed I'd ever see this much money at one time. I can't even begin to imagine how much good can come from this money." Clayton just stood there, beaming once again.

Vit walked along 39th Street against the buildings, trying to avoid the glare of the streetlamps. He stopped and looked in every direction to see if anyone was around before he scampered to the door of the Dante League Social Club. It was still under reconstruction, so fewer people would likely see him change his social stature in the neighborhood forever. He opened the door and was bowled over by the pungent evidence of sex. J.R. was buckling his belt while some Dominican whore was tugging her skintight dress back down. "There he is!" J.R. shouted out. "Vit, do me a favor, will ya? Open some of those windows. It still smells from the fire in here."

"Sure, Mr. Albanese," Vit replied, eyeing his companion.

J.R. turned to her and said, "Millie, why don't you go clean up in the back bathroom?"

"Alright, J.R.," she said, returning Vit's stare with the same intensity.

Albanese let out a belly laugh. "Calm down. She's all yours. I'll send her along with you when you go. Just make sure she whips your dick... and, no, I didn't say suck. She literally whips your *pene* with her tongue. It's incredible. But first, business. So tell me why you want to do this?"

Vit thought for a moment. "Because I think my friends have their heads up their asses. Don't get me wrong, I love them, but they all think that scumbag, Kelly the Mick shits gold or something... and that *frocio*, Colin Garvan, is just as bad. I know they're all going nowhere, but I want to be somebody. I'm pretty good on my feet, good with my hands and willing to learn."

J.R. said, "Yeah, but you know it's probably going to get dangerous."

"With all due respect, Mr. Albanese, waking up in Hell's Kitchen is dangerous, so what's the difference?"

"So what about that Doonan kid... Francis?"

"Truthfully," replied Vit, "he's the only legit one of them all. He marches to the beat of his own drum, if you know what I mean, and he really doesn't bother nobody."

"Yeah, that's kind of the impression I get. What did you think about what happened at Gleason's Gym the other day?"

Vit paused for a moment. "Honestly, your son got what he deserved. He had it coming for awhile. He's a bully, and I would've done the same thing if I'd been in Francis' shoes." He stopped for a second and swallowed hard. "Sorry. I know that might piss you off, but that's the truth, and I didn't think you'd want someone working for you who lies to you."

"You're fine," J.R. replied. He actually liked the way the kid opened up. He knew he'd be a good little rat. "Okay, so I want you to stick close to this little gang, you got it? I want to know everything that's going on or is about to happen... especially if they're going to move on me or any of my operations. Understand?" He reached into a drawer and brought out what looked like a small black block with a clip on it. "Do you know what this is?"

"No, sir," Vit responded.

"It's a way to communicate. When I want you, I'll call it and it'll beep. The number I want you to call back will be on it. If anyone asks you why you got it... just tell them you're a surgeon, on call." J.R. bellowed out another belly-laugh. "And here," he pushes five $100 bills into Vit's hand. "That's your first pay as a member of my crew."

"Thanks, Mr. Albanese. You won't be sorry."

Millie appears behind J.R. with her hair slicked back. She stroked her fingernails down his back and kissed his neck, but her stare never left Vit the whole while. J.R. grabbed her arm as she walked by, put some money in her hand and whispered something in her ear. She nodded and he slapped her ass hard. "I'll be in touch, Vit," he said, stealing one last kiss from Millie. They exited the club while J.R. was walking into the backroom.

As soon as they were outside, Millie spit on the ground and rubbed at her lips with the back of her arm. "Nasty, fat fuck," she said under her breath while raising her hand to flag a passing cab. As she hopped in the cab, she told the driver, "23rd and Seventh, papi. Drive slow." Vit got in next to her and she just smiled, undressing him with her eyes. She removed her Dentyne and stuck it behind her ear while her hand unzipped his fly and exposed his raging hardon. "Mmm. I been needing me some young cock," she moaned, sucking his turgid member into her mouth and whipping it – just as J.R. reported she would – from 39th Street all the way down to 23rd Street. From the slurps and moans coming from his back seat, even the cab driver thought he was going to cum. As her head and hand bobbed up and down on Vit's prick, he never noticed her free hand reaching into his pocket and removing the $500 that Albanese had given him. Almost like clockwork, Vit started convulsing with orgasm as soon as they'd passed 24th Street, bracing himself by gripping both door handles.

As the cabbie announced, "23rd Street, beautiful," Vit shot a dozen spurts of creamy goo and Millie swallowed the deposit hungrily.

She sat up and air kissed Vit near the cheek, saying, "That was on the house, sweetheart. But you know what? I think I just want to go up and go to sleep, if that's okay. We'll do the full run some other night. Is that alright with you?"

"Sure," wheezed Vit like any typical guy who had just dumped his load and couldn't have given less of a fuck about anything else. She got out of the cab and stroked the driver's cheek, making him smile. She turned to Vit and winked, but he just sat there as though he were paralyzed.

"You going to get out or give me a new destination?" the cabbie snapped Vit back to reality.

"Oh, yeah. 43rd and Tenth." The car pulled away as Vit rode up Tenth Avenue, leaned back in the seat like a lord surveying his land. He thought to himself, "Now I'm a bona fide <u>man</u>. It won't take long. I'll move up in the organization, run my own crew, have a string of broads like that... whatever I want."

When they reached 43rd Street, the cabbie said, "Twelve dollars, kid."

Vit leaned forward with a whole new manner about him, talking like a wise guy, "All I got is hundreds."

The cab driver was unimpressed. "I can handle it." Vit dug into the pocket of his sweat pants, but at that moment, his $500 was being used to buy a round for everyone at the bar in the Chelsea Hotel. As he continued to search his pockets and the backseat of the car in vain, the cabbie asked, "What's the problem?"

Vit's voice was back to normal. "I don't know. I had it a second ago. I must've dropped it. Shit. I'm really sorry."

"I don't give a shit what happened to your hundreds, Al Capone. You owe me twelve bucks... plus tip... and I want it. Now."

"Can you wait here for a second? I'll borrow some money from my friend and be right back."

"Do I have a sign that says, 'Asshole' on my head?" the driver asked sarcastically.

"You don't need the sign." Being back in his own neighborhood had brought the tough guy attitude back out of Vit. "Look, if you want your fucking money, nigger, you're just going to have to wait for me to go borrow it." He reached for the door handle, but before he could pull on it, the automatic locks clicked down.

"Did you just call me a nigger!?!" he roared, jumping out of the driver's seat, ripping open the back door and pulling Vit out like a rag doll. "You can keep the $12, you motherfucker, because I'm gonna take it out of your ass... plus tip." Vit had unfortunately decided to become a rat and a punk all on the same, rare night in Hell's Kitchen: one where no one was around on what was usually a very busy corner. The cabbie proceeded to beat Vit half-senseless, leaving him twisted, and with a shiner that would probably leave his eye closed for a few days. By the time the cabbie decided he'd had enough, Vit was left leaning against a parked car, bellowing like Kowalski in "Streetcar." The cabbie got back in his car and pulled away.

With all of his might, Vit leaned back and screamed, "You nigger!"

The cabbie instantly hit his breaks and put the taxi in reverse as Vit took off down 43rd Street on shaky legs.

Clayton and I were roused from a dead sleep simultaneously when a rooster began crowing somewhere in the nearby countryside. Light was filtering through the old, wooden shutters in a strangely beautiful way, but all we could think about was that damn bird. "Is that seriously a fucking rooster?" Clayton asked groggily. "We damn sure ain't on Tenth Avenue, huh?"

"No," I chuckled hoarsely. "If we were, someone would have to be either cooking it or placing bets on its fighting skills."

As if cued by the rooster, Fr. Healy's voice pealed up from the foot of the stairs. "Up and at 'em, boys. C'mon. It's going to be a beautiful day. The rain's gone with the clouds, so there'll be nothing to keep us from our rendezvous with a roller today." He provided the lone chuckle to his own joke as Clayton and I rolled our eyes at each other. "Breakfast in fifteen, so give us your best Lazarus imitations on the double."

"Alright," Clayton answered back. "We're up!"

I remained prone a bit longer than Clayton. *it's hard to believe it's already wednesday. yesterday was a complete blur. probably because we were all so tired and spent most of the day asleep!* The Heavens had opened up the night we arrived in Mahopac, baptizing all of Putnam County through the following day. Sister Mary Margaret had even mused about breaking out the plans for the ark. It kept us all confined to the retreat house, which was probably for the best anyway since Sandra had scarcely opened her eyes long enough to do more than dry heave or be helped to the bathroom... and we had all worn a path to and from her room to monitor her progress. *when clayton and i weren't snoozing our brains out in boresville.* It took a little while longer for Clayton's ears to adjust to the country than it had for mine, but the unnerving din of the silence contributed mightily to our stir craziness. We'd eaten our fill, flipped through every *Sports Illustrated, Life, Time...* and even *Highlights* magazine in the house, talked about playing Monopoly, Trouble and Stratego, and bitched about the storm keeping the antenna from receiving a clear TV signal. Maybe it was just pure exhaustion, but sleeping had been a retreat from the other 23 hours of insanity all the same.

"Think the sister's frying tomatoes again?" Clayton asked, slapping at my foot beneath the blanket in "get your ass up" fashion.

"If she does, I'll eat them for you this time. Chill out." I hopped up and pulled on clothes, following Clayton down the stairs and into the kitchen. Fr. Healy had whipped up a quick breakfast of eggs and toast. Neither Sandra nor Sister Mary Margaret were anywhere to be seen.

"Good morning, you two," Fr. Healy greeted us. "We're getting a head start on the day because we need to make up for yesterday, gentlemen. Painting the retreat was our cover story, yes, but it still needs to be done. You'll need your strength, so eat up and then follow me out to the garage."

We had reclaimed all the pieces of the scaffold from the weeds alongside the garage just as the morning sun climbed high enough in the sky to burn the dew from the grass. While Clayton and I were finishing up assembling the scaffold, Fr. Healy was mixing up a whitewash concoction called Thoroseal, which we would be spending the better part of the day applying with rollers and enormous brushes. After less than an hour splattering as much of the paint on ourselves as on the building, it was clear that Fr. Healy's part in the process was going to be purely supervisory. It didn't bother me, though; it really felt good to work out in the sunshine like that... and it was almost successful at keeping the demons in hibernation. As Clayton was wrapping his shirt around his head like a turban, Father came out with the radio on an extension cord. I wiped the midday sweat from my forehead with my shirt sleeve and said to Clayton, "I could sure use a cold beer and a fat dube right about now."

"I second that emotion," Clayton replied.

"I know you brought some bud with you; we just have to figure out how to get the brew." Clayton made no response. "You did bring herb, right?"

"You saw him take my stash at the hospital, yo. That shit was humiliating. I didn't want to go through that again."

I stared at him with disbelief. "You have gotta be fucking kidding me. You were afraid of being embarrassed?"

"Fuck you," Clayton said. "Maybe I wanted to show some respect."

I was disgusted and, more to the point, the demons were pissed. "Don't talk to me, pussy. Who are you now, Aretha Fucking Franklin?"

"Fuck you," Clayton responded as silence fell over the scaffold like fresh snow.

We continued painting for another hour or so with only the radio providing the soundtrack to our efforts. *what i wouldn't give to be on the stoop with howie right about now. he'd know what i was talking about. he'd know how to have a good time. i've gotta get the fuck outta here and soon. it's getting on my nerves being around all these holier than thou types... clayton included.* When Aretha Franklin's "Until You Come Back to Me" began playing, I turned and looked directly at him, to which he responded only with a single finger and a half-concealed smirk.

Looking just past Clayton, my eyes focused on a towncar in the distance, parked beneath a tree alongside the road at the edge of the retreat house property. I stared for a moment at the driver who was leaning on the car while reading a folded-up newspaper, and knew for certain that it was Benny. It wasn't long before he looked up and saw me turned in his direction, giving a little flip of a salute with the newspaper and then motioning me over with it. I waved back and replaced my brush in the large bucket of whitewash before starting to climb down the scaffold.

"You're going for another piss? You just took one not ten minutes ago," Clayton asked. "I'm not painting this motherfucker all by myself, yo."

"I'm taking a break," I replied, pointing a finger. "See? That's Benny over there under the tree."

"What's he doing here?"

"Well, that's what I'm going to find out, genius. He'll probably take me to go get some lunch."

"But Healy said they'd be serving lunch in 30 minutes or so," Clayton protested.

"What? Are you my mother now or something? Just tell Fr. Healy I went to grab a bite with Benny and you can have my food. He is my boss after all, remember? He probably wants to talk about some business stuff."

"Yeah, right, Mr. Businessman. Whatever." He paused for a moment before adding, "If he's taking you somewhere good, Francis, ask him if I can come too."

"Who invited you?" I shot back over my shoulder as I jogged up to Benny's car.

"I'm not taking you away from anything, am I, kid?" Benny asked as I drew up next to him. "I saw you two up there when I pulled up and thought I'd just sit here and wait until you were through."

"Nah. It's good to see you, Benny. How long ago did you get here?" I asked.

"Maybe half an hour, 45 minutes. Not that long."

"Why didn't you come up to the house?"

"I just sort of came up here on the spur of the moment, but I didn't want to interrupt anything by showing up unannounced. I just thought I'd touch base with you and see how things were going since we haven't seen each other in several days."

I chuckled and said, "And you drove yourself up here? Wow. I'm honored. I didn't even know you knew how to drive."

"I try not to make a habit of it," Benny replied. "So, are you through? Can I take you to grab some lunch?"

"Yeah, we were getting ready to knock off anyway. Me and Clayton, that is," I said, thumbing back towards the scaffolding.

"Well, would he like to come too?"

"No," I replied, thinking for a minute. "He's having lunch with Fr. Healy."

"Okay, then. Hop in," Benny said, sliding behind the wheel and starting up the car. As he made a u-turn to head back towards town, Benny continued, "So, fill me in, kid. I've only gotten these brief phone calls and messages from you for the last week. 'I'm not gonna make it today, Benny.' 'I won't be in today, Benny.' 'Going to Mahopac with a girl and a priest, Benny.' I figured I had to see you in person in order to get more than a couple of sentences out of you."

"Oh, sorry about that. I really didn't mean anything by it. I've just been really busy and things have been so crazy since I got back from Woodstock with Karen."

"Yeah, I heard that your visit was restful."

"What? Karen called you? Why? What'd she tell you?" I asked as we pulled into the parking lot of a little mom-and-pop eatery in town. *shit. sounded way too defensive, like i've got something to hide.*

"Actually, I called her. I just wanted to see how your trip was." To change the subject, Benny added, "Is this okay? I really hope they have some good chicken and rice soup and this looked like it had potential."

"Sure," I replied, stepping out of the car and heading inside. "You grab a table and I'll join you in a second. I have to go to the restroom." The demons were starting to wake up from their afternoon nap and I needed to splash a little water on my face.

When I joined Benny, the waitress was already filling his coffee cup. "Ah, Francis, I ordered a soda for you."

"Actually, do you have any wine?" I interjected without a pause, seeming to startle Benny a little.

"Nothing fancy," the waitress responded, "but, yes, we have wine and beer. But are you old enough?"

"Well, I'm 18," I lied... making it worse by adding, "but this is my dad."

Benny wasn't going to appear startled twice, but he didn't see the harm in covering my ass. "That actually sounds like a great idea, son. I'll have a glass of your house red too."

"Why not just bring the bottle?" I added without Benny's objection. "Can I get the meatloaf and mashed potatoes?"

The waitress nodded and looked at Benny. "And for you, sir?"

"I'll have a bowl of the chicken and rice soup and a grilled chicken sandwich with lettuce and tomato."

"Coming right up," the waitress said, walking away.

"A bottle of wine for lunch? It's not even two o'clock."

The demons made sure my reply had more snap than it needed. "Who made that a crime? Those rules about when you can have a drink during the day are stupid. Besides, I've been slaving in the sun all day. I don't think it's that weird to want a drink, is it?"

"No, I guess not," Benny replied with a slight look of concern on his face that grew less subtle after the wine arrived at the table and I downed the first glass like water. An uncomfortable tension hung over the table as we ate and I consumed the entire bottle of wine, minus the half-glass Benny had poured himself and hardly touched.

I was struggling to keep it together, but the demons were screaming for attention and I had no choice but to Willy Loman them. When the waitress returned to the table and asked if we wanted another bottle, the demons screamed, "Yes!" before either Benny or I were able to register the question. Rather than embarrass himself... or, more to the point, embarrass me, Benny excused himself to go to the restroom. Failing to recognize his polite gesture, I took advantage of his absence when the second bottle arrived and quickly downed two glasses and was pouring the third as Benny returned.

I started to pour some more wine into his glass. "That's okay, kid. I've had enough." I stopped and set the bottle down with a messy, drunken thud. "And I think you've had enough too."

The tannins and demons were in lockstep by that point, and they both spoke for me. "Oh, I get it. So you're my father now? I can't have a drink or two? Karen ran her mouth about the trip Upstate. Yeah. That's it. I tied one on a couple of times and all of a sudden, it's an issue? Wasn't I supposed to be on a trip to relax? Isn't having a couple of drinks relaxing? I just lost my best friend, for fuck's sake."

Benny had sat silently through my tirade, and it was his motionlessness that stopped me. Unaccustomed to enduring such scenes, he stood up, laid a hundred dollar bill on the table and said quietly, "I'll be waiting in the car when you're done drinking your lunch."

wow. did i ever just fuck up. Still, I sat there for another two or three minutes... just long enough to finish my meatloaf and the new bottle of wine.

I stepped lightly out of the eatery and into the passenger seat of Benny's towncar, fumbling a bit with the door handle. I sat there without speaking for a couple of minutes before I finally said like a petulant child, "What?"

Benny didn't reply or look over for a minute. Instead, he just stared through the windshield with a pained expression. Finally, he took a breath, cleared his throat, and said, "Did you hear yourself in there, kid? I just made an observation and you went on a ten-minute rant. Well, just so we're clear, Karen said nothing other than that you two had a great time and it was very relaxing.

"And I know you lost your best friend. I would never try to trivialize that. I'd just rather see you talk to me or someone else who cares about you... and not a bottle." The tension inside the car had seeped down both of our throats and choked back any words so that the drive back to the retreat house took place in utter silence. He pulled into the driveway but then seemed to think better of proceeding, putting the car into park.

"Where's Sonny Blue when I really need him?" I spit out under my breath, adding, "but I'm sure he'd have a sermon or two to preach my way too."

"Excuse me?" Benny inquired.

"Nothing. Look, Mr. Levine, I'm sorry, alright? I'm sorry that I haven't been to work lately, but my friends are more important to me than work... even if it's working for you. I know you put business first, but I don't. So, sorry for that. And I just think that with everything that's been thrown on me lately, it's not that big of a deal to want something to take the edge off." I didn't know whether it was my demons, the wine, or my insanity, but I spoke to one of the men whom I respected more than anything in a fashion I'd never even thought about, much less dared, before. Part of me wished I could grab all of the words that had just left my mouth and reel them back in... but that part of me was somewhere, cowering in a corner. I continued, "And I'm sorry if I didn't call you enough when I was in Woodstock or up here. And I'm sorry if I didn't act the way you wanted me to at lunch. And I'm sorry that you came all the way up here, but I didn't ask you to. I didn't ask you for anything, did I? I mean, you're not my dad, Mr. Levine. Why do I have to justify myself to you when I'm just doing the best that I can? I don't ask you to justify yourself to me, and we both know that there are some things you do that you're not proud of either, right?" I stopped, horrified.

"Right," he replied softly.

"Well..." I tried desperately to fix what I'd just done. "So you can cut me some slack. I mean, I don't deserve.... Right?"

We sat there with the rumbling of the engine underscoring the rumble in the car. I wanted to cry or scream or something, but the best I could manage was, "I have to go." Benjamin Levine reached into his jacket pocket without ever looking over at me and pulled out a pair of Franklins, tucking them into my hand. I looked at the money. "What? Is this a buyout? You buying me out? Giving me the heave-ho?" I was able to stop myself before the rant started this time.

"No, kid," Benny said softly. "Go finish your whitewashing."

The phone rang for the tenth time at Gleason's Gym when Seamus Boylan finally snatched it off of the hook with a grunt and growled into the receiver, "What?!? What?!? What?!?"

"Seamus, it's Benny Levine."

"Ah! Benny! My friend! How are you? Sorry about all that. I just had to run all the way up here to get it."

"It's not a problem, old friend," came Benny's reply.

"I hear from you twice in the same decade! To what do I owe this honor? Is it about that kid? I gave him a call... or at least I thought I did... right after his fight, but I never heard from him after that. Can't do anymore than that, right?"

"No, no, Seamus. I appreciate you calling him, but there's actually something else I need to pick your brain about."

"Well, I can't promise you that there's much more than rocks and bats up there, but shoot. What do you need?"

"Two words," Benny replied: "Sonny Blue."

"Sonny What? What's that? This a tip on a horse or something?"

"No. Sonny Blue. Wasn't he a boxer? Wasn't there a Sonny Blue out of Harlem back in the late 50s?"

"Oh, yeah, yeah, come to think of it. You're right," Seamus replied. "Now there's someone I sure haven't seen in years. Seems to me that something popped up about him this time last year... or maybe back around the Thanksgiving before that. One of my fighters hopped on the "H Train" and took it to Overdose Station and I remember Sonny's name being mentioned in connection with all of that, but I have no idea whatever came of it."

"Sounds like that may just be the same Sonny Blue I'm thinking of too. What do you know about him?"

"Well, he was an old junkie. Unless he cleaned up, I'd be surprised if he wasn't dead by now." Seamus thought for a few moments. "I thought I heard someone talking about a shooting gallery he used to haunt over on the river in the low West 70s. Basically just a burning barrel and plenty of places to pass out, but whether he's still there... or the spot's still there, I have no idea. I can't believe the cops wouldn't have shut it down."

"I remember him as being quite the brawler. A lot of potential," Benny said. "Whatever happened to him? Why'd he disappear?"

"Dunno, Ben. Could've been the smack. Could've been the drink. Could've just been a case of being Black and abandoning the frustration over that for some other pursuit. I don't think he ever got tied up with the mob or anything like that, though. But you never know."

The silhouette of Sonny Blue's haggard old frame shuffling around the U.N. could be seen against the lights of the New Jersey riverbank as the day began to slip from The City. Sonny was tidying up in preparation for the daily offering. It was a Wednesday night, but he expected that the crowd would still be decent. As he dropped an armful of wooden clothes hangers into the barrel and set their newspaper bed aflame, he looked up to see a pair of headlights glaring at him from the mouth of the unkempt path that led from the highway to the barrel. "Now what the fuck this is?" Sonny growled to himself as the lights approached slowly.

As he stood in the middle of the clearing, bathed in the flood of light from the car, Sonny debated whether or not he should make a break for it, but he knew he wouldn't get far. No one ever drove back this far, but he knew it wasn't the police; they would've come up with more than their headlights flaring. If it was somebody underground, his meager attempt to run couldn't match his pursuers, much less their bullets. So, he stood his ground, stoking the barrel as the driver exited his vehicle and walked down the middle of the headlights' beams, keeping Sonny from getting a clear look at him. Finally, he could tell as the driver was only paces away that he had a hand secreted beneath his overcoat, clutching something hidden from view. Involuntarily, Sonny started to tremble slightly. He'd been through a lot in his life, but never a gunshot wound. He wondered what it would feel like, if he'd go instantly or if he'd linger... painfully or not.

The figure reached the barrel. "Sonny Blue." It was a statement and not a question. Sonny nodded uncomfortably. "If you'd have only weaved and then thrown the left, you would've won the belt." The man withdrew his hand from his coat, producing a purple bag-covered bottle of Crown Royal. "Benjamin Levine."

"You saw that fight?" Sonny asked.

"The last time I saw you in the ring," Benny responded.

"Probably the last time I really was, tell the truth. But I's betting you didn't really come all the way out here to this neck in the woods to shoot the shit about boxing history. And somebody as important as Benjamin Levine don't really get lost, so what can I do for you?" Benny chuckled and Sonny added, "You ain't the only one who knows the reputation of the other."

"I just wanted to share this bottle and have a little chat." Sonny stoked the barrel as the wooden hangers began to blaze. "A fire in the middle of the summer?" Benny asked, taking a swig from the whiskey and passing it to Sonny..

"It's like ol' Lady Liberty's torch. It show the way for them tired, huddled masses. ...And it can give you a little warmth if you ain't got nobody helping out with that in the first place. Even though you prolly ain't here for the evening's offering, I guess you know we all don't come out here to sing 'Kumbaya,' so what's the topic of our chat?" He finished swallowing his long drink and passed the bottle back.

"Francis Doonan," Benny replied.

"Francis. The Irish kid? And his friend with the big nose... um, Howie?"

"Howie's dead." A swig and a pass.

"Okay. I understand you now. You're out here to settle things on that Howie kid? Well, I tried to stop them. I did everything I could short of beat 'em off with a stick, but everybody's here for a reason, Mr. Levine. If they hadn't gotten they fix from me, they would've gotten it from somewhere. I told them the shit was heavy... particularly what I was holding that night... but they didn't listen. I can't be held responsible for that kid's overdose. It wasn't even me who shot them up. It was this Spanish whore that comes 'round here every such often."

Benny raised his hand as Sonny tipped the bottle back and took several long gulps. "Wait, Mr. Blue. I think I've misspoken. Howie Nesto didn't die of an overdose."

"Aw, shit. So it was the Irish kid? No. I really liked him."

"No, he didn't overdose either. The boy who died, Howie Nesto, got mixed up in an organized crime turf war and was beaten to death on the railroad tracks down in Hell's Kitchen. I came here to talk about Francis. He's still with us, thank God, and I'd like to keep it that way."

"I don't know for how long though," Sonny interjected, passing the Crown Royal back.

"I agree with you there," Benny replied with another sip. "That's why I'm here. Francis is on a downward spiral and I don't know how to stop it. I don't know how to help. I was hoping you could enlighten me there."

Sonny took the bottle back and thought through the grimaces after each swig of whiskey. "Well, for starters, you can keep him away from here."

"I can't really do that in all reality," Benny said.

"I can ban him from here, Mr. Levine, but if he really wants it, he'll go somewhere else. I may have the U.N. here, but there are other countries on the Island if you follow me."

Benny took a deep, pensive drink. "True."

Sonny slurred his new rationale. "But if you talk to him.... If I talk to him and show him some of the zombies that come here... shit, that'll be here in only a couple of hours... maybe he'll see for himself. Whatever we try, the only way it's gonna take is if he sees it and figures it out for himself. Nothing else. I don't know much, but I know that he gotta do it on his own."

"We should keep in touch, Mr. Blue. Communicate between ourselves about where things stand with Francis and what we can do to keep him off of the mortician's slab."

"Yeah. Irish seems worth it."

"And I will happily compensate you for whatever financial loss you'd experience," Benny offered.

"I'm not just about the money, Mr. Levine. I can care about the boy too."

"I meant no offense, Mr. Blue." Sonny nodded, clutching the bottle with its finger of whiskey left swilling about the bottom. Only the sounds of highway traffic mixed with the lapping of the river's waves and the popping of the barrel's burnt offerings for a few moments until Benny broke the silence. "I have another bottle. Why don't we go have a seat in my car and talk a little boxing history?"

Sonny looked at Benny with amusement and cracked a gap-toothed smile. "I'd like that... at least 'til my customers begin showing up."

Long after the wooden hangers had burnt into ashy cinders, the first of the zombies stumbled toward the U.N. without the torch of the burning barrel to lead the way. Happening upon Benjamin Levine's town-car, he found it running, with both the driver's seat and passenger's seat occupied by the passed out pair, drunken heads flung back onto the rests, mouths agape, snoring. Outside the car, the zombie's pulse quickened as he looked about to see if the man or men who'd hit Sonny were still in the area. Sprinting back toward the highway, he rationalized that there was no sense in making the mob whack an unwitting witness too.

The smell of food wafted up to our room, filling our noses. Clayton's eyes snapped open. He remained motionless, putting together the menu based on the aromas. It wasn't long before I moaned appreciatively in my sleep and stretched awake. "You just went like 'mmmmm mmmmm mmmmm' like a little bitch, Francis. And in your sleep too. Is that what you sound like when you're getting nailed?" Clayton laughed to himself, but never let his thoughts drift far from the sweet scents filling our room.

"Fuck what you heard; do you smell that?" We both leapt from the bed and scurried downstairs to find Fr. Healy in his robe and Sister Mary Margaret in her Winnie the Pooh slippers shuffling around the kitchen in complete sync with one another in their effort to cook the perfect hearty breakfast. I was thrilled to see Sandra sitting at the table, even if she did look a little pale and tired.

The sister paused long enough to see us enter the kitchen. "Well, wouldn't you know now that you two would finally pull yourselves from the beds once all the work was done down here."

"And a good morning to you too, sister," Clayton replied with a chuckle. "Please tell me those are banana pancakes I'm smelling."

"On the nose," Fr. Healy said. "Have a seat. We'll be ready to eat shortly."

I sat down next to Sandra, but she scarcely looked up, probably from lingering embarrassment. *doesn't she know i couldn't care less?* I bumped her knee with mine underneath the table and she looked up. I winked and watched the self-consciousness melt away. "How you doing?" I asked, pouring a glass of freshly squeezed orange juice.

"Okay, I guess," she replied, hemming and hawing in an attempt to find the words to thank me.

I rested my hand on top of hers firmly. "Stop. Come on. You would've done the same for me, right?" She wiped away the tears that rolled down one cheek. "We'll have plenty of time to talk later. But you look good, Sandra."

"Liar," she shot back softly. "I look like shit."

I wiped away the tear that trailed down her other cheek. "On your worst day, you couldn't look like shit." She looked deep into my eyes. *my god, why has she never looked at me like that before? it's like she's seeing me for the first time. i can barely breathe.*

"We'll be cleaning up the language at the breakfast table, if you please," Sister Mary Margaret said with a smile in her voice.

After everyone had eaten their fill, Fr. Healy pushed back his plate and said, "Alright, troops, now that your batteries are fully charged, here's the battle plan: Sister Mary Margaret and Sandra are going to be heading into Mahopac to get some fresh produce and some fresh air... that is, if you feel you're up to it, sweetheart." With her mouth full of scrambled eggs, Sandra just nodded emphatically. "And the three of us are going to resume painting," he said, eliciting glances and eye rolling between Clayton and me. "And if you have any issues with that plan, you can feel free to write them down and drop the cards in the Kitty Box."

"The Kitty Box?" I asked. "That was a new one on me."

"KITTY: Keep It Totally To Yourself," Father replied, wiping his mouth and getting up from the table.

Clayton groaned. "That was terrible. You think of that yourself, Healy?" Everyone laughed.

Within an hour, Sandra and the sister were walking slowly through the small downtown streets of Mahopac. There was not a great deal being spoken, but a lot was being said. Mary Margaret knew that, although Sandra was no longer in such extreme physical pain, her emotional and spiritual pain was still excruciating, and the good sister was trying to find a way to communicate with her. They stopped at a local farmer's stand and were examining the fruits and vegetables when the nun struck upon an idea. "Aren't these just so colorful and gorgeous?" she asked.

"Very much so," Sandra replied.

"They're kind of like society in a way." Sandra gave her a puzzled look as Mary Margaret continued. "They come in every shape, size, color and texture, right? Take this pepper, for example." She reached into a box and removed a bright red bell pepper. "I sort of identify with it. It's kind of like me."

"You've lost me," Sandra replied with a curious smile.

"Well, it's got an awkward shape, first of all." Sandra giggled. "But it's got a tough skin, and when you shake it, that noise inside means it's got a heart. It's sweet, but it's also bitter... and yet it's plain enough that it can still go with almost anything." Sandra remained still, her gaze seemingly lost in the quilt of produce. The nun saw her chance. "So which one would you be, then?"

Off to the side of the boxes of produce stood the farmer, picking out the bruised fruits and vegetables from the pristine. Sandra reached over and picked up a badly bruised tomato from the wooden railing. The flesh was drawn and beaten in, and the stem was missing, which had allowed the seeds to ooze out. The farmer saw her pick up the rotten tomato and said, "Oh, miss, you don't want that one. It's no good."

"Exactly," she whispered, staring at the sister and dropping the tomato into the farmer's trash basket. She walked away from the stand, finding a bench upon which she collapsed and began weeping quietly.

Sister Mary Margaret paid for their produce and then followed her, sitting down next to Sandra and asking her gently, "Do you want help, child?"

The sobbing teenager looked into the nun's eyes and mouthed the words, "I want tomorrow."

"Okay, dearie," came the reply. "You've just taken the first step towards that. Now let's get back to the house; we've got hungry men to feed."

Clayton and I had managed to get almost all of the exterior painted since there was very still little conversation to distract us. I wasn't sure if there was lingering tension from our little spat the previous day or if I was just preoccupied by the horrible way things had been left with Benny, but I was definitely in a world of my own until the station wagon pulled up and I watched as Sister Mary Margaret, shopping bag dangling from her forearm, came around to the passenger's side door and helped Sandra step out of the car and walk into the house. I could see through the window as she sat at the kitchen table and began laboring to open cans of tuna while the sister was washing and cutting up the produce they'd gotten to make a salad. After the tomatoes and cucumbers had been washed and sliced up, Mary Margaret busied herself cleaning the lettuce and then turned back to the table to dice the onions. She realized instantly that the knife she'd been using was no longer resting on the cutting board where she'd left it. She thought to herself that the knife would be of little use in combining the ingredients for tuna salad, and watched quietly as Sandra stared alternately at her own reflection in the blade and her wrist. Ready to jump in at a moment's notice to stop whatever may happen, the little old nun observed several torturously long moments of Sandra conducting a debate within herself. The sister prayed silently as she watched the teenager's back, watched her breath rise and fall... and seem to stop at one point... right before Sandra laid the knife back down on the cutting board and inhaled deeply. Mary Margaret waited for just a moment more and then stepped over to the table to dice the onions as though she'd seen nothing. "As soon as you've finished, sweetheart, would you mind getting down the Wonderbread and spreading the tuna salad on a few slices? I'm sure we can assume the boys will want at least two sandwiches apiece. I'll be done with the salad quick as you please, so we can call them all in shortly."

The rest of the day seemed to pass quickly. By the time the sun was setting, everyone was exhausted and more than ready to settle down for the night... everyone except for my personal demons, who had begun strumming tin cups against the gates like never before. Sister Mary Margaret had decided that she felt comfortable enough not to have to sleep in Sandra's room that night after she'd hooked her up to an intravenous bottle of Vitamin B12 and I counted Fr. Healy's footsteps on the stairs as he took his glass of warm milk up to bed with him. Once I was sure that everyone was tucked in for the night, I began to implement my escape.

I walked into the living room to find Clayton looking like a little boy with big, bright eyes, battling fatigue and illuminated by the flickering light from the TV. They're all out. "Are you ready to party?"

"I don't know, man," Clayton said, shifting his focus to me. "I'm really tired. Besides, what about Healy?"

"What about him?" I shot back, annoyed. "We ain't under house arrest, are we? We're helping out here voluntarily. Fuck, it's Thursday night! If we were home, we'd be torn up by now. C'mon, man. Let's go. I need to get fucked up." I could feel my demons preparing to regroup and cause some havoc.

"I'm too tired," Clayton replied, returning his focus to the television. "And I don't really feel like getting high anyway. I wanna see what it's like to be straight for awhile, I think."

"You've got to be kidding me," I said. "You're a fucking dealer. Your father was a dealer. Your mother is a dealer, and now you wanna pull a Little Lord Fauntleroy on me? You want some fucking cookies and milk too?"

"Not a bad idea," Clayton responded without looking at me.

I fumed out of the room and then out of the house. *i just want to freak the fuck out, slam the fucking door so hard that all the windows break... but then i'd get caught and that'd defeat the purpose. fuck clayton.* I gently inched the door closed and avoided the noisy gravel in the driveway on my way to the garage where I'd come across a bicycle earlier in the day and left it leaning up against the building. I walked it through the grass and around to the front yard. I passed by the window and saw Clayton inside, reclining on the couch like a little kid with a bag of Oreos and a glass of milk, laughing in the dark at Benny Hill. *i can't really be mad at him. this moment might be the closest thing to normalcy he's ever known. besides, clayton is my boy, and he'll cover for me, whatever the case.*

Once I reached the street, I hopped on the bike and went pedaling into the night, through the scents of the trees and the summer bloomings. I thought about Howie a lot during the three-mile trip into town. *he would've loved this area. he was always kind of the "grateful dead"-head type of hippie at heart.* But I knew that he would've been as annoyed as I was by the fact that everything – including the sidewalk – rolled up at around 9 p.m. in small towns like Mahopac. *but it's got to have its dysfunctional side too; if i'm lucky, maybe i'll find some cute girls there. i could use a little pussy.*

I'd been pedaling quickly as I approached the small, darkened downtown area, so I stopped pumping my feet and ended up gliding right past a Dairy Queen. Although the lights were off inside the ice cream store, a half-way decent-looking girl caught my eye through the window. I doubled back slowly and could see that she was counting money, so I figured she must be the manager. I could see no one else in sight, so I decided to wait and try to talk to her. I didn't want to spook her, though, so I rode to a general store at the end of town... which was still close enough that I could see the Dairy Queen. I hopped off of the bike and sat on the building's front steps, waiting for her to come out. *ah! there's just nothing like a stoop. it ain't tenth avenue, but it'll do.*

I hadn't been sitting there for long before I watched a couple of guys come into view, look around, and then disappear down the driveway area behind the Dairy Queen. *are they fags?* In less than a minute, though, they reemerged without ice cream or anything else in their hands and headed back in the direction from which they'd come. *i doubt they're fags. there's no way they had enough time to do anything back there.* Strangely enough, a girl followed them out through the mouth of the driveway and stopped at the curb to smoke a cigarette as the men walked off. She seemed to be looking up and down the street periodically. *i don't think she sees me, but i can't be sure.*

In just moments, a different girl approached her and the two vanished from sight down the driveway together. *i'm starting to get the picture.* Soon, the second girl exited alone and continued down the sidewalk. *looks interesting. i know a buy-spot when i see one.* My interest was no longer with the manager.

Like clockwork, still another guy approached the Dairy Queen just as the manager was leaving. He stopped in his tracks, walked across the street and tried to look like he was peering in a store window. The manager disappeared down the driveway herself, and came put-putting back out seconds later in a Volkswagen. I could see that she was alone in the car when she drove right past me. As soon as she was out of sight, the man crossed the street again and walked down the driveway, only to reemerge a minute or so later.

I waited for a few more minutes before remounting the bike and gliding behind the Dairy Queen. It was dark back there and it stank of sour milk. I could see nothing but black trash bags and empty Coke bottles, but I got off the bike and said, "Is anyone here?" Silence. "There doesn't look like there's any other way out of here than the way I came in, so there's got to be someone back here."

I heard a small shuffling noise and then saw two sets of eyes shining out at me like raccoons. I just froze on my bike and waited. One by one, three girls came out of the shadow, each of them about my age. The first was a willowy beauty who looked like she may be from Woodstock. The second girl was the one I'd seen smoking the cigarette, and the third was a squat girl with a crew-cut and tattoos on each bicep that read "Fore" and "Play." She spoke first. "Who the fuck are you? What do you want?"

I replied as non-threateningly as I could, "Just hanging. Looking to get high."

"Oh really, officer?" she shot back.

"Do I look old enough to be a cop?" I replied.

"You could be working for Sheriff Fatass."

One of the others interrupted. "That enormous retard? He couldn't handle a bee sting, much less a drug sting."

"Shut up," Foreplay ordered. She turned her attention back on me. "We've never seen you before. You could be a narc or a plant. This all smells like a trap."

I was getting tired of their bullshit. "Look, I'm none of those things. I just want to do some partying."

"Oh, yeah?" Foreplay wouldn't give up. "Where you from? What are you doing here? We know all the dead beat boys; either fucked them or kicked the shit out of them."

"I'm from NYC," I explained. "I'm up at the Holy Cross Retreat, helping a priest friend of mine."

"You got priest friends and you want to score?" the pretty one asked. "Bullshit."

I'd run out of patience. "Look, here's $100. I just want to get some party supplies. I'll even smoke it in front of you. Would a cop or a plant do that?" I could hear them talking to one another in the background.

Foreplay stopped the debate. "Well we don't have any. If we can get some... and I'm not saying we can... we'd have to go somewhere else to get it. But we can get anything you want there... allegedly."

fucking amateurs. "All those people I saw walk out of here left empty handed?" I fired back.

"Hey!" the smoker chimed in. "Take it or leave it, narc!"

"Fine. You can go get it."

The pretty one made an attempt at charming me. "You give us the money and we'll get you whatever you want."

I laughed out loud. "Do I <u>look</u> stupid?"

"Do you want the grass?" she replied immediately.

I took a deep breath. "You said you could get anything. Can you get coke?"

Smoker giggled, "Yes."

"Maybe!" shouted Foreplay.

"And is your weed good?"

"It's the best, shit brick." *good. foreplay's getting tired of this game too.*

"Bring me back $50 of blow and $25 of weed, and you can have the whole hundred."

They chattered amongst themselves again before the pretty one said, "Alright. Wait for us here. We'll be back in a little bit."

"I'll be here," I said with a sigh.

"Yo!" Milk shouted, skating into the middle of the handball court. "C'mon! The harbor police are pulling a dead body out of the river!" The whole crew went tearing off towards the piers, trying in vain to keep up with Milk.

They arrived at about the same time as Det. O'Casey, who lifted the yellow tape and went straight to the bloated and discolored corpse of what appeared to be an Hispanic woman, pulling back the cloth that covered her. "Jesus Christ," he said. "Now that's fucking disgusting. Anybody know what happened?" All the kids from the neighborhood crowded around to see as much as they could.

"A jogger spotted the body floating near the wall around 10 a.m.," a patrolman responded, reading from his notebook. "Best guess is that it's been in there at least three days. Forensics will have to say for sure, but the deceased is believed to be a Female Hispanic, somewhere between the ages of 18 and 35. Tattoo on her left breast reads, 'Carmen.' She has what appears to be a large knife wound in the stomach and her throat's been slashed. No I.D. or purse, but there are still several pieces of jewelry on the body, among them, a sizable necklace and diamond earrings, all of which look to be the real deal. Whoever cut this lady up didn't want to rob her; he wanted to kill her in the most painful way possible. We can't tell for sure because of the bloating, but she looks like she got thrown a pretty vicious beating before she was gutted. The throat wound seems to have just been insurance."

"Alright," the detective said as the patrolman began to recover the corpse. "Wait a minute," O'Casey ordered, walking over to the crew. "Any of you guys recognize her? What about you,... um... kid?"

"I'm not no 'kid,' Detective. The name is Andrés, but my friends call me 'Caliente' or 'Cal,' for short."

O'Casey rolled his eyes. "Okay, then.... Andrés... can you tell me if you recognize her? She's Hispanic."

Cal shot back, "Oh, I get it. And so the Spic is supposed to know everyone else in New York who's brown?"

O'Casey was losing his patience. "Sorry. No. I just thought you might know her from the neighborhood or from church or something.

"What about you?" he asked, looking at Milk.

"Man, I'm black, not brown!"

"Are you fucking kidding me?" the detective growled. "Anybody? She's got a tattoo. It says 'Carmen.' Anybody know of a Carmen in the neighborhood?"

"She's not from Hell's Kitchen, man," Redbone said. "I don't know of any Nuyoricans named Carmen around here... and there's no way anyone from this neighborhood could afford those leather clothes she's got on... and all that jewelry." Everyone else in the crew nodded in agreement.

"Same goes for El Barrio or the Bronx," Vit chimed in. "Unless she's one of those high-priced call girls. Whoever did her just drove down the West Side and stopped to pitch her in the Hudson."

Romeo T spoke up. "Maybe talk to the winos or some of the bums who sleep down here. See if they saw anything."

"Now why didn't we think of that?" the detective asked sarcastically.

"Man, forget you," Romeo responded. "You were asking for our help."

"Well, if any of you think of anything or hear anything, stop in at the precinct and let me know. Or you can tell Sandra you want to see me and I'll find you."

"Yeah. That might actually happen," Min quipped.

Patty Boy asked, "Where is Sandra, anyway?"

"She's doing some charity work for the church," her father replied.

"Yeah, genuflecting on Danny Albanese," Patty Boy responded under his breath, leaving Brian coughing from a fit of laughter.

Det. O'Casey glared at Patty Boy. "Show's over, kids. Clear out."

As everyone headed back towards the stoop, Milk asked, "Do you guys think the Albaneses had anything to do with that?"

"I don't know why they'd kill someone none of us have ever heard of," Vit replied.

"I don't know why either, but you never know anymore. They're killing anybody for no reason. Any one of us could be next. You never know."

"Yeah, well, don't worry about Johnny Rugs and his retard of a son," Brian said. "Kelly the Mick and Colin Garvan are going to make sure we're plenty prepared to handle whatever they try."

"What're you talking about?" Romeo T asked.

"Let's just say that there's more than floor hockey sticks and volleyball nets in the sports closet over at the Hell's Kitchen Youth Organization these days." Patty Boy shot Brian a worried look.

Redbone said, "You're so full of shit, Brian. You'll buy anything those two say."

"So I guess I'm not the one with the key to the sports closet then," Brian responded, holding up his key chain and jingling it.

"God damn," Milk chimed in.

"But don't say anything to anyone," Patty Boy added. "Kelly the Mick wouldn't think twice about putting all of us in the river to keep that Carmen bitch company."

"True," Redbone said. "We should go see if Francis is back yet and then grab some Mad Dog and hang on the stoop."

"He disappeared again," Milk replied. "I went by there last night and today. No Francis. But I can't hang out anyway. I'm supposed to meet up with that girlie from Union Square once her moms leaves out to go to the doctor."

"I hafta pass too," Vit said. "I don't have two nickels to rub together and my dad's been on my ass about taking all this shit out to my aunt's place in Queens."

As most of the crew continued on down Eleventh and over to the stoop, Milk and Vit broke off and went their separate ways. Vit stalled at the corner of 45th and Tenth, ducking into a storefront and heading for the diner's old wooden phone booth. He dialed the number to the Dante League Social Club and asked for J.R.

"Who's speaking?" the elder Albanese demanded on the other end.

"It's Vit, Mr. Albanese."

"Well, if it isn't my superstar! How'd things go over with that D.R. whore, Millie? She give you a whipping?"

Vit chuckled. "Oh, yeah. She was a lot of fun. Listen, you told me to let you know if I found out anything."

"Right," J.R. replied. "I want to know what you found out, but tell me as though somebody else is listening... somebody else who maybe we don't trust. *Capisce?*" He was obviously worried about his line being tapped.

"I got you." Vit thought for a second. "The two guys we were talking about... Mr. Gold and his faggot sidekick? You got me?"

"I do."

"Well, they've got some stuff... loud equipment, I think, stashed nearby."

"Do we know where this loud equipment is?" J.R. asked with interest.

"I do, sir."

"Well, perhaps we should claim this loud equipment so it does not hurt our ears. And it would make me feel very good to repay my debt from that poker game last Sunday."

"That's an excellent idea, Mr. Albanese."

"This is good stuff, kid, real good stuff. I'm proud of you. And be sure to remind me to give you a nice bonus tomorrow night. Be here at

8:00 sharp. We'll have dinner in Little Italy and you can fill me in further. Then we can go and claim the loud equipment."

"Yes sir, Mr. Albanese."

The line went dead.

I sat down in the darkness on a milk crate to wait for the three girls. I leaned my head back against the building and closed my eyes in the hopes that the demons would relax as well... but my mind was working overtime. *those girls weren't half-bad-looking... even foreplay; and the one was really kind of pretty. this could be fun yet.* The demons were pushing all sorts of buttons and forcing eruptions, flare-ups, crazed thinking in every way and place imaginable. *i'm just so scatterbrained; i don't know how to control these feelings of sadness, of hurt, of that deep pain that throbs like an ache in my upper body. i feel like i'm going to explode most of the time.* I heard a sound. *is that something coming from the driveway? thank god they're back.* The sound stopped. *that's weird.*

I got up to check out the situation, looking down the driveway, but I saw nothing. *great, now i'm hearing things.* I walked back into the darkness, found the milk crate and sat back down, my heart pounding. *how the fuck did i end up alone behind a dairy queen?* Suddenly the screech of tires filled the night and the back of the Dairy Queen was bathed in red light as a sheriff's car screamed into sight, almost crashing into the back fence. I jumped up, but was trapped in the driveway. The extremely rotund Sheriff hopped out as quickly as his fat frame would allow, yelling, "Don't move or I'll shoot you!" But, because of the width of the car in the narrow passageway, the corpulent sheriff was wedged into the partially open door, and he couldn't even draw his service revolver to make good on the threat. Although the only exit was entirely blocked, the irony was that Sheriff Fatass couldn't get to me anymore than I could get out. "I was watching you sit out in front of the general store. You think we don't recognize strangers around here? You don't think I know you were waiting for those three girls to leave for the night so you could rob the Dairy Queen?"

"Sir, you've got this all wrong...," I started.

"You have the right to remain quiet!" he shouted. "I suggest you use it or there's no telling what'll happen to you."

this guy is a fat retard, but he hasn't caught me doing anything.

"Now listen to me, you. I want you to put your hands above your head and come to me." I raised my arms and started toward the patrol car, but then stopped abruptly. "No funny shit!" he practically screamed.

"But, sir, I can't get to you. You've got me blocked in."

"Don't argue! I want you to approach the vehicle."

"I have, sir," I replied imploringly. "I'm touching it with my legs. I can't approach it any further." *this guy is unstable. he's gonna fuck around and shoot me and then say i was going for his gun or something.*

"Well, I want you to climb across the hood towards me," he said while trying to step backward to unwedge his fat ass and draw his piece at the same time. His gun hooked on the door and scuttled off behind him.

can he arrest me for trespassing, maybe? Unsure of what to do next, I stepped on the bumper and then on the hood. Momentarily blinded by the flashing red lights, I could only see a silhouette of the sheriff, but it looked as though he was hunched down slightly, with his back to me. I didn't know if he was similarly blinded by the lights, but I didn't think he could see me, whatever the case. *fuck it!* I took a leap directly at Fatass, landing on him like a wrestler doing one of those moves off the ropes.

Tubby went down face first faster than a preacher's daughter in the back row of the movies.

Glancing back, I saw that the impact had knocked the sheriff out cold so I stopped and looked around quickly. *no one is watching.* The beauty of Dairy Queen alley was that no one could see anything from the street. *well, i'm not waiting for him to wake up and arrest me for assault!* I went tearing down the driveway, practically bowling over the three girls. "Get out of here!" I shouted. "The sheriff's back there! He tried to bust me!" The girls didn't wait for another syllable. They scattered as I ran out to the street.

I'd been forced to leave the bicycle since I couldn't get it past the car and its fat driver, so I just ran as fast and as hard as I could in the direction I'd come. When I'd gotten as far as my legs and lungs could carry me, I slowed down long enough for questions to cloud my thoughts, some of which I could scarcely believe were going through my head. *i have to make a decision. should i go back to the retreat? for what, to be a goody two-shoes? fuck that. that little cunt is going to be okay; she'll just go back home and be the same anyway. i've got my own life to lead. and i'm getting sick of fr. healy's holier than thou bullshit. that guy thinks he's fucking perfect. he can hire some fucking painters anyway. i gave him enough money... and so did clayton. what does he think we are, niggers? fuck him.* There wasn't a soul to be seen or heard as I ran as fast as I could on my way toward the NY State Thruway. *i'll just run down the south ramp and stick out my thumb. fuck it. i'm going home. there's only a couple of miles to go to the ramp and i want to beat the sunrise. but who the fuck is going to pick me up? what am i doing? where am i going? what the fuck is happening to me?*

Sheriff Fatass had no idea where he was or how long he'd been there as he started to regain consciousness. He felt his forehead and could tell there was an enormous goose egg on it. Getting to his knees slowly, he realized that his patrol car was still running... but he wasn't sure why.

His brain was scrambled and he was having difficulty putting everything together. The sheriff grabbed the car door and pulled his considerable dearth the rest of the way up. When he was standing again on his own two feet, he reached for his gun from force of habit, but there was nothing there. That woke him right up. Sheriff Fatass let out a bone-rattling yell of "Fuck!" that echoed through the little town. He leaned in to grab the radio, but stopped. He knew that he couldn't tell anyone or go anywhere until he found his gun. It was way too embarrassing. Suddenly the idea hit him that the thief who attacked him might have taken it. He wondered if the thief had breached the Dairy Queen... if he might still be inside. He wondered if he really wanted to know the answers to any of those questions. "Real crackerjack police work, Don," he told himself, tears welling up in each eye. "You sure are a winner." At the moment, that particular civil servant felt like the biggest piece of shit in the universe.

Clayton's eyes fluttered open and strained to focus as his ears were filled with the top stories of the CBS morning news. He must've fallen asleep on the couch the night before because Sandra had been standing over him, shaking him gently. "Do you know where Francis is?" she whispered.

It took a second for his mental cogs to start spinning, so he paused before responding, "He's in his bed, isn't he?" Sandra shook her head and Clayton stretched. "Well, he's gotta be around here somewhere."

"I overheard Fr. Healy and Sister talking just now. They're in the kitchen, making breakfast. I got up and was going in to help when I heard Father say something about not needing as many eggs because there were only going to be four of us for breakfast. When Mary Margaret asked what he meant, he said that he got up before daybreak to go for a ride, and that, when he checked in on us and saw that you and Francis were missing, he looked around and found you on the couch, but no sign of Francis. And then, when he went out to the garage, the bike was gone too."

"So maybe he went for a bike ride or something."

"For more than four hours... and without leaving a note?" She persisted. "I'm worried. When was the last time you saw him? Did he say that he was going anywhere?"

Clayton debated whether or not to keep the previous night's conversation to himself. "He was just a little stir crazy. He said he wanted to go out, but I was tired."

"When was that? Last night?"

Clayton nodded. He was starting to get worried too. "I don't know if he took the bike or not."

Sister Mary Margaret walked into the living room. "Ah, you're up, then. Good. Breakfast is ready. Come join us."

Clayton and Sandra followed the nun into the dining room and sat down. Francis' absence was glaringly apparent. Fr. Healy greeted them. "Good morning, you two. I hope it didn't hurt your back to sleep on that couch, Clayton."

"Nah, I'm fine. My bed at home is harder than that."

"Any idea where Mr. Doonan might be? We thought he might have gone for a bicycle ride this morning, but he's been gone far too long for that."

"Did he say anything to either of you about leaving or when he might be returning?" the sister added.

Clayton and Sandra were both awkwardly silent, keeping their eyes in their laps. Finally, Clayton responded. "If he's not back by now, he's not coming back. I mean, I know that he wanted to go out and do something last night, but he didn't mention anything about a bike. And it's not his style to just stay gone all night and not say something. He probably went back to the Kitchen."

"On a bicycle?" Mary Margaret said in disbelief. "What're we going to do? There's no way he'll make it all the way back to New York City on that old bike."

"He probably took an early morning train," Sandra suggested.

"Perhaps, but without returning the bicycle? That just doesn't make any sense. What was he so all fired-up, needing to get back right away for?"

"I think he was probably wanting for something very important." Fr. Healy stared right at Clayton until he looked up with confirmation in his eyes. "Whatever the case, Francis would've said something before he left had he been able, I'm sure. And that old bike was hardly worth returning. If I remember correctly, when it was donated to us several summers ago it was already used anyway, wasn't it?"

"So we're not going to do anything?" the nun asked.

"Oh, Francis can take care of himself. I'm sure that we'll see him on that stoop of his as soon as we get home. He'll be okay."

"I hope so, yo," Clayton murmured.

The rest of breakfast was fairly quiet, but once they'd all finished, Sandra said, "Why don't the two of you relax while Clayton and I clear the table and do the dishes?"

Sister Mary Margaret was pleased to see how much better Sandra was feeling. "Well that'd be lovely dear, thank you."

As Sandra started filling up a sink with hot, soapy water, Clayton started carrying the dishes over to the counter. "I don't understand why Francis acts so crazy sometimes," she said, breaking the silence.

"It's not that he's crazy. He just does his own thing," Clayton explained. "He's like the definition of 'unique' ... an individual. I actually respect that about him a lot. He's not a follower, no matter what."

"No, he's definitely no follower, but he's not really a leader either. So what does that make him? I don't mean that in a bad way," Sandra added. "He doesn't fit into any definition or type. He's just... Francis."

Clayton stopped for a moment to reflect on what she'd said. "No, I know what you mean, but in a way, Francis is no different from you or me. He's young, kind of fucked up, not sure what to do, not sure what's next. You know... not a kid anymore, but not an adult yet either. You know what I mean."

"Definitely."

"Wow. Thanks, you guys. This is looking great," Fr. Healy said, looking around at the kitchen. "When you get done, I'd like you to go upstairs and get cleaned up. Now that the painting's been taken care of, I'd like to take you guys on a little field trip instead of just finding something else for you to do around here."

As they were finishing up with the dishes, Fr. Healy went upstairs to the room Sandra had been sleeping in and placed a pamphlet on her bed. The title of the pamphlet read, "This is AA.... An Introduction to the AA Recovery Program. When he went in to do the same for Clayton, he looked over at the bed where Francis had been sleeping and felt a sincere pang of regret. "The Lord helps those who help themselves," he said aloud. "For wherever you're going, Francis Doonan, Godspeed."

I walked down the ramp and onto the Thruway, where I saw a sign that said "New York City 60 miles." Those sixty miles felt like they might as well be 60,000. I was overcome with so many different emotions and feelings, all flying at me like bats from a cave. I felt overwhelmed, hopeless, afraid, resentful, guilty and desperate, among others... but more than anything, I was just enraged. I wanted to eat. I wanted to puke, to fight, to make love. I wanted to laugh, to weep, to drink, to shoot up... *to JUST FUCKING DIE!* I couldn't tell who was talking inside my brain anymore. Was it I or was it the demons? Their rants and their screams had taken on my voice. They'd taken over my brain. *who would miss me, and for how long?*

I sat down next to the NYC mile sign and started bawling with every fiber of my being. My chest was heaving violently as my breath spasmed from my mouth in place of wails. Had someone told me at that moment that my tears were of blood, I wouldn't have questioned it at all. *fuck me. i'm in such serious trouble.* "Howie!" I screamed so loudly that I thought my vocal cords would snap and my temples would cave in. I jumped up as though I'd been stung and began to stagger and spin aimlessly along the roadside path, unintentionally kicking crushed rock everywhere. *hey, howie, maybe i should be with you. nobody fucking cares, least of all me. i try to do the right thing, but i'm a complete fuck up.* I looked south, toward the city. *and what waits for me there? more bullshit, people wanting me to be who i'm not... violence, jealousy, total fucking mayhem. please, god. please. someone tell me what to do. howie! howie?*

"I can't take this anymore," I whispered... to whom, I didn't know.

Light broke across my face while the rumble of an approaching vehicle filled the air – a truck heading for the Big Apple. I stood, frozen. The idea crept into my head: I simply had to step... once... to the right... directly into the truck's path. *i'm close enough. it will all be over.* The demons had won. They were gathered in a large group, screaming at me, "Do it, you piece of shit! You useless piece of shit, do it!" They were getting louder and louder in my head. The fear within me was beyond belief, but it decreased with each interminable millisecond that the truck took to come closer. I had just about committed to doing it, to taking the step. *there is no going back.* I wondered for a moment why my life wasn't flashing in front of my eyes on the entrance ramp. *i can't even have a ending like they describe in books and movies.* And then I saw my mother's eyes. I saw my father's smile. *i can't do this to them.* The truck's air horn was deafening as I flung myself off of the asphalt River of Styx and onto its grassy banks.

I stayed there for a few moments, a shaken young man... but alive. I didn't know if it was God or Howie or my parents or what, but something had gotten the demons back behind their gates. I finally rose to my feet, arms outstretched, as cars whizzed by. I dropped my left arm and stuck my right thumb up, finally taking my first step backwards... back towards home. I felt like Dorothy. I turned around, and each step was powered by thoughts of what I'd do when I got there. *...oh, and the shower i'll take... for two hours.... there will be so much steam coming from my apartment that someone will phone the fire department. and i'm going to sleep for a whole day.*

Suddenly, I saw the unmistakable silhouette of a State Trooper approaching me in the opposite lane. I swallowed hard. There was nowhere to go, nowhere to hide. I was caught. I could feel the demons start to rally. The car seemed to speed up as the trooper flipped on his red lights. I stopped... and waited... as the car breezed by. *the fucker had himself a speeder.* I laughed and it suddenly dawned on me. *that fat fuck won't tell on himself.* But perhaps I had spoken to soon. A car pulled up, just behind me, its lights throwing my shadow out onto the pavement like a corpse outline. I turned around slowly, blinded by the headlights. "Sorry," I heard a voice say as the lights dimmed, revealing a red Cadillac Coup Deville. "You need a ride, don't you?" I could hear The Temptations' "I Wish it Would Rain" playing softly in the background. I didn't move. My poor brain just couldn't appreciate the entirety of the situation. "Hey, little brother, are you looking for a ride or are you some kind of motherfucking census counter?" He let out the wheezy laugh of a smoker and I finally regained my senses. I chuckled too, stepping forward to grab the handle of his car door and get in.

"Thank you so much."

Milk was running out of his place to join the rest of the crew behind P.S. 72 to play some sponge ball when he stopped at Vit's apartment and knocked. He figured that he might as well since they lived in the same building and no one had seen Vit all week. Vit's father answered the door and informed Milk in an intentionally loud voice that his "Lazy ass son is still in bed." Just feet away, Vit was indeed still under the covers, but it had little to do with laziness. He hadn't been able to sleep at all the previous night. He'd begun to feel a little bit like a Judas, but it was too late to turn back. He sincerely doubted that J.R. would take kindly to a bout of amnesia or a sudden spate of conscience.

"I went by Francis' apartment on the way over here. He didn't answer the buzzer at all," Milk reported to Brian, Redbone and Patty Boy, already in the midst of a game. "And I stopped by Vit's too, on the way out. His dad said he was still in bed. Maybe he's sick."

"Maybe he's got a lady," Brian offered.

Patty Boy snapped back immediately, "That's impossible. He likes to suck cock."

"What the fuck?!?" Redbone said, putting down the bat and straightening up.

"I'm only fucking around, you retard," Patty Boy said, laughing and throwing the sponge ball at him.

Redbone whipped the ball back at Patty Boy's head. "Laugh at that, bitch."

"Just for that, I'm gonna 'Nolan Ryan' your big, black ass." Patty Boy threw the sponge ball high and inside so that Redbone had to hit the deck.

He jumped back up, though. "You honkey, Irish, potato-eating cocksucker, don't make me go 'Willie' on you."

The other three boys feigned laughing hysterically. "Yeah, 'Willie Mays' me, you spear chucker." Patty Boy leveled the ball in at the box painted on the wall and Redbone swiveled into it, ripping the ball into the midday sun, literally splitting it in half. One piece ended up down on the train tracks while the other flew up and landed on top of the apartment building across the street."

"Game over, cracker!" Redbone said, dropping the bat, "And that shit counts as a double home run, bitch."

"Way to go, 'Willie.' Now what are we gonna do?" Brian asked.

"I've got a couple of joints," Milk offered. "Why don't we stop at the bodega and get some Bud tall boys and hang out on the stoop?"

"Sounds like a plan, Stan," Brian replied.

———————————— ⁂ ————————————

I closed the door and reached over to the driver. "Thank you very much, sir. You're a lifesaver."

"Nah, I'm Richie Kingston, but I also answer to Richie the Skimp, the Poor Girl's Pimp. All the same, you're welcome, youngblood. And what do they call you?"

"I'm just Francis"

"Well, alright then, Just Francis. I'm heading for Harlem Town, USA, God's Country. How far can I take you?"

"Harlem would be fantastic," I replied.

"Cool. I got me two days off, and I plan on getting torn up and tearing up as much pussy as possible."

I smiled despite myself. His attitude was infectious. "Sounds like a plan, man," I said, trying to look back as discreetly as possible to see if there was any law enforcement behind us.

"Don't worry, little brother, I got you covered. Keeping an eye out for Mr. Charlie is second nature when you a Black man in America. As long as I keep it under the speed limit and don't let too much reefer smoke get out, we're cool." He let out a great, distinctive laugh. "You get high?"

That was music to my ears. "Is Nixon a crook?"

Richie smiled from ear to ear and produced a big, fat joint from under his seat. "I haven't tried it yet, but this shit is supposed to be real good. I got it from this Jewish cat who's a big dealer out where I work on Long Island."

"Oh, yeah?" I asked. "Where at?

"Monticello. I'm a cook at Grossinger's Hotel and Resort. You ever hear of it?"

"No, but my family just moved to Long Beach recently."

"Cool, cool. Working in a kitchen is hard work, but it's honest money. The whole joint is Jewish folk. I cook special for some of them so they're real nice to me. And then, in the winter, I go down to Miami and work at the Fountain Blue Hotel... and would you believe it's the same people down there?" I laughed. "Are you going to light that thing or fuck it, baby?" he asked.

"Shit. Sorry." I pushed in the car lighter, and when it popped a few seconds later, I lit that beautifully rolled joint and took a long hit. Holding my breath and doing my best to stave off a coughing fit, I passed it back.

Richie made smoking a joint look like both an art form and a form of science all at the same time. He reached under his seat again and produced a fifth of Hennessey. "When the weed is this good, youngblood, you gotta have some 'Henney' to go with it." With a joint in one hand and the brandy in the other, it was impressive how he could drive that beautiful Cadillac with his knees. He spun the top off of the bottle and took a swig. "Ahh! Now that is what I call breakfast." He passed the bottle to me and the demons sang along with The Temptations to "Ball of Confusion" while they were having their morning shower.

"So if your family lives out on the Island," Richie asked, "why are you heading to Harlem?"

"I actually live in Hell's Kitchen," I replied.

"Oh, really? A kid your age lives there by yourself? You'd probably be safer in Harlem!" We both chuckled. "Well that's not too far. I'll just drive you to your place."

"Thanks, man. I really appreciate it."

Before long, we were both drunk and high, and our conversation during the trip had run the gamut from sports to politics to women. We'd had some serious laughs by the time he pulled up in front of my building, so I knew it'd be cool to ask him why Black guys didn't eat pussy. I howled and knew I really liked Richie when he looked at me and said, "I don't know what Black guys you been around, but I don't just eat it... I suck it like a fucking mango, baby! You take care now, youngblood!"

No one was within sight from the stoop, so I headed indoors and stopped to check the mail. I had two delivery attempt notices for a package at the post office, so I pulled out the roach that Richie told me to take from his ashtray and headed over to the branch by the Port Authority. I was still fairly well fucked up, so the couple of hits I got off of the dube made me exceptionally contemplative about 42nd Street, eastward from Times Square. *i wonder if all the talk of improving this area will ever really happen. hell's kitchen is just looking so old and tired anymore. even on a sunny, blue skies kind of day, the view from the ground looks like dresden. god damn this weed is good! the people walking behind me must be getting high from the fumes!* My chuckle turned into an all-out guffaw when I crossed the street and turned towards the post office. It was odd that the thing prompting that laughter was the sight of funeral attendees filing down the stairs of Holy Cross. The memory they stirred was of the time Howie wanted to see what it was like to be an altar boy... even though he was Jewish, born and raised. I remembered helping to sneak him into vestments before mass and then laughing my balls off as he rang the bells in all the wrong places and the congregation was popping up and down like jacks-in-the-box. *although i doubt he'd admit it now, even father found it amusing.*

The thought of Fr. Healy made me stop for a second. *i hope that father isn't too mad at me. i hope he understands that <u>sandra</u> is the one with the problem, not me.* Lost in thought, I almost neglected to spot Mrs. O'Casey coming out of the church, and remembering that she thought I was in Mahopac with her daughter, I bolted for the door of the post office. In the amount of time it took me to claim my package, I was able to make sure that Sandra's mom was nowhere in sight. There was no return address, so I took another look at the postmark after I'd stepped out onto the street and was waiting to cross the street and head for that Hell's Kitchen staple, Dwyer's Bar and Grill. *canada? who the fuck do i know in canada?*

I wanted to keep my buzz going, so I'd downed two shots of "Henney" in honor of my guardian angel, Richie, and took a swig of my Heineken before I started to rip away the tape on the manila envelope that contained what appeared to be a standard apartment key and a purple velvet bag holding something cylindrical. I looked inside the mailing envelope and saw a note that had remained lodged inside. I unfolded it and saw Mrs. Nesto's signature at the bottom. I had to stop twice while reading her touching words to get myself under control and avoid having a repeat of the Thruway meltdown of earlier that morning. When I'd finally absorbed the note four times and wiped my eyes and nose, I opened the velvet bag and removed the purple bottle with the pewter crown. I set it before me on the bar and rested my chin on my folded arms. *i cant believe it. sitting right there. that's howie. shit, how weird.* I removed the silver stopper from the bottle and shook some of the contents into the crown. It looked like a grayish-white cross between sand and gravel. I could feel the demons slamming against their cage doors as my heart rose further and further up my throat. "Who do you have to fuck around here for more brandy and beer?" I demanded, prompting the bartender to sneer at me. While I chugged the rest of my beer, awaiting its replacements, I folded Mrs. Nesto's note around her key and shoved them in my pocket.

keep it together, francis. don't lose it. might be possible, but i'm gonna need a lot of pain medication real fucking quick.

"So where are we going, Father?" Clayton asked after they'd been driving for only a few minutes.

"Not far, Clayton. Did you see the pamphlet I left on your bed?" Fr. Healy asked.

"Yeah," Clayton responded.

"And did you read it?"

"...Yep," came the less-than-convincing response.

"How about you, Sandra? Did you read it?" Father asked.

"I didn't really have time before we left," she replied. "But I brought it with me to look at in the car."

That was what the priest was hoping to hear. "Why don't you read it out loud for a few minutes? We're almost to our destination."

Sandra began to read. "One. We admitted we were powerless over alcohol, that our lives had become unmanageable. Two. We came to believe that a power greater than ourselves could restore us to sanity...."

As Fr. Healy was pulling into the driveway of what appeared to be a school, they could all see a group of people standing about, most of whom were chain-smoking, drinking coffee, or both. All of them had a look about them like they were hurting. Clayton and Sandra exited the car and followed Fr. Healy warily. Until Clayton's stomach intervened with growls of hunger, his mind was preoccupied about what sort of field trip the priest had brought him on. Sandra, on the other hand, was trying to be open-minded and take in the experience as a whole. She had figured out in the car that their field trip had something to do with the pamphlet.

Fr. Healy heard Clayton's stomach rumble. "Goodness. Was that you?"

"Sorry, but I'm hungry, yo. I didn't really eat all that much at breakfast."

Father seemed to remember things differently in that area, but he still said, "Well, there's some coffee and snacks inside... cake and cookies, that sort of thing."

He'd barely gotten the word "snacks" out of his mouth before Clayton parted the crowd like the Red Sea on his way to the door. Just inside, he was greeted by a guy who looked like he was breathing nitrous. "Hi there, friend. I'm Gerry Clayton."

Clayton was a little startled, but he covered it by saying, "Yo, what's up, Gerry?"

"Nice to meet you, Clayton. Can I have a hug?"

"What the fuck?" Clayton started, his face all screwed up. "What kind of fruit do I look like to you? You better step back, man." Gerry recoiled, but it didn't deter him from greeting the next person through the door in the same fashion.

Clayton spotted two large coffee pots on a table in the back and went to investigate, finding an assortment of less-than-appetizing-looking cookies and an unopened box containing an Entenmann's crumb cake. He picked up a knife off of the table, opened the box with it, and then cut the cake in half, removing one of the two slabs of powdered sugar-dusted pastry. He took a Styrofoam cup and filled it with milk that had been intended for the coffee when a rather masculine-seeming woman approached him and said, "Hey, that cake's for everybody. You're not the only one here."

"Well, I'm the only one eating it," Clayton replied as powdered sugar sprayed from his mouth in little puffs with each syllable. "And everybody had a chance to grab some, so what do you want me to tell you?" Everyone had started coming into the cafeteria of the Mahopac Children's School, so Clayton walked over to where Sandra and Fr. Healy had chosen chairs from the circle in the center of the room, leaving a trail of sugar dust in his wake. Clayton was finding it difficult to concentrate on what the people seated in the circle were saying, choosing instead to alternate opening and closing each eye while looking at two side-by-side signs on the wall that read, "The Twelve Steps" and "The Twelve Traditions."

He finally grew bored of his little eye exam game and listened as the leader of the meeting stood and identified himself as "Richard, a grate-fully recovering alcoholic." When everyone in the room answered, "Hi, Richard." Clayton was a little startled.

"Whoop-dee-doo. Up with fucking people," he said under his breath. As Richard told the story of his own personal struggle with alcohol, everyone else seemed genuinely interested... all except Clayton, who continued mumbling things under his breath. When Fr. Healy heard something along the lines of "Yo, don't be such a bitch, mother-fucker. You're crying like a cunt," he gave Clayton a stare to which Roman Catholic priests have owned the patent for centuries. Uncomfortable, Clayton got up and the priest was convinced that he was going to leave. But when Clayton headed back to the coffee and snacks to take the remaining half of the crumb cake and then return to his seat, Fr. Healy allowed himself to continue to hope. The woman who chastised Clayton about the cake the first time, however, glared daggers into him from the table all the way back to his seat.

As soon as Richard finished speaking, he added, "Not to embarrass anyone, but simply to get to know you, do we have anyone new here today?"

Six hands went up. A large, Black woman stood up. "Yeah, family. I'm Sue. I'm cross addicted. And I have two days. The room responded to her in the same way Richard had been greeted: "Hi, Sue."

Three other people identified themselves as Sandra was thinking about how moved she had been at Richard's sheer honesty about his struggles. It made her feel a little forgiving of herself, that perhaps she was not the only one who'd made mistakes. Somehow, the room made her feel safe, and she suddenly found herself on her feet. "Hi. I'm Sandra. I don't know for sure, but I think I might be an alcoholic and a drug addict." Great tears welled up in her eyes. "And I'm glad I'm here." She sat down as Fr. Healy threw his arms around her and Clayton just looked on, mystified.

He realized that he was the last person who had put up his hand, and that he was expected to introduce himself. He had been genuinely moved by Sandra's example. He stood and cleared his throat. "Yeah, um, my name's Clayton. I drink sometimes and use sometimes... but I don't know that I'd say I've got a problem with it. But... um... I guess I'm glad I'm here too." He sat down but then stood back up immediately. "Oh, yeah, and I'm from Hell's Kitchen." He looked back down at Father. "Were we supposed to say where we're from?" The room cracked up as Fr. Healy beamed at Sandra and Clayton. When he sat back down, a couple of people near him leaned in and patted him on the back. He still didn't know what in the hell all of that was about... but he guessed he didn't mind so much.

Richard said, "A special welcome to our new folks. Alright. We're going to open it up to a show of hands." Many people raise their hands and Richard pointed at one.

He stood. "Hi. I'm Brian."

As with everyone who introduced themselves at the meeting, the room answered back, "Hi, Brian."

"First off," he continued, "I want to say I'm really very grateful to be here, but I've been going through some unusual shit lately. My life has been good for some time now, but there's this feeling I get. I don't know if it's loneliness or idleness, but it makes me act out, and honestly, how I've been dealing with it is by calling hookers."

"Damn," Clayton thought. "I like this guy."

"Being that this is my home group, many of you may remember that, when I first came in here, I was broken <u>and</u> broke. I didn't have a quarter to my name. Many of you, in fact, brought me sandwiches and coffee... and I'm forever grateful for that, but now that I find myself with money in my pockets again, I'm calling Asian escorts at $200 a pop, and when they arrive... to see their pain and loneliness... it just makes me feel like... I don't know... like I'm looking in a mirror." An egg timer sounded and Brian added, "I don't want to hog time, but although I feel shameful and guilty about it, and when I ask God for help, he does... talking about this out loud... it's one of the few other things that seems to help too. Thanks."

Richard called on Fr. Healy and he stood. "I'm Michael, a grateful recovering alcoholic. Welcome to all of the newcomers." Clayton and Sandra just stared at the priest in disbelief. "I've been feeling the urge lately to drink, and it's strong... very strong. I haven't used altar wine in the sacrament of mass for almost fifteen years. A part of me started to tell myself that it was necessary to use the altar wine because that was the way I was taught, and that I should be able to separate my malady from my duty. But I know what's really making me say that... and that alcohol can be both cunning and baffling. It's just got me feeling guilty about my vocational duties again lately. But, I thank God that it hasn't happened because I was able to pick up the phone, get on my knees and ask for the power and the courage and the direction. ...Thank you."

Clayton found himself deep in thought. He had always believed that priests and nuns and teachers and doctors and so forth had it all together. Finding out that they were human was moving. Fr. Healy looked at Clayton and he smiled genuinely. The priest returned his own as a gesture of appreciation... and just as sincerely.

The first several minutes in the station wagon on the ride back were completely silent until Sandra asked, "Fr. Healy, do they have meetings like that back home?"

"Of course," he replied. "Lots of them; everywhere in the world, in fact. I can give you an NYC meeting book when we get back, if you'd like."

"I would," Sandra said. "Thanks."

Fr. Healy continued driving, wondering if Clayton was going to speak. He didn't know if the teenager would open up at the meeting or not, so he was pleasantly surprised when it happened. Clayton finally stopped staring out the window and broke his silence. "Father, if it's okay with you, I think I want to go home tonight."

"Sure, Clayton. I can't begin to tell you how much I appreciate all of your help, but I wonder if you could do me one more favor once you get home."

"Name it," Clayton replied. "Anything."

"I'm going to give you back half of the money that you brought up here. I'd like for you to take it to an administrator named Carmel Ryan at St. Clare's Hospital and tell her that I sent you to give her the money. I'm sure she'll put it to its best use... for a room renovation or new windows or a new piece of equipment or something, but would you ask her to please include a note with it somewhere that says it's "from a friend?"

"You got it, Father," Clayton replied, "if you drive me to the station later."

The priest laughed as he pulled in next to the retreat house. "You've got a deal."

While Clayton went upstairs to pack his things, Sandra went to the kitchen to place a call home. Clayton made a final check around the house to make sure he hadn't missed anything and then hunted down Sister Mary Margaret to say goodbye. Doing so was harder for both of them than either had imagined it would be. She gave him a hug and a kiss on the cheek, and then handed him a brown paper bag. "I've prepared you some food for the train ride back." He looked up at her and smiled. "I know how you like to eat." Clayton gave a little laugh and then threw his arms around the sister for one final hug.

"All set? Have you got everything? The next train isn't for half an hour, so you have time to double check."

"Nah, I'm all set," Clayton replied as Sandra came into the room.

"I just got off the phone with my mother. She'd like to come up a little early… this evening, in fact. She said she'd like to spend a few days helping too. So she wanted me to ask if it'd be okay for her to stay. Do you think it's a good idea?"

Fr. Healy looked deeply at Sandra. "That's a question only you can answer. How do you feel?"

Sandra thought for a moment before responding, "I think I'll be okay."

Sister Mary Margaret kissed her on the forehead. "Yes, my dear. I think you will too."

Sandra turned to Clayton and asked. "So you're all ready?" He nodded. "Mind if I go along for the ride to the train station?"

"Not at all," Clayton responded with a smile.

Later that afternoon, as Sandra was pacing back and forth on the porch, nervously awaiting her mother's arrival, Dorothy O'Casey pulled up in the family car and gave a brief honk as a greeting. She turned off the car and stepped out as Sandra scampered over to hug her. "Your father didn't want me to wait until the morning and have to deal with all the traffic, so I came right after my Holy Name Society meeting."

Fr. Healy came out of the house. "Hello! You must've made great time, then!"

"Oh, yes, I did. And the car is stocked to the top with food and other goodies that might help you get through the season."

"Thank you as always. Why don't we go inside?"

Sandra walked along with her mother's arm around her shoulders instead of with the daughter's arm around her mommy's waist. Somehow Dorothy knew that something was different. She thought, but wasn't sure, that it was just her little girl becoming a young woman, but if there was something else her daughter wanted to say, she would allow her to do so with time and dignity. Sandra kept in step while tears fell down her cheeks. Her mother looked at her, touched by the truly lovely moment. "Sweetheart, what's wrong?"

Sandra sniffled. "I'm just so happy to see you."

Sister greeted the pair at the door as Fr. Healy began unloading the car. "Mary Margaret!" Dorothy exclaimed. "It's been too long!"

"Well, I hope there's a bit of sweet cake in that car because I've already put the kettle on," she replied.

That night, after they had all talked themselves into exhaustion and Fr. Healy and Sister Mary Margaret had gone off to bed, Sandra and her mother were in the living room with steaming hot chocolates. Sandra remembered the courage that she'd summoned at the meeting earlier in the day and announced, "Mom, I'd like to talk to you for a minute."

Dorothy put down her hot chocolate, folded her hands in her lap, and gave her daughter her full attention. Sandra began to tell her mother everything in a mature, yet sensitive fashion. She revealed everything from her first time with Danny Albanese, all the way up to the A.A. meeting. Her mother never spoke a word, but that couldn't keep the tears from streaming down her face.

"Are you okay, mom?" Sandra asked.

"Yes, my dear. I'm just listening," her mother replied.

"It may sound weird to say this, but 'That's it.' That's everything."

Dorothy sat quietly for a moment, took a deep breath, and then began to speak. "I am your mother and I love you, so I won't pretend that it was easy for me to hear all of the things that you just said. I'm not angry and I'm not disappointed. I'm glad you felt you could share those things with me. I knew it was hard to be a kid these days..." She got a little choked up. "...but I guess I didn't know how hard."

"Please don't tell Daddy," Sandra said quietly.

"That will be hard, Sandra. I have to be honest with you about that," her mother responded. "I've never lied or kept a secret from that man since the day we met, but I have no idea what that kind of knowledge about his princess would do to him... or what he would do to the others involved in your situation. But for your good... and for his... you have my word that I'll never betray your confidence."

"Thank you, Mommy," Sandra cried, throwing her arms around her mother's waist and hugging her tight.

"Strangely enough," she replied. "I think this will make us even closer. God works in mysterious ways indeed. But, as strange as this may sound, coming from your 'ol' Irish mother,' I want you to see someone... someone who can help you professionally to deal with the scars you've been given that no one can see on the outside. Okay? I want you to focus on school and make your life's dreams a reality."

"Yes, Mommy," her daughter replied, wiping away a tear. "And I hope Francis gets some help too. He deserves it. He's such a sweet guy, and he gave up so much to help me."

"Only he can make that decision."

I staggered out of Dwyer's in time to see the sun slip behind the row of buildings unfortunate enough to be in New Jersey, realizing that I had drunk my entire morning and afternoon away. I suddenly felt the urge to hear my mother's voice, so I held onto the payphone on Ninth Avenue and emptied my pocket on the shelf in search of change. I dialed my family's new number... with their new area code... and it rang twice before I heard the voice of my sweet mother, Agnes, say, "Hello?"

"Mommy?" I slurred.

"Hello, Francis. How are you, dear?" In that way that only mothers know, she could feel my pain by hearing one word. There was a long moment of silence. I just didn't know what to say.

"Mommy?" I repeated. Silence.

"When are you going to come and see the house? Daddy and the girls would love to see you too. Why don't you come and spend a few days...

swim in the ocean.... I'll cook some of your favorite foods and put some fat on those bones."

My slurring made, "I will," almost indecipherable.

"Go see your Uncle Patsy too, okay? He's been trying to call, and he's gotten worried about you."

I could tell that calling had been a mistake. My conduct and state had my mother upset. She was being a trooper and not calling me on it, but I knew. I summoned all the strength I had in an attempt to pull it together for even a few moments. "Everything's alright here. There's nothing to worry about. I'd love to come out." Another pause went on forever. I could hear the tears collecting on her eyelids. "I miss you... and I love you... very much."

A crack of thunder prompted her to ask, "What is that noise, dear, a storm?" I grunted an "uh huh," so she continued, "Well, for God's sake, take off your chains and rings; you don't want to get hit by lightning."

I started to laugh. My mother had eased my pain for a moment, and she was obviously relieved to hear my laughter too. "I'll talk to you soon, Mommy. ...Thank you."

"Okay. Goodbye, Francis." I hung up the receiver as the deluge began. Rain started falling as if out of buckets, and I just huddled in the open phone booth until it slowed up. *after all, where do i even have to be, anyway?*

I was a little wetter, but not much more sober when I started across 43rd Street on my way home. All I wanted was to pass out for about 24 hours. I hadn't slept for a day and a half, and I couldn't remember ever being so tired as I dragged one foot after the next along the sidewalk. All of a sudden, a series of whoops sounded into the air as I came into the focus of Brian, Milk, Romeo T and Redbone, who had just come from his apartment and were hanging out on his stoop. *a nice stoop but not as nice as mine.*

"Look who's back! If it ain't the prodigal son," Redbone yelled out.

"What's up, fellas?"

"You look like shit, man," Brian said.

Romeo chimed in, "And you smell like it too! Whew! You are fucked up, Doonan! Did you take a bath in Budweiser, dude?"

"Nah, nah, I'm just tired. That's all," I replied.

Rome shot back, "Yeah, and tired smells like hops and barley!"

"Where you been? I've gone by your place every day this week," Milk barged in.

"Um... that's a long story," I said. "Let me get some sleep and I'll catch up with you knuckleheads tomorrow."

"Yo! Before you go, though, you gotta take a hit of this. It's exotic. My cousin sent it over from Thailand in Kodak film canisters. The customs people can't open them because of exposure or something." Romeo handed me a joint. "They call this shit 'pussy hair.' And we see why. It's just as good!"

I took an enormous hit and flew to another planet. "Okay... later," I slurred, continuing to sway back and forth down the street. The boys headed off towards Times Square, and within seconds, the rain had returned with a vengeance. I was standing right in front of the door to the 453 building... Howie's place... when I remembered the key and the note in my pocket. I walked through the front door, which had never been locked as long as I could remember, and staggered up to the third floor, step by step. With a great deal of concentration, I finally got the key in the lock of the door to apartment 3-C and swung it wide open.

It was warm and stuffy inside, but I knew that the rainy air outside would wash that away quickly. Hoping to find something to satisfy my munchies, I opened the refrigerator, but saw only things that couldn't spoil: condiments, things in cans or bottles, a jug of water... and beer. The demons were celebrating. "That'll work," I said, grabbing the remaining eight cans of Budweiser, Howie's favorite. "It's cool. This was actually Howie's beer." I was talking out loud, but I wasn't sure who I thought was listening. "Maybe I should call Benny and check in. Let him know everything is alright." I thought to use the phone in Howie's room, but I wasn't prepared for the assault on my mind and heart when I opened the door and everything in there contributed to overwhelming me with memories of my best friend. The room started to spin and I collapsed on the bed in place of the floor. I took a couple of deep breaths, not knowing whether I was going to puke or not. Whatever the case, exhaustion claimed me long before I could pick up the phone... or remember to pull off the ring tab on my can of beer.

In a thick Sicilian accent, Dominic approached Johnny Albanese and said, "That kid, Vit is here."

"Well show him in," J.R. responded.

Danny protested. "Hey, pop, are you sure we can trust him?"

J.R. gave his son a ghoulish smile, forming a gun with his thumb and forefinger and putting it to his temple. "Son, I trust him with his life." Danny understood what his father was saying, and it made him feel better.

Dominic showed Vit into the backroom. He was wearing a black leather jacket that he figured made him look the part. "There he is... Mr.

100% Gen-u-ine Wiseguy," J.R. mused. They all laughed, making Vit feel a bit stupid. Oh, I'm just breaking your stones, kid. C'mon. The rain's stopped, so we can take the top down on my Delta 88."

A short while later, the four men were seated at an outdoor table on Prince Street, in front of Alfonso's Italian Restaurant in the heart of Little Italy. The patrons there practically populated the wish list of every law enforcement agency in the country, and near the top of each of those lists was the quartet's newest dining companion, Vincenzo, another Sicilian and also a stone-cold killer. J.R. made the introductions all around before turning to Vit. "So, tonight we're going to boost the micks' arsenal. Now what we need from you, my young ace-in-the-hole, is the location of said arsenal."

"It's in the sports closet at the Hell's Kitchen Youth Organization. The only difficulty that I wasn't able to tell you about on the phone is that it's locked... but my friend, Brian has the key. If you can give me some time, I could probably get it from him."

"Where'd you get the zip? Topeka?" asked Vincenzo.

Johnny replied, "Take it easy. He's a new friend of mine." Turning back to Vit, he continued, "My young friend, keys and locks were made for honest people. We'll simply take the fucking doors off, and then, tomorrow, you will bring an envelope to the Hell's Kitchen Youth Organization as sort of a donation to the repair fund."

Vit nodded, even though he was already scheming to keep the money since they'd have to replace, not repair, the doors. They sat for a few hours at Alfonso's, even though J.R. had insisted that none of them have wine or anything alcoholic. Vincenzo and Danny busied themselves by flirting with a pair of girls who looked like they could be fashion models while J.R. chatted with the owner and Vit could only look on and learn.

It was rather late by the time J.R. asked for the check and then argued with Alfonso over the right to pay it. The five men had piled back into J.R.'s car and headed west on 23rd Street toward Eleventh Avenue. Danny's friend, Chuckie, worked at the U-Haul Rental Agency there and had agreed to leave the gate unlocked and a key in the ignition of the truck that Vit and Vincenzo were going to "borrow" and drive north on Tenth, up to 52nd and the Hell's Kitchen Youth Organization.

Dominic and Danny sat lookout with J.R. in his car as Vit hopped out of the truck, crowbar in hand, and walked toward the club's door. Vincenzo just sat in the cab, staring at him with a look of disgust until Vit turned and saw that the Sicilian was motioning to him with a single, beckoning finger. He walked over and Vincenzo rolled down the window. "If you're going to do something, at least do it the right way. Use your head for something other than a hat rack. Be smart. If you wrap the crowbar in a towel, you don't hear nothing. *Capisce*?" he said sarcastically.

Vit resented being talked to that way, but took the offered towel all the same and wrapped it around his crowbar. They walked over to the door and tried unsuccessfully for several minutes to pry it open. Vincenzo put down his crowbar and used the towel to wipe his forehead as Vit looked over at the Delta 88 with an expression that said, "What now?" J.R. said something to Dominic, who got out of the passenger seat and proceeded to charge like a bull straight at the door, taking it down as though he were Dick Butkus. An ear-splitting noise echoed through the streets of the West Side as Vincenzo stuffed his towel in his pocket and transferred the look of disgust to his fellow Sicilian. Vit led the two of them through the darkened gymnasium, so nervous that he thought he'd just about jump out of his skin. They finally reached the supply closet, and Vit pointed to the huge padlock on its doors.

"Fuck!" Vincenzo hissed. "I left the crowbar at the front door."

It was Vit's turn to be condescending. "Smart move, you zip." He'd just picked the wrong person to whom he could be condescending.

Vincenzo grabbed the teen by the throat, his knife resting millimeters from Vit's jugular. "Who the fuck do you think you're talking to?" he demanded. "I should slice you open."

It wasn't until that moment that Vit truly appreciated the type of men he'd thrown in with. He hadn't sold out the crew from the stoop; he'd sold his soul to the Devil, himself. Tools in hand, Danny stepped into the room in time to see Vit suspended in the air, on the verge of death. "I told my father not to waste his time with this fucking kid," he said to Dominic. "Can we do this please? It is why we're here, Vincenzo."

He released his hold on Vit's throat, but whispered in his ear, "I'm not done with you." In a matter of moments, the doors had been removed from the closet and the four men had each grabbed an edge of the King's tarp to carry the cache of weapons upstairs and onto the truck. Dominic jumped behind the wheel of the U-Haul while Danny returned to his father's car. Vit and Vincenzo headed for the truck's passenger side when the Sicilian grabbed Vit's forehead from behind and slashed his throat, shoving the body forward to crash onto the pavement and bleed out into the gutter. "You should've listed to me," he said, wiping his blade on Vit's leather jacket.

Clayton gave one of those stretches that a person can only manage when he's woken up early in his own bed after some time away... and realizes it's Saturday. He hopped in the shower and headed immediately to Francis' building and pressed the bell to 4RS. "Crazy Irish fuck," he muttered. It did nothing to alleviate the worry over his good friend that Clayton's curiosity about what happened to Francis remained unsatisfied.

He had only loitered on the stoop for a bit before he saw Brian, Redbone, Milk and Romeo T get out of Kelly the Mick's car and head in his direction. It would probably be more accurate to have said that Clayton smelled them before he saw them, but they'd had a rough night all the same. The first of the mutual greetings were drowned out by the sirens from an ambulance and two cop cars that went whipping by, but he had embraced each of his friends and he filled them in on what had happened and where he'd been in short order. Finally, Clayton asked, "Have any of you guys seen Francis? He disappeared from the house two nights ago and no one's seen him."

"Oh, yeah," Brian confirmed. "He was seriously fucked up when we saw him, which was weird because I think he was coming from the post office. Anyway, we were hanging out at Redbone's yesterday afternoon. He came by, we smoked a little weed, and then he said he was heading home to crash out."

Clayton felt better, but rang Francis' buzzer again anyway. "Still no answer. This nigga must be zonked."

No one saw the black, undercover cop car pull up in front of the stoop until it was too late. Brian's asshole clenched when he realized they'd find the weed and pipe he was holding if they did a search, but he remained still. All eyes were on the sloppy, bloated frame of the infamous Det. Perez as he sort of heaved himself from the car firing questions. "You kids know Vittorio di Cicco, right?" No one responded. "Let's try this again. I know you know Vittorio di Cicco. When was the last time any of you saw him?"

"I don't know... a couple of days ago, I think," Milk responded. "I stopped by his place yesterday morning, but his dad said he was sick. Why?"

Brian just stared at the detective while he tried to rip a hole in his pocket so he could drop the pipe and weed down his pants leg. Although he didn't believe they knew anything about their friend's murder, Perez just shifted his gaze from one boy to the next until Clayton got tired of the performance. "Yo, he asked you why. Vit didn't do whatever bullshit you guys are trying to say he did."

Perez focused on Clayton and then lifted his chin so he could sneer down his nose at him. "You guys are all pretty close, yeah? Well, what bad luck. Your group seems to be getting smaller and smaller. First, the Nesto kid and now the di Cicco kid."

"What the fuck?" Romeo blurted out. "What are you talking about?"

"I'm asking the questions here. Where is the other one? The pale Irish kid... Doonan or whatever?"

"We don't know," Clayton shot back. "Yo, what the fuck happened to Vit?"

Perez spit out his response as insensitively as he could, "Oh, yeah... um, we found him with his throat cut in front of the Hell's Kitchen Youth Club early this morning... well, a smacked-out hooker did, actually. We just cleaned up his blood and piss... and his shit." The detective was paying close attention to gauge their reactions, looking for any of them to receive the news... or how the detective had delivered it... strangely. He got no such satisfaction. As soon as the initial shock had turned to numbness within each guy, they all reached the same conclusion silently: J.R. Albanese. "Oh, shit. You didn't know yet?" Perez feigned regret. "Wow. Sorry about that. And sorry about your friend. Look, I have to get back to work, but keep close in case we need to talk to you some more... and it might not be a bad idea to travel in packs. Seems like it's open season on you poor souls who are unfortunate enough to be trapped here in Hell's Kitchen."

As Perez was getting back into his car and talking to his partner, the boys were chatting amongst themselves about going down to the Dante League and "doing what they had to do, with or without Kelly the Mick" as Brian put it. None of them really knew what that entailed, but they'd made a group decision to meet back on the stoop early the next morning and go "handle business."

After Det. Perez had turned to give one last look at the crew before pulling away, Kelly the Mick came storming up to the stoop from across the street, where he'd been watching the boys talk to the cop. "You rat cocksuckers! I knew it. A bunch of cheese eaters! Like Pac Man with fucking whiskers! All of you!" He looked right at Brian. "Ten million pigs sitting in front of the HKYO and I come back to find you sucking that fat fuck detective's withered prick."

"No, man!" Brian insisted. "He was here to ask us about Vit. They killed him this morning. The Albaneses. We didn't say shit about the Youth Organization. That's just where they found Vit's body."

Brian's words eventually sunk through Kelly the Mick's rage. He walked to the curb and yelled "Fucking wops!" into the street, stalking back to the stoop. "Well, if they want a war, they've got one. Brian, you go find out if the stuff is still at the HKYO."

"There's cops all over up there. I'm not...." he began to protest.

Kelly the Mick interrupted him. "<u>You</u> fucked this up, so <u>you</u> are going to fix it! Prove to me that I was a jerk-off for trusting you." As he said "trusting," Kelly shoved the teen as hard as he could, sending him back into the building's door.

Redbone inhaled deeply to pump up his girth, stepped in front of Brian and said, "Back off, Kelly."

Kelly the Mick glared back, furious. "What? Who the fuck do you think you're telling to back off? You work for me. I own you, nigger."

Redbone didn't think. He just reacted, connecting with a short right to his chin, sending the gangster down, bouncing his head off of the pavement.

"What in the fuck are you doing?" Brian screamed. "What? Are you fucking crazy, man?"

Redbone spoke calmly. "This motherfucker's had it coming." Assuming a "sho nuff, boss," drawl, he finished, "And Missa Lincoln say dat after da war, we all's free."

Brian understood what his friend was trying to say. "But what happens when he gets up? And what about Colin Garvan? They're both just as fucked in the head."

The boys huddled on the stoop, afraid and unsure of what to do. Clayton spoke first. "Shit. They got Vit. I wonder if they got Francis too."

Milk added, "I won't believe it until I see it... but we sure can't hang around here until that crazy fuck wakes up. Somebody grab his gun just in case."

Romeo crept to the downed heap that was Kelly the Mick, lifted his coat lapel and pulled out his piece, shoving it down the front of his pants. "Let's get fuckin' gone," he said, leading the pack racing up Tenth Avenue.

As soon as he'd risen and could remember where he lived and what year it was, Kelly the Mick groggily made his way over to Rudy's Bar to find Hughie Horgan, a once infamous IRA gunman, who now resembled a soused version of the Lucky Charms leprechaun. He sat down, but struggled to keep his voice down. "Hughie, I need your help. I need some shooters... tonight."

Hughie strained to focus on Kelly the Mick, but managed to respond, more to get Kelly to leave than to help him. "Well isn't this your lucky day, then?" He pointed at two pale characters with jet black hair.

"Those are the Leahy Brothers. They're fecking lethal... and if you've got the money, they'll do anything you want."

Kelly the Mick ordered a bottle of Bushmill's and a bag of ice for his jaw and then went to the payphone to summon Colin Garvan. Colin told him on the phone that he'd heard from Brian, who said that the sports locker had been cleaned out, but not by the cops. More enraged, Kelly approached the Leahy Brothers with the bottle and said, "By the time this is empty, I want to have mapped out the plans for how we're getting rid of the Albaneses, once and for all. We're finishing this shit tonight." The brothers were overjoyed at the chance to make some cash, but that idea in particular practically left them salivating with anticipation.

The Albaneses and the Sicilians had bedded down at the Dante League Social Club that morning and had all woken up at different times. J.R. had just finished going through the weapons and explosives in the late afternoon when his son approached them, yawning and wiping sleep out of his eyes. "Well, good <u>evening</u>, Little Baby Naps-a-Lot. So glad to see we're all still alive... no thanks to you."

"What'd I do?" Danny asked. "Nothing happened, did it? You guys could've woken me up if you needed me. It's not like I had a clock or nothing."

"Why did the Church have to be against abortion?" J.R. muttered, leaving Dominic and Vincenzo snickering behind their fists. "You know, these mutts are going to try and come at us eventually, Daniel. They'll know we did this."

"I know that, Dad," Danny responded, "I'm not saying they're stupid. But if they were any less stupid, they would've already hit us. It'll take them a couple of days to put something together. But we can take them out first with Dominic and Vincenzo along for the shooting."

"Absolutely," Dominic replied. "It'll be a walk in the park."

"Well, I don't want anything taken for granted," J.R. replied. "That's why I want everyone to stick close. You should all go in the back and have a shower... take whatever you want to wear off the racks back there, but bring your other clothes back here and put them in this bag. Later, I want to order some food later and strategize... put down a plan to end this Irish infestation for good. Yeah?"

The trio nodded. "I'll place the order," Danny offered sheepishly. "Where's the Calvecchio's menu?"

"No, it's a special occasion. Tonight let's order from Giovanni's instead," his father replied. "But are your eardrums clogged with shit, Daniel? I just told you to go shower up and change first." He grabbed Vincenzo's right sleeve, pointing to a bloodstain. "Or is that a marinara spill? You fucking morons." J.R. Albanese was clearly still unhappy about losing his pet rat.

I had to remind my body to wake up, part by part and limb by limb after I opened my eyes and found myself drenched with sweat. Once I realized that I was in Howie's bed and my mind began piecing together the events that had led me there, it took several nearly panic-stricken moments to put together how much time I had actually been asleep. It seemed that the amount of alcohol I'd consumed, coupled with not having slept at all the day before, had overridden my body's internal alarm clock and I had ended up comatose for almost 24 hours. I scanned my mental calendar in vain to see if there was anything I'd forgotten to do during that lost day as I walked down the hallway to the bathroom for a long piss. I didn't feel good at all, and suddenly started to battle back the same impulses I'd faced on the Thruway. I grappled with the unbearable urge to go to the spot where Howie had been murdered, contemplating how I'd climb the cement wall between Tenth and Eleventh, just a few doors from where I stood.

i've got to get high. now.

Howie hadn't been my best friend for nothing. I knew he had to have something for me somewhere in that apartment. I started to pull the drawers out of his dresser, one at a time, dumping the contents on the bed and sifting through them like a prospector seeking gold. The best things I found were a stale pack of Kent cigarettes and a number of corn cob pipes that Howie had loved customizing, each clogged with resin and sporting screens that were similarly coated by the dark, sticky goo. I put the pipes on the desktop and cracked each one open with one of Howie's old baseball trophies, harvesting the gunk with a pen knife. By the time I'd finished scraping the pipes, night had fallen and I had a nice ball that resembled an asphalt rock from a paving crew.

Remembering that Howie had always described his mom as something of a hypochondriac, I decided to search the medicine cabinet next and was rewarded with a brand new bottle of Robitussin. ...*with codeine.* I brought the bottle with me back into Howie's room and twirled a few of the cigarettes between my thumb and forefinger to make the tobacco snow down onto the tar-like glue ball. Using the knife to mix the concoction all together, I ended up with a black and brown lump about the size of a super-bounce ball. I started rolling it slowly with the palm of my hand, leaving permanent, shitty stains wherever the ball touched, until I had a perfectly spherical object, which I quartered with the knife. I dropped that into the only clean pipe I'd found in his room and held the flame from my lighter over the pipe, inhaling until it began to smolder. The harsh mixture of the residue and all the crappy tobacco ensured that the huge hit I took left me straining to cough violently while trying desperately to hold it in my lungs.

When I finally allowed myself to exhale, I chased my phlegm with a beer and waited for the relief. I couldn't tell if I was still fucked up from the day before or if I was experiencing a whole new buzz, but the remedy was not enough for the demons. Snatching up the bottle of Robitussin, I spun the cap from the bottle and stuck the opening in my mouth, preparing the pipe with another section of the resin ball while the bottle dripped and drained down my gullet. The demons were running free and had overrun my nervous system, leaving me feeling as though I'd explode at any moment. I scrambled desperately to smoke the three remaining quarters of my resin-tobacco ball to keep them under control, but soon realized I was losing the battle; I was losing the war.

and there is only one place to go for help if you're losing a war: the united nations.

As Saturday night fell on Hell's Kitchen Hughie Horgan unlocked the front door to his apartment and let his four business associates file through. They waited in the living room as he disappeared in the back and reemerged with a pair of .45s, a shotgun that had had its barrel sawed off and a handful of smoke bombs. Since the Leahy Brothers already came loaded to the teeth, Kelly the Mick took the two handguns and put them in his belt, Wild West style. Colin Garvan laid down the spool of rope and rolls of duct tape that he'd gotten out of the car and filled his pockets with shotgun cartridges. Hughie handed him a belt to fashion something of a sling for the scatter shotgun. Kelly the Mick put several money notes in the old man's hand and said, "Thanks, Hughie. I won't forget it."

"That makes one of us," the old drunk responded, cackling at his own joke.

Nearby, in the kitchen of his restaurant that smelled like an authentic Tuscan neighborhood, Paulie Giovanni was giving instructions to his delivery guy. "Mr. Albanese doesn't order from us often, so I've made sure this is perfect. Make certain it gets to him the same way, Nino. And don't screw around. Go straight there so it'll be still be piping hot. And no matter what you do, don't accept a tip, no matter how much he tries to get you to take it. Insist that it's your pleasure, yes?" Nino nodded as they both wiped sweat from their brows. Although the delivery boy stood to lose his job, Paulie stood to lose a little bit more in light of the note for fifty grand that Johnny Albanese held over him.

A short while later, the Giovanni's delivery van pulled up in front of the nearby Dante League Social Club. The driver got out and knocked on the door. Dominic took his pistol off of the table and headed to answer it. "It's the food," he yelled into the back.

"It's about time!" J.R. shouted his reply. "Help the kid bring the shit in. We ordered a lot for tonight and tomorrow."

Dominic pointed at the large, bullet-shaped object and asked Nino, "What's in this silver thing? A fucking bomb?"

"N-no," the boy stammered. "It's a Thermos bottle."

"The fuck you say," Dominic replied.

"It is, sir. Full of fresh pasta fagiole. You guys ordered a lot of it."

Sounding like a little kid, Dominic responded, "Oh, I love pasta fagiole. Fuck me. This thing is heavy as shit."

Having parked his car a block away, Kelly the Mick rounded the corner onto 39th Street just in time to see Dominic and Nino each carry a handle of the large container into the club. He stopped immediately and backtracked, running into the other three who were right on his heels. "The fucking door is wide open. They're getting take out." He waited for a minute more, peering around the corner of the building as his breathing grew more and more rapid. Once Dominic went back inside, carrying a stack of aluminum pans filled with Italian delicacies, passing Nino, who was on his way back out to retrieve another stack, the four gunmen bolted down the block. One of the Leahys happened upon Nino first, just as he was turning around with his hands full. He didn't want to give up the element of surprise, so he kept his gun trained right on Nino's forehead. "Not a fucking word or you die." The other three rushed into the club and found the main room entirely empty, but the door to the backroom wide open. Kelly the Mick saw Dominic disappear through that door so the gunmen crowded next to its opening and waited, firearms at the ready.

The Sicilian came back through the door, saying, "Where the fuck did that kid...." but Kelly the Mick cut short Dominic's thought by painting the door with his brains. They all rushed in, catching J.R. and Danny with plates in their hands and Vincenzo opening up one of the aluminum pans.

Although he was trembling terribly, Colin Garvan plugged the barrel of the sawed-off shotgun against the base of the seated Sicilian's skull and growled, "Move, motherfucker and you're gone." Kelly the Mick and the other Leahy brother had a pair of .45s trained on each of the Albaneses as the first brother directed Nino to reenter the club after closing the van's doors and then closing and locking the building's doors.

With all four of the Italians seated around the table and staring at the business end of various firearms, Kelly the Mick ventured a smile of satisfaction. "Tell me, Albanese, in that pig-nigger language you people speak, how would you say, 'We're fucked?'"

"So much for your theory that these cocksuckers couldn't organize this quickly, huh?" J.R. sneered at Danny with disgust. As thanks for the backhanded compliment, Kelly the Mick began pistol-whipping the elder Albanese until his head was a gleaming, frothy pulp that clung to his skull. Danny cried out with fear and rage, paralyzed by the twin .45 muzzles aimed at his forehead.

Nino began begging for his life in a mixture of English and Italian. "Shut the fuck up!" Kelly the Mick shouted, smacking the delivery boy in the back of the head. "We know you're not one of them." He threw the rope and duct tape onto Nino's lap and ordered, "Tie them the fuck up... and if any one of them gets loose, then you <u>will</u> die." With trembling hands, he even bound the barely recognizable J.R. Albanese, unconscious from his vicious throttling. "Colin," Kelly ordered, "check them for weapons. Start with that greaseball you've got there."

Colin leaned over to search inside Vincenzo's jacket when all of a sudden he tried to head butt Colin. Little did the Sicilian realize that, although the shotgun had shifted to an upwards angle, it was still resting at the base of his skull. When his forehead connected with Colin's face, the shotgun discharged and sprayed large pellets through Vincenzo's skull and soft tissue, practically erasing his head altogether. And like some surreal, violent minstrel show, the air in the room had become instantly filled with a strange, black, powdery mist from the pressurized carbon dust inside the obliterated Thermos bottle. Everyone and everything in the room looked like it had been dipped in roofing tar. Faces, clothes and hair were all jet black. "What the fuck!?!" Kelly the Mick screamed. He couldn't tell who, if anyone was still alive.

He could eventually make out Danny crying and saying, "I'm shot, Dad. He fucking shot me in the shoulder." One of the Leahy brothers was lying at Kelly the Mick's feet, unmoving, while the other one made horrible gurgling sounds for a short while before he went silent.

Nino finally spoke. "Am I dead?" He seemed to have missed being shot, as had J.R. Albanese.

"Colin?" Kelly the Mick called out. A slurping, groaning, moan came from the middle of the table. "Colin? Are you hit?"

Somehow Colin Garvan pushed himself up from the tabletop. Since he'd been facedown, his face was not covered with the black powder... but more difficult to make out all the same. Blood, bone and snot dripped from a gaping orifice that used to be his mouth and nose. Kelly couldn't even find one of his eyes into which he could look. In a horrid, slurping voice that was almost impossible to understand, he screamed, "What? You fuck! What fucking ideas do you have now? You asshole!" Colin somehow still had the shotgun in his hand and started to swing it around when Kelly the Mick raised his loaded .45 and emptied it into his childhood friend. Realizing what he had done, he rushed over and cradled what remained of Colin Garvan, wailing.

I pulled on my shoes clumsily and started glancing around Howie's room to make sure I had everything before I sprinted off to Sonny and the burn of the can for my anesthesia. Something moved in the corner of my eye and I snapped my head over to look at the doorframe. *fuck. i could've sworn there was someone there just now.* My eyes began darting involuntarily around the room as I sprang to my feet and searched down the long, dark hallway, listening for any intruders. That eerie feeling of unexpected company made me spin back around and I found myself staring at a picture of Howie and myself as kids, arms around one another's necks, waiting in line the first time we were allowed to ride the Cyclone at Coney Island. My view snapped from picture to object to bit of memorabilia, almost every piece of which I recognized and could explain its back story. Tickets from concerts, faded certificates from school, a small yarmulke and a menorah he'd made out of roach clips. Photos of us on the pier, on the stoop, on the prowl. Everywhere was Howie. *but howie's nowhere... except in my pocket. fuck me! in a small purple bottle!* My eyes began to tear up as my head went into full spin and the demons began an all-out assault on the gates that held them at bay.

I blew out of the apartment, hearing the bang of the door shut behind me, but only slightly aware that I hadn't locked the door. I nearly knocked one of the Nestos' neighbors into a wall as I tore down the stairs and flung myself into the sticky, humid air of that Hell's Kitchen night. My stomach began doing flip-flops to match my brain as I staggered instinctively west on 43rd Street and realized how close I was to where Howie had been murdered. The demons had howled that Thruway impulse back to life and I started running as best as I could toward the cement wall that overlooked the train tracks.

Under normal, less affected circumstances, I could scale it like a cat, but that was not quite the case at moment. Although my motor skills and coordination were for shit, what was left of my brain kept ticking, trying to come up with a solution. There was one of those large trash dumpsters up the street, near Tenth, upon which I saw a set of four massive casters. Although it was unwieldy and stunk like pure rot, I was able to push it down the street and slam it into the concrete wall to stop it. Stepping on its various nooks and shelves, I mounted the oversized bin and steadied myself as it moved like the world's most bizarre skateboard. When I hopped from its top, up onto the wall, the motion set the dumpster rolling down the hill toward the river, careening right into someone's brand new, midnight blue Chevy Nova.

I swung my legs over and sat atop the wall, staring down into the darkness. As high as I was, I half-expected to lose either my balance or my consciousness and plummet down onto the tracks. It didn't seem like a bad idea, honestly, and the demons were excited that I was once again considering it as an option. *fuck. how am i going to get down? why do i even give a fuck? what would be so bad about being done? the alternative has been a fucking nightmare. even i don't know who i am or where i'm going. my family has all moved on and i blew it, staying behind to ruin myself without anyone else to blame. i'm not their son anymore. i'm not benny's son. howie's gone and sandra would've rather had a child with danny fucking albanese than me! how could anybody love me? i sure as fuck don't.* The sound of an approaching train brought me back from my introspection for a moment, but I wasn't giving up on my plan to give up that easily. *fuck it. i'm done. i'm just going to jump.* The demons were screaming their approval and my brain was too clouded to resist. The buildings began to shake and I could see a halo of light appear around my shoes. "Now," I said aloud, scooting away from the wall with all of my might. I closed my eyes and realized that the air rushing through the tunnel and that sensation of falling were the last two things I'd ever feel....

Until I landed atop the train's coal pile and various craggy chunks of black stone poked me all over my back and legs.

The train chugged along with its newest passenger, screaming Uptown through darkened tunnels. "I can't even kill myself right," I moaned, doing my best to lean up into a sitting position on the jagged pieces of coal. I knew I had to get off the damn thing somehow, or else risk ending up back in the Upstate... or going all the way to Canada. The more I moved around and the more the train rumbled along the track, the more I was choked and being covered in coal dust. Struggling to keep my watering eyes open, I saw a bright light up ahead on the right. I recognized it as the marker for 125th Street. Just beyond it was a little patch of green grass that was similarly lit. *that's my only chance. i've got to hit it or else choke to death... or worse.* The irony wasn't lost on me, that I was making decisions to save my life when I'd just been looking to end it only minutes earlier. *i am so fucked up. but this might be the answer you're looking for, francis. you hit your mark, and you live. you miss, and you're dead.* I stood up on shaky legs and jumped with all the strength I had. My whole world went into slow motion before I landed with a thud on the patch of green grass. I distinctly remembered hearing the sound of metal on metal as the train passed and left. I knew that I couldn't move, but I lacked any true realization that I was blacking out.

After Kelly the Mick had gotten himself under control, he instructed Nino to drag Danny Albanese, wounded and still bound, out into the main room so they could get clear of the black dust that continued to hang in the air of the backroom. The junior Albanese was trying his very best to catch Nino's eye in an effort to enlist his help, but the delivery boy was actively avoiding the mobster's gaze. He wanted nothing more than to save his own life, and had already figured Danny's situation was terminal. Kelly the Mick had begun searching the club and came across his stash of weapons and explosives from the Hell's Kitchen Youth Organization almost immediately. "What a waste of $10,000," he commented. "Didn't even need them."

Danny was getting nowhere with Nino, so he thought he'd try to find an "in" with Kelly the Mick. "You don't have to do this, man," he said. "There's got to be something you need more than killing me."

Kelly the Mick hadn't even been listening. As he continued to ransack the club, he found himself dwelling more and more on how the Albaneses had gotten his gun stash. "How'd you do it?"

"What?" Danny asked.

"How'd you know about the guns at the HKYO? It was the kids, wasn't it?"

Danny nodded, grimacing with pain. "That kid, Vit. My dad recruited him and he came over, singing like a bird." Rather than getting him the leniency he was hoping for, Danny's confession earned him a couple of whacks to the head with the butt of Kelly's .45. "What'd I say? I didn't do it. I was just telling you that you had a Benedict Arnold in your midst."

"And that fucking group of pussies is up there right now, crying about it, pulling their hair out over a fucking traitor!" He gave Danny a kick in the stomach as Nino sat quietly, staring at the floor.

"What can I give you to just walk away? Not to kill me?" Danny asked. "Weapons? Drugs? Money?" Kelly the Mick turned his attention back to the younger Albanese at the mention of money. "I could give you a lot. You could take it and go anywhere. I'd never say a word. I'd say I have no idea who did this, that it was a robbery. You've already won. What reason would I have to go on fighting."

"Where's the money?" Kelly the Mick asked quietly.

"Are you going to let me go?" Danny replied.

"My God. What's wrong with you? Look at what a pussy you've become. I thought you were supposed to be a tough guy, and now you're here, willing to suck my cock for me to leave you alone. You'd do it, wouldn't you. You want that? You want to suck my cock?" Danny remained silent. Suddenly, Kelly the Mick was overcome with rage and began to smash his gun into the side of Danny's head with each word he spoke. "Where... is... that... fucking... money? Tell... me... and... I'll...."

"In the bar!" Danny cried out. "A safe, built into the ice chest. You slide the left side open, tilt the tub of ice into the right side and then pop open the bottom of the left tub. You just push it and it pops up."

Kelly the Mick walked over to the bar and followed Danny's instruction while the younger Albanese wept openly. "Holy shit. You were telling the truth." He pulled out a duffel bag containing a large sum of cash, took it over to Nino, dropped it in his lap and told him to count it. As Kelly the Mick continued searching the club for anything interesting, Nino counted away, eventually looking up and reporting that the bag contained a little more than $275,000. "Not bad at all," Kelly the Mick said. "You know what, Albanese? I've decided that I'm really not going to kill you. Although I don't know that you'd want to if you saw what you looked like right now."

Danny launched into a new round of tears. "Oh, thank you. I swear I'll never say a word."

"And you know what else? I've actually decided that I'm not going to kill your dear old pop either," Kelly continued, turning his focus to Nino. "Hey, kid, go in there and drag what's left of his old man out here. Let's see if he's still breathing." With a great deal of effort, Nino did as he was told, and to everyone's surprise, J.R. was still making weak little wheezing noises. "Here," Kelly said, pouring two drinks from a bottle of Johnnie Walker Black off of the club's bar and then tapping a pile of money that he'd taken out of the duffel bag. "Have you ever seen that much money before?" Nino remained silent. "You know, I don't even know your name. What's your name, kid?"

He debated whether or not to speak before finally saying, "Nino."

"Nino. Nice name there, Nino. Well, tell me now: what would you do if you had more than $75,000? Yours. To keep."

"I would leave NYC and open a pizzeria somewhere."

"Why? You hate New York that much?"

"No," Nino replied. "It's just that I have no family here... and the people, they can be unkind sometimes." Kelly tilted back his head and laughed with complete lack of feeling. "I heard that it is not that way elsewhere...."

Kelly the Mick put his hand up to stop the young man. "Hold on. Hmm. Let's try this again. Maybe I'm not getting through to you." He straddled Nino, who had sat back down, and raised his .45 to put its end right between the teen's eyes. "What would you do with $75,000?"

Nino was afraid to breathe, let alone speak. "I don't know what you want me to say," he blurted out. "I'm sorry."

"The answer I'm looking for, ... Nino... is that you would disappear and no one would ever hear from you again. It would be like this never happened. You understand now?"

Nino nodded his head up and down emphatically. "Of course. No one would ever see me here again... ever."

"Good answer. See? I'm a fair guy. No one can ever say I'm not. Now grab one of those sacks from your restaurant and put your money in it. Then go wait by the door. We're about to leave." He did what he was told as Kelly walked over to the bar, pulled bottle after bottle off of the shelves and started to unscrew the tops, walking around the club, pouring the alcohol everywhere, particularly on the dead bodies.

Danny started to cry when he understood what Kelly the Mick was doing. "But I gave you the money. I said I wouldn't tell." Kelly walked over to the Albaneses with an open bottle of Johnnie Walker in each hand and dumped the contents onto the father and son. "For the love of God!" Danny screamed. "You said you wouldn't kill us."

Kelly the Mick opened the box on a carton of cigarettes, lit the flaps with his Zippo and walked around, igniting all of the racks of clothes as Danny screamed for help.

"We had a deal! You said you wouldn't kill us," Danny screamed again.

"I won't," Kelly the Mick responded, dropping the flaming carton of cigarettes next to the Albaneses. "The fire will." Danny let out one inhuman scream after the next while Kelly the Mick picked up his duffel bag with the $200,000 in it and walked towards the door. Kelly stuck his head out and looked up and down the deserted street. "You're driving," he said to Nino, stepping outside and hopping into the passenger seat. Nino walked around and got into the driver's side and put the keys in the ignition. "Nino, where's your money?" he asked, laughing. "You just really don't want that cash, do you?"

Nino ran back inside just as the flames began spreading all around the club and Danny's screams were trailing off. He grabbed his bag of money and headed back out to get behind the wheel of the van, leaving the door open... and fanning the frames. Little did either of the two men realize, though, that a lost tourist had just stepped into view and saw Nino exit the club, get into the van and peel away. She could see the glow from the flames while the smoke was billowing out, so she made a mad dash to a payphone across the street and dialed 911. As the operator answered, small explosions began to sound from within as the cases of booze ignited. She stayed on the line to answer the operator's questions about what she'd seen until the wail of sirens filled the neighborhood and the fire reached the cache of weapons and explosives... and the Dante League Social Club ceased to exist.

West 39th Street was once again completely blocked off with all of the emergency services vehicles and personnel trying to battle the blaze. Det. O'Casey stood near Det. Perez, watching the remnants of the Dante League Social Club vanish... and the better part of their evidence along with it. "The Fire Department will be getting more out of there than we will, I suspect, Jack," David Perez chimed in.

"Not that we'll need it. You and I both know who did this... just like we both know who killed the Nesto boy... and the di Ciccos' kid."

"Well, now, I don't know that I agree necessarily," Det. Perez replied. "Might be a different story on this one."

"What? Where's your head?" O'Casey fired back. "Those kids were just bowling pins, caught in the alley. Killing J.R.'s English enforcer was the spare. This was the strike."

"Too many things just don't fall into place, though. The witness saw only one person leave the scene... a teenage boy."

"Whom she described as a dark-skinned <u>Black</u> male."

"He could've had on a ski mask."

"She would've seen a ski mask," O'Casey argued back.

"So why was Kelly the Mick's car parked a block away? And why is it still here... the same as J.R.'s Delta 88? I'm sorry, Jack, but if you ask me, there are just too many things that suggest a third party lured the Irish crew here to the Italian's club and whacked them both. Who do they both hate? And who hates them back? The Blacks. And where does the white getaway van come into your theory? Neither of them had anything like that. Anybody put out an APB on white vans in Harlem? The Bronx?"

"I don't know, but we won't be collecting any evidence from inside there anytime soon. That much is certain. And even when we do, I'll be shocked if it's much beyond bones."

"True, but how many sets of bones is the question," Perez said.

"Do you see how you're all over the place, David?"

"As far as the investigation is concerned," he replied, "we might as well do what we can in the meantime."

O'Casey rolled his eyes, "Umm... okay...."

"Well, 'night, Jack."

"G'night." As Jack O'Casey watched his fellow detective lumber away back to his car, one face in the crowd struck him as peculiar. He made his way past the other police officers, fire inspectors, FBI Anti-Crime Mob investigators, arson experts... none of whom were making any headway figuring out what had happened there... and sifted through the sea of regular Joes from Hell's Kitchen on gut instinct to pick out the strangely anxious face of Paulie Giovanni. "Hiya, Paulie. Funny seeing you here."

"Funny? How do you mean?" the restaurateur replied nervously. "I'm just nosey, I guess. ...Like everybody else."

"I'm just surprised you came all the way over from your restaurant to watch a building burn. Did you know Johnny Albanese?"

Paulie had been wondering if he should mention Nino's trip to the Dante League that evening. If the boy had been inside, there wasn't anything he could do for him... and he hadn't had any family to come wondering. And if he'd gotten out of there, chances were that no one would ever see him again. Whichever the case might be, Paulie knew that his $50,000 debt went up in smoke along with J.R. Albanese's laughable toupee... so long as he kept his mouth shut. "Know him?" Paulie answered back. "Not really. His son ordered from us once in a blue moon, but I'd heard that they preferred Calvecchio's."

"No accounting for taste, right?" O'Casey joked.

"Right," Paulie replied with a big smile on his face.

Det. Perez's car slowed down while driving back past the stoop between 43rd and 44th Streets. "It's interesting that those boys from earlier are all still there," Perez's partner said, glancing over. "None of them went down to rubberneck at the Albanese fire."

Det. Perez replied, "It's more interesting to me who's <u>not</u> there. See Francis Doonan anywhere? Same as this morning. I wonder if he's going to be one of the crispy critters they find on 39th Street... or if he's driving a white van as fast as he can away from it?"

As the delivery van crossed over the bridge and into Queens, Nino finally got up enough nerve to ask Kelly where they were going. "I'm open to suggestions," Kelly the Mick replied with a less-than-confident chuckle.

"We should dump the van," Nino answered back decisively, an idea that Kelly thought was splendid. "My best friend, Salvatore, he works in a junkyard over on Willett's Point Blvd. He can make the van disappear. But first we should wash up. We can't go there looking like this."

"Good point," Kelly said. "There's a joint over near Shea called the Mets Motel. It's a 'No-Tell Motel.' They rent by the hour to hookers and hustlers. We could go there and get a room to shower up and get this stuff off of us while we're waiting to hear from your friend about when we can meet him. Follow my lead and they'll just think we're into some extra-kinky shit."

They pulled into the motel parking lot and did a little preparatory work with some of Kelly's rope and duct tape. Moments later, Kelly the Mick was standing before the motel clerk, holding a rope "leash" that was tied around Nino's neck. Duct tape served as a blindfold and "restraints" for the delivery boy as well. In his most bizarre voice, Kelly the Mick lisped, "We need a room pleassssse."

The clerk didn't even look up. "For how long?" he asked.

"Just a few hours," Nino responded, for which he got smacked across the chest with the loose end of the rope.

"Did I tell you that you could ssspeak, ssslave?" Kelly the Mick was laying it on thick.

"No, master," Nino responded.

"I'll teach you, ssslave," Kelly hissed again.

The old clerk still never batted an eye. "Pay on your way out, then."

Kelly giggled crazily all the way to their room, abundantly pleased with the success of his trickery. He pulled some of the clothes from the racks at the Albanese's out of his bag and started into the bathroom to turn on the shower. "Call your friend while I'm in the shower and then you can hop in while we wait."

Nino picked up the phone as Kelly took his bag and clothes into the bathroom. As he stood under the water, letting it wash away the black powder that had covered them, head-to-toe, he could hear the sound after Nino turned on the TV. Channel 7's Eyewitness News was leading with a story about "...a mob hit turned into an inferno on the West Side last night. Police are seeking a young, Black male in connection with the crime. A witness reported...."

Kelly could barely believe his ears. "There had been a witness after all...," Kelly said out loud, "and the black powder had actually helped us! It made their witness think we were niggers! Niggers! Did you hear that, Nino? They thought we were niggers. They're probably combing Jamaica or Hollis right now, looking for us." Kelly the Mick turned off the water and walked out into the room with a towel around his waist, but Nino was nowhere to be found. "I guess the kid wanted to be sure I didn't change my mind." He could hardly begrudge Nino his decision, but Kelly still knew he had to get out of there as soon as possible... just in case.

A few hours later, after the Giovanni's van had been crushed to the size of a small refrigerator and piled up with all the other junk, Nino was waiting in line with his best friend, Sal, to board a flight at LaGuardia to start their dream pizzeria in Pittsburgh. His blood ran cold, though, when he saw the unmistakably insane eyes of Kelly the Mick as he walked the terminal thoroughfare toward him. Time, like Nino's breath, seemed to stand still until, to his great relief and surprise, the gangster walked right past him and headed for a gate to board an Eastern Airlines flight bound for Miami. "And they say crime doesn't pay," Nino mused to himself.

When I finally opened my eyes and looked around, I had no clue how long I'd been unconscious, but it had to have been a good long while. I could hear the squeal of rats dancing around me, sniffing to see if the black-lung, turned inside out, might be a meal. Everything on my body hurt, but still, I began crawling in what felt like an upward direction, over garbage, broken glass, tires and refuse of every kind. I didn't know if it was because of the unbearable smell through which I was inching, or the poison I'd put in my body all day long, but I started to vomit violently, emptying my stomach all over my arms and hands. *it's just adding to every other substance i've got sticking to me right now.* It wasn't until the acid from my stomach seeped into my unseen cuts that I realized how badly my hands were bleeding. My wounds were filled with sick and my lungs were filled with charcoal dust; I stopped to rest on a bed of broken glass.

By the time I'd fought my way up to the top of the incline, the effects of the intoxicants I'd been experiencing had all but worn off. I managed to get to my feet, resembling something like a garbage heap at midnight. Starting to walk very, very slowly across 125th Street, I must've looked like I was in a horror movie to the people who lived there. *but there aren't many people out. it must be incredibly late. i must've been knocked out far longer than i thought.* I began to trudge downtown in search of a subway station. I had little hope that a cab would pick me up in my state.

As the demons forced me to do the math in my head and figure how far I was from 72nd Street and Sonny Blue, I noticed for the first time that dawn was slowly breaking. I raised my hand to keep the sunbeams out of my eyes and a cab screeched to a halt next to me. *if this guy's name is richie kingston, i won't be the least bit surprised.* I reached into my pocket and, although I could've sworn I had a bigger roll, I found that I only had ten dollars on me.

I loaded myself into the back seat and said, "Thanks so much, man. I really appreciate it. I want to be honest with you, though. All I've got is ten bucks. Just take me as far as it'll get me and I'll walk the rest of the way."

"You look like you've had a shitty day, mon," the Jamaican cab driver said, "or maybe you're finishing a shitty night, but Gabriel 'ere is gonna make sure you get 'ome safe and sound. Ya 'ear? Now where we 'eading?"

"Just keep going down West End, all the way to 44th, and then make a left. I'll be getting out on Tenth Avenue."

The cabbie gunned it, and in what seemed like seconds, he announced, "'Ome sweet 'ome, my friend. 'Ell's Kitchen. 'Ope you 'ave a better tomorrow than you've 'ad a today," Gabriel said.

"Thanks," I replied, seeing my beloved stoop as if a mirage. I began to trudge down Tenth, only steps from home.

Across the street, Det. Perez almost choked on his bacon and egg sandwich when he realized that what he thought was a bum from the river was actually me... and that, covered in coal dust, I matched the color, age, and body type that the witness in the Albanese blaze had given. "Well, whattya know? Perez, one. O'Casey, zero." He picked up his radio and called for back up while he came running out of the deli and across the street, weapon drawn.

I'd taken one step onto the stoop when I heard a voice say, "Doonan, don't you move a fucking muscle. Put your hands against the door where I can see them." I had no idea what was going on, but I just wasn't in the mood to be shot right then, so I did what I was told. The detective started firing questions at me without giving me any opportunity to respond. "Why do you look like that, Doonan? Why are you painted all black? Where did the cuts on your hands come from? And the vomit? Where have you been for the last 48 hours?" In just those few seconds, the street filled with police vehicles and eight cops had their weapons aimed at me. Det. David Perez had finally finished giving me the third degree and waddled up behind me to put a handcuff on my right wrist. I offered no resistance at all because there just wasn't any left in me. When he reached to handcuff my left wrist, I fainted dead away, coming down hard on the stoop. "Call a wagon. He's out. We need to get him to St. Luke's right now."

By the time the ambulance arrived, half of the neighborhood had assembled to see what was going on, including the crew. Clayton and Patty Boy gave each other confused looks. "Did you see him? Why'd he look like that?"

Patty Boy replied, "I've never seen anything like that before. I almost couldn't believe it was him."

Clayton started barking orders. "Go tell his Uncle Patsy and have him call Francis' parents. I'm gonna call Benny Levine." After he had instructed Clayton to meet him on the stoop in an hour, Benny picked up the phone and called Patsy, who had been told by some of his police friends that the slaughter at the Albanese place was being pinned on Francis. Benny's next call was to the Doonans.

As I was being wheeled into the emergency room, handcuffed to the gurney, Det. David Perez led the effort to parade me past the news crews who were all clamoring for a scoop. At the last second, the Director of St. Luke's Hospital saw what was going on and instructed the detective to remove the cuffs. Filled with delusions of grandeur to come, Perez announced that I was his prisoner and I would remained restrained. The doctor grew very quiet and leaned in to say, "Listen, you asshole, you have the entire New York press corps behind this door, and standing right over there is my very good friend, District Attorney, Robert Morgenthau. You decide how you want this to happen."

Perez broke out in a cold sweat from the look in the doctor's eyes as he fumbled for the keys to unlock the cuffs. As they wheeled me in, photographers from every newspaper in The City started snapping pictures as the crowd surged forward and D.A. Morgenthau replaced Det. Perez in order to handle questions about the person the press had already dubbed the "Hell's Kitchen Killer."

Benny skimmed the article in the previous day's paper about Roberto Duran's defeat of Sugar Ray Leonard on Friday night in Montreal as he imagined how the headlines in tomorrow's papers would read. Mr. and Mrs. Doonan sat next to him in the back of the limo. No one really knew what to say. According to Patsy, Francis had already given a full confession to killing the Albaneses, but Benny refused to believe it unless he heard it from Francis himself. Apparently, Francis had simply answered "yes" to all of Det. Perez's questions, which made the District Attorney's office extremely uncomfortable. There were sincere doubts about the kid's guilt, but the assembled throngs of news people had to get something to calm a city on edge about a spike in violent crime. Whether he did or not, Francis Doonan had waived his right to representation before writing and then signing his own confession. The crime had a perpetrator. All that remained was to alert the media and determine the court and sentencing dates.

As soon as the Doonans and Benny arrived, they were met by Det. Jack O'Casey, who escorted them directly to Francis' room, going straight through security and around the media. The detective didn't know what to say any more than anyone else; he knew as well as Benny and the Doonans that there was no way Francis did what they were saying… but since Francis was saying he'd done it, that was all that mattered. The detective waved off the security personnel outside of Francis' door and stood watch himself.

The three people who cared most about me walked in the room and did their very best to keep "stiff upper lips." My mother sat in the chair closest to me, rubbing my forehead and feeling so guilty and inadequate. They pretended not to notice that both my hands and feet were chained to the bed. *as though i'm strong enough to get out of this bed even without the chains.* My father called my name quietly and I began to wake up, realizing who was there with me. I tried my best to give them a little smile, but we all seemed to realize at the same time that we were each employing the same nicety. The room was filled with a strange silence until my father spoke again. "We're going to try to do everything we can for you, Francis. Mr. Levine, here, has a lawyer friend who's very good and knows the D.A. quite well."

"A Marty Wolf," my mother said softly, crying as she added, "Your sisters all send their love."

I nodded and closed my eyelids slowly a couple of time to feign fatigue. I hoped Benny got my hint. "Maybe we should be going and let him rest for awhile," he said finally. *good old benny. i can always count on him.* My parents came up to the bed and grasped either of my hands, leaning in to kiss me.

"We'll be back when you've got some more strength, son," my father reassured me.

Benny stepped into the hall and asked Det. O'Casey if someone could escort my parents to his car while he took a minute to pass on some legal advice that his friend had offered. Benny stepped back inside and pulled up a chair. "Well, sir, we are in some deep shit, kid. I've got the best criminal attorney that money can buy just waiting for the word, 'go,' but something tells me that you're not going to let me say it, are you?" I smiled and shook my head. "When I heard you'd confessed to something we both know you would never even <u>think</u> about, I had a feeling you wouldn't let me get this situation set right. Mind telling me why?" I detected a note of anger and frustration in Benny's voice. I could certainly understand where it was coming from.

"Benny, it's what I want. I don't know how to make you understand that, but it is. It's what I want. It's what I need. There's no other way."

"You want <u>two decades</u> in prison, Francis? That's what you need? Excuse me if I just can't believe what I'm hearing. Do you have any idea what this is doing to the other people in your life… and you want them to go through twenty years of it, day in and day out? Those friends of yours from the stoop are calling you the hero-prince among men. You're the new standard for courage and machismo now that you took revenge on the animals who killed your friends… except you didn't, son. You didn't. And you know it. And Clayton knows it too, just like the rest of us. Your parents, your Uncle Patsy are all beside themselves. Sandra O'Casey has spent her every waking moment in the back of St. Paul the Apostle's, lighting candles for both you and Danny Albanese, and wondering if she should feel guilty about that."

"I don't know how to say it, Benny. I just don't."

"Francis, I hear you. I hear the sound in your voice and I know you're not crazy or stupid. But you and I are old buddies, and will be forever, but… well… you just didn't do this." I just continued to stare deep into Benny's eyes. I wished more than anything that I was no longer able to hurt other people with my actions. Benny continued, "Kid, do you realize what we're talking about here? Twenty years in prison! Jesus Christ, is that what you want?" He stood over me, becoming more upset with the frustration of trying to make me see his point. "They will take twenty years of your life away from you. That's more than you've had already."

"I know, Benny, and look what I've done with it."

"And that's really what you want? To be locked up like an animal?"

I looked up at my friend with tears in my eyes and said, "Yes, Benny. They won't be locking me up like an animal. They'll be locking the animal out."

"Kid, tell me I'm hearing things." He collapsed to his knees on the side of the bed, all the air removed from his sails. I'd never seen him like that before... helpless. "I don't know what to do for you, kid. Your poor parents are heartbroken. I'm heartbroken... and I just don't know what to do." Benny buried his face in my blanket and sobbed.

"Benny," I said with a new found lucidity, "I want to tell you something, but I need you to do something for me. Please. You can't interrupt me, even if you don't like what you're hearing, okay?"

He looked at me with respect in his eyes and replied, "Alright, Francis."

"Benny, you know me better than anyone left in the world. You know the truth, and I know the truth, but I'm taking the rap for these deaths because I want to save my life. I know that seems bizarre. I know it's difficult to understand, and it may sound crazy, but I've been facing down death a lot lately... and sometimes, I've gone knocking on his door. In the last few days alone, I've tried to take my own life... with intoxicants, on the grill of a truck, and even by throwing myself in front of a train where Howie met his maker.

"But you know what, Benny? I had to face wanting to die three times in order to realize that I really wanted to live. It's clear that I have been spared three times for a reason. And I want to have a chance... but you know what it's like around here. The way things are, I never will. Danger and trouble wait for me on every corner in a tough neighborhood with a lot of tough problems. I'm only eighteen years old, but I feel like I'm a hundred. My body, my brain and my soul are completely controlled by booze and drugs. I don't even know who I am. Honestly. I know that may seem cliché, but I've either been drunk or high... or wanting to be drunk or high for so, so long that I don't remember who Francis is anymore without that.

"I just want to go away, Benny. I know it'll be hard, but what isn't? Maybe I can get some help to stop drinking, stop drugging... go to school and actually learn something so that I can make something out of myself that I'll be proud of. And, of course I know that you want to tell me that I could do all of that here, but I can't. I'm just not put together that way. I wasn't raised that way. The ways to help someone like me don't exist in this world, on this side of the fence. The only thing waiting for me here is trouble and violence and death. I can't wait around, wondering how long it will be before someone finds me dead on a rooftop... or O.D.'d in my bed. I can't end up like Howie or Vit... or even Danny. I can't.

"So I want your word, Benjamin Levine. I want your solemn word that you'll let me stand up and be a man the only way I know how. Let me do this, and if I survive it, it will be because I was meant to survive it. And I'll still be relatively young, able to have a chance at a life and a family. But it has to be on my terms. It has to be Francis doing this for Francis... not for drugs or booze... wanting to feel like someone else. Please."

Benny sat, dumbfounded. He'd never heard anything like that before. He'd never known more respect for anyone than he felt for a single Irish kid. He took my manacled hand and said softly, "Remember when I predicted that Duran would win 'The Brawl in Montreal?'"

"Oh, yeah," I responded. "That was a couple of nights ago, right? I forgot all about it. Did he win after all?"

"Of course, of course. And after all the shit he and Sugar Ray were talking back and forth to one another, Duran got the last word in after he won the decision. I just read in the paper that he said he beat Leonard because he was 'the better man.' Well, if that was indeed the case, then you would have tamed 'El Animal' that night. I don't know of a better man, my friend." We both took a minute to let Benny's sentiment sink in. "You have my word, Francis. I'll respect your wishes. And I give you my word too that I'll keep an eye on your family as well."

"I'd be grateful if you could keep an eye on the crew too. Oh!" I interjected. "Almost forgot. That includes Howie." Benny gave me a confused look. "If you go to his building, the front door of his apartment is still unlocked. Inside, there is a key, wrapped inside a note from his mother. I think it's on his bed or his desk. Will you please take care of her request since I won't be able to do it?"

"Of course, Francis."

"And will you visit me, Benny?"

"I'll visit you, kid. Never doubt that I'll always be by your side."

Three weeks later, I, Francis John Michael Doonan, was sentenced to twenty years in Dannemora Prison for the murders of J.R. and Danny Albanese... and four of their unknown associates.

I feel the bus jerk before its ascent into the Port Authority bus terminal, exactly two blocks from my home. As I walk through the Port Authority, I can see some of the changes they always talked about making. I'm really nervous, stepping out onto Ninth Avenue. I hope not to run into anyone I shouldn't. The City looks and feels pretty much the same as night falls. There's the hustle and bustle, the same energy.

I cut across 41st Street to reach Tenth Ave. I'm really not ready to see anybody just yet. My heart is pounding out of my chest as I cross Dyer Avenue, carrying the little gym bag that has all of my belongings. I remove the envelope from my mother that contains my apartment keys and a note that starts, "Welcome home, my dear Francis. I cant wait to see you." *i can't wait to see her too. how weird. i left here a boy, and now i return a man. now that i'm older, i can truly understand why benny tried to talk me out of my decision. it wasn't easy, but i'm home now... after only fifteen years, though, thanks to excellent conduct. i've got a masters degree, and i think i want to try being a writer.*

I find myself standing on 42nd Street, at Tenth Avenue. I turn and look up to see if I can spot my beloved stoop. I have only one more block to go and my body must realize it too because sweat pours out of every part of my body. As I cross 43rd Street, I think of the letter in my inside jacket pocket, sent by Benny Levine in Miami Beach. His note arrived the day after my mother's. Its opening lines read, "Welcome home, kid. Here's the number to a bank account I had set up for you while you were away. $500,000 should help you a little to figure out what you're going to do. When you get your feet on the ground, come and visit Miami."

Before I even realize it, I am standing in front of my stoop.

My stoop.

In a way, it looks like someone I could've shared my bed with that morning. In another way, it's foreign and inaccessible. There are a whole cast of characters assembled there, all of whom look like they could be my friends from childhood, never having aged. I rub my eyes and look again as the thumping beat from the Notorious B.I.G.s hit, "Suicidal Thought bangs out from a big boom box and shakes me back to the reality of another generation of Hell's Kitchen kids... on my stoop, the smell of weed fresh in the air.

They all seem to stare back at me. One kid who could be Howie's twin says, "What are you? A cop? Toledo, this guy's a cop."

The husky, ebony-skinned kid he addressed looks me up and down. "No. This cat's righteous. He's just an old Hell's Kitchen 'G.'"

They all step off of the stoop to let me pass.

"Thank you," I say, stepping through the outer door and inserting my key into the lock of the inner door. I turn and look through the glass to see that Toledo and I are watching one another's every move.

I nod at him and smile.

He returns the gesture by tilting his head back.

just another stoop to conquer.